# The Last Red Wolf

**Kurtis Dolman**

*To my husband,*
*Thank you for always being there for me and always supporting my dreams.*
*&*
*For all the people who aided in supporting a dream.*
*A few special acknowledgements to;*
*Adam Schulties*
*Erin Gwinn*
*Josi Geary*
*Emily Gomez*
*Taylor Hall*
*Katerina Ianacone*
*Paige St. Pierre*
*Kynda Skyes*
*Jennifer Vandecar*
*Tina Casias*
*Megan Brantley*

Even a man who is pure in heart and says his prayers by night
may become a wolf when the wolfbane blooms and the
autumn moon is bright.

— Curt Siodmak

# Content Notes

These notes are made available so readers can inform themselves if they want to. Readers will encounter;

- LGBTQ+ Themes
- Bad language: mild, infrequent
- Sex/Nudity: Several scenes that discuss nudity and briefly described sex scenes
- Violence: some references to violence towards major characters (assault, kidnapping, sexual assault)
- Suicide Ideation
- Childhood Trauma

# Chapter One

THE ROOSTER CROWED SEVERAL TIMES and as it called I began to rouse myself from the grip of sleep. Even in the early morning twilight of spring I could feel the heat setting in on the day and knew that sweat would already be collecting underneath me on the sheet. Outside, I could hear the trucks on the gravel road and the animals calling for feed, sounds I had grown accustomed to during my last three years in southeast Washington. I twisted and moved for the edge of the bed. Mr. and Mrs. Johnson, my employers, had allowed me to live in the small trailer on their property as a portion of my compensation for the farm work they had hired me on for and I was grateful. After having moved through the foster care system, this small trailer had been my home during the longest stretch of consistent housing I had been granted in my life thus far. This was still not the life I wanted for myself, however, not the one I had dreamed of since graduating from school.

In the foster system, I witnessed a series of other boys and girls like myself transitioning from foster home to foster home until one or two would end up in juvie, continuing on through the justice system toward a life behind bars. By keeping to myself, doing what was asked of me, and keeping my nose clean, I did my best to avoid ending up on a similar track. Someone once told me I was lucky to not have my parents around — continuing to screw me up through their own infusion of problems and drama as had happened with some of my counterparts. I didn't know if that was true. They were right that I never knew my parents but being better off never having them was a point I couldn't agree on. I had always thought it would be better to have parents, to have someone that at least wanted you in their lives enough to keep trying for you, even though most of the examples I saw failed again and again.

As I grew older, I had learned that my father died of a drug overdose before I was born, and my mother, stricken with grief, took her own life after giving birth to me. Another foster parent informed me that, when my mother was pregnant with me, she had the sense to take care of herself and move into a rehab center and that if it was not for that I wouldn't have fared as well as I had and would not have done as well in school. I couldn't tell you for sure if that was true or not but if I went to school, followed along, and completed the work that they asked me to do then my grades stayed good enough for me to never be in trouble for them. I never acted rebelliously or behaved in a challenging way like some of my foster siblings did, but I also never developed any close attachments. When I was young, I would try and stay put, but for one reason or another, I always found myself in a new home, with new siblings, and a new school before I could ever experience a sense of permanence. So, once I finished school and turned eighteen, I knew I needed to beat the odds for myself, create my own home, and get myself through school so that I wouldn't be chucking bales of hay and living in farm-owned trailers for the rest of my life.

Reaching out from the bed, I grabbed a pair of jeans and a shirt. I quickly smelled the shirt to determine if it was clean and decided it was good enough until my next trip to the laundromat. I put on my clothes and went into the small corridor that doubled as both kitchen and living room. As I did, I stopped and briefly glanced at the acceptance letter and notification of my scholarship I had gotten a month before.

> *Dear Lyle, CONGRATULATIONS! I am delighted to offer you admissions to the University of Washington's Class of 2017. We are also pleased to offer you a full scholarship package as requested with your application material to join us this fall.*

*I did it*, I thought to myself as I tapped the letter with a sense of accomplishment. I'd already rented a university apartment for the entire year and in a few weeks I'd be able to move in. I sighed contently at the thought and then filled my stomach with a quick breakfast and headed out to complete the daily tasks.

Thankfully, the weeks went by quickly as we worked through the rest of the season and the day had come where I would leave the Johnson's farm and move one step closer toward my ambitions. Mr. and Mrs. Johnson gave me a ride to the airport and, over the last three years, I had grown somewhat close to them both. I never saw them as parents, but they were kind to me and I tried to do everything they needed, even if that meant helping with household maintenance and other duties that would typically fall outside the scope of a farmhand.

"Be sure to let us know once you get settled," Mrs. Johnson said as we reached the airport. "I know we aren't your folks, but we would like to know when you get there and how things are going for you every once in a while."

"I will. Thank you both again for everything," I said. Mrs. Johnson turned and smiled at me as we pulled up to the gate. They both continued to pass on words of wisdom as we exited the car and I grabbed my suitcase and backpack.

"You'll always have a home and a job with us should things not work out." Mrs. Johnson added as we went to say our last goodbyes.

"I appreciate that and will keep that in mind." They both were very kind people and I enjoyed all the time I had spent with them.

They supported my goals and ambitions as much as they would their own kids, if they'd had any children of their own.

Mrs. Johnson's eyes started to collect water in the corners as she gave me one more hug and climbed back into the car. Mr. Johnson was a quiet man, like me, and never had too much to say. He grabbed me by the shoulder and said, "Good luck." He then pulled out a folded envelope and handed it to me, "I know we are not your family, but we have high hopes for you. Here is the last of your pay and a little more to help get you going once you get there." I took the envelope and inside found exceedingly more than what I normally received. I tried to give it back, saying that I would be fine, but Mr. Johnson refused.

"No, you go on and keep that for yourself. We would not have it any other way. When you get settled, let us know, and if you need anything, call me. You have a bright future and knowing where you come from and seeing where you are going, we can't think of a better use for this money than to help you. Now go on and catch your plane." He gave me a one-armed hug and said goodbye. They would never be my parents, but I couldn't think of two better people to have spent the last three years with.

# Chapter Two

I was a bundle of nerves and excitement as I took my first steps out of the Uber and onto the sidewalk of my new Seattle residence. Taking hold of my suitcase and backpack, I turned back around and said "Thank you" to the driver who had driven me all the way from the SeaTac airport to my apartment in the U District. He waved back at me before speeding off back into traffic and up the road. Coming from a small town on the outskirts of South Eastern Washington, the sights, sounds, and smells of the city differed from those of the place I last called home. I took in my surroundings. Trees, buildings, and people were stacked on top of each other like building blocks. It had just stopped raining and I could smell water evaporating off the cement. I could hear sirens in the distance, traffic scurrying along busy streets, and other students walking and laughing as they all returned to campus. Classes would not start for another couple of weeks, but I couldn't wait another second to leave my previous life of a small-town orphan boy who jumped from foster home to foster home and to start a new life that was wholly my own. I reached the front doors of my new university apartment building and stared through a line of older windows that looked in at some dated furniture before turning and seeing a small call box on the outside. I pushed the office button and with a loud ring a girl's voice came through the call box,

"Hello" she shouted through the box, "How can I help you?"

"Uh, hi... My name is Lyle. I am.. uhh.. supposed to move in today." A long pause passed by,

"Lyle Larson?" the girl shouted back.

"Yeah, sorry" I replied.

"I see your name here. Pull the door when you hear the buzz." The girl responded.

A loud buzzing noise came from the door and I reached out to grab it. It was solid and heavy as I pulled it open and moved inside. I swung my suitcase and pushed it through the doorway following behind. After entering the building, I moved toward a small door that had been left ajar with "Office" printed in black above it. As I reached for the door, it swung open. A tall blonde girl with her hair pulled back walked forward with a clipboard and a manila envelope. She looked up from the clipboard and smiled politely at me.

"Hi Lyle, I'm Jesse. Welcome to the UW Apartments."

I smiled back, "Hi Jesse, nice to meet you."

She looked back down at her clipboard and then back up at me before saying "I have here that you are going to be in apartment 626, that's honestly one of the better ones we have here, a lot of students request that apartment because it has the best view."

"Oh. I, uh, didn't know." I replied, as I went to follow her down the hallway to the right of the office.

We walked down the hallway to a small elevator, where she pushed the call button.

"The only downside is that it's on the 6th floor. This is the only elevator for the complex, and sometimes it goes out, so hopefully that doesn't happen because the stairs can be a bit much," she chuckled.

I returned her smile, "Oh, okay, that's fine with me. I don't mind."

The elevator doors opened and as they parted, Jesse took the first step in - I followed. She looked me over as we stood in the elevator. As usual, I was wearing my dark blue jeans, a white t-shirt and a flannel. I looked in the mirrored wall of the elevator and saw that my hair was a little disheveled. I reached up and ran my fingers down and through it to push the stray tussles of dishwater blonde hair back into place. She smiled again at me when we made eye contact in the mirror.

The door opened and we headed into the hallway. I turned to follow Jesse down the hallway as she continued dispensing pleasantries about how my roommate was scheduled to move in tomorrow, detailing the events that were put on by the student staff and relayed that she was one upperclassman who worked in the front office. As she talked, I took in my surroundings. The carpeted hallway running down from the elevator was a dark gray color and looked similar to carpet that lined some classrooms I had seen in several of the older high schools I attended. We started walking and I noticed beige walls lined the corridor, which were decorated with some framed inspirational posters that hung in between dark wooden doors. I followed Jesse to the end of the hallway before she stopped in front of one of the doors and opened the manilla envelope she was carrying. Behind her stood a floor length window that looked out over part of the city. As I started looking out at the window, Jesse pulled out a set of keys and unlocked the door.

"Here we are." She said as she opened the door and we walked through the entryway. I looked around as we entered, the apartment had a small dark blue couch with a coffee table that faced an entertainment stand- *it all looked so clean.* A small matching dining table stood nearby, with four chairs pushed neatly into place. The kitchen had a small refrigerator, stove/oven, dishwasher, sink, and microwave all arranged amidst the white and brown cabinets.

*Simple,* I thought to myself as I walked through the new space that would be my home for the next year. Definitely a far step up from the trailer. As I looked about the space, feeling excited about all the opportunities this next journey would hold, Jesse snapped me back to reality.

"You're in room A" she shared as she walked over to the door with a big black "A" hanging on the front of it.

"Great" I exclaimed as I followed her toward the door.

She opened the door and inside the room was a simple queen-sized bed stripped to just a mattress, two matching bedside tables and a dresser at the foot of the bed. The furniture in the room appeared to match the living room furniture. Straight across the entryway was a small little bathroom and to the left of the bed was a small closet.

*What a perfect little bedroom*, I thought to myself as I followed Jesse into the room, placing my suitcase and backpack near the closet door. Jesse continued to walk to the far side of the room and opened the blinds of a rather large window.

"This is the best part," she stated as the blinds pulled up, revealing a spectacular view of the city skyline, including a small side view of the Space Needle far off in the distance.

"Wow," I said, "you weren't kidding about the view. It's amazing."

Jesse turned and smiled toward me, "Isn't it fabulous?"

I nodded as she continued, "If you'll follow me back into the dining room, I'll grab your signature on a couple of things and hand you your keys."

We turned and walked back into the dining room. She laid out her clipboard and asked me to initial in a couple of places and sign at the bottom. As I signed the page, she grabbed the manilla envelope she pulled out a white card and placed it next to two keys.

She continued to run through some lines and then explained the keys, "The white card will get you into the building and both keys are for your apartment," I nodded. "If you lose your keys, there is a number to call for someone to let you in, but there will be a charge associated with that, so I'd recommend not losing them."

I nodded again and said, "Thanks" I smiled and took the keys from her and fumbled them in my hand.

"Why Seattle?" she asked me as she picked back up her clipboard and empty envelope.

"New opportunities," I stated. "I don't think I could ever leave Washington, but it was also the furthest place I could get from where I was with more to offer."

"Farthest away from family?" she asked, with a hint of humor in her expression.

"No, no family to move away from back there, so I couldn't tell you." I said, with an attempt at being humorous in return.

"Oh, I'm sorry," her face turned toward concern, humor having left her tone.

"Oh, no worries." I shrugged.

"Do you know anyone in the city?"

"No, but it's okay. I bounced around a bit growing up and you get used to being in places where you don't know anyone. I tend to meet people along the way, ya know?"

"Oh, definitely." She agreed with me. "In the spirit of meeting new people, I'm going to meet some friends of mine after my shift soon. You are more than welcome to join us if you'd like."

"Oh, I'm not sure. I think I may want to get settled for a bit here first."

"You have a suitcase and a backpack. I hardly think that will take you forever to settle. If you change your mind, we are going to the pizzeria. It is up the road a couple of blocks and we would be more than happy to have you join."

We exchanged phone numbers, and she told me that, if I could get settled, they would all be meeting there at 8. I smiled and told her I might come. She left the apartment. I looked around again at my new surroundings and felt content.

Several hours later, I had finished unpacking, gone to a second-hand store up the road, and had turned my bedroom into my first humble home.

*Mine.* I thought to myself as I laid out on the bed and felt a large sense of pride in the accomplishment. It may be silly, but I had never owned my own bedding, lamps, or furnishings before. For most of my life, all I had was the suitcase a previous foster parent bought for me, my clothes, and my essentials.

I looked at the time on my phone and realized it was nearing 8. I laid there and contemplated going to bed but considered that meeting new people would not kill me. It may be nice to make some new friends. I tossed my phone onto the bed, tugged my shirt over my head, wriggled out of my jeans, and went to take a quick shower. Rubbing the towel in my hair as I stood in front of the mirror, I realized that the past three years had been good to me. I was never the fat kid through school, but I always had a few extra pounds. My arms and chest now had more definition and shape to them, my chest hair had filled in along the lines that defined my pecs, and, while I still had a small stomach that lacked any definition, it was now covered with scattered trails of dark blonde hair that spread along my abdomen.

*I've changed a lot*, I thought. Continuing to look in the mirror, I threw some junk in my hair and messed it into a short tangle of blonde brushed to the side. I noticed that some dark blonde stubble had started appearing as a shadow across my cheeks, jaw, and chin. I considered shaving it off for a second but rejected it in favor of beginning a new style in this new period of my life. After I finished getting ready, I threw on some clothes, grabbed my phone and noticed that I had gotten a new notification from Jesse.

JESSE

Hey Lyle, getting ready to head to the pizzeria. Hope you had enough time to get settled. See you there?

LYLE

Ha ha I just finished funny enough. Yeah, I think I will join you all if that is still okay.

I stuck my phone back into my pocket and headed for the door.

As I reached the front door, my pocket buzzed with another text from Jesse.

JESSE

I thought the whole "See you there?" implied we still wanted you to join us, so yes, it is okay. See you soon. :)

I smiled at the sassy retort and laughed slightly.

As I walked a few blocks up the street, I noticed a small neon sign glowing in the shape of a pizza and assumed that this must be the place. I pulled open the door and walked into a small parlor-like space that was rather small and cozy. From the back corner, Jesse stood out to me with her wave, accompanied by three other people at her table. I walked to the back and joined the four of them.

"Hey Lyle," Jesse said as I took the seat next to one of the guys at the table.

Jesse did a round of introductions. A guy with reddish brown hair, matching beard, and beer gut sitting next to Jesse was her boyfriend, Reese. The two guys sitting across from them were Hunter and Phisher. Hunter, the taller one, had black hair and shockingly blue eyes. Phisher sat slightly shorter and was completely opposite Hunter, having short blonde hair and green eyes. As I settled into my seat, all had greeted me with a warm welcome as Jesse continued to introduce me.

"This is Lyle. He just moved into the UW apartments today and is new to the city. I invited him to come hang out with us since he doesn't know anyone in the city yet."

"Welcome to the city." Reese boomed as he reached out to shake my hand.

I reached back and shook his hand, saying, "Thanks." I settled in as Jesse returned to her conversation with Hunter and Phisher. As I worked my way into the conversation, I learned that Hunter and Phisher were dating each other and that the group of friends were all two years ahead of me in school. As I was freshly 21 and joining college, however, we were all relatively close in age.

"What were you doing the last few years then?" Hunter asked as I told them I was just starting school.

"I was working as a farm hand in a small town on the other side of the state and saved some money to move over here." I shared.

"Oh well, that explains why you are so freaking hot then." Hunter shared. I flushed at the compliment. Never having thought of myself as hot in any context prior. It never had really come up. I was quiet, kept to myself, and rarely had any time to make any great friends, let alone find out if anyone thought I was hot or tell me to my face that I was. I retreated into myself a bit, not knowing how to process the compliment.

Phisher reached over and nudged Hunter's shoulder. "Hunt, you are too much. You cannot just announce things like that to people you just met."

"Well, why not?" he exclaimed. "I did it to you and look where we are. Besides, I was just trying to compliment him for taking the long way to get here, which also produced the sexiness we see before us."

I continued to flush and retreat into myself. *Sexy? Hot and now sexy? A guy is calling me hot and sexy?* My mind was blank, and I had to keep talking, so I said "I..... uh, am not sure." I gulped, feeling uncomfortable.

"Oh, I am sure you were beating off boys and girls all the time," Hunter continued. I choked as I took a sip of water and said, "Oh, no, I haven't" and uncomfortably chuckled.

Jesse intervened just before Reese added, "He is trying to sus out if you're gay or straight." Jesse turned and smacked Reese's shoulder and said, "Lyle, I am so sorry about them. Feel free to completely ignore them for being so rude."

"It's okay," I shared as everyone chuckled. As a joke, I gave a non-committal answer, but I had put little thought into it, so I assumed I was into girls. I felt drawn to friends and colleagues I had known, but I never gave it too much acknowledgement. As I contemplated the question, I thought either option would be okay with me. I had never met any gay men before now and decided that they were both great and that I was happy to have met them. They asked me several more questions about being a foster kid and choosing to come to Seattle before moving onto the topic of the upcoming semester and what classes everyone would be taking. I found out that I was going to have one class with Hunter and one class with Jesse and was glad to already know at least two people that I would have a class with. Our night continued with other small conversations and then finished with some pizza and beer. The rest of the group and I exchanged phone numbers and we made plans to hang out again in a couple of days.

The rest of the night was uneventful. I went back home, climbed into bed, and passed out. The next morning, however, I woke up to noises coming from the living room. I turned on the light, threw on some sweatpants and a shirt and went into the living room. After opening the door, I saw a larger woman with big red curly hair unpacking boxes of kitchen things into the drawers and cabinets and a shorter balding man with a bit of a gut hooking up a flat screen and entertainment system in the living room. I turned my head toward the front door and a short, thin boy was signing papers with a girl from the front office who was helping him with his move into the apartment.

The woman with red hair turned and grinned an enormous smile at me, "Well hello there, you must be Lyle. They said you were checked in but we didn't see any boxes or things anywhere, so we assumed you may have been out. I am so sorry if we woke you. I am Susie, this is my husband Paul, and my son, Andy. He is your new roommate."

I waved back at them, a little overwhelmed at having such a bright and shiny response after just waking up. "Oh hey, no I.. uhh, finished unpacking yesterday. All moved in."

Susie looked at me with a shocked expression, "What do you

mean you're all moved in? Everything is still empty. Where are all of your things?"

Andy turned to his mom then and said, "Mom." Paul chimed in and said, "Suze."

"What?" she said, "I was just asking him a question."

"It's okay." I said, "I, uh, didn't come with much other than some clothes."

Susie continued her rounds of questioning, "Your parents didn't help you get anything for your apartment?" Andy cried out "Mom," in protest again and looked over at me with embarrassment on his face and mouthing, "I'm sorry."

I replied, "Nope, no parents to speak of, just me."

"Oh, I'm so sorry to hear that sugar. Well, no worries then we may have over spent some on Andy and you can use whatever you want in here. We got it all for you boys to share anyhow."

Paul finished plugging in everything and tucking it all away before joining in, "Yuuup. We got you boys all set up with your entertainment needs as well."

"That's right." Susie shared. "Paul here owns a small electronic store up north in Bellingham and we got you boys the best." As Andy's parents continued going over all the things they had gotten for Andy's and now my first place as well, the office gal had left and Andy shrunk down into a chair at the dining room table with a look of pure terror and embarrassment on his face.

He cried out, "Mom! Dad!" they both stopped and looked at him, Susie responded, "Well excuse me for paying forward your manners, this nice young man and you are going to be living together all year and hearing that he came with nothing it is all the better we over spent for you."

I responded, "That's very kind of you and thank you, I can get some of my own things."

"Nonsense sweetie, it is a mother's and father's job to help get their son's first apartment all set up. Oh, you sweet boys, we will take care of everything, don't you worry. You need anything you let us know, and we will get it for you two."

I didn't know what else to say other than, "oh, uh. Thank you." Suddenly feeling a little uncomfortable with all this unfounded hospitality, "Is there anything I can do to help?" I asked sheepishly.

"Oh sugar, no need to thank us, and aren't you so sweet? If you wouldn't mind helping Andy take some of these empty boxes out to the trash. That would be super." I reached for the empty flattened boxes and grabbed an armful. Andy grabbed the remaining few and followed me into the hall.

As soon as the door shut, Andy ran up beside me and exclaimed, "I am so sorry about all of that. They are so embarrassing. I hope they didn't offend you."

"No worries." I turned and smiled at him. "They seem nice. I am Lyle. It is nice to meet you." He smiled and responded, "Nice to meet you. I'm Andy." I smiled at his response.

We continued to walk down the hallway toward the elevator and as the doors opened Andy chimed in, "It is true though what my mom said, you're more than welcome to use whatever you want. They always just buy stuff for me and my friends; they have done it my whole life."

"I appreciate that. I am sure using what you brought would be a lot nicer than anything I would get from the secondhand store, so thank you." Andy smiled at me and nodded. Though being honest, I would not have minded getting some things on my own as well. Having everything already provided as part of my living situations all my life, I guess I was just used to it by now, but I did not want to be rude by not accepting the hospitality they were showing me.

On the way down, I learned Andy was 18 and a freshman as well. He had just graduated from high school and was coming to study technology. He was shorter than me, slender, with a crop of brown hair and deep brown eyes. He acted just like his parents, being overly friendly to people he did not know. They reminded me of a family I once stayed with when I was much younger, kind, eager to give to others, and very overbearing. I had thought once that I would stay with them forever, but she had gotten pregnant with another child of their own and they moved me into another house. I liked Andy. He seemed very young, sheltered, and naïve as an initial impression, but I felt like our first meeting had gone well. Odd, but well. I already had the feeling that I had made the right decision and that I was well on my way toward my next step in life.

# Chapter Three

Over the next couple of weeks that led up to classes starting, I got to know Jesse, Reese, Hunter, Phisher, and Andy. I spent most of the time hanging out with Jesse and Reese that first week, as Jesse seemed to take a specific interest in wanting to know more about me. Andy, not knowing anyone either, was never far behind, he seemed to become a shadow that followed me wherever I went. I had learned that Jesse was a psychology major and that she was passionate about pursuing a career in mental health counseling.

"I love psychology." She would say. "Knowing why and how people do the things they do, the different distortions in which our minds can lead us, and how it can be used to help people. Ultimately, that is what I would like to do - is help people."

It made me happy to know that one of the psychology courses I registered for, to meet a general requirement, would also be the class that Jesse and I would have together. I had never given much thought about psychology before and her passion for it made the subject sound more and more appealing. She told me earlier that she was estranged from her parents because of their Conservative beliefs and their refusal to accept that certain populations deserve equal rights. She said that, at that point, she decided that you can only scream at people for so long before realizing they won't ever change. I understood her passions but struggled with her choice of estrangement. Never having parents, I felt like maybe that bond should not be something to throw away. I kept it to myself though because Jesse was very strong in her convictions. I wondered if maybe she and her parents had more in common than she realized. They just were on opposite sides of the field. She and I had a very similar sense of humor, we ended up leaving ourselves in hysterics and laughing fits while others would stare, looking at us like we were crazy. I had worried once or twice about how close Jesse and I were becoming and how that might make Reese feel, but it didn't take long for me to realize that Reese was one of the most secure, down-to-earth people I had ever met and that he and Jesse loved each other. I thought it was odd at first because Jesse was so clean, nicely dressed, and more-or-less a type A personality while Reese was very laid back, more thrown together over being presentable and clean, and had a dying love for video games and sci-fi that was as strong as his love for Jesse. He and I grew close while I schooled him at Mario-Kart and Smash Bros, beating his overall high scores. The rest of the group was shocked — none of them had ever beaten Reese at anything video games related since knowing him.

Andy became my unofficial little brother in a lot of ways. There was another boy like him in one of my foster placements who idolized me and tried to do everything that I did. His parents did not care for how my presence made such a follower of their son and I was moved to a new home a little less than a month later. I wouldn't say that I made Andy a follower, but that he tried a lot of new things he had never tried before and our friend group pushed him to go outside of his comfort zone. Jesse and Hunter agreed I was having a positive effect on him and shared with me that I was 'corrupting' him, but in a good way. The small group I met on my first night in the city took to Andy just as quickly as they took to me. Hunter did the same thing to

Andy that he did to me on the first night and called Andy a twink! I was not sure what that meant until I looked it up later, which I regretted. It was not long after the semester started that Hunter and Phisher had Andy coming out of the closet as bi-sexual and Hunter doing anything and everything he could to play matchmaker for whoever was single. Andy was also an only child and after my initial meeting with his parents I understood what people meant when they called certain parents 'helicopter' parents. Andy, though, did not act spoiled. He was humble, shy, and apologetic to everything and everyone. I thought at a couple points that he appeared fragile in a lot of ways, but I grew to care for him as a great friend as the first several weeks went by.

I was a little more hesitant to go out with Phisher and Hunter absent from Jesse and Reese only because of our initial interaction which left me feeling self-conscious and unsure of myself. That faded away as the three of us bonded over a newfound love for iced coffees and was aided by how incredibly kind they both were to everyone they met. I had learned that Hunter had been out of the closet ever since he was 12, at which point his parents had disowned him and kicked him out of the house. I had thought my upbringing was unfortunate, but I couldn't imagine what that would have done emotionally to someone so young. It made me angry for him, even though he did not harbor any ill will toward other people including his parents. He inspired me with his perseverance and that, like me, he wanted a better life for himself and pushed to make that happen. We had a lot more in common than I had thought on that first night at the pizzeria. Phisher was shyer and more reserved than Hunter. He had come out later in life, after he met Hunter. They met their freshman year at the university, and he fell for Hunter's buoyant personality and charismatic attitude. When he came out, his parents were very supportive and they too fell in love with Hunter. I felt relieved when Phisher told me his story that both he and Hunter at least had one supportive family on their side. Though if they hadn't, I supposed they would still have had each other. They had been together for three years and

I couldn't imagine that any two people could be more right for one another. They both studied history at the University, Phisher was more interested in American history and Hunter described his interest as being a man of the world and wanting to know more about the histories of other cultures and the development of our kind.

It was so weird how different my life felt as the semester started. I never had strong relationships with others. As I was growing up, I did my best to be friendly to other kids and I had a couple of opportunities to make friends. However, the most certain thing about my life was how uncertain it was. I never understood why everything happened like it did, but I was grateful for my time now in this place with these people as I opened myself up to them and they not only accepted me for myself, but also would share things about themselves in turn. At one point, a month into the semester, Hunter announced that they were officially adopting Andy and me into their little group of four and while we all chuckled at the joking jester it meant more to me than I was ready to share. In my head, that is what they had become: my family.

As the semester moved from the first month into the second, I made some new self-discoveries. I was terrible with biology, stayed afloat in my college algebra course, was doing well in world history, thanks to Hunter, and I loved psychology. It was Psychology 101, in a lecture hall, with at least 150 other students seated in rows in what looked like a small auditorium, but as the teacher moved through studies and theories with Freud, Skinner, Jung, James, Pavlov, and Adler things just clicked. Jesse was the teacher's aide for the course and when I told her how much I was enjoying the class, we both nerded out. She started sharing advance notices of things that would come up in the class so that we could discuss them together prior to the topic being brought up in lecture.

"So, wait! You're telling me that Pavlov could condition a dog to drool at the sound of a bell alone just because he had conditioned him to do so?" I asked in disbelief.

"Not only a dog, though that is one of his most famous experiments, but with many animals." She spoke. "Not only that, but it works on people too. Psychologists have been able to repeat the study with people and we can condition ourselves to respond to a stimulus in the right circumstances."

*Amazing.* I thought to myself. I was just beginning to learn a whole new world of knowledge that I had yet to explore and I was already hooked. Jesse was so excited to have someone else just as thrilled as she was about psychology, and she was already mapping out the next series of courses I would need to take. I appreciated her.

Into the second month of courses the six of us fell into a routine. It was Friday night and it was Andy's and my turn to host a movie night. This was our 2nd time hosting everybody at our apartment and I was still learning how to have people over. For Andy, it was easy. We went out and bought a few 2-Liter bottles of soda, some chips, and would order a pizza once everyone arrived. We did not have enough space on the couch for everybody to sit, so we pulled out an inflatable mattress that Andy's parents had purchased for him, just in case he wanted to have a sleepover with friends. I chuckled to myself when it had arrived in the mail with a note explaining its purpose. Andy had been so embarrassed, but it served as great additional seating once pushed up against the back of our dining table chairs with a bunch of pillows for a backrest. We had rented two movies to watch, a romantic comedy about a guy and a girl and his efforts to woo her and make her his and a horror movie about a witch that lived in the forest and three college students making a documentary about her. At 7:30, Hunter and Phisher arrived in their pjs and brought along a pack of cookies to add to the food amassing on the dining table.

"Oh man! We are the first ones to show up. Phish, I told you I need to be fashionably late for these things," Hunter whined jokingly as he moved in to hug Andy and me. He had a flair for theatrics.

"I'm sorry Hunt, I guess I told you the arrival time was 15 minutes early again." Phisher stated as he winked at me and walked through the door.

"I didn't know there was a right or wrong time to show up to anything." I added as Hunter wrapped his arms around my neck and gave me a small kiss on the cheek. It made me flush every time. He did it to all of us every time he greeted us and when he said goodbye. It was his thing, and I didn't want anyone to know that was the first time that anybody had kissed me. Even though it was not a genuine kiss, just a sweet, friendly form of greeting.

Phisher followed Hunter in and gave my shoulder a squeeze as he set the cookies they brought down on the table. As he was doing so, Jesse and Reese arrived and walked in the door.

"Who's ready to watch movies?!" Jesse said as she entered, shaking a bottle of wine up in the air as she walked in. She enjoyed drinking and bringing wine to everything I had learned. However, it couldn't be red, it had to be cold, it couldn't be dry, and it always had to be sweet.

Hunter turned to look at her, "Yass. Werk." he said with returned enthusiasm.

We exchanged a few more greetings as everyone gave each other a hug or a squeeze and we all shuffled into the apartment and found a seat around the tv. Andy started ordering pizzas, after asking what everyone wanted, and submitted our order, Hunter and Reese started up their continuing debate about pineapple on pizza. With Reese being for pineapple and Hunter taking up the rebuttal.

"What movie does everyone want to watch?" Andy asked as he held up the two options.

"Ohhh! Let's do the romantic comedy!" Hunter said as he snuggled closer into Phisher's side. "I've been wanting to watch that one."

"I'm more inclined toward horror." Reese stated.

"I agree with Reese," I added as we went around submitting our votes.

Jesse smiled at me as she submitted her vote for the romantic comedy, and Phisher, as expected, chose whatever would make Hunter happy, and with that, the romantic comedy won.

As Andy put in the movie, Jesse returned to sit between Reese and me, handing me one of the small glasses of wine she had poured for everyone except Andy, because he was one underaged and he said he thought it smelled gross. I never thought it smelled bad, but I was not too big on the taste of it. *Bitter*, I thought to myself as I took a sip. Alcohol was not something I found enjoyable most of the time. I really didn't care for the taste, but occasionally, I would drink a few with them and have a good time.

The movie rolled on as it set up the guy to be super kind, funny, nerdy, but un-dateable in the movie's intro. He meets a new girl that he has never seen before and finds her attractive and starts falling for her. Then a funny scene, rejection scene, funny, and then first date.

"We really need to find you a girlfriend, Lyle." Jesse suddenly announces as the movie sets in on the date.

"What?!" I gulped with a pit in my throat that just appeared.

"Or a boyfriend. Jesse, you can't just keep assuming everyone is straight." Hunter added back in, agreeing with Jesse, but always offering the alternative.

"I... uhhhh, uhhhh," I groaned, going blank with nothing to offer to the conversation.

"Oh, come on, you two, let him be. He will find someone when he's ready." Reese stated with a smile.

"Oh, come on, Lyle, it's been two months since classes started. Isn't there anyone that you've met that you have at least found attractive?" Jesse asked.

"I... uh. I don't know." I said as I felt a nervous sweat gather near my lower back.

*Play it cool, they will drop it soon*, I thought to myself as I tried to think of something to say.

"Oh, sure you have Lyle, there are tons of cute boys and girls all over campus right now. You have not seen one person you are at least kind of interested in?" Hunter replied.

*They are not dropping it this time*, I thought.

"I guess there was this one person...." I started. "So, it is a guy!" Hunter screamed with glee.

"He didn't say guy dummy, he said person," Jesse stated back.

"Lyle, will you please just tell us if you like guys or girls before Hunter has an aneurysm trying to figure it out?" Phisher asked.

"I don't know," I said.

"You don't know?" Hunter repeated the question slowly.

"I just... it's like.... look it's....," I said.

"It's okay, Lyle. You don't have to be attracted to anybody. Some people just aren't," Andy added, trying to reassure me.

"It isn't that either. I guess what I am trying to say is both? I have been attracted to people and I find both men and women attractive, but I don't know if there's anyone that has... you know."

"Taken your breath away?" Phisher asked.

"That's so romantic." Jesse added.

"Yeah, yeah, but what I am hearing is that you have never been on a date. Like ever." Hunter asked.

"No." I sighed in defeat.

"Let me set you up with this guy, Lyle. Please, can we please get you one first date and then, like, we will never bring it up again?" Hunter asked with excitement.

"He is like a dog with a bone, Lyle. It is one date and he'll shut up about it. I would take that if I were you." Reese added.

"I.... okay," I said.

"Better make sure it's one hell of a good match then Hunt." Jesse added with a smile.

"Oh, don't worry about that. I will handle everything." Hunter let out a squealing sound of excitement before continuing, "you are going to have such a good time." Hunter was ecstatic to once again play matchmaker.

"One condition." I added.

"What?" Hunter asked.

"If you are setting me up with somebody, set Andy up with somebody too." I stated, Andy's eyes going wide.

"Oh no. I don't need to." Andy started. "Deal," Hunter said, cutting Andy off. Andy flushed and smiled at me. He was happy to be set up. He'd already had three crushes that he'd told me about in the last month alone and, if Hunter is a legendary matchmaker, he would find someone great for Andy.

With the deal struck, we returned to watching the movie. I took pleasure in convincing Andy to join me in this venture, but a significant problem haunted me. I had just agreed to go out on a date with a stranger, someone I had never even seen, and, as the thought settled, the nerves set in.

*I will deal with those later*, I thought to myself as the doorbell rang and the pizzas were delivered. Andy jumped up, answered the door, and returned with three boxes of pizzas as I stuffed my nerves away for the rest of the night. We continued through the evening, stuffing our faces and laughing along with the movie. I was so happy to know these people, to call them my friends, and to feel that I not only belonged with them, but they cared about me in ways that no one else ever had. They were the best friends I'd ever known and thought that they must be the best friends anyone could ever have.

# Chapter Four

The sun shone bright in the sky as it rose in the east and peeked through the tops of the evergreens that towered around Lake Crescent. It was a rare occasion that the western peninsula of Washington State had clear skies and sunshine.

"Chess......?" a woman's voice called out in the distance.

"Chess......?"

I awoke with the calls of my name ringing in my ears. The sun was touching one side of my body as I laid on the ground. I stirred and stretched out across the bare earth beneath me as I sat up. I pulled my knees to my chest, looked out across the lake, and I took in the beauty of the crystal blue waters of Lake Crescent. My family had lived here for generations and one day it would all be mine. I had been home with my family for the summer and it was close to ending. Soon I will be returning to the University of Washington to continue my family's legacy. It occurred to me that I should jump into the water to wash off the dirt that still clung to the side of my body. But, "Chess....," my mother, Emily, was calling me home. As I turned away from the lake, I took a final stretch and relished the feeling of the sun's warmth on my skin and the sensation of my body stretching all the way out to my toes. I ran back through the woods and enjoyed the sensations of my feet against the soil as I passed through the ferns and trees on my way home. I reached the edge of the trees right before they revealed the clearing containing our house and paused for a moment to take one last breath of the woods into my lungs before stepping out into the clearing.

"There you are Chess, we have been looking for you. Your father would like to speak with you. He is up in the study." My mother said as I bounced up the steps of our porch.

"Okay, yeah, sure. I'm just going to take a quick shower first." I replied as she reached out her hand to touch my shoulder. She moved her hand up and ran it through my hair, knocking out some foliage that hung behind my ear before saying, "I wouldn't keep him waiting too long darling, you know how busy he is." Then she brushed at some dirt that still clung to my shoulder.

She sighed. "Did you at least have the decency to not ruin another fine outfit before going out for a midnight run in the woods or are your clothes lying torn up somewhere?"

I smiled childishly, opening the door, and headed inside without answering. My mother was one of the kindest and noblest wolves, many in our pack looked up to her. She encouraged my siblings and me to never shift in clothes, as they would tear and be ruined, and she took a lot of pride in staying well-manicured and clean. We didn't always follow that rule, but no one ever really enforced it either. As I entered the house my younger brother, George, ran up to my side and attempted to tackle me.

"Where did you run to last night?" he asked as I hastened him into a headlock and scratched the top of his head.

"To the edge of the sea and back." I responded as I pulled him back up to standing and moved past him toward the stairs.

"Will you promise to wake me up so I can run with you next time?" he asked as I started climbing to the top.

"Only if you promise to not get expelled from another boarding school by the next time I see you." He smiled at me before heading back down the hallway and out of sight.

*That boy was some kind of trouble,* I thought to myself as I followed the curve of the stairs up toward the landing. I mean, I was a troublemaker through school as well, but he had me beat by recently being kicked out of his fourth high school.

*At least he was 18 and this will be his last year,* I thought to myself. Dad would have his work cut out for him this next summer, getting him whipped into shape before sending him to intern at the Union of the Wolves. Not the cleverest of names, but it was the organization that was founded and operated by the Alpha's of each pack. I had done an internship out of high school as well and it had allowed me to learn more about the packs outside of our own.

At the top of the stairs was my sister, Valorie, holding a towel and reaching out to hand it to me. I took it from her and wrapped it around my waist as she snarled. "You know, you could at least have a pair of shorts stored in the mudroom for when you come home. In normal families they don't just walk around in their skin all the time." I thought being the older between her and George, even by 3 minutes, she would have reached an age where sarcasm would stop being the only language she was fluent in. I corrected my earlier thinking, it was with Valorie that Dad would struggle the most, she was not one to easily fall in line without a fight. With her fierce attitude she could damn near be an alpha all by herself. I chuckled to myself as I reached the end of the hall and went into my room. I hopped into the shower, rinsed off, and threw on shorts and a tank top before heading back into the hall toward the study.

I reached the two large wooden doors that opened into the study and could hear my father speaking on the phone. A woman was on the other end of the line. I pushed my ear to the door and listened for a moment before entering.

"Noah, I really must press that it is of the utmost importance that he chooses a mate soon so that we can make the proper arrangements. He is of age to take a mate and to begin learning the ways of your pack in order to be its next alpha. I am afraid I must insist on encouraging him to take care of this matter as soon as possible, it is his duty." The woman stated over the phone.

My father grew irritable at being pressed for any agenda other than his own and said, "I take great pride in ensuring that my pack and its members will do what needs to be done to take care of itself, this includes my son. He will take a mate when I am sure he is ready to do so and then he will do his duty for our family and our pack. Do not call to pressure me again. I will let you know when to make the arrangements." He growled into the phone before he hung up from frustration and to assert his dominance over whomever it was he was speaking to.

"Yes, sir. I apologize, sir. We will wait for your call."

The phone disconnected and the tone went out. "Come in Chess." My father said as I stood by the door. I pushed open the door and walked inside. My father stood across his desk standing and staring out of the window into the woods, "I assume you heard all that?" he asked as I went to sit in the chair he had in front of his desk.

"I did," I replied.

"Chess, I don't know what to do with you sometimes." He turned to face me and walked around the desk. He rubbed his hand through my hair and squeezed my shoulder. "It's hard for me to blame any of the girls when you won't even attend the appointments to meet them."

"That isn't how I want to choose a mate. It isn't natural to have the other packs send their daughters for me to choose from, like some auction house." I protested.

My father returned to the other side of the desk and sat down. "Son, we've been over this numerous times. You are to be my successor and with that comes certain duties, including carrying on our family's legacy. It's a tradition for you to take a mate from another pack and carry the bloodline. Your mother and I met this way and your grandparents before us did the same."

I argued, "just because something has been done does not mean it should be done or should continue to be done."

"Chess, when you take my place, you will understand. You will choose a mate before you finish school, and you will take my place as the head of this family. I will give you that much time to make your choice. When you finish with your degree, you have to choose. If you do not, you will leave your mother and I no choice but to choose for you."

I growled deep in my chest at his orders, to which he returned an equally forceful growl. I submitted and left the study.

My father is a great man and alpha to our pack. In my early teens, when we started my alpha training, I noticed how many people respected and admired him. Even when I started sitting in on alpha meetings with my father, the other alphas would defer to him and show him respect, even when they would so easily undermine and argue with each other. He radiated an aura that no one ever saw, but all could feel. It demanded attention and would compel others to submit, even when they didn't want to. I wondered if I would ever have that type of influence over others, if I could live up to being the next alpha. My father's reputation earned him respect and admiration from all the packs in America, his support of the last leader influenced her election.

I was aware of what the UOW and my father expected from me, but I had never felt comfortable with it. This day had been coming since my training began so long ago. I had hoped for something to change before I would have to choose. It made me resent being a wolf, but thinking that at this moment, I knew it wasn't true. I loved everything about it. Running through the forest, the connection I felt toward nature and toward my family, the smells, the speed, and the strength. Wolves never get sick, and mostly, people would always follow my lead. The thought of being a prized puppy for the archaic system that the alphas of every pack created for the conservation of our kind made me feel like I was living some kind of nightmare. I would have to though, eventually; it's just the way things work. I growled again. My wolf was becoming increasingly agitated. I could hardly resist the urge to shift. On the skin of my hand, fur grew and spread up my arm. Normally all wolves controlled their shifts, but the wolf has a mind of its own. It's primal, instinctual, and will take over if we aren't careful. I steadied and felt the bones in my face start to twitch and stretch. I took deep breaths and tried to pull the shift back, but I couldn't control this one. My wolf rejected the thought of forced mating as much as I did. Feeling like I was going to be unable to stop the shift, I hurried down the stairs and out the front door. The full weight of the shift hit as I opened the front door, and the pressure within my body grew as my morphology changed. Leaping off the porch, I felt my paws hit the ground first. I ran into the tree line and headed north. I didn't run far, though. The excess frustration started draining away into the forest floor with each stride I took north. Being in nature had a heavy influence over us, and we always found solace when running through the woods. I stopped on top of a cliff's edge that overlooked much of my family's land. I regained control and shifted back and sat down, hanging my feet over the edge, and listened to the sound of nature around me.

I turned when I heard another wolf walking up the side of the cliff and watched as the giant gray and white wolf approached. At first glance, I thought it was my father coming to talk through the end of our conversation, to apologize for his gruffness like he used to when I was younger, but it wasn't. As the giant wolf reached my side, I could tell that it was my Aunt Jenn taking a seat beside me.

"Hey Jenn" I said as I turned to her and smiled.

She looked back at me and then nuzzled her nose into my arm. I sighed and scratched between her large gray ears. It was almost impossible to tell her wolf apart from my father's. They were shockingly similar in size as wolves, had nearly all the same markings, except for a white diamond formation on the top of my aunt's head. She shifted back from the wolf and rested her legs over the cliff like mine.

"I thought I might find you here." She said as she settled into place.

I looked over at her and smiled. Jenn was my dad's older sister. Like him, she had dark brown hair, but differed in her soft facial expressions and much more forgiving eyes. She was like a second mother to my siblings and me. She moved in after my 11th birthday with my younger cousin after hunters killed my uncle. I remembered her being so sad when she arrived. She had stayed in a shift longer than I had ever seen before. My mother and father cared for my cousin while my aunt grieved the loss of her mate. When she had finally shifted back, she took on a greater role within our pack. Teaching pups to navigate the forest, how to make use of herbs from the wild to enhance our healing abilities, and teaching other basic survival skills. As I got older, I could see that her pain was never too far away. It stayed with her and she never truly healed from the loss. I had asked my mom once, when they first arrived, why aunt Jenn stayed in shift. She had explained to me that when your mate dies, a part of yourself dies, and while we can find solace in family and pack, our lives will never be truly full again. My aunt had found a new purpose, it was enough for her to continue.

She whispered again. "Do you want to talk about it?" looking over at me with a side smile.

"Not really." I sighed.

"Okay," she stretched back, turning her face up toward the sun.

"That's it?" I asked.

"Yup," she smiled. "You're 25 now, Chess, I don't need to force you to talk about things you don't want to." She laughed.

"Just say it. I know you want to say it." I said, waiting for her words of wisdom.

"Not much to say Chess. You challenged your father because you got mad, and lost control of your shift, but you got it back, and now here we are enjoying this beautiful day." She kept her eyes closed and continued to grin.

"It's more than that, though." I sighed, pausing and reflecting. "Did anyone else see?"

"You mean did anyone else see you lose control of your shift like a pup, shred another outfit your mother bought for you, and ran off into the woods?" She paused for dramatic effect and looked at me. "No, just me." She smiled. "I got rid of your clothes and told them you ran to get something for me."

"Thank you." I sighed. Another moment of silence passed as we soaked up the sun and listened to the world.

"I don't know if I can do it, Jenn." I groaned.

"Do what?" she asked, self-assured and smug.

"Pick a mate like how they want me to. It's just not right. They shouldn't force wolves to mate this way. It is all business and blood-lines and bullshit. It is against nature." I blurted out.

"You're right." She agreed with me. I looked at her, waiting for her to say more, but she didn't.

"What do you mean I'm right?" I asked after a few moments of silence passed.

"You are right. We find mates the way we do out of necessity. I will tell you a secret, though. It isn't as bad as you may think." She responded. I remembered my uncle and her; they had been arranged through this system, but I had always believed that fate had blessed them to feel love for one another from the beginning.

"You know. I couldn't stand your uncle when I first met him." She sighed. She never talked about him, and if she did, it was only because she felt she had to.

"Jenn, it's okay you don't." She raised her hand at me to stop. "I couldn't stand that man," she laughed. "He was arrogant, pompous, and I never thought I could ever love a man like him." I listened closely as she spoke. ".. but the night we were mated, something changes in you. The wolf falls for the one you mate too. While it was not love at first sight, once we were mated I loved him as fiercely as I do today. I could never imagine my life going any differently than it did with him, but you are right wolves are not meant to mate in the way we do." She smiled at me again, a tear not too far behind her eyes. "Did your dad ever tell you about your Great-Grandparents?"

"Yes, and no. He said they were from a different time and that their generation established the UOW." I responded.

"Well, yes, that is true, but what he failed to mention is they were true mates. They found each other the way wolves should and their love was powerful. Not that your parents' love and my love were not powerful because it is, but for all the love I held for your uncle, I never believed we held a flame to them."

"See, why can't it be like that Jenn." I asked her.

"Well, I wondered that too and when the alphas made their decision to match mates, your great grandmother told me that what they had was very rare and couldn't be guaranteed to happen in a lifetime. Wolves are too few, we are dying out. Wolves can only be born and we need to ensure the survival of our kind." She paused. "She told me that once mated, the wolf will find love in their mate, even if it was not the same as it was for the traditional mating bond. The union binds the souls together and the love you have for a chosen mate will be no less than the love created by the traditional mating bond." She looked back into the sun and smiled. "She was mostly right, but man, those two shone brighter than any mated pair I have yet to see."

"Dad told me something similar about what happens during the union, but Jenn I still don't believe it. There is something different for me. I just feel it and I don't think I can mate like that."

"I know it seems wrong, Chess, but I promise you it's not. You will see in time. Trust in us Chess." She grabbed my hand and gripped it.

I sighed. I knew how it worked and I knew what would happen, but everything inside me fought against it and would continue to fight it untill I was left with no other option.

"I trust you." We looked out into the distance as the sun settled into its place in the late afternoon setting and she smiled at me.

"When do you plan to go back to Seattle?" She asked as she

leaned back, soaking in the last of the sunshine that now showered us in its golden afternoon light.

"In another week. Maybe sooner if there is more talk about choosing a mate." I replied with a grin.

"Oh, come on now," she patted my knee and jumped up from her seat. "I need a run. Will you come with me?" she asked.

"Absolutely." I responded by leaping up from the edge and heading back toward the trees.

She leaped out ahead of me before I got to my feet and I leaped out behind her. When we fell back to the ground, our paws crashed into the earth and we ran down the cliff side, bumping into each other playfully as we ran toward the coast.

# Chapter Five

In a few weeks I would return to the Seattle home our family had purchased for us to live in while we attended the university. Beyond the expectation of choosing a mate, we were all expected to go to college and choose a field of study that matched our pack's prestige. I found the expectation of an education much easier to meet than that of choosing a mate. My father had gone to school to be a lawyer and my mother had studied ecology. They both were very successful in their fields. My father had worked his way up to partner in his firm faster than anyone in the firm before him. My mother chaired committees that championed laws forcing companies to go green. In addition, she consulted with many companies regarding eco-conscious practice changes and helped to plan their implementation. It was the wolf. The wolf propelled us to be the best in everything we did, it was a surprise to no one to see a wolf succeed in their chosen field.

My family expected me to follow in the path of my father, but I found a passion for biology and natural sciences. I excelled in every class that I took before being granted an independent study course and a lab that allowed me to study DNA and genome mapping. It satisfied my family because after I pursued my interests I could attend some prestigious medical school with my dual bachelor's degrees in biology and chemistry.

During the last few weeks before my return to Seattle, I spent a lot of time helping my mom with harvesting her garden: picking, cooking, canning a wide variation of berry jams and vegetables, and prepping the beds for the fall and winter which would come sooner than expected. I spent as much time as I could with the twins and my younger cousin as well. I made continuing attempts to convince my rock head of a brother to keep his grades up and to stay out of trouble when he returned to school and listened to my sister discuss all her plans for what she would like to do after high school.

We had one last family dinner the night before I returned to Seattle. After I headed back to school the rest of the family would disperse. Even though we were never far from one another, our wolves found more peace when we were together, here, in our territory.

"When do your classes start, Chess?" My brother asked as we all started eating.

"Two days from tomorrow." I responded, giving him a grin.

"What courses are you taking this next semester?" My father inquired, probably trying to ensure I was taking a full course load.

"I will continue my independent study and take advanced micro-cellular biology, anatomy, and I will be a teacher's assistant for the first year's bio-series."

"Very good." He nodded.

"Do you think you'll come home for the winter break?" My mother asked.

"I will be back over this way in November, remember? I told my friend that he and some other friends could come this way to see the property and go camping near the lake."

"Oh, that is right. We will be in Portland then. I am sorry we won't be here to meet them." She said,

"That's fine. We won't be coming to the house, anyway." I responded.

"You'll keep everyone near the lake?" My father stepped in.

"Yes, sir." I responded.

"Good. I do not want anyone to go too far into the woods. It is too rough for humans and I don't want anyone getting hurt if we won't be here."

"Right. I remember the rules."

"No shifting while you are here, either. There won't be anyone nearby to run interference should any of them go looking for you. Are you sure you will be able to do that?" he asked, hesitant to grant his permission for a second time.

"Yes. I don't shift during the semester in the city. I think I can manage to not shift for a few days."

"Yes, but you will be home, and your wolf may feel more inclined to shift forms being in our territory. Especially if you lose your temper over anything."

My aunt Jenn interjected, "I think he will manage it just fine Noah." She gave me a wink and put her hand over my father's.

"I have it under control. There is no need to worry."

The dinner continued with conversation about what everyone would be up to after we all left. The night was uneventful. We played some games and the family all went for a run together late into the night before returning home. I would miss all of them tomorrow when I would leave to go back to school, but I was also ready to return to the city and regain the independence that distance granted me.

# Chapter Six

My stomach was sour as I waited to see the results of the first round of assessments that were about to be posted online. I was sure I would be pleased with my grades in psychology and history classes since I was doing well. Hunter's guidance in history made me sure that I had done enough right to at least do decently on the first test. Math and biology made me more nervous, I felt uncertain about where I stood with Math, and I knew I was not understanding much of the biology course at this point. I refreshed the page on the computer and the scores were in.

> Psych 100- Intro to Psychology- A
> Hist 203- World History- A
> Math 201- Introduction into Advanced
>     Algebra- B
> Bio 201- Intro to Biology- F*

"Shit," I said to myself, sitting at the library computer. I sank deep into my seat, seeing the "F" at the bottom of the screen. There was an asterisk on it which showed a note from the professor. I slid the cursor over the failing grade and a small window appeared.

Please see Dr. Derby for problem solving.

I sighed and moved the cursor to close the window. As I was closing out the window, Jesse was walking toward me so that we could grab lunch before going to our Psychology class together.

"Hey stranger." She said as she walked up beside me.

"Hey" I said in a deflated tone.

"What's wrong?"

"I failed the first biology test. I don't know what I am going to do. The professor wants me to go talk to him about it and find a solution, I'm scared he is going to tell me to drop the class."

"Oh man, that is rough. I doubt he will ask you to drop the class though. He will probably offer you some type of extra credit or something to make up for it."

"I don't know." I responded, feeling defeated. "It's just not making sense to me. I have never struggled with a subject this much before."

"Well, how did you do with all your other classes?" she asked optimistically.

"I passed them all." I half smiled back at her.

"Well see then, you're doing fine. You will figure it out with the professor. Just go talk to him, and he'll help you."

"Where do you want to go eat?" Changing the subject from my failing grade to something more positive.

"Hmm. I don't know. I could honestly probably just go for coffee if that is fine with you."

"Sure," I said. I felt like that was a good idea, given I still was feeling a small pit in my stomach over getting such a terrible score. I was feeling thankful, however, that it was Friday, and that I would have the next two days to not think about school.

It was raining outside as we reached the automated doors leading out of the library. I had grown to love the rain since the fall settled into the city and the warmth of the summer had dissipated, giving way to chilly mornings, changing leaves on the trees around campus, and lots and lots of rain. Jesse pulled an umbrella from her bag and she unfolded it as we stepped out into the rain and headed down the street toward the café. We walked inside, only having gotten slightly wet from the downpour that was occurring outside. The café was relatively empty and we moved to the counter. She had ordered a venti Americano, I ordered an iced white chocolate mocha. She smiled at me.

"Hunter has got his claws in you deep." She laughed as I paid for my coffee.

"What do you mean?" I asked, confused.

"Iced coffee even in the rain. That is definitely Hunter." She said, amused.

"It isn't," I disagreed, amused. "It's just fantastic."

*Yes,* I thought to myself, *Hunter and Phisher had me order it first, and yes, I agreed it was better iced than it was warm.*

*She's right;* I thought and admitted that they had definitely had an influence on me, but I couldn't help liking what I liked.

She continued to tease me a bit about it and we laughed as we waited and got our orders. We took a seat at a small table next to the window.

"Are you looking forward to your date?" she asked with a clear sense of amusement as we raced through general topics.

"No, not really." I admitted. It had only been a few days since I agreed to go on Hunter's blind date and he already had a guy who he knew thought I was cute and had arranged for us to go out tomorrow night.

"Why not?" she asked.

"I'm honestly not sure, I just..." pausing and taking a moment to plan what I wanted to say. "... I just haven't dated anyone before. I have no clue how to handle a date or what we should talk about."

"Wait! You were serious then? You have never been on a date

before? You're 21?" she said, as if my age made it weird that I have not already experienced things that normal people do when they are in high school.

"It just never happened. There has never been anyone that has asked me out or that I had any time to have a deep connection with. I moved a lot."

"What do you mean? I know you told me what happened with your parents and that you were in foster care."

"I was, but I was never in anyone's foster placement longer than maybe a couple of months."

"What? That can't be right. I don't even think that would be legal."

"It just was what it was. I move in and everything would go well, I thought, and then my case manager would show up and would take me to another home."

"Lyle, that's terrible. I am so sorry."

"It's okay," I smiled, giving her some reassurance. "I did all right."

"That makes sense now that you have not been on a proper date. Don't be nervous. It's just dinner with a stranger. Ask them what they like to do and their hobbies and just get to know them."

"I know how a date is supposed to go, Jesse. It's just there's been nothing I have found more than maybe friendship with others and if you could even call it that. You all are the first real friends I think I have ever had."

"Lyle..." she said with a tinge of joy and sadness in her voice.

"Sorry," I said, not knowing what else to say.

"You do not need to be sorry about anything. I am just thrilled that we met you." She smiled at me. "Knowing Hunter, he will have made sure that you and he had some things in common before setting you up together. So, I would imagine at the very least you could make a new friend. I think you will have a good time."

"We'll see." I said, shrugging my shoulders. "We better get going."

We gathered our things and headed for the door. It had stopped raining and we walked toward our next class. On the way there, Jesse encouraged me to go meet my biology professor after class to find out what I needed to do about my grade before heading home for the weekend. I agreed with her as we entered the auditorium and found seats toward the back.

We discussed more in depth information about the founding fathers of psychology and we were learning more about Freud. I sat and fidgeted with my pencil as I listened to the professor review some key components of his ideology.

*What a weirdo*, I thought to myself as she went into detail about his initial ideals and beliefs pertaining to psychology and all things Freud. The hour went by quickly and as the professor was wrapping up her final thoughts on Freud, I packed my notes into my bag.

"What did you think of Freud?" Jesse asked me as we walked back out into the hallway after class.

"Really interesting guy" I laughed, and she smiled.

"Oh, just wait, it gets better. Are you going to head to the science hall?"

"Yeah. I think you were right. It would be better to know everything I need to do rather than worry about it all weekend."

"Do you want me to go with you? I was going to go meet Reese for dinner. You can go with us afterwards."

"No, that's okay," I responded. "Go have fun. I'll text you later what all he says. "

"Sounds good. Let me know if you want any help tomorrow before your date. I could help you pick out what to wear."

I laughed, "I'll let you know." She gave me a hug, and we parted ways.

While making my way to the science hall on the other side of campus, the rain began again. I sprinted toward the hall, but by the time I got to the doors, I was completely soaked. I pushed through the second set of double doors that led into the building and looked up at a sign hanging on the wall for the direction of the professor's offices. The lights in the building were shut off for the weekend already, but as I reached the hallway of offices, several lights were still on. I started walking down the narrow corridor until I reached the office that had Dr. Derby written in black on a gold plaque outside the door. It was open just a smidge, and the lights were still on. I knocked on the door and paused.

"Come in," Dr. Derby said before I opened the door.

"Hey Dr. Derby. You wanted to see me?"

"Ahh yes, Mr. Larson, come in and have a seat." I moved into the office and sat down in the chair he was gesturing toward. "I've been noticing that you have been having a difficult time in the class, Mr. Larson, and with your first test score coming in so low, I want to make sure that you're getting connected with resources to help you." He stated.

"Yeah, I have been having some trouble understanding some of it." I admitted cautiously.

"That's okay; you're not alone in that. There are always a few students every semester that struggle in this class." Dr. Derby replied, "We have resources set up to help students who are struggling though and I wanted to get you connected with some before we get too far into the semester. I have reached out to my TA, Mr. Beck, and have requested that he meet with you and help tutor you. He has some time tomorrow mid-morning if you are available to meet with him. I know it's a Saturday, but I think you would benefit from some extra help. We don't want you falling too far behind."

"Oh, yeah. That... that works fine for me. Thank you, Dr. Derby." He smiled at me before handing me a piece of paper with the room number and the time to meet Mr. Beck.

*11:00 AM*

*Lab 214*

"He has a small lab on campus for independent study. He requests students meet him there for tutoring."

"Ok, yeah, great. I can do that."

"Sounds good Mr. Larson. If you need any more help, please let me know and I will see what we can do. Since the tutoring is on Saturday, I am going to give you a few extra points every time you attend to help with buffering this first test score."

"Thank you." I said as I got up to leave the room. I was thankful that Dr. Derby had offered help and not a verbal tongue lashing, maybe I would make it through his course after all. My goal was to succeed, but I knew that if I didn't try, I would fail the class and I was just relieved to not have to drop it.

I left the science hall and headed back to the apartment, feeling better about my first round of tests and knowing that I had made it through the first set of challenges the university had put in front of me. *Checklist,* I reminded myself. *Go to class, do the work, be on time, and all should be fine.* Upon returning home, I found that Andy was still out and was surprised to have some time to myself. It was 7:00 PM and it was still overcast outside. It, thankfully, had stopped raining during my walk home, but I could tell that it would start again soon. I went into my bedroom and collapsed on the bed. I looked out the window at the city skyline in the distance.

*How amazing is this?* I thought to myself. I had been in the city only a few months, but my life had changed quickly into something I could only feel was spectacular. It was a strange feeling, that I had so quickly grown to love this new life of mine, albeit so different from what I had experienced in my life thus far. I could no longer think of my life before which seemed strangely far away. I didn't understand how I had gone all that time without the friendships I had created since I had arrived in the city. Jesse, Reese, Phisher, Hunter, and Andy filled a void in my life that, until now, I didn't realize even existed. It started to rain again and, as the droplets hit the window, I slowly drifted to sleep.

I awoke the next day with my phone buzzing in my pocket, checking the time I realized it was nearly 10:00 AM. I was astonished that I had been asleep for so long. Checking my phone more thoroughly, I saw I had two notifications from Hunter.

HUNTER

Gooooood morning! I hope you are ready for your date tonight?! I set up reservations for you both in the U-Village for 6:00.

You are going to have so much fun. Be nice and report back as soon as it is over. I have to know how it goes. Luv you.

I rolled my eyes and sent a response;

LYLE

Good morning, U-Village at 6 got it. I'll text you tonight.

It made me chuckle a bit as I set my phone back down. I had one hour before needing to go meet with Mr. Beck. After glancing in the mirror, I decided I should take a shower. I dried off quickly, threw some paste into my hair, put on some fresh clothes, and checked the time again. 10:20. I hastened my pace and headed out the door. I hurried across campus and was walking up to the science hall right at 10:55, I sighed in relief knowing that I had made it on time. For some reason, I didn't feel complete relief. Something inside me shifted as I opened the doors to the empty building. Pushing through a strange sense of discomfort that felt like electricity shooting through my body, I made my way through the double doors. I took out the folded scrap paper where Dr. Derby had written the time and place of my meeting with Mr. Beck.

*11:00 AM Lab 214;* I read to myself. I attempted to use the elevator to go up a level to the labs, but it, like many of the lights, had been turned off for the weekend. Turning from the elevator, I walked down the hallway past classrooms and took the stairs. As I approached the 2nd floor door, I felt uneasy again. I pushed through the stairwell door and walked down the hall, passing several empty rooms that I assumed must be other labs.

208... 209... 210... 211... 212... 213....... 214. I fumbled with the piece of paper in my hands and the tingling throughout my body intensified.

*What is going on?* I thought to myself. I had never felt this way before. All my senses were awake and screaming. While I felt like they were screaming at me to run, there was something just a little louder pushing me forward. I hesitated again before reaching my hands out to open the door. The hair on my arms stood up and the sensation continued to climb up my arm until it reached the nape of my neck. I felt my flesh start to goosebump along my legs and thighs just before I opened the door and walked in.

The lab was far nicer than any of the others I had been in for our initial labs at the beginning of the year. For starters, it was cleaner. There were stainless-steel countertops filled with equipment I had never seen before. There was some kind of high-tech gear with a large section of what looked like plexiglass hanging in the middle of the room. My hair still stood on end as I moved toward the back of the room. I could see near the back of the lab there was a door open slightly with light pouring out of it into the space. I felt a lump form in my throat and the air seemed to turn very dry as I went to speak.

"Mr. Beck?" my voice cracked as it left my lips. No response. I moved closer toward the light and tried again. "...... Mr. Beck?" sounding a little less cracked, but I couldn't shake the feeling of the lump in my throat moving up and down as I spoke.

"Who are you?" a voice asked me from behind. I turned around with a startled gasp. I stared at the figure blankly as my heart and eyes settled from the initial jolt of adrenaline that shot through me. My eyes adjusted to meet his gaze and I flushed. My body temperature climbed and my heart no longer continued to settle back into my chest. If it was even possible, my eyes felt as if they dilated as they stared into his gaze.

*One blue eye, one green eye,* my mind thought to itself as it had processed the large man that stood before me.

*Tall.* My second thought stretched into place as I tried to look for the words I needed to say.

"Are you Lyle?" he asked sternly, while I continued to stare blankly into his unusual eyes.

*What is happening?* I thought to myself. It took everything to formulate, but I let out a small "y... yes." His gaze never left mine. He had an expression on his face that I couldn't read. I felt a weight in the room as he spoke. My ears had started ringing and I couldn't make out what he said. His mouth moved and all I could notice was a subtle cleft in his chin that rounded back into a broad jawline. My mouth went dry again. He looked at me, confused. His eyebrows shifted into a position that I couldn't process and then a stray piece of his well-kept dark brown hair fell out of place to rest across his forehead, drawing my gaze as he pushed it back into place.

I gulped hard, *say something,* I thought to myself.

"I. I'm failing biology" the words escaped my mouth. He shifted his stance a bit and continued to look at me. I could feel him staring at me as intensely as I was looking at him. The hair on my body stood on end and every nerve felt like it was tingling, radiating, and warm. After my outburst, his body appeared to relax a little and my body seemed to respond in turn. It felt like hours had moved with each second. His lips twisted into a toothy grin and he spoke again.

"I'm aware you're failing, I asked you how you were doing," he said matter-of-factly. He moved around me and as he moved, his eyes stayed connected to mine, his nostrils flaring slightly.

"Oh, uhh, yeah. I... I'm good?" It came out sounding more like a question than a statement. I felt my face flush, *Get it together man!* He continued to stare. "Are there any other students who are supposed to meet for... uhh, tutoring?" I asked.

He looked at me puzzled, "other students?"

"Dr. Derby said that there were others that would be... uh coming for extra help?" I still felt hot, but my words had returned to me and I started finding it easier to speak. The heat continued to climb gradually increasing along with the pressure I felt surrounding me. I could feel sweat gathering at my low back and the palms of my hands felt clammy.

"No, no other students. It's just you." He said, leaning against the counters lining the windows. He broke eye contact and I felt him look me over again. His expression remained quizzical. He looked at me in a way that made me feel like he was trying to figure something out.

I felt... I felt.... *How did I feel?*

"Oh... uh." I started staring around the room, looking at my exits in case I needed to run. My heart quickened, I felt lightheaded. And what was that smell? It smelled intoxicating and at the same time was making me lightheaded. I took another deep breath.

"I think... uh. I think," I said as the room started spinning.

"Lyle?" he asked before feeling the electricity inside of me disappear. My nerves went numb, my heart felt like it skipped, and my head went dark. I fell forward and Mr. Beck moved quickly to catch me. One hand grabbed my shoulder and the other my rib as he stopped my motion in one fluid movement. I regained my composure and looked up at him. He stared back at me just as confused as before, but now a look of concern spread across his face as well. I regained my footing and he kept a hand on my arm for a moment longer before I took a step back from him. "Lyle, are you okay?"

"I'm, I'm fine." I said, pausing to take inventory of my current bodily functions. "Yeah, I am fine." I said, answering his question, but also trying to reassure myself.

"Mr. Beck, I uh.."

He cut me off again. "Chess."

"What?" I asked.

"My name is Chess. Only my father goes by Mr. Beck."

I looked at him again, my senses restored. "Chess, I uhh... sorry."

"For what?" he asked.

"For all that," as I gestured to the area in which I lost my footing and fell.

He smiled again. "Oh, don't worry about it. Are you sure you're, okay?"

"Yeah. I'm fine." I was back in my head again. Completely embarrassed and looking like an utter fool.

Silence filled the room.

*Why was he looking at me like that?* I couldn't place the expression settled into his face, but I flushed again and said, "So... tutoring."

He snapped back a bit and responded "Y-yes, Dr. Derby let me know you failed the first test and that you've been struggling with the first unit. He is going to give you extra in-class points for coming and meeting with me, but for today I just wanted to get acquainted and set up a standing time for lessons." He took a few steps forward and then to the side of me to grab a medium-sized messenger bag I hadn't seen on the counter next to me. As he leaned in close to grab the bag, the smell returned, my stomach lurched, and I started getting lightheaded. The smell, it was coming from him. I felt my arm go fuzzy again, I shifted to the right in an effort to create a larger distance between us all while willing my arm to stop. Chess pulled out a phone and turned it on. He pressed his finger to the screen and said, "I can do Tuesdays, 6:00 in the evening, if that works for you."

"That works." I replied.

"Would you want to meet here in my lab or somewhere else?"

*Not here,* I thought to myself. I want to be somewhere with other people and not here in an empty building with him — alone.

"We could... meet in the library?" I offered as an alternative.

"That works. There are offices in the back we can work from. I will schedule to use one for the next three weeks. We can reassess then if your grades necessitate that we need to keep meeting."

I nodded and thought to myself a table in the front would work too. Somewhere more public. I didn't know if it was my deep shame from what had happened within minutes of meeting him or if it was something more, but further thoughts of being alone with him made my nerves twitch uncomfortably. I continued to feel tension in the air between us and fluttering jolts of electricity hummed in my stomach as I stood next to him.

He smiled at me and said, "Okay, then we are all set. Is there anything else?", returning his eyes to mine.

"No." I responded quietly. He smiled at me again and I felt my lips turn into a small smile back. "Well, I will see you on Tuesday then." I said, turning and heading toward the door.

"Lyle?" He asked as I took a few steps toward the exit. The hair on the back of my neck standing up on end again. Turning back around I responded, "Yeah?"

"Are you sure you're, okay?" he asked again.

I flushed and responded, "Yeah, I'll be fine," and gave a small smile while continuing my walk toward the exit. Each step I took away from the door and down the stairs gave an increasing sense of both relief and regret. I made my way out of the building and into the fresh air, taking in a big breath. The chill that clung in the air filled my lungs and it felt like the fire within me slowly extinguished. I stood in front of the building for a moment trying to figure out what had just happened but could find no explanation. I had never experienced anything like that before and couldn't decide whether it had been a sense of excitement, anxiety, or something else entirely that I couldn't even begin to describe.

On the way home, I replayed every moment that had occurred in the lab between Mr. Bec... Chess and me. I continued to recall the details of his face in my mind. I waved my card over the box at my apartment building and blindly pulled the door open when I heard the buzz. I started toward the elevator before hearing, "Lyle! Hey Lyle." I turned and Andy was coming in with several bags of groceries that looked like they may tip him over. "Would you give me a hand?" he asked. I twisted around and grabbed several of the bags from him, then helped hold the door open while he passed through.

"Thanks!" He smiled up at me. We continued to walk toward the elevator together and on the way up he asked, "Lyle, what's wrong? You look worried?"

I shook further thoughts of Chess from my mind as I looked at him, smiled, and said, "Nothing. I'm fine." He looked at me, a worried expression on his own face. We made it into the apartment and unloaded the bags in the kitchen.

"Lyle, I may have not known you forever, but I know that was the first time have you ever lied to me," Andy said abruptly as I moved to put a box of cereal on top of the fridge.

"What?" I asked.

"Don't 'what' me. I asked you what was wrong and you lied." I flushed as thoughts of Chess returned to my mind.

"No, I.." Andy gave me one hell of a look and I stopped myself and sighed. "I went to the science lab to meet with my tutor. I felt something I have never felt before and I don't know what happened or why." Andy sat down. I walked him through the events that had happened less than an hour ago in excruciating detail about how hot I felt, the way I couldn't speak, that I fell, and how Chess caught me, including how embarrassed I was. When I finished explaining what had happened, Andy started laughing at me.

"This isn't funny Andy" I said, "I think there is something seriously wrong with me."

"There isn't anything wrong with you, Lyle. It sounds to me like he turned you on." Andy continued to laugh.

*WHAT?* I thought to myself.

"No, that isn't what that was, Andy. It couldn't have been. I..." heat ran to my face as I turned red with the realization that he was right. Andy continued to laugh.

"You seriously have never felt that way about another person?!" Andy asked. "I feel that way anytime someone attractive starts talking to me. You have the hots for your new tutor," he chuckled.

"Oh my God, I do." I admitted out loud. "What am I going to do now?" I asked.

"Nothing, except feel the same way every time you're near him."

"Oh God," I groaned. My phone buzzed in my pocket, and I pulled it out.

JESSE

Hey how did everything go yesterday with Dr. Derby? Did you get everything taken care of?

Another Buzz.

JESSE

Also, did you want help getting ready for your big date tonight? Let me know!

LYLE

Yup, I did. I have a lot to tell you, but I'll tell you tomorrow when we all go out to dinner. For tonight - I think I'm good. I'm just going to go in what I have on.

Three little dots started bouncing across the bottom.

JESSE

What is there to tell?! Okay, sounds good. Let me know how it goes!!

I put my phone back in my pocket and Andy continued to put groceries away. "I'm going to take a nap," I announced as I stood from the table and headed toward the door. It was 2:00 PM and I had several hours before I needed to head to the U-Village to meet my date. Andy said nothing as I opened my door and headed for the mattress. My comforter cushioned the impact as I slammed into the bed. Suddenly, I was flooded with so many emotions, but paramount was the embarrassment. I rolled over, closed my eyes, and drifted to sleep.

# Chapter Seven

*W*hat the hell was that? ran through my head as Lyle stepped out of the lab and the door shut behind him. I turned away from the door and took a few steps toward my office before seeing a small piece of crumpled up paper on the floor. I reached down to pick it up and, as I unfolded it, the scent that had radiated off Lyle infiltrated my nose again. My head went light. It had taken everything I had to control my wolf from leaping through from the moment I caught his scent coming up the stairs. If I hadn't gone into the chemistry lab and inhaled those toxins, I didn't know if I could have controlled the shift that had almost started as he grew closer to the second floor. I read the note.

> *11:00 AM*
> *Lab 214*

The little note looked like he had all but torn the thing to shreds with folds and creases all over the tiny piece of paper. Waves of his scent leapt off the small piece of paper and I had to shove it in my pocket to stop the wolf from tearing at my insides again.

*Control yourself, Chess,* I repeated to myself again and again. How could a human like him drive my wolf so crazy? It didn't make sense. I had been exposed to humans my whole life and had never once felt my wolf so much as stir. With Lyle, all my primal urges had bubbled to the surface and pushed me to bite him. Thankfully, I think I had played it cool enough that he didn't suspect anything was off.

I was so mad at him, enraged at this person I had never met. There must be something wrong with him, I concluded. Why did he continue to sweat like he did? He kept getting warmer and cooler, every time he got warm I could feel it from across the room and his scent came along with it. It made my mouth water. He'd even had the nerve to fall, I should have let him hit the ground. It was a close call; I was lucky that he didn't feel my claws on his side when I gripped his rib. How could he be so stupid? There was no way for him to know the danger he was in just then, but why did he keep looking at me like that? Did he know? He looked so scared one second, then confused, and then normal again. My head raced at how the meeting had gone. This couldn't be normal.

*Should I call Dad?* I thought briefly. No, he would make me leave UW and go somewhere else. I've worked too hard here to leave everything behind just because of one stupid human. I could control it, I could keep my wolf at bay. Three sessions with him and he will have caught up with the class and I will be done with him. If he wasn't caught up by then, I would pass him off to another TA. It would be okay. Three more meetings. I could do that.

My phone chimed in my pocket. I quickly pulled it out and brought it to my ear. "Hello?" *Oh God,* my mind screamed as I realized the note had passed its scent to my phone. My spine shuttered. I held the phone away from my face and pressed the speaker.

"Hello? Chess... you there,"

"Yeah. I am here. What's up?".

"Are we still meeting at the gym to work out or are you bailing?"

*The gym?* I had completely forgotten, but yes, that was exactly what I needed right now to burn off what I was feeling. "Oh no, I'm coming, I'm on my way there now."

"Cool, see you soon."

I hung up the phone and returned it to my pocket. A jolt of energy ran through my body one more time and then I felt my insides settle. I turned off the lights in my office, grabbed my bag, and exited the lab. When I got to the gym and made my way to the locker room, I felt like my old self again. I changed and as I went to put my pants into the locker, the scent returned.

*Holy Nature!* I quivered again. *Why did he smell so good?* My mouth was flooded with saliva again and I could feel my teeth beginning to sharpen. I slammed the locker shut, startling the man next to me. "Sorry," I said, acknowledging that I closed it too hard.

From the locker room, I went up the stairs and jumped on the treadmill. I nearly maxed it out to get rid of the pent-up frustration I was feeling. I ran for about five minutes straight, before a girl looked over at me and noticed that I hadn't even broken a sweat. I lowered the speed and pretended to be winded a bit until she looked away.

"Hey Chess." I turned toward my name.

"Oh, hey Phisher, what's going on, man?" I stopped the treadmill, hopped down and we clapped our hands together.

"Nothing too much, man, just ready to get in a workout. Are you ready to head for some weights?" he asked.

"Absolutely, let's do it."

I followed him toward the weight wall and grabbed a free bench press. "Will you give me a spot?" Phisher asked as he loaded 45-pound weights to each end. "Let's do it."

Phisher laid down and lifted the set free from the bench. I kept a hand softly underneath the bar as he went for 10. I counted, "1... 2... 3... 4... 5... 6.... 7..... 8..... 9....... 10." He struggled on the last two and I helped him push the bar back into place to its rest. He took a quick five-minute rest and then went for two more reps. We switched places, but I added two more 45-pound weights to each end. Phisher looked at me wide eyed and said, "Man, are you sure you can press that?"

I looked at him and smiled, knowing that I could easily press double this weight, but this would be heavy enough for me to forget Lyle and sweat out some of this feeling. "How many do you want to go for?" Phisher asked.

"15" I said, laying back on the bench and putting my arms up to the bar.

"Okay man, here we go." He placed both hands under the bar lightly as I pushed it free from its rest and pressed. Phisher counted in time, with me pushing the bar back up all the way. I easily went for the first 15 and then took a quick three-minute break between sets. I broke a small sweat and the scent of all the other sweaty humans in the gym broke up the lingering scent of Lyle. We took turns on the weights for about 30 more minutes and then went back to cardio to finish. We each found a treadmill and started at a slow jog.

"How's everything going with Hunter?"

"Really great man, thanks for asking. He's not so thrilled to go camping next weekend, but he's happy that you said we could bring the rest of our friends along, so thanks for that," he replied.

"For sure, no worries. It's going to be great. You are all going to love it," Phisher responded with a breathy smile as he began to breathe heavier and pick up speed. We ran for ten more minutes before calling it.

"Hey Chess, is everything alright?" Phisher asked as we headed toward the locker room.

"Yeah, man, what do you mean?" I asked.

"You just went really hard this time, and you seem irritated," he said, glancing over at me.

"Yeah. Just some freshman failing bio and I am adding some extra time to my course load to tutor him. Didn't think that fell within my duties as a TA, but whatever," I smiled and opened my locker. A small growl grew in my chest as the notes' scent permeated the locker and my clothes. I grabbed a towel and shut the door. I took off my gym clothes, wrapped myself with the towel, and folded my gym clothes on the bench so as not to get them marked with Lyle's stench. Phisher took off his clothes and followed me to the shower.

"What else have you got going on this weekend?" Phisher asked as we turned on the water and washed.

"Not much. Just going home tonight and then nothing tomorrow."

"Would you be open for dinner tomorrow night? You could meet the rest of the gang that we are planning to bring camping with us?" he asked.

"Sure, I could do that. What time are you meeting?"

"We are going to the pizzeria. We should be there around 6."

"Sounds like a plan," I smiled at him. We finished showering and returned to the lockers. I put my gym clothes back on. Phisher gave me a side eye but didn't ask why I wasn't changing. I reached into my locker and shoved the tainted clothes into my bag and carried it at my side. Phisher and I said goodbye and I headed home.

I ran back to my building, keeping my bag close to me so that my wolf would not sense what it held. After buzzing myself into the building, I headed to the old freight elevator and raised the slotted wooden gate to step inside. I resealed the gate before buzzing my floor and feeling the slow lift ascend. My mind returned to thoughts of Lyle. The problem he posed was much larger than I had wanted to admit initially.

*Why couldn't I stop thinking of him?* My wolf howled internally, and I felt him bubble toward the surface again, he would not take a break, he wasn't edging me toward a shift, but I could feel him flipping and dancing in my chest wanting to sniff the tiny little piece of paper that was tucked away in my bag.

*No,* I said to myself, chastising one of the best parts of me for jumping and playing gleefully at one of the biggest threats we had faced to our security and the possibility of being exposed. I pulled the gate open, exiting the elevator, and my primal self continued its naive dance. I slid the door to the loft open and walked inside.

I took a deep breath again, tossed my bag next to the desk, and flopped onto the large leather couch with feelings I couldn't process. I groaned as I rolled over, facing the ceiling of exposed steel and wood. Lyle was going to be a much bigger issue than I had initially thought.

*Maybe I could pass him off onto a different TA now, rather than wait.* I began to think, my wolf growled. Even if I had wanted to and my wolf had agreed, I couldn't pass him off to someone else. It wouldn't look good and Dr. Derby wouldn't look favorably if I passed him to someone else before even working with him a few times. I was stuck. Inside, my wolf didn't feel stuck and jumped for joy at the thought of smelling him in person again.

*You idiot! You wanted to bite him. We do not bite humans.* I groaned again with frustration. *I will make you a deal.* I finally felt him settle. *We will see him again, but you must control yourself. You cannot bite him, and you cannot force your way through a shift. You must let me keep control.* He growled a bit, but settled again, and I could finally breathe. *We will see him again,* we both agreed. I rose from the couch, climbed the stairs to the landing, climbed into bed, and went to sleep.

# Chapter Eight

"Lyle?...... Hey Lyle?" Andy startled me awake from an afternoon nap.

"Hey Andy, what's up?" I asked as I let out a yawn.

"Are you still going on your date tonight? It's like 5:30," he asked, cautiously.

*Oh shit*, I thought to myself as I jumped out of bed. "Yeah... I, uh yeah, I am. I just need to get ready." Andy smiled as he left the room. "Have fun," he shouted, closing the door behind him. I hurried over to the mirror and gave myself a quick assessment. There was no time to shower, but I could fix my hair, brush my teeth, and change into a button-up shirt. I rushed through my list before running out of the door. There was no helping the fact that I would be a little late, but I was doing my best to get to the U-Village as close to 6:00 as possible. I left the apartment building and headed down the street, pulling out my phone to check my messages.

4 New Notifications

HUNTER

Heeeeeyyyyyy, hope you are getting excited. I just talked to your date and he is so excited to meet you. He will meet you in front of the plant store right at 6. Have fun!

JESSE

Lyle, try to have an enjoyable time tonight. I know you are probably stressing right now. Honestly, just act like you are going to dinner with us and you will be fine.

REESE

Hey man, have fun tonight.

PHISHER

Have fun tonight. Cannot wait to hear how it goes later.

I sighed and rolled my eyes a little. It felt nice to have so many people care about me and encourage me to do things I normally wouldn't do. I'd probably be single forever without the help. I opened the message from Hunter and sent a text asking him to let whoever I was meeting know that I was on my way and that I would be a few minutes late. He quickly responded.

HUNTER

A little late huh?! Playing a little hard to get? Haha

I would not be playing anything, but I knew Hunter was teasing me. I sent back a little laughing face and could see the U-Village in the distance. At 6:05 I went to the plant shop, but there was no one outside. I started looking around me to see if I could see anyone who looked like they were waiting for someone, until someone approached me from behind.

"Lyle?" a voice asked from behind me. I turned in response and saw a guy who looked oddly familiar standing in front of me.

"Yeah." I said kindly, offering him a small smile. "Are you who I'm supposed to meet?"

He flushed and said, "Yeah, I am Jacob. It is nice to finally meet you." He smiled shyly; I searched my memory from where I had seen him before. He was appealing. I mused as I scoured my memory for information. He was shorter than me, although that was not uncommon. He had auburn hair, green eyes, and slight facial hair that he clearly maintained well. Although his appearance was not athletic, he kept himself in shape and took care of himself. I couldn't place him, so I asked, "Have we met each other before? I feel like I know you from somewhere."

He smiled again. "No, we have not ever officially met, but we do have biology together. I sit bottom right and you sit top left."

*That's it*, I thought, immediately linking him up with the missing information, finally recalling him in the enormous crowd of students that make up the lecture hall.

"Oh, awesome," I added, smiling at him. I felt a little awkward before asking, "Do you know where our reservations are at?"

"Yeah, I do. Should we head that way?" I nodded in reply and we started walking toward dinner.

We exchanged casual conversation about our day's and the recent arrival of fall before walking up to an Asian style restaurant with dumplings and an assortment of other delicious looking food. We walked up to the podium and Jacob told the hostess we had a reservation for two at 6:00 PM. The hostess greeted us nicely and smiled as she asked us to follow her. The restaurant had dim lighting and they spaced the tables out from each other to add a small amount of privacy to those dining in the restaurant. They sat us at a table in the back corner near a window that looked out over some small shops across the street. I took the seat facing the window and Jacob sat opposite of me. The hostess handed us each a menu and let us know our server would be with us shortly.

"Have you ever been here before?" Jacob asked as he opened his menu.

"No," I replied, "but it smells fantastic."

"I've been here a couple of times and it's great," he smiled at me again.

"So... how do you know Hunter?" I asked.

"We had some classes together last year. He is a really great guy." Jacob was a year ahead of me in school but was a year younger than I was in age.

"How are you liking our biology class?" he asked, after I agreed that Hunter was a good guy.

"Oh... It's... uh... It's alright," I started. I didn't really want him to know that I was failing the class at the moment, so I downplayed the challenges it held for me and asked him how it was going for him.

"It's going well. Pretty good overall." He smiled again and the waiter approached, taking our orders. We continued with small talk while we waited for our food to arrive. The date had been going well overall, I thought, but I already knew in my head that while Jacob was attractive, there were no sparks for me. I glanced out the window for a moment while Jacob talked about how he really likes plants and how he maybe had too many of them in his place.

My heart skipped a beat when I saw a man leave a bookstore across the way. *Chess?* My eyes traced the man's features quickly hoping to make an identification, but it wasn't him. The hairs that had risen on the back of my neck laid back down and my heart stilled in my chest. Jacob was still talking, and I was doing my best to listen to his story about a time he had gone hiking with friends, but images from this morning danced through my head of Chess's toothy grin, his handsome face, and his eyes. I had never seen eyes like his. One blue, one green. It had been entrancing how stunning they were and how they elevated his appearance substantially, making him unique. The waiter disrupted my inappropriate thoughts and snapped me back to the present by delivering our food. I had gotten pork dumplings and Jacob had gotten.... Something?... I felt guilty. I wasn't being very kind and I felt like a terrible date. Jacob's stories were humming along and he didn't seem to notice that my attention had wandered away from him and the table. It wasn't right though. I pushed my attention back to the table.

"Wow, this looks great," he said as we opened our steamed basket of dumplings and started eating. He was right; it was fantastic. He continued telling another story about the first time he had eaten here with his friends and I tuned in as we ate. Once he finished, he looked at me and smiled, "I'm really glad Hunter set us up on this date." Smiling back at him, I said, "Yeah, this was fun." I was having an enjoyable time. He was nice, the food was good, and the setting was pleasing, but still no sparks.

"I have to admit, I was super surprised when Hunter told me you liked guys." He flushed as he gave me a flirtatious smile. I suddenly felt myself shift awkwardly.

"Uh... ye, yeah. It is, umm, sort of new?" I started. "I, uh. I like both?" It came out as more of a question than a statement of what I was.

"Oh, so you are bisexual?... That's cool," he laughed a little. I agreed with his conclusion.

He had done it again, flushing and smiling, making eye contact, looking down, and then making eye contact again. He was flirting. "I, umm. I must admit, I had the hots for you the moment I saw you at the start of the year." He turned a little redder having admitted his secret. It made me shift in my seat a little as I thanked him and smiled back. Then he asked, "Did, did you notice me too?" He looked up at me like he hoped I would say that I had.

I had to be honest. I saw him that day and had grouped into a nice-looking category, so I said, "Yeah, I saw you," he blushed.

*I hope I am not leading him on*, I thought to myself. I was relieved when he started telling another story about a time when his friend and he had gotten caught doing something in class. As the story went on, I thought to myself privately again about Chess' eyes. His smile. *Stop it, Lyle*, snapping myself into the present. The date was nearing its end. I had given my card to the waiter, and we were waiting for him to come back with it so that we could leave. Jacob was telling me that he had a delightful time and was so happy to have been able to get to know me better. I kind of thought it was funny, because he hadn't really gotten to know anything about me since he had been talking the entire time.

When the check returned, I left the waiter a nice tip, signed the ticket, and we left the restaurant. Outside, Jacob thanked me again and gave me a hug. Then, I was nearly blindsided when he asked, "My place isn't too far from here, if you want to come over and, I don't know, continue getting to know each other, that would be cool." He had unbuttoned the top of his shirt and was clearly making passes as to hint how we would be getting to know each other if I were to agree.

"I. uh. That would be great, but it's getting kind of late. I have some things in the morning I need to take care of," I said, trying to be convincing and not hurt his feelings.

"Oh, okay. Another time then," he stated, sounding self-assured that there would be another time.

He hugged me one more time and we went our separate ways. I felt a little relieved that it was over as I headed out of the U-Village and started toward the direction of the apartment. I pulled out my phone again.

2 New Notifications

> JESSE
>
> How did it go?
>
> Call me when you head home!

I opened my phone and hit the call button near Jesse's name, I heard it ringing on the other end.

"How did it go?"

"Uh, it went."

"Uh oh. What happened?"

"Nothing. I just. Okay, this is going to sound so awful, but I kept thinking of someone else the entire time and Jacob mostly just talked about himself."

"Oh Lyle, that's a bummer. Who were you thinking about?"

"My new Biology tutor, he is the TA for my class". I began detailing what had happened that morning including how nervous I was and how he made me dizzy, how I fell and he caught me, about the electricity in my body, the way he smelled, looked, and his eyes that had just mesmerized me.

"Sounds like you have a crush," she laughed.

"I... uh, yeah, maybe? I felt terrible, but I just couldn't get him out of my head the entire time. Does that make me a bad person?"

"No, it doesn't make you a bad person. It just means Jacob isn't the right person."

"Jacob asked me to go home with him after dinner."

"He what?! That's crazy. Guess the date went well for him then," she said with a chuckle.

"Guess so."

"Well, you will have to tell him eventually that you don't feel the same way, but you don't need to worry about that yet."

We continued talking about Chess and my date and how we were both looking forward to dinner tomorrow evening.  As I walked up to my building, we said good night and disconnected the call.

*What a day*, I thought to myself as I slipped out of my clothes and climbed into bed. I can still remember the days where the only exciting thing I did was re-shoe a horse or clean out the mouse traps in the hay barn. Now I'd had my very first date and my very first crush and on top of that they were with totally different people.

As I went to sleep, I retraced what had happened with Chess that day, including how I had totally screwed up any chance of redeeming myself in his eyes. He probably wasn't even attracted to guys. *Great, I probably had no chance with someone I was actually attracted to. Amazing Lyle, you can be such an idiot sometimes.* I finally fell into a fitful and turbulent sleep as thoughts raced through my mind.

The next morning and afternoon sped by without too much

effort. I caught up on some laundry, did some other chores, and then, before I knew it, Andy and I were getting ready to go meet the gang for dinner. We walked into the restaurant right on time, and per usual, Jesse and Reese were already at the back corner table. It had unofficially become our spot by now and having a spot with friends made me happy. Jesse had already told Reese about how the date had gone and that I had the hots for my new tutor. He was thoroughly enjoying teasing me about it all and I just flushed and tried to take it in stride. It was humorous and, had it been any of them, I would have done the same. Not too much time had passed before Jesse was waving toward the door at Hunter, Phisher, and someone else wit... *oh my God.* The moment we made eye contact, my heart stopped in my chest, the electricity came back, and I turned back toward Jesse with a speed I had never moved with before. She gave me a weird look as the three approached. Andy turned and looked at me, curious as to what was happening. With every step he took closer to me, I could feel more electricity and the heat started climbing again.

"Hey everyone," Hunter announced as they reached the table. Phisher and Hunter took their usual seats and Chess took the only other empty seat next to.... Me.

"Hey guys, this is my friend Chess Beck," Phisher said as they sat down. Phisher started going around making introductions and, as she heard the name, Jesse turned to me with wide eyes. I couldn't react to her. I couldn't even breathe with Chess sitting next to me. Everyone made polite introductions around the table until Phisher got to me and he started in with "and this is...,"

Chess cut him off, "Lyle."

"Oh, you two have met?" Phisher asked. The rest of them started noting my apparent oddness. As he said my name, a lump grew in my throat again.

"Yeah, we met yesterday. I am helping him with some of his biology work," he said in acknowledgement.

"Oh, so you're the tutor," Reese said with an inflection in his voice as he connected the dots. Hunter, not missing a beat, started automatically filling in blanks. I could see him putting it together in two-seconds flat, even though no one had told either of them anything.

I couldn't say anything, if I spoke, my voice would crack and it would just make the whole thing worse. So instead I smiled and took a sip of the water in front of me. "Well, that's cool," Hunter interjected. I knew he would grill me about information and details later, but God bless him for knowing how to change the topic when he figured out how uncomfortable I was, sweeping in to save me.

"You guys, I have got to tell you about the cutest thing that Phisher did for me yesterday," I loved him for that — knowing just how to move things along. He glanced over at me and in his eyes, I knew he was telling me, *I got you.*

He went into detail over an insignificant thing that Phisher does all the time, Chess leaned in toward my side and whispered, "Hey Lyle, are you okay? I'm sorry if I shouldn't have said anything about helping you with biology." I turned to look at him. His eyes and brows shifted, looking concerned that he had upset me somehow.

"It's okay," I said, barely higher than a whisper. *Relax, Lyle, relax.* The group continued talking about how everyone's week went, but I couldn't really follow everything that was being thrown around the table. I was focusing on my breathing, staying cool, looking interested in the conversation, and pretending that everything was normal, but I knew it was not. I glanced over at Chess, trying not to get caught, and he was looking at the group, getting to know everyone new.

*He is incredibly handsome,* I thought to myself. He had great posture, dressed nicely, and as I continued to stare, he turned to look at me again. We locked eyes and I spun my head toward Jesse. She smiled at me humorously and I felt warm. I had never felt this way before about anyone. Why now, suddenly, did I feel so intensely about him? I couldn't understand it. My body felt like it called out to him, I was doing everything I could to keep what I was feeling on the inside from showing on the outside.

"So, Chess. This is the crew that will be going," Phisher started.

"Great," he said, smiling and looking at everyone.

"Going?" I asked. I looked around at their faces, clearly confused.

"Camping," Jesse said matter-of-factly. "Remember, Lyle, we are all going camping next weekend?"

I did remember, they had been talking about it for a couple of weeks now, but I hadn't known it was with him. I hadn't met him yet. I didn't know the way he made my insides burn and how it was hard to breathe when he was near me. I didn't think I could spend an entire weekend feeling like this.

"I.... I don't have any camping stuff to go." I said calmly as I turned back to the group.

"You already said you were going to go, Lyle," Hunter retorted, hinting with annoyance in his utterance. "You can't back out now. It won't be the same if you aren't there with us."

"Plus, I have extra you can use. You should come," said Chess. Hearing the words come out of his mouth made my skin burn. Electricity shot through my stomach, nearly making me double over, but I couldn't bring myself to look over in his direction. I slowly turned to look at him again, he was looking back at me, flashing that bright, toothy smile of his. "My family has more than enough stuff. You will be very comfortable," Chess said, raising his eyebrows slightly, awaiting my response.

*Was he hoping I would say yes?* I turned again to the rest of the group, who continued to stare me down, only this time Hunter was smiling from ear to ear at Chess's offer of help.

"Okay," I relented, "I'll go." As soon as the words came out, I felt like swallowing them whole again. I turned slightly and saw Chess smile, although for a moment I thought I saw a look of regret in his eyes and it tore me up inside thinking that he didn't actually want me there. He already has to tutor me and now he was going to be forced to spend a weekend with me just because we had some friends in common. Then, just like so many times before, I felt the sting of rejection, but it hurt more this time than it ever had previously because this time I had hoped that maybe, just maybe he may have felt the same way about me that I did about him. I pushed the thought to the back of my mind and decided I had to force myself to stop these feelings. I could be nice, accept his help with biology, spend a weekend camping with him and my close friends, and that is all this would be.

# Chapter Nine

After the dinner on Sunday ended, Jesse and Andy filled the rest of the crew in on my incredibly embarrassing crush. Hunter was elated, because I was finally attracted to someone, but also said that if I was going to be a proper bi-sexual and date men then first I needed to make sure the guys I found attractive were also interested in men. Phisher had told him that Chess was about as hetero as they come and that even though he shipped the idea that it would not work out.

On Monday night, I went over to Phisher and Hunter's place where they all but confirmed Chess' preferences by telling me that Chess had said something to Phisher about having to tutor "some freshman" in biology. I didn't tell them much more but hearing that he said it the same day we had met had my head and heart spinning.

*I'm not going to go,* I thought to myself on Tuesday morning, *to tutoring or camping.*

*He did not have to DO anything;* I thought to myself. I would just fail the class or ask Dr. Derby for another option, although I knew I couldn't do either. Tutoring was still an option, but I'd have to lie to get out of the camping trip and my friends would be furious if they ever found out why. I didn't want to take the chance of losing them by attempting to find an excuse not to go. I thought maybe if I was honest with them about how I felt that they would let me out of going, but I didn't want to do that either. Instead, I did nothing and continued to feel trapped by it all.

The days came and went in an instant and, before I knew it, I had to decide whether I should cancel tutoring or go. It was 5:00 PM and I was standing in between the library and my apartment. I started pacing in the small courtyard in front of the library, fretting about doing any option at this point. It felt so complicated, but it wasn't. I had never been in my head so much about anything up to this point in my life and it was giving me a headache. I sat down on one of the small cement benches nearby and it started raining.

*Good*, I thought to myself. The weather outside is just as unpredictable as how I feel on the inside. I sat in the rain for a moment and let it soak through my hair, turning my gray t-shirt dark where the drops hit. I checked the time on my phone, 5:45 PM. I couldn't believe I had been sitting here for forty-five minutes trying to decide what to do in a situation that should not even be that complicated. I decided I would just send him an email that I wasn't feeling well before getting up from the bench and leaning down to grab my bag.

"Hey Lyle!" I shot up and, before turning around, the hair standing up on the back of my neck had already given him away. I turned and standing in front of me stood Chess, all tall and gorgeous, with an umbrella above his head. "What are you doing out here sitting in the rain?" he asked.

"Uh, nothing," I said, bewildered.

"You're all wet," he replied, looking me up and down through his stunning eyes.

*Thanks, captain obvious*, I thought to myself.

"Yeah, well..." I looked down to acknowledge his statement and added, "... I like the rain." He smiled at me before taking the few quick steps that had been separating us and held his umbrella above my head.

"That's something we have in common then," he smiled, "... but you probably don't want to be soaking wet while we review biology, do you?"

*You don't know*, I thought to myself as I looked up at him.

"I guess not," I shrugged, he continued to grin at me in a self-satisfied manner.

"Well, we can walk to the library together, we'll share my umbrella," he gestured toward the library and I followed. I had literally just decided to go home and cancel this meeting, but now here I was walking shoulder to shoulder with him walking toward the library. I kept trying to move away from him, to keep my distance and continue to break down this attraction I had created in my mind, but every time I tried to inch away, he would move toward me again, ensuring I stayed covered under his umbrella. We didn't speak the entire walk to the library and, as we approached, all the lights were off with a note hung on the doors.

Closed due to power failure.

*Thank God.* I felt so relieved, now I could go home. I turned toward Chess and said, "Oh no, I guess we can just meet another time," he looked a little angry facing the door and I felt like I heard him make a noise before he turned to me and smiled.

"Nonsense, we can just go to my place. It's right around the corner from here," he said. The idea made me tremble a little. I did not want to go to his place. Especially after just deciding that I wanted to spend as little time with him as possible. I needed to get away from him so that I could stop feeling like he was the most attractive human on the planet. My heart stopped at the idea and the electricity returned, feeling like it grew from my stomach and rose until it was shooting out my shoulders.

"I uh. I don't know," he stopped smiling and looked at me "I mean..." I didn't know what else to say. He just continued to stare at me, those peculiar eyes penetrating my core. I turned to look away and wondered what would happen if I just started running. Would he think I was super weird or would he try to stop me? Looking at him I felt like it could be either.

"We don't have to," Chess said, breaking the silence. The rain poured a little heavier and hit his umbrella with louder thuds than before. He looked up, "I would feel better if you would come over at least until it stops raining like this. I don't think you should walk home in this amount of rain." Before I even had a moment to reply, a flash of lightning cracked in the sky and he immediately reached out, grabbed my arm, and pulled me in slightly. He looked at me again and said, "Please." His hand around my arm compelled me to agree with a nod and, with that, he took my arm and led me forward to his place.

He wasn't kidding about it being just around the corner because we had easily walked to a building that he said was his home within ten minutes. I looked up at the old building, thinking that there was no way this was an apartment building, but continued to follow him through a door on the side of it. We walked down a short hallway before reaching an old freight elevator. He lifted the wooden gate up and we walked in. He smiled at me softly before turning to close the gate and pressed the button to move the elevator up. We had passed several floors before realizing that he was taking us all the way to the top of the building. I stared at him from behind and realized that he was much bigger than I had originally thought, I could see the muscles run down from his broad shoulder into his back. I suddenly felt a little nervous, but before I could go too much into my mind, we had reached the top floor and he was opening the gate. I followed him into the hallway, waited for him to re-secure it, and then followed him toward a giant sliding door. He unlocked it and slid it open before gesturing for me to go inside. As I walked in, the beauty of the place stunned me and I realized it was one of the nicest places I had ever seen. I turned to him as he slid the door shut and locked it again. He turned around and smiled.

"This is your place?" I asked him, clearly in shock.

"Yeah, this is home." He slipped his shoes off and walked ahead of me a bit before flopping onto a large, light brown leather sectional which was centered in the middle of the room. I looked around and took in the impressive industrial space. Two of the walls were brick and all the outer walls were old factory set windows that displayed an impressive view of the entire city skyline, currently being pelted with heavy drops of rain. I started walking toward the far side of the sofa when a large flash of lightning illuminated the loft even brighter. I stared up at the winding staircase that led to a platform that sat over the kitchen. Everything was so nicely decorated, it looked like someone had styled the space professionally, down to every nail. He observed me as I examined his space, and his eyes followed me as I walked to the other end of the sectional and slowly sat down.

"What is it?" I asked him as the silence began building in the air, creating a thick layer of pressure.

"You're soaked," he replied casually, and I realized he was, in fact, correct. My shirt was dark gray and as the water weighed it down it clung to my body tightly. I looked back up at him and shrugged my shoulders.

"Oh well," pausing for a moment, "it'll dry." I dug into my backpack to pull out my biology text and when doing so, Chess stood up from the couch and started walking away. I felt so nervous being here with him. *Why did I agree to come here?* My mind was running as I reached for a notebook and pencil. I set my backpack down beside my leg and leaned it against the couch, looking around waiting for Chess to return from wherever he had just gone. I watched outside as the rain continued to come down in waves before hearing Chess climb back down the winding stairs.

"Here. Change into this," he instructed, handing me a purple Huskies hoodie.

"Oh no, I am okay. Really... my shirt will dry" he looked at me disapprovingly.

"Not for a while, it won't. Just change into something dry so we can get started," he looked, frustrated, and before I thought to turn down the dry shirt again, I complied. I stood up from the couch moving behind it, all the while, his eyes followed. I hesitated. I felt embarrassed with him watching me and just before I went to slip my shirt over my head, I stopped. He continued to stare in my direction.

"Can you like.... turn around for a second?" I asked him nicely. He looked at me curiously, like my request was one of the oddest things he had ever heard.

"We are just guys, you know?" he looked at me with a grin, "Are you shy or something?"

*No.* I thought to myself, *I just don't want you to watch me because you make my skin hot every time you look at me.*

"Or something," I said sheepishly. He smiled, still looking confused, and he turned away as I had asked. Taking off my soggy shirt, I put on the purple hoodie. I shuddered, sticking my head inside the sweatshirt because it smelled like him, it made my skin rise into small bumps all over my arms and legs as the scent filled my nostrils. I pushed my arms through the sleeves and pulled it down, sliding my head into the hood. When I opened my eyes, he was looking at me again. I flushed. The hoodie was a lot larger on me than I thought it would be. I expected us to be approximately the same size, but it was clear he was more muscular. After getting the hoodie pulled down, I leaned over to grab my wet shirt and moved back around to sit on the couch. I threw the shirt into the empty front pocket of my backpack and looked over at him.

"Ready?" I asked him, sitting upright and grabbing my textbook. He smiled at me and said, "Sure thing."

He moved in closer and we reviewed the first unit from the beginning. We spent the next hour reviewing the details we had gone over in class. Only this time, the way he explained it, made more sense than the entirety of the lectures I had sat through over the last few months. We had wrapped things up and, as I was slipping my things back into my backpack, he suddenly started talking about the camping trip.

"So... this weekend should be fun," he said. I looked back up at him and couldn't seem to get a read of what he was getting at from his expression.

"Yeah? Phisher said it was your family's property?" I asked.

"It is. It's one of the best places in the world," he said, seeming enthusiastic.

"Well, I've never really been anywhere, so, to me, this has been the best place I have ever been," I admitted. His expression grew blank, and he looked at me.

"What do you mean you've never been anywhere?" he asked.

"This is the farthest I've ever been from where I was living," I said.

"So, you've never traveled?" Chess replied.

"No, I've never even been camping before either." I said, laughing a little.

"Well.... I'm glad you are coming with us then," he said sincerely.

"You are?" I asked. I felt the electricity jolt a little in my stomach.

"Yeah, I think it will be a good time for everyone. The lake is beautiful and I think you all will really enjoy it," I deflated a little at his emphasis of everyone enjoying themselves over just me.

"Well, thank you again for offering to let me use some of your camping stuff. I don't know if I ever did thank you properly," I said.

"Don't mention it," he said, smiling at me and our eyes connected. I thought I saw him flush a little, but his eyes shifted away from mine, and he leaned back into the couch. We continued to talk for a little while and I learned he had two younger siblings, that his mother and father both worked in the city, and that they were all very successful.

*Explains the beautiful loft*, I thought to myself. He seemed like a different person than what I had previously thought him to be, he was suddenly much more real, down to earth, and family oriented. Honestly, getting to know this side of him made him that much more attractive, which was a big problem seeing as he would never feel the same about me. At the very least, maybe we could be friends. During our conversation, I held some things back about myself. I didn't tell him about my sad upbringing and moving around from place to place and just that I didn't really have a family. I had learned previously, from telling friends, that it made others feel sorry for me and I didn't want him to feel that way about me. Instead, I told him about the Johnsons and how I had worked for them for several years and how great they were. He inquired about my real parents, and I told him the small amount of truth I knew about them which, like my friends, gained me some unwanted sympathy but mixed with his sympathy was something more, something I hadn't felt from another person before and I couldn't quite place it, anger maybe? I changed the topic somewhat quickly to shift the mood and learned how he had met Phisher.

"Intramural sports." Chess said, his attitude shifting back to normal.

"Oh, really?" I said, "What sport?".

"Flag football, he was our team's captain and we just clicked well. I was one of the first people he had talked with about Hunter and how he had feelings for him," Chess admitted.

"Oh, wow, that is really cool. I can only imagine how that went" I stated.

"Better than you might think, I could tell from the moment he started telling me about Hunter that they were going to be together," he smiled to himself, "I think everyone deserves that, someone that makes them light up when they talk about that person. Who challenges them to be themselves, even if that is different from who they thought they were before." He seemed envious of Phisher, but I could also tell he really had a lot of respect for him and the connection he had with Hunter.

"I wouldn't know what that's like," I admitted. He looked over at me with curiosity. An awkward silence fell on both of us and I shifted in my seat a little.

"I should probably get going," I said as I started to stand, grabbing my bag and making everything a little more awkward.

"It's still raining outside," he said, standing up.

"That's okay. I don't mind. Plus, the rain has lightened up a lot from earlier," I looked up and smiled at him, but he didn't look pleased. His expression made something shift inside of me and the hairs on my neck rose a little.

"Are you okay?" I asked. He looked at me, surprised.

"Yeah, I'm fine," he said shortly.

"You don't look fine?" I said as he shrugged a little. "Really, I am fine to walk in the rain. It's not a big deal," I said, he said nothing.

"Do....... Do you want me to stay?" I finally asked him after a few more moments of silence. He relaxed a little.

*Why is he acting so weird now?* I thought to myself. He was fine one minute and then so tense the next.

"At least until it stops raining," he said, nodding and I set my bag back down.

"What do you want to do then?" I asked.

"We could... uh, watch a movie?" He mumbled.

"Okay, let's do that," I said. I really didn't understand what had suddenly happened or why he didn't want me to go home in the rain. Something danced inside me slightly at him not wanting me to leave yet. We sat back down on the couch and he picked up a tablet from the coffee table, pressed a couple of buttons, and what I had thought to be some sort of accent furniture began to move and a flat screen emerged from inside.

"Woah," I said, "that's cool." He looked over at me with a grin. He continued to push buttons on the tablet and the tv turned on and he opened a selection of movies to stream. He slid through the choices before picking an old horror movie in black and white about were-wolves. I leaned back and said, "Classic horror, good choice." Chess smiled again and said, "Thanks," as the opening credits started to roll.

A little more than halfway through, I drifted off to sleep. I woke up suddenly and the room was dark. The only lights that lit up the room were the lights of the city in the distance. I had a small blanket draped over me and when I turned my head I saw Chess snuggled up on the couch, fast asleep next to me. My mind started cursing at me for falling asleep. I pulled out my cell phone and checked the time.

12:00 *AM?! What the hell is wrong with me?!* Looking out the windows again, I saw it had stopped raining. Carefully, I removed the blanket and pondered if I should stay or go. I sat quietly for a while before I decided it would be better if I snuck out quietly rather than try to fall back asleep. I quietly got up, grabbed my things, and left. On the way home, I kept replaying the entire afternoon in my mind, and how hot and cold Chess had been all evening. I was still kicking myself for falling asleep and knew that I would hear all about it from Hunter when Chess told Phisher all that had happened.

Great, now I am the annoying freshman he is tutoring in biology who also fell asleep at his place. He was the one who got weird and asked me to stay though. It was all so bizarre. I made my way back to my building, went upstairs, crawled into my bed, and fell right back to sleep.

# Chapter Ten

The rest of the week I was waiting for a barrage of text messages from the gang with inquiries about my tutoring session and what had happened with Chess. At the very least I had expected Hunter to hit me up trying to fish for information, but the days passed with little significance. I texted Jesse and Reese a bit on both days and Hunter a bit on Thursday, but no one mentioned anything about what had happened at Chess' loft. I could have sworn Chess would have said something to someone, but so far, nothing.

Friday morning finally came, and we would take off for the weekend of camping in just a couple of hours. I pulled out my phone and already had a couple of texts from Jesse and Hunter.

JESSE

Good morning! Hope you slept well! Hunter and I are coordinating who is driving with whom. Are you going to skip your morning class to head out? We are thinking we are going to leave here in about an hour.

HUNTER

Hey boo, so I think Jesse, Reese, Hunter, Andy, and I are going to head out this morning since we all don't have classes today. Jesse said she texted you. If you're cool with it, you can still go to your morning class and then ride over with Chess. He said he has a couple of things he has to do in the lab this morning before leaving too.

I felt a little uneasy at the thought of skipping class and felt similar about riding over with Chess. I responded to Jesse first.

Lyle to Jesse:

JESSE

LYLE

Hey good morning. Yeah, I'm still going to go to class. Hunter said I may be able to catch a ride with Chess.

HUNTER

LYLE

Good morning. That sounds alright. I'm fine riding over with Chess, if that's fine with him. I don't have his number, though. Are you sure he is okay with that?

I got out of bed and headed toward the shower to get ready. I thought about the long ride, we would be driving to the coast and heading all the way down to the lake with Chess. This would either be fun, awkward, or tense, depending on which Chess I ended up getting today. Shortly after getting dressed, I heard my phone buzz.

HUNTER

Yeah, he is fine with it! Phisher talked to him this morning. I will send you his contact information next.

CHESS

Just like that, Chess's contact information pulled up on my

phone. I sent Hunter back a quick reply saying thanks and that I would see him in a little bit. He quickly responded by telling me to have fun and that they would see me later this evening. I pulled up a new message to text to Chess before heading out to my morning class.

LYLE

Hey Chess. This is Lyle. Thank you for being willing to take me with you today. My class will be over at 10. Do you want me to meet you somewhere?

I hit send and threw some things I wanted to take on the camping trip into my backpack along with my notebook for class. Before leaving for my lecture, I saw Andy and brought him up to speed on the situation and let him know that I would leave after class with Chess to head to the lake. He smiled before teasing me about it. I paid no attention to him and responded in jest before leaving. By now, I had gotten used to being teased about Chess and while I still had the hots for him, I ultimately couldn't get a read on what was going on with him. I didn't know if he liked me, if I annoyed him, or even worse, if he hated me and just put up with me because he had to. Stepping out into the fresh morning air, I heard a buzz coming from my pocket. I grinned a bit, knowing that it would most likely be Chess and the feeling it gave me to pull out my phone and see his name on the screen gave me that electric feeling in my core that I had grown to enjoy.

CHESS

Yup. Meet me in my lab after your class.

*Well, that was less than optimistic sounding,* I thought to myself. Maybe he was irritated or angry at me, I restrained my enthusiasm for texting him and my mind started running the text over and over in my mind, trying to read between the lines and discern some meaning from the words. I resented the way he could live in my head causing me to obsess over some hidden meaning and I couldn't help but fret about the vagueness of the message he had sent. It would have been nice to drive with my friends as opposed to Chess, but that opportunity had passed. I continued walking toward campus and hesitated, trying not to respond too soon, but inevitably sent back an 'ok' to confirm that I would meet him there. I found my way to the math building, walked inside, found my seat, and class started. The professor spent the hour reviewing the last unit we had been working on and helped us create a study aid that we would use on our next test. As he finished talking about what to expect next week, I pulled out my phone to check for any missed messages. Nothing. I pulled up my messages and sent a quick update to Chess.

LYLE

Class is wrapping up. I will head your way soon.

I put my phone back in my pocket, re-packed my notebook, headed into the hall, and BUZZ.

CHESS

K.

My chest tightened and I grew a little irritated. This is the first time I was ever sent a "K." message. I mean, I had never been in a position where that would have bothered me either, but he was being a bit of a jerk. It's not what I expected to get, yet perhaps my leaving in the middle of the night had a bigger effect on him than I had expected. I felt restless and uneasy as I stepped into the science hall once more. This time I didn't feel the pins and needles and nervousness like before. I was a little hurt and a little upset. I didn't feel like what I had done was that bad and that it certainly didn't make up for him being passive aggressive. Why had he offered to give me a ride knowing that we had a three-hour drive together if he wanted to act like this? I didn't hesitate this time and walked up to Lab 214, arriving on time. When I entered, he was in his back-office packing things into his bag, getting ready to head out.

"Hey," I whispered. He turned to look at me.

"Hey. I am almost ready - give me a sec," he responded, turning back around, and continuing to put things away. I had turned away from him and looked around the lab again. This time I could see that the giant contraption in the middle of the room was some type of two-sided computer and he had a bunch of information pulled up on it. I really couldn't make much of what it said, but it looked complex. I took a couple of steps closer to it before feeling his hand touch my shoulder.

"You ready to go?" he asked.

"Yeah," I said as I turned to him and smiled. He looked back at me and then looked back at the monitor before powering it off.

"I'm studying differences in genealogy patterns across generations and the variations in DNA changes across different lineages," he said politely, answering my unspoken question.

"Neat," I replied, pretending to understand what he had just said, as I followed him past the giant monitor heading into the hallway.

"How was your class?" he asked.

"It was fine," I answered, continuing to follow him down the stairs and out of the science hall. We began heading for his loft and continued to walk in an awkward silence. I looked at the back of his head and felt total confusion over how complicated it was to feel what he was thinking. I had tried to get rid of my emotions for him in the hope of making things less difficult and, in the past, I had a tendency to pay little attention to what others thought of me which complicated trying to put my finger on how he felt. So many people had come and gone in my life, but I felt like I'd never forget his face. We walked a little further before he reached into his pocket and pulled out a set of keys that unlocked what looked to be a practically new gray Jeep Wrangler parked along the sidewalk.

"This is your car?!?" I asked him, a little shocked but also not too surprised after seeing his loft. He turned around and smiled in my direction. He opened the back seat and reached his hand out for my bag. I handed it to him and he tossed it in. Then he opened the passenger door for me and waited for me to climb in.

"You don't have to do that," I said, climbing into the passenger seat as he held the door open.

"Do what?" He looked at me, confused.

"I could have opened the door myself," I said and he flashed another toothy grin before shutting the door behind me. While he was walking around to the driver's side, I looked around the car and thought to myself that it was probably one of the nicest vehicles I had ever been in. The seats were leather and the Jeep had all the bells and whistles, it even smelled new. He pulled open the driver's side door and climbed in, buckled his seat belt, pressed the start button, and the car roared to life. He looked over at me one more time and asked me if I was ready. I nodded and he pulled out onto the street and went down the road. We drove for about twenty minutes in silence before he finally broke the quiet with a question.

"So.... I think we should probably talk about what happened on Tuesday night," he said, sounding flustered and I could tell it had been on his mind.

"What about it?" I asked, fully knowing what he was going to say next, and not giving him the satisfaction of thinking that it had been on my mind as well. He looked over at me with a bit of a furrowed brow.

"You just left. I didn't even hear you leave. If I had I would have..." his voice trailed off and went silent.

"Would have what?" I asked him.

"Nothing. It doesn't matter," he said, sounding upset and angry. I could tell I should stop talking, but I didn't.

"Wasn't I allowed to leave? You know, you can be really confusing. First, I'm annoying, then you're nice to me, now it seems like you're angry with me, and we haven't even known each other that long," I said as he continued to sit quietly, his eyes on the road, staring ahead angrily.

"I didn't even ask to be tutored, you know. The class is hard for me and I am just trying not to fail. I don't have a lot of nice things and I haven't had many advantages in life, but I'm doing my best. I apologize that I was thrust into your life, but we have the same friends and it would be nice if we could just get along. But if you don't like me and this is how it's going to be, that's fine. We can just stop."

*What was I doing? Stop Lyle. Shut up.*

"That might be a good idea," he whispered. That hurt, deeply. We sat quietly for a couple of minutes as he continued driving.

"Okay," I finally responded, a hint of contempt in my voice. He continued to proceed along the route, passing several exits where he could have turned back toward Seattle, eventually dropping me off and excluding me from the camping trip altogether. I kept my head turned away from him and looked out the window, not wanting to see his expression. After about forty-five minutes of driving in silence, we pulled into the ferry line and waited to board. I continued looking out the window while the ferry docked and unloaded. The entire time we sat parked in the queue, I could feel Chess glancing over at me, trying to assess what I was thinking or maybe feeling. We continued to sit in silence as he put the car back in drive and followed the directions of a man in orange to load the Jeep and board the ferry. Chess pulled the car onto the ferry and parked. The ferry ride would be about an hour from Seattle to the Olympic Peninsula and, I don't know why I did it, but, as soon as he put the car in park, I opened the passenger door and headed for the passenger deck. It had been a while since I'd had this much pain inflicted on me by another person and the feelings of rejection settled into my chest. I suspected that there was more to what I was feeling than just rejection, but I didn't want to face those thoughts and risk revealing to myself the true depth of the pain that Chess had caused in me. Leaving the car, I walked up the stairs onto the passenger deck and headed toward the front of the boat to stand on the balcony and lean against the rail as the ferry launched. I had never even been on a ferry before, this moment was something I had only seen in movies. As the boat launched, I felt the ferry lurch forward as the wind and the slightest spray from the waters of the Sound hit my face. Looking around I noticed that the ferry must have been relatively empty because there were only a couple of other people on the passenger deck and I was the only one in the observation area.

*Well, it is freezing,* I thought to myself, hugging myself tightly in my sweatshirt. Roughly fifteen minutes passed and I felt the familiar feeling of the hairs on the back of my neck beginning to stand on end, signaling that Chess must be coming up behind me. I continued staring outward at the Sound, all the while feeling his presence as he stood behind me and looked at me. I waited for him to speak, but he didn't. After a few more minutes, I turned slightly to look at him, acknowledging that I knew he was there, and then turned back to the Sound. He looked sad. I wasn't sure I had seen that expression on his face before, but he was clearly upset too.

"Lyle I......." he started and then trailed off. He clearly wanted to say something to me and was struggling to find the words.

"You know, this is my first time on a ferry," I said, leaning back over the railing, "I have never seen a place more extraordinary than this." He moved up to join me, leaning on the bar and looking at me. His eyes burned into my side, but I focused on the horizon before shifting my attention to him. He looked at me, the same sad look on his face. His unusual eyes bore into me, making the electricity ignite, and I was right back where I was before.

"I'm sorry," he finally said, staring at me. I stayed quiet, allowing him to say what he had been holding back for the past week.

"I want to be your friend, but it's complicated. I don't... I don't know how to stop myself from wanting to be around you and it's dangerous, because I like you. I can't like you in the way that I do...." he trailed off, biting his lip, turning outward toward the horizon, and took a deep breath. Hoping he would keep going, I waited a few moments, but he remained silent. I turned back, staring down to where the ferry split the water, watching the waves push back as we were propelled forward.

"I like you too and that is scary to me too, because I have never really liked anyone that way. I understand your fear, but it's okay. I know you're not gay," I said. He started laughing at that and he clearly was getting a little emotional.

"Who said I wasn't gay?" he said, looking at me, amused.

"Well... Phisher said that you weren't into things like that," I said as he continued to smile.

"So, are you... gay?" I asked quietly.

"No, but I'm not straight either. I don't think or feel in those terms. Gender doesn't define anything in my world" he said, stopping again.

*Why does he keep stopping?!?* He clearly has things to say, but keeps stopping himself from saying them. "It is just.... I generally don't care for people at all, but I'm inexplicably drawn to you for some reason. Despite my best efforts, I can't help but want to spend time with you. I'm not sure if I can give you more than friendship though" he said, not giving away his reasoning. I thought over what he had just said and decided I could accept that as enough. He was trying to make a connection and my insides were leaping in my chest, dancing at his admission to feeling what I felt, which let me know that it wasn't just me. There was something that existed between us and while it may only be friendship, that would be okay. I grinned shamelessly as I looked out toward the coastline, feeling a little victorious at his admission, acknowledging our connectedness and the awkward tension that had plagued our interactions. We stood there for a few moments longer in silence, both satisfied with the successful conversation after clearly butchering our earlier attempt at expressing what was going on between us. I shivered slightly, feeling the cold breach my hoodie, and, as I did, he grabbed my hand that had been resting against the rail. I jumped a little and my initial instinct was to pull away, but his hand was so warm.

"You're freezing," he said, taking hold of my hand with a firmer grip.

"It's just a little cold," I admitted. He moved my hand to his other and then moved around me, positioning himself behind me before grabbing my other hand. He pulled me in from the rail and held my hands crossed in front of me.

"What are you doing?" I asked comically.

"Warming you up," he said, sounding matter of fact as if it was not even slightly odd that he had grabbed me and pulled me up against him. He was so warm and his heat radiated from everywhere on his body. He smelled so good. I leaned my head back against his chest and felt a heavy wave of spruce, cloves, and spice hit my nostrils, beginning to feel lightheaded again.

*This isn't something friends do*, I thought to myself, but pushed the thought aside. If he didn't think it was weird, then I wouldn't stop him. He leaned down a little and whispered into my ear. "Next time you fall asleep at my place, don't leave in the middle of the night." I turned my head slightly and looked at his face. He was stern, like he was administering a warning that I accepted with brief hesitation as I nodded. I took one last look out at the horizon and then turned back to look at Chess. He muttered, "Let's go back to the car. We will dock soon." I nodded in agreement.

He let go of one of my hands, but to my surprise would not relinquish his grip on the other. He walked and I followed. Once we got back to the car and disembarked from the ferry, we continued talking casually all the way to the lake. In that time of casual banter, I learned that his favorite color was red, mine was green, he loved everything that had to do with being in the woods, and I did too. He liked pizza, pasta, and carbs, but only if it was fresh and homemade. He loved his family and wanted to be a doctor. We shared small things about ourselves that sometimes take a while to learn. He was a different person now, almost, still himself, but his previously rigid walls were more porous now, letting me peer inside of him. He was still holding things back, but this may have been the most relaxed and like himself he had been since we had met. It felt like only mere minutes had gone by, but before long we arrived at the campsite and were pulling in next to Jesse's car.

I tore my, what had seemed to be never ending, gaze away from him and looked out to see the view. It nearly took my breath away. Chess' description of the place had in no way undersold its beauty. The water was near turquoise in hue and clear, with the bottom of the lake visible as it stretched out over colorful pebbles until the depths turned to a slightly darker blue. Giant evergreens, mountain cliffs, and stone surrounded the water, adding to the majesty. It caused an indescribable feeling inside of me that felt like I was both at home and connected to all of it somehow.

"This is beautiful." I said as the view engraved itself in my mind. Chess smiled at me before opening the car door and walking over to open mine. I wasn't sure why he insisted on doing that, but it clearly mattered to him so I let him. A little way off from the cars, I could see smoke rising from a campfire. We grabbed our bags from the back seat and each took a large bag from the trunk before starting toward the campsite. Our friends had already settled in. I followed Chess closely as we walked off the dirt road onto a small trail that led through the fern covered forest floor. As we walked closer, I could smell the campfire and hear our friends' voices and laughter. Walking  up to the campsite, the group was all seated in folding camp chairs, their tents creating a small horseshoe on the outer perimeter of the clearing with two spots left on the far side for us to set up. Chess gave a warm wave in greeting as we approached and everyone turned to greet us with giant smiles on their faces.

"Finally!" Hunter said, exaggerating our having taken so long to get there. Phisher stood giving Chess a hand clap and bro hug. Jesse stood and gave me a hug looking me over as if to examine that everything had gone well on the drive. I smiled at her and gave a nod in acknowledgement to show that everything was good. Chess and I each went around the circle, giving everyone warm greetings before Chess pulled out two camp chairs and set them up next to each other. I walked around and took my seat beside him.

"How was the drive?" Jesse asked, already knowing the answer.

"It was good. Long," I laughed jokingly. "What time did you all get here?" I asked.

"Uh, maybe two hours ago. We just finished setting our stuff up and got the fire going," Reese responded.

"You two should probably get your tents set up. It is almost four and it will start to get dark soon," Phisher said. Chess nodded, getting up from his seat and I got up to follow him. The group returned to their conversation, picking up where they had left off, a boisterous discussion of the University's football team and how the season was going. I started helping Chess empty two enormous bags we had hauled from the Jeep when he turned saying, "Do you even know how to set up a tent?"

"No," I replied, "But I'm willing to learn." He smiled at me before pulling out what I assumed must be a tent and a bunch of poles from the bag.

"Well, you help me do this one and then I'll help you with yours," he said as he started unrolling the tent and spreading it out over the ground. I grabbed one side and helped him lay it flat, then he pulled out the poles and started unfolding them so that they clicked together into one long line. He began feeding one of the poles through a corner and I helped as it ran through the pole casing finally coming out the other side where he secured it into place. We followed the same process for the other pole, after which he raced around the perimeter, securing the tent with small stakes into the ground, saying it was so it wouldn't blow away. "Not much to it," Chess mused as he pulled out the second tent. I looked over at the group and saw Jesse and Hunter watching us closely and whispering back and forth. Chess hummed softly and I turned back to continue setting up my tent in the space next to his. The tent was up and standing in no time. Chess pulled out two foam mats and he laid one in each tent, unrolling a sleeping bag over top of them. He moved quickly and efficiently, revealing his expertise in his ease. Just as he had finished, the sun sloped over the western side of the lake and behind the tops of trees. We took our seats back at the campfire. Sitting around the campfire for a couple of hours talking, laughing, and having a great time. We roasted hot dogs for dinner and had s'mores for dessert. I laughed when Hunter accidentally burned his "perfect" marshmallow and Phisher came in with the save — giving Hunter his. Chess would periodically turn and look at me, smiling as the sun set, the moon and fire embers illuminating our faces.

*What was he thinking?* I wondered. Every time he looked at me the electricity would hum in those spectacular rhythms that made me light up inside all glee and nerves. Everyone began to fade as the moon rose higher in the sky. Phisher and Hunter tucked in first, followed by Andy, and then finally Jesse and Reese. Leaving Chess and I alone again.

"It really is beautiful," I said, looking out over the lake. Staring into the reflection the moon cast onto the serene blue water.

"It's even better now," he said, looking at me with the view in the background. My cheeks flushed brighter than ever before. I didn't think he had ever flirted with me before, so I turned around and smiled at him.

"Don't do that," I said, smiling at him.

"Do what?" He asked, amused.

"Flirt with me," I mouthed back at him, as to make sure no one could hear us in their tents. "It will make it very hard for me to be 'only friends' if you do that," I whispered softly, looking at him. He flashed a toothy grin and I was sure I saw him blush.

"You should probably get some sleep. It has been a long day," he said, the last flicks of flame from the fire turning into glowing embers.

"What about you?" I asked, stretching my arms out with a yawn.

"I'm going to put the fire out and then I'll head to bed, too," Chess replied. I accepted his response, rising from my chair and moving toward the tent he had set up for me earlier. Hurriedly, I changed into a pair of sweats, a challenge to do while in a cramped tent before crawling into the sleeping bag. It was cool outside, but the sleeping bag was warm and it smelled like Chess. I closed my eyes and fell asleep. As I was drifting off to sleep, I heard Chess unzip his tent and climb into his sleeping bag.

Startled awake, I heard the sound of someone leaving their tent. I sat up quietly, staring out into the darkness as a feeble attempt to see who it was.

*Chess?* I thought to myself, looking to my right. The front of his tent was unzipped and I looked around from the inside of my tent to see if I could see him, but I couldn't. He probably just needed to use the bathroom, I thought, laying back down. Laying in the tent, I relaxed, enjoying the sounds of the woods at night from outside until I started hearing what sounded like Reese snoring from the other side of the campsite. I tried to remain alert hoping to hear Chess return, but as time went by I realized that he had not come back or that maybe I just didn't hear his return? I fought off sleep a while longer until, inevitably, closed my eyes and drifted back to sleep. Opening my eyes the following morning, it was cloudy and cold, but I could hear a few people already up and back around the campfire. As soon as I got out of the sleeping bag I shivered from the cold. Reaching for my backpack I  opened it up, reaching inside and pulling out the purple hoodie Chess had given me to change into the other night. A quiet sigh of satisfaction escaped me as I put on the hoodie. I hadn't known what was going to happen this weekend, but I'd brought it to either give back to him or to wear. I pulled out a new pair of slip-on rubber shoes I had purchased for the trip, slipped them on, and unzipped my tent.

"Good morning!" Hunter said as I emerged from my tent. Walking over to join them around the campfire.

"Good morning," I replied.

"Coffee?" Jesse asked as I sat down in my chair from last night.

"Yes, please," I responded. She grabbed her French press and one of the mugs she had seated next to her on the cooler and poured me a cup. I reached over to take it from her and took a big sip.

*Ahh, that is good,* I thought as I savored the coffee as it began to warm me from the inside. I looked around and didn't see Chess anywhere or Phisher for that matter.

"Where are Chess and Phisher?" I asked.

"They went for a run around the lake," Hunter replied.

"Last night?" I asked. Hunter and Jesse looked at me funny.

"No, like maybe an hour ago?" Jesse responded. *Huh*, I thought to myself. I was certain I'd heard Chess unzip his tent last night. Leaning back in my chair, I sipped the coffee Jesse had given me and listened as she and Hunter continued their conversation from last night about queer representation in movies. I continued to look out over the lake and felt at peace being here. It had a warmth to it that I had not ever felt in a place before. Even though it was cold outside, my insides felt warm. It wasn't much longer before Chess and Phisher came jogging up toward us from behind. I turned and saw that Chess was running shirtless in only a pair of joggers. He was coming in first with Phisher right behind him. I had never seen Chess without a shirt on and, instinctively, my mouth fell open a little.

*Was there no end to how perfect this man looked?* I groaned in my head. There was a strong definition along every muscle trailing down from his shoulders to his waist. He had been sweating and he glistened slightly as he stopped and grinned at me. He had a slight layer of body hair that clung to his chest and trailed down his torso into a soft line of dark brown hair over his navel. I felt lust hit me hard. It had never happened before and I felt myself stir slightly. Chess started walking toward us coming around the side of my tent.

"Good morning everyone," he announced brightly, clearly energized from his run. Everyone turned and greeted the pair. Phisher was still huffing and puffing from the run and sweat was visible through his shirt, with even a little still dripping off his brow. Chess looked unfazed. Jesse poured Chess a cup of coffee while he went into his tent, coming back out fully clothed again.

"Thank you," he said to her, grabbing the cup. She smiled up at him and then grinned at me. He moved around the chairs, taking his seat next to mine. As he settled in he took a big sip from his cup. Phisher was in Hunter and his tent changing and Hunter had followed. Reese, Jesse, and Andy started talking again, and I was following along until Chess leaned over and whispered, "nice sweatshirt."

I blushed before turning to him and saying, "Thanks, some dude gave it to me because I was all wet." It sounded cooler in my head and a lot less cheesy, but he grinned and touched my side all goofy like.

"Where did you go last night?" I asked him.

"What do you mean?" he turned his eyes toward me, looking a little concerned.

"You got up last night and left your tent. I couldn't see where you went, but you were gone for a while. I never heard you come back."

He grimaced a little. "Lyle, I didn't go anywhere last night. I was here the whole time. Did you maybe have a dream or something?"

"No, I was awake. I heard you...." Hunter interrupted me, announcing that we were going to go on a small hike and to get ourselves ready. Chess jumped up from his seat and headed into his tent to get ready, I looked around a little confused.

*Why would he lie to me?* I reflected. I knew he had gotten up and left last night, I had seen his tent unzipped, and I knew I'd never heard him come back. It wasn't a dream. I got up from my chair and went to my tent to get ready. I kept the sweatshirt on because I was still cold, but slipped on a pair of jeans and replaced my shoes with the boots I had been wearing the day before.

"We are going to go in two groups," Phisher announced. "Chess, Reese, Andy, and I are going to go to the right, and Jesse, Lyle, and Hunter are going to go to the left. We will meet around the other side of the Lake at the base of the cliff in the distance."

"Why don't we all just go together?" Hunter asked, touching Phisher's shoulder slightly.

"Because the four of us are going to beat you three to the other side." Reese explained. Jesse scoffed and said, "Oh, you better believe the three of us are going to get there way before the four of you ever do. We will probably have to go looking for you boys before too long after you get lost in the woods."

I felt a little anxious inside because I wanted to talk to Chess about last night and now we were going to be split apart for the better part of the day. "I think maybe we should all just go together. Like Hunter said," I started.

"Oh no, not if they are going to claim they are better than we are, Lyle. Come on, we got this." Hunter said competitively, stretching his arms back and forth. I looked over at Chess and saw that he was avoiding eye contact with me.

*What the fuck....* I thought to myself quietly.

"Okay then, we'll see you guys in a while then," Phisher said as the four of them headed off. I turned and followed Jesse and Hunter in the opposite direction. We walked for about thirty minutes quietly, gossiping about the other group. As we walked, I was slightly worried about why Chess would lie to me, especially after the drive yesterday and with how well the second half of the day had gone. While locked in my mental battle about Chess evading my question, I was also taking in the spectacular views around me. It was just beautiful, all of it, and it felt more and more warm to me as we walked around the lake.

"Soo.... Are you going to spill the tea on what all is going on between you and Chess now or what?" Hunter asked sarcastically from the front of our line.

"There's nothing to talk about."

"Oh please. That man never takes a shine to anyone and now he can't stop looking at you every time you move. What did you two talk about?" He asked again.

"School and stuff."

"School and stuff?" Jesse repeated. "Let's talk about the stuff."

"I don't know guys. It's just, kind of, complicated."

"Complicated means there's stuff, Lyle. Come on, we are YOUR friends. You can tell us."

"Well, we got into a fight that ended with us deciding that maybe we should just tolerate each other for the sake of y'all and then on the ferry I got frustrated and kind of stormed off."

"Well, clearly you made up. So, what happened?" Jesse asked.

"I don't know you guys. Maybe I shouldn't say anymore," I said, hesitating.

"Lyle, we won't repeat it, but maybe we can help you if you tell us," Hunter shared.

"Well... okay, I was up on the viewing deck, and he followed me. Then he apologized. He told me he wants to be my friend and that he likes me, but he can't be anything more that that. I said I was fine with being friends, but then he wrapped his arms around me from behind and then held my hand basically the rest of the ferry ride,"

"Well... I'll be damned. Phisher was wrong, he is a closet gay," Hunter announced.

"No. He said he wasn't gay, but that he doesn't think or feel in those constructs," I corrected him.

"So, like, are you two a thing, then?" Jesse asked.

"I don't think so. We just said we were friends."

"Friends don't tell each other they like each other like that and then hold hands for over an hour, and honey, he doesn't look at you like a friend," Hunter said, pointing out the error in my thinking.

"I don't know," I said, confused. A thought crossed my mind that I should tell my friends about the incident last night and how he had denied leaving his tent before we all went on the hike, but I wasn't eager to keep discussing it.

"Well, Jacob is going to be super disappointed then," Hunter said. I hadn't even thought about Jacob. The date hadn't really gone great for me and he had totally slipped out of my mind.

"What do you mean?" I asked him.

"He is totally infatuated with you. Said it was the best date he had ever been on. Could have sworn you two would have worked out. I can't believe I'm saying that I was wrong," he said, continuing to talk about what Jacob had said about me, and how great he thought I was. I felt bad. I couldn't say the same about him, and to be honest, I couldn't really remember anything he had been talking about on our date.

"Oh well, that's unfortunate. I definitely didn't feel the same," I said sadly.

It took us a couple of hours of walking before we could make out the bottom of the cliff right in front of us. We could hear that the other group had already arrived. We walked up and everyone was there except Chess. I looked around in the distance for him, but he was gone. Jesse and Hunter reunited with their partners and I greeted Andy. Jesse looked around and asked, "Where's Chess?"

Phisher responded, "He had to run to his family's house for something and said he would meet us back at the campsite in time for dinner."

I felt a little frustrated. *Did he do that to avoid me again?* I wondered silently. We all sat on the rocks for a moment, taking a small lunch break with the sandwiches that Jesse had packed. *That girl thinks of everything,* I thought, smiling and thinking of what a great person she was; about how great they all were. I had never confided in other people like that and it felt good that I could trust them.

We finished up our break and decided that we would all walk back to camp together. Everyone chatted on the way back and we arrived back at the site within a few hours. We walked a lot slower on the way back, the sky darkening a little as mid-afternoon passed. Phisher and Reese began stoking the fire, Chess hadn't come back yet, and I was becoming filled with mounting frustration. It had gotten dark and Jesse put a pot over the fire to cook some mac and cheese. I thought it was a little odd, but cool. It wasn't until dinner was cooked and Jesse was passing out bowls that Chess wandered back into camp.

"There you are," Phisher said jokingly. "We were just about to send a search party." Chess laughed.

"Nope, all good. Sorry it took so long everyone," Chess replied. Taking a bowl from Jesse, he returned to his seat next to mine.

"Did you have fun today?" He asked me as he took a bite.

"Yeah, it was a good time. We missed you, though," I said with maybe a bit of frustration escaping in my voice. Definitely more frustration than I had meant to express.

"Are you okay?" he asked, turning and looking at me for the first time since this morning.

"Yeah, I'm fine," I replied, looking into the flames and taking another bite of food. We didn't really talk after that for the rest of the evening. We all finished eating and I went to bed early. Feeling flustered, I laid in my sleeping bag and listened as everyone else slowly followed suit and went to bed. Chess was the last one to climb into his tent - again - and I laid there a while longer before eventually falling to sleep. I woke up again at what felt like the same time as the night before and sat up to look around. Chess's tent was open again, but this time he was already gone.

I decided to look for him, to learn why he had lied to me the night before. Putting on his sweatshirt, I grabbed a small flashlight and left my tent. I looked around the campsite and out across the lake. The sky had cleared and the moon was out, which helped illuminate the perimeter of the lake, but I couldn't see any sign of Chess. I checked his tent to find he was not in there and I made my way toward the trees. To prevent anyone from being startled, I held off on switching on my flashlight until I was further into the woods. I waved the small light around between the trees, trying to see if I could spot any signs of where Chess had gone. I walked a large circle, still near the camp, to see if he was anywhere near. After searching for about ten minutes, I glanced back at the campsite and noticed both his and my tents were still open. Walking to the shoreline of the lake, which was slightly further out, I finally spotted Chess' shirt and pants folded up neatly about a quarter mile from camp at the edge of the woods. Looking back I could see the little tent mounds in the distance. I wondered why he would have taken his clothes off to go into the woods.

"Chess?" I said quietly, trying to see if he was nearby.

"Chess?" I said again, a little louder.

No response. Making my way through the edge of the woods, I

shone my small flashlight around looking for him. I moved forward a little, the lake was still visible through the trees, I continued to look and still couldn't see any sign of him. I had just about given up when I heard rustling further in the woods.

"Chess?" I asked again, "If that's you, I'm not mad. I just wanted to talk to you and find out what's going on." I walked toward the noise and felt a push on my back, knocking me forward onto the ground.

My ribs jolted against a rock as I hit the ground and the air came gushing out of my lungs. I gasped for breath. I scrambled to the ground before feeling a sharp pain in my calf. Looking down, I saw teeth puncturing my skin, tearing into my flesh. I tried to scream but I still hadn't been able to get the air back into my lungs — the scream was there, but there was no power behind it. Terror ripped through me as I whipped around to fully catch sight of whatever had attacked me, but the creature had already disappeared. My leg was bleeding through my sweats and I felt the fabric stick to my skin, heavy with blood. I finally pulled air back into my lungs before releasing a loud scream into the night. I pulled myself up into a seated position and held my calf, trying to apply pressure to stop the bleeding. I continued to scream for help and then could hear my friends running in the distance, but it was Chess who came running through the trees from the shoreline to reach me first. He was shirtless and wet, but had his pants back on. He looked down at me in shock.

"What happened?" he yelled as he bent down and picked me up off the ground with ease.

"Something attacked me. It bit my leg," I groaned and tried not to cry or curse at the burning pain I felt on my calf. He carried me out of the woods to the shoreline before setting me back down near where he had left his clothes. I could see my friends running down the lake toward us as he ripped the leg of my sweatpants off at the knee and pulled the torn fabric down my leg carefully and over my foot. My calf stung as the cold air hit the puncture wounds with their continued bleeding. Chess grabbed his shirt and wrapped it around my leg tightly, applying so much pressure it felt like he might break my leg. I let out a loud cry of pain again as he gripped my leg.

"I'm sorry," he said, "I am trying to stop the bleeding, it has to be tight. I'm so sorry." He continued to hold pressure on my leg as our friends arrived.

"What the hell happened?" Jesse asked, leaning down at my side and examining the scene.

"Lyle was attacked by something in the woods," Chess said, sounding angry.

"What was it?" Phisher asked

"I don't know, I didn't see it," I said. "It knocked me down from behind, bit my leg, and before I could turn around to defend myself, it was gone."

"Sounds like maybe a mountain lion?" Reese questioned.

"I don't know, Agh" I said, letting out a small cry as Chess let go of my leg and checked to see if the bleeding had stopped.

"The bleeding has stopped. We need to take him into town so they can stitch him up," Chess said, picking me up off the ground again and holding me close. Everyone turned and followed as he walked back toward the camp with me in his arms. Everyone continued to ask questions and ask me if I was okay. We were far from camp, but Chess held me tightly and carried me the entire way. I was confused about how he could possibly do that, but I was so grateful that I didn't want to think about it too much. My calf felt like it was on fire and my ribs started to hurt as we got closer to camp. Chess walked past the campsite and headed straight for the cars. He put me into the passenger side of the Jeep carefully, I winced as my ribs shifted in the motion, taking in a sharp breath again. He grabbed the side of my face and looked me in my eyes. "I am so sorry, Lyle. This shouldn't have happened. You're safe now and everything is going to be okay. Give me a minute. I'll be right back and we are heading straight to the emergency room." I nodded back at him as he shut the passenger door and headed back to where our friends were standing. He talked to them before they turned and headed back to camp. He climbed into the driver's side and started the car.

"Where is everyone going?" I asked, as he started backing up.

"They're going to pack up the campsite and then they will meet us at the hospital," he said.

"Oh. I'm sorry," I said back to him.

"You're sorry? For what? You did nothing wrong, Lyle. This shouldn't have happened. I'm sorry. I'm so sorry," he said. I looked close and I thought I saw a small tear rolling down the side of his cheek as he sped out of the woods and back onto the small highway.

"I... I ruined the rest of the trip," I whispered.

"What? You didn't ruin anything," he said, sounding angry. "Why did you leave camp so late at night?"

"I went looking for you. You left again and you hadn't come back. I got worried so I thought I should try and find you to make sure you were okay," I responded. "Where were you though I... I found your clothes?" I asked.

He sat quietly for a second. "I... I went for a swim," he answered.

"But the water is freezing?" I spoke. "You went skinny dipping in the cold water?"

"Yeah, it was refreshing," he explained. It made some sense why he was so wet when he found me and why he didn't want to say anything in front of everybody earlier this morning.

"Oh.... I'm sorry," I said again. Chess finally stopped gripping the steering wheel tightly and grabbed my hand.

"You didn't do anything; stop saying sorry," he said, squeezing my hand as he raced down the highway. "What hurts?"

"My calf burns and my ribs hurt. I hit them against a rock when it knocked me over" I said, trying to shift a little in the seat and quickly feeling the sharp pain shooting through my side again.

"Probably broken," he replied. "Anything else?"

"No, I don't think so," I was trying to take a mental inventory of my body's condition to confirm it was just the two things. Chess pulled into the nearest town sooner than I had expected and continued to speed until he parked his car as close to the ER doors as possible. Quickly, jumping out of the car, he rounded back to my side before picking me up and carrying me into the hospital. He set me down in a wheelchair at the entrance before going up to the counter and explaining what happened to the triage nurse. They quickly wheeled me into the back and Chess followed. The staff tried to tell him he couldn't be there, but they soon realized that he was not leaving. He moved me from the chair to the bed and the nurse took my vitals. Mostly normal which was a surprise considering everything that had happened. In triage, they had worried that I may be in shock, but my vitals indicated that wasn't the case. The nurse requested that I change into a patient gown and asked if I needed any help.

"No, I think I can do it," I told her and she smiled at me.

"Do you want some privacy? I can show your friend to the lobby?" She said politely. For a moment I thought Chess might yell at her, but he sat quietly at my side fuming at the thought that he would possibly have to leave.

"No.... No, I'm fine. Thank you," I said, smiling at her. She smiled back before pulling the curtain closed and shutting the door. I grabbed the gown in my hand and twisted to the edge of the bed, inhaling sharply at the pain in my ribs.

"Can you.... maybe... umm, close your eyes for a second?" I asked Chess, as he was already standing.

"No," he said, "you need help."

He grabbed the gown, held it out, and looked to the side. "Okay..." I said. I went to grab my shirt and pull it up, but lifting my arms sent shooting pain through my torso and I breathed in sharply again. Chess set the gown down at the side of the bed.

"Can I please help you?" he asked me quietly. I looked back up at his face and seeing how sad he looked, I nodded.

He reached behind me carefully and started pulling my shirt up gently. Moving the back of it over my shoulders. My face came in close proximity to his chest and I turned away, resisting the urge to lean my head against him. He grabbed the collar of the shirt and stretched it carefully so that he could pull the back of my shirt and collar over my head. Then he carefully slid my shirt off my arms, setting it to the side. With his head still turned, he held out the gown so I could slide my arms in before he pushed it onto my shoulders. He moved in close again and tied the gown in the back at the neck, securing it in place.

He pulled back and looked into my eyes. "I'm going to take your pants off now. Can you lift your hips a little?" I gulped hard and nodded. He squatted in front of me before reaching his hands up the bottom of the gown and grabbing the waist of my sweatpants. Pulling them down carefully, he made sure to not let them touch the gown or side of my calf as he eased them down to my ankles and finally off. The tips of his fingers touched my waist just before a jolt of electricity shot up into my core. I was desperately trying to hide any semblance of arousal, but this was the most erotic moment of my life up until this point.

*Sadly*, I thought to myself, given the current circumstances involving an animal attack and being in a lot of pain, but even so, I think he may have seen more of me than I was ready for him to. He didn't say a word or give any attention to anything being wrong with it. All he wanted was to make sure I had everything I needed. He carefully lifted the blanket on the bed next to me and I moved my legs back up on the bed and covered them.

"All well?" he asked quietly.

"Yeah. Thank you," He gave a small smile, but overall, still looked sad and worried. We sat quietly for a few minutes before the doctor arrived.

"How are we doing this early in the morning?" he asked politely. "I hear we have an animal attack on our hands?"

"Yeah," I responded, feeling a little foolish for it having happened.

"Well, let's look," he said, moving around Chess and lifting the blanket. He then moved the gown up to look at my ribs. "These definitely look broken, but we'll order an x-ray to be sure," he said, lowering the gown. "I'm going to take the shirt off your leg so that I can see the bite and to visualize the area to determine if we need any stitches." I nodded and he unwrapped the t-shirt carefully from my leg. When he pulled it off, we could all see little puncture wounds where the teeth had perfectly pierced the skin. "Oh well, that's interesting," the doctor said.

"What is?" I asked.

"Well, normally animals will thrash when they bite to tear at the flesh. Here it looks like whatever it was bit and then just let go. You got very lucky; these won't need any stitches. I will have the nurse come in to clean it and then re-dress it with some gauze and wrap it up before you go to x-ray. Do you need anything?"

"No. I think I'm okay." I replied.

"Okay then. The nurse will be back in soon," he said, leaving the room and shutting the door behind him. I looked down at my leg and I could see the little puncture marks better now, twisting my calf around so I could see them all.

"At least I might have some cool scars." I said, trying to lighten the mood. I turned smiling at Chess, who was sitting in the chair quietly. He looked so sad and angry, but I didn't understand why. "Hey," I said to him and he looked up at me, "I'm going to be fine," smiling at him again.

"It should have never happened, Lyle. It could have been avoided and then you would have never gotten hurt," he stopped himself, getting choked up.

"You couldn't have prevented this. It was a freak accident and the only person who could have prevented it was me. I shouldn't have left in the middle of the night to go look for you alone," I said to him, trying to make it better.

"No, Lyle, do not put this on yourself. This isn't your fault...." He said, appearing like he was going to say more, but the nurse walked into the room.

"Knock, knock. Are you ready for me?" She asked politely before entering, carrying a small tray with instruments to clean the bite.

"Also, I was told that your other friends have arrived and they are asking how you are doing. Would you like for me to send someone to update them?" she said, as she walked up to the bed and set the small tray down on a metal stand nearby.

"No, that won't be necessary. I will go out and talk to them," Chess said as he stood up from the chair, heading out into the hall. I went to say something, but he just walked out without looking back.

"You've got a great friend there," the nurse said as she pulled up a small swivel stool to the side of the bed and grabbed a pair of gloves.

"Yeah," I said, "he is." The nurse worked carefully to clean the wound and before too long, she had finished and wrapped my leg with bandages. She let me know I would need to change the bandages again later and how to do that. As she finished, the x-ray tech showed up and helped me into a wheelchair to go to the x-ray machine. I had half expected Chess to be sitting in the chair when I got back, but he wasn't. I sat in the bed for a while before the doctor returned telling me I had fractured two ribs. He went over what I needed to do for the next week and let me know that they would send a referral over to the student's doctor office at the university so that I could follow up with a doctor in a few days. He went to get the discharge papers and the nurse came back in with a wheelchair to take me out. As we entered the lobby, Jesse and Reese were sitting in two chairs, but I didn't see anyone else.

"Hey stranger, how are you doing?" Jesse asked as the nurse rolled me over to them.

"I'm alright. Where is everyone?" I asked her.

"Oh, Chess took everyone else back to the city. We wanted to be the ones to wait for you and take you home," Jesse said. Reese nodded.

*He just left me here,* I thought, feeling disappointed.

"Oh okay. That sounds great," I said, trying to hide some of the disappointment.

"You ready to go, man?" Reese asked, standing from his chair.

"Uh yeah," I said, turning to the nurse, "do I need to pay anything for all of this?" I asked her.

"Oh no sweetie, your friend from earlier already took care of all that. You are good to go."

"Oh, umm. Okay then. Yeah, I am ready to go." The nurse continued pushing my wheelchair out to Jesse's car and helped me get into the back seat. Jesse and Reese thanked her and got into the front seats, putting the car in drive and heading back to Seattle.

# Chapter Eleven

Waking up in the city, I realized I had slept all the way home. Reese helped me up to my apartment and into bed. Andy was already home and had finished unpacking. He was watching something on tv when we passed him on the way to my room. I crawled into bed, said goodbye to Jesse and Reese, thanking them for their help, and apologized for ruining the trip. Neither of them would accept my apology and insisted that I just get some rest.

The next morning, I woke up in considerably less pain than the day before. When I looked at my phone, I saw notifications from Hunter, Phisher, and Jesse, but nothing from Chess. I responded to the three of them, letting them know I was fine and that I was going to stay in bed another day. I rolled over and went back to sleep. Later that evening, after waking up again, I reached over for my phone and still saw nothing from Chess. I pulled up a message to him and sent a small text.

LYLE

Hey, I made it home yesterday. Feeling a little better.

After a brief pause, I sent it. I rolled over to the edge of the bed and pulled out the extra bandages the nurse had given Jesse for when it was time to clean and redress the bite. I laid them out on the bed and unwrapped my leg so that I could rinse off.

*This can't be right,* I thought to myself, taking the bandage off. The little puncture marks where the teeth had pierced my skin looked like they had practically healed. There were no scabs and all that showed on the skin were little dark red spots where the holes had been. I rubbed over the biggest one and felt no pain. I reached up to touch lightly where my ribs had broken. I could still see bruising on the skin, but when I touched it, I didn't wince in pain or feel like it hurt to breathe anymore. *What the hell?* Standing up, I felt minor discomfort as I walked over toward the mirror. Gazing into the mirror, I kept rubbing my broken ribs and observing that even though the bruising was quite severe there was almost no pain. I shoved it out of my mind and headed into the shower.

I leaned my head against the wall slightly as the hot water ran over my bruises and started worrying myself about what I had done that would make Chess leave the hospital like that. Maybe he didn't want to be there the entire time and he was just waiting for our friends to get there so he could get out. That didn't feel like the right explanation either though. He always acted like he was on the brink of telling me something, but that he never could get it out. I was frustrated and sad about everything that had happened, the pain inside actually hurt worse than any of the physical wounds I had sustained from the attack. After I finished showering, I checked my phone again — still nothing from Chess. Jesse had texted me though.

JESSE

Hope you are doing better. I'm going to be working in the office tonight and will bring you some dinner. I should be there in a couple of hours.

I responded quickly with an 'Ok' but really eating wasn't on the forefront of my mind, I just wanted to go back to sleep. I laid back down and closed my eyes.

Jesse showed up a couple hours later, like she had said she would, and I woke up to her seated at the edge of the bed.

"Good evening sleepy head. How are you feeling?" She said as I opened my eye slowly.

"I'm doing alright," I said, pulling myself up in bed and yawning.

"Oh, that looks painful," she said, observing the bruising around my ribs as she pulled out a folded up Chinese take out box.

"It's not that bad, actually. It doesn't even really hurt anymore," I said, taking the box from her.

"Huh. That's interesting. Have you eaten at all today?" she asked, pulling out a set of utensils.

"No. Not yet," I admitted, sheepishly. She gave me a disapproving look as she handed me some chopsticks.

"Well, I got you some Phad Thai. I figured you should eat something heavy that ought to last you for a while," she said, her tone showing her disapproval at my not having eaten yet. I felt so grateful to have someone as amazing as Jesse in my life. She cared about everyone and always went above and beyond the call of duty whenever help was needed, in my book this made her a great friend.

"Have you heard any news about Chess?" I asked quietly as I took a bite of food.

"No. Hunter said he was acting weird on the drive back, that he dropped everyone off and then left. You could text Phisher if you wanted to check and see. So, you haven't talked to him?" she asked.

"No," I sighed, feeling a heavy weight in my chest. I knew I was falling for him and I also knew that I shouldn't be. He was complicated, secretive, and his personality would change so fast it practically gave me whiplash.

"That is weird. I mean, I for sure thought from his actions that it would be near impossible to pry him away from you after everything that had happened. He seems so intense when he's with you Lyle. I've only hung out with him a few times, but usually he keeps to himself and is just kind of... there. This trip was the first time I had ever seen him legitimately have a  good time. It was the first time where I felt like he really interacted with us." Hearing that made me feel good knowing that maybe my presence had a positive impact on him, but it also brought up more questions in my head.

"Interesting. Well, maybe I'll give him a little space. He seemed freaked out about everything that happened over the weekend. Maybe it was just too much all at once," I said, shrugging, Jesse agreed. "Well, I'll see him tomorrow for our next tutoring session, so maybe I can figure out a little more then," I added.

"Are you going to be back in your classes tomorrow?" Jesse asked.

"Yeah. I'm honestly feeling better already and I really don't enjoy missing class," I replied.

"That makes sense," Jesse said, "Well, let one of us know if you need any help. You know we're all here for you. We love you and we are here." She smiled, reassuring me once again and I felt warm all over. They'd each said  that they loved me before, but, what they didn't understand was that, before they had come into my life no one had ever told me they loved me and it still felt so alien for me to hear it every time. I felt like I had adjusted well to having friends and maybe even some kind of chosen family with them. I think maybe I still held back and that is why they continued to remind me. Repeatedly letting me know that I could come to them, that I was one of them, that I had value, and that they loved me. It felt comforting.

"I will," I said, smiling at her while taking another big bite of food. Jesse checked the time on her phone and it was time for her to head back downstairs for her shift.

"Do you want me to come back afterward? I could text Reese and we could come watch a movie or something?"

"No, I think I am just going to go back to sleep and rest before my classes tomorrow. Thank you, though, I really appreciate you all," I said. She gave my leg a small squeeze and told me to get well. She asked that I text her tomorrow after school and to keep her updated in case I needed anything and I agreed.

I finished eating the Phad Thai she had brought and checked my phone one more time. Still nothing. I sighed, stretched back into my comforter, and fell back to sleep.

I don't normally dream or, at least, don't normally remember any of my dreams if I do have them, but during the night, my dream jolted me awake. I couldn't remember the dream, but, upon waking, I sat up breathing heavily in bed. I was drenched in sweat that had soaked through to my sheets. *Gross*, I thought to myself. I rolled over and checked the time. Midnight. I climbed out of bed, pulled the sheets off the mattress, and pulled out my clean pair from the closet to spread back out. Moving to the sink in the bathroom for a drink of water, I saw my eyes in the mirror and it seemed like they were flashing in the reflection. I moved in closer to look, but no, I looked normal. It was just a dream; I reminded myself as I took a big drink of water and returned to bed. I woke up again to my phone alarm blaring, I couldn't remember if I'd had another dream. Grabbing my phone, I quickly slammed down on the screen to make it stop. I sat up in bed and unwrapped the bandages on my leg for the second time. The dark red marks that were in place yesterday were now light pink. I checked my ribs again, the bruising that was there yesterday was now a dull yellow color.

*What the hell?* I thought again. There was no pain or discomfort anywhere, my body was making it look like the attack had never even happened. I quickly got ready for class, re-wrapped my leg, and wrapped the ace bandage around my ribs as instructed. I walked out of my room and headed toward the kitchen.

"He's alive!" Andy said sarcastically, coming out of his room and into the kitchen with me. He smiled and asked, "how are you feeling?"

"Good," I replied honestly, "really, I'm alright."

"Awesome!" He said enthusiastically. "What do you have going on today?"

"Just going to classes and then tutoring tonight again," I replied. "How about yourself?"

"Same," he started, "no plans tonight though. Do you want to hang out when you get home?"

"Yeah. That sounds nice," I responded. It had been a while since Andy and I had hung out in our apartment together. He had taken to hanging out with Hunter and Phisher a lot recently and I had been so tied up in everything I had going on that we really didn't get to see each other much. I made some toast and ate quickly before saying goodbye and heading to class. As I left the apartment I had to admit that I felt a little strange. Strolling around campus, I felt a faint dizziness in my head and had a strange sense of smelling odors that weren't really there. My first class came and went, it felt hard to pay attention to what the professor was saying. My second class, psychology, went well even though Jesse was not there today, I felt a little more normal again sitting at the back of the auditorium listening to the psychology lecture. I checked my phone on the way to history, no messages. Hunter greeted me as I walked into the history hall. We caught up quickly and I told him what I had told Andy and Jesse. He gave me a quick kiss on the cheek again. I blushed and we went to class. Afterward, Hunter had caught me up on what I had missed on Monday, it had turned out I hadn't missed too much. He gave me a copy of his notes and asked me to let him know if I wanted any explanations. He gave me another quick smooch goodbye and was off to meet Phisher. We didn't talk about Chess, I didn't want to ask. Not having heard from him since he'd left me at the hospital hurt me inside, it was the only thing that hurt at this point. I tried to push it out of my mind as I entered the science hall and grabbed a seat toward the back again.

"Hey Lyle," Jacob said, pulling my mind back into focus. He grabbed the seat next to me and smiled brightly.

"Hey," I smiled back, "how's it going?"

"Good. I heard you went camping this last weekend. Did you all have fun?" He asked politely.

Clearly, no one had told him what had happened. "Yeah, it was a good time," I shrugged, not wanting to talk about the attack.

"I was hoping I might have heard from you. Did Hunter ever give you my number?" He asked hopefully.

"No... He didn't," I responded politely.

"Oh well, that's okay. I could... uh... give it to you now?" he blushed again and I felt awful. However, this time when he blushed, I kept smelling something. It smelled nice, but I couldn't really place it and it made me feel like I might need to sneeze a little.

"Oh yeah, sure," I said, pulling my phone out, and he inputted his number into my contacts.

"You can text me whenever. I have plans most of this week, but if you wanted to hang out, we could probably find some time," he said, pushing his hand up through his hair and smiling awkwardly. He was clearly unsure of himself, this may have been the first time he had ever been.

"Oh okay. Yeah. I'll... uh... text you sometime then," I said. He blushed again and the smell returned. My head had gone a little fluffy. The professor walked into class and turned on the projector. He whispered, "Cool." Before settling into the seat next to me and paying attention. Admittedly, he was a really nice guy, he wasn't ugly, and was really into me. I thought for a second that maybe I should really try to give him a chance, especially if Chess was going to continue to be so hot and cold. I shook thoughts from my head and tried to pay attention. As the professor ran through the lesson, I continued to think about what Chess had said last week during tutoring. It had really helped out this time because this was the first time I felt like I understood some of what the professor was reviewing. I kept feeling Jacob's eyes drift to the side of my face, but doing well in this class mattered and I tried to ignore it. The class went quickly when it usually felt like forever because I was so lost. Afterward, Jacob followed me out of class and continued to tell me about what he had going on this week with his friends, me just listening along. He seemed to have a lot to say and I did my best to keep up with him. Given how nice he was, I couldn't help but think that maybe he didn't realize that he talked a little too much.

"Well, I've got to get going," I said, interrupting him finally as we left the science hall.

"Oh, where are you off to?" He said, interested.

"I... umm. I get tutoring for this class on Tuesdays." I admitted, feeling a little embarrassed.

"Oh, you know I had tutoring for a class once last year, that can really help." *There he goes again,* I thought.

"Oh yeah, it is helping, but I don't want to be late. So, I'll see you later?"

"Yeah, of course. I will see you tomorrow. You know I could always help tutor you too if you wanted," he offered politely, but I couldn't help but think any time spent tutoring with him might end up talking about something he really liked instead.

"Oh yeah, maybe. I'll... uh... keep it in mind," I said as I started walking away and felt him watch me as I left.

*I don't know about him,* I thought to myself and weighed the pros and cons of spending time with him again. It made my head hurt. I reached the place on campus where only a week ago, Chess had met me and caught me just before I'd left to go home.

*Has it only been a week? How could so much change in a week?* Sinking back down onto the bench, I took a few moments to catch my breath. I could see off in the distance that the library lights were on, so at least this time we would actually meet each other there. I continued to breathe and recenter myself, feeling better with each breath, and I felt more comfortable being outside in the cool breeze than having been inside all day.

*That's funny,* I thought, *I'm not cold.* I usually always felt a little chilled, and enjoyed the feeling, but right now I don't feel the cold the same way. I felt the cold air in my lungs when I first breathed it in, but didn't feel the cold air kiss my skin like it normally did. *It must be a little warmer today,* I admitted to myself and I stood up, heading toward the library. I checked in with the librarian about the office reservation and she said I was the first to show up. She gave me the key and pointed me in the direction of the study room. I opened the small little room and pulled out my textbook and notebook. I waited a bit and checked my phone. No message and he was already 5 minutes late. I pulled up our message history and thought to send him another message before the door opened and a short woman with curly brown hair and thick black-framed glasses walked in.

"Lyle?" she asked politely as she shut the door behind her and sat down in the chair across from me.

"Yeah?" I asked her hesitantly.

"Hi, I'm Jamie. I'm going to be taking over your tutoring sessions from now on. Mr. Beck has gotten busy with his lab and the department arranged for me to take over." She smiled, but assessed my expression growing angry and added, "Did anyone tell you about the change?"

"No," I said shortly. My head fumed and my frustrations turned to fury in a blink. Not at her, but at Chess. *How could he just completely disappear on me like this? Where the hell does he get off just dropping me like that after everything that happened this past week?* Jamie shifted a little in her seat uncomfortably, rightly so because I felt a movement in my chest I'd never felt before, something deep and it growled inside of me.

"Lyle... Umm... Are you okay? Are you okay with this?" she asked nervously and I realized that I was making her nervous and reined it back in.

"Ye... umm. Yes... I'm sorry. Yeah, that's fine. Thank you for being willing to take over," I said, trying to smile at her a bit while I continued to bury the feeling of heat and anger that was still sitting in my chest. This wasn't her fault and it was not okay for me to act that way toward a total stranger. I knew better. Jamie relaxed, pulled out her textbook, and we started with the session. I followed along, still feeling like it was helping. There were parts where I struggled to follow, but she was still helping me understand the missing pieces and I appreciated that. We wrapped up after an hour and set the time to meet again next week. The same deal applied to her as it did with Chess. She would report on our meetings and I would get the extra credit. The moment I got outside, however, the anger returned, I felt the stirring in my chest again and it flushed my mind with anger toward Chess again. I tried to rationalize it, but I couldn't at that moment. I felt like if I did, I would make it okay. The stirring in my chest continued refueling my frustration and with that all my chances for rationalization were crap. I pulled out my phone and sent him a message.

LYLE

I cannot believe you. At least have the balls to tell me to my face you don't want to see me again.

I hit send without hesitation and stormed my way home. Andy was waiting for me patiently and was excited to hang out. He could sense my mood had shifted sour and wanted to talk about it, but I cut him off.

*I would not have done that before*, I thought briefly. I apologized and told him it was nothing. Afterward, I joined him in the living room and tried to have a good time watching a movie and chatting about the day. He had apparently met someone and was really excited about it. His name was Kay, he was a trans-man, and he made Andy feel super special. He had expressed he never had met anyone who was trans before, but that he really liked him and that's all that mattered. I told him I was happy for him and that he should not treat it any differently than any other person he'd date. I told him he sounded like a really great guy. Andy beamed, it was clear he was infatuated. Seeing Andy happy made me happy and with that the feeling in my chest finally cooled, retreating to rest. I didn't understand this strange shift that had come over me, but something was definitely off.

# Chapter Twelve

L yle's text was like a shot to the heart. It tore a hole inside me bigger than I had ever felt before.





I couldn't see him again. I.... I.... I... had bit him. I felt so much shame and regret. My wolf howled in mourning knowing I had completely cut Lyle off. I couldn't have these feelings for a human. It wasn't right. I had to put an end to it. I was putting him in so much danger just by being near him. I had never lost control like that. My wolf had never lost control like that. I thought I could be his friend, but I knew better. That night.... That night, I'd brought him back to my place. I knew I wouldn't be able to stand it. I felt like I needed to protect him. I could sense there was something off that night. There was someone watching him from somewhere I could feel it. I should've just let him walk home and left well enough alone, but I couldn't do that either. He needed me, I'd felt it. I had to do it.

Bringing him home with me was the only way I knew he would have been safe that night, but being near him killed me. He'd gotten his scent on everything. It had run through the entire loft and I could still smell him a full week later.

*How could a human have this sort of pull on me?* If I could've just stuck to the plan, none of this would have happened. If he'd never come over that night, I would have been fine. He just looked so ridiculous and cute dripping wet, I couldn't have him sitting there soaked and seeing the way the shirt stuck to his body had made it hard to breathe, but then having him put on my sweatshirt and smelling my scent mixed with his had torn me through to my core. I needed to know him. I had to understand what had made him so irresistible.

*Maybe if I'd let him leave after studying it would've been okay, but I couldn't have been sure if whomever was following him hadn't followed him here as well. What if he'd left and then gotten hurt? I couldn't let that happen. Why did he have to fall asleep though? Why did I put on that werewolf movie? Why did he have to like that movie? Why... why? Why?* I was going insane. I needed to run.

I threw on sweats and a hoodie and left the loft. I ran through the streets at full speed. I was glad it was late. The streets were mostly empty. I tore past the university and ran up toward Capitol Hill, through Volunteer Park, under the interstate, and down toward Pike's Place. I stopped when I reached the aqueducts and breathed heavily against one of the stone pillars looking out toward the pier. I didn't know what to do. I slowly slid down the pillar and sat on the ground. I replayed the drive to the ferry. Boy, did he have a bit of a temper. I liked that. He'd laid into me about how often my mood was shifting and he was right - he made it shift a lot. I didn't like that he'd yelled at me or that I'd made him angry. I liked his fire; he had spirit and he could stand up for himself. He was strong, but he didn't know how strong he was. At that point, I'd known he could take care of himself, maybe he didn't need the protection I thought he did. He would be fine without me in his life. I didn't like that he had stopped talking to me though after I'd agreed that we shouldn't be friends - he looked so sad. I could smell how sad he was too. It was painful that I'd made him feel that way. My wolf had cried inside the entire time, but I'd kept it in. I should have let him feel the pain. It would have stopped me from getting too close, but I couldn't let him feel the pain and then see him sad all weekend. I shouldn't have taken his hand though. I shouldn't have pulled him into my chest like I did. It all felt too nice. I'd resisted nuzzling my face through his shaggy blonde hair and from rubbing my scent into him just because I'd wanted to. I wanted him to be mine. His hand felt nice in mine; like it was meant to be there, and I didn't want to let go. I didn't let go. He had been so happy then; I'd made him so happy. *How could I have made him that happy?* He'd laughed. I liked his laugh; he liked movies and ice cream and food and nature. He liked family and friends and me. He made me blush. He liked that I'd blushed because he blushed too and I liked that.

*Nature, what is wrong with me?! Let him go. He's gone, you hurt him, he's gone because you hurt him. You can not have him; you'll break him. You have duties and he is a human.* I stood up and started running again. I ran south, past the pier, along the street, and followed it down. I took the turns and ran toward the signs toward the Seattle Bridge. I crossed the bridge moving into West Seattle, stopping again at Alki Beach. I sat down again on a big stone slab that looked out over the beach and toward the city skyline. It was dark now and the Space Needle was lit up with the rest of the city, it was beautiful. As beautiful as Lyle in the camp chair with the lake behind him, with my lake behind him. He'd looked so happy sitting next to me with our... his... friends. He'd laughed and had fun and so did I. I had fun because of him. He was so amused when Hunter had burned his marshmallow. He looked so attractive, the way his eyes squinted with his smile and he'd smelled so good when he laughed. I shouldn't have gone for a run that night. I wasn't supposed to; I knew it was against the rules, but Lyle was there in my territory and he was happy and my wolf had to run. He needed to feel the joy that I did knowing Lyle was there, knowing that we could smell him in our woods near our lake. I shouldn't have done it, though. Lyle shouldn't have been able to hear me leave, either. I was so quiet; a deer wouldn't have even been able to hear me if I was on the hunt.

I sprinted again. I had to keep running. I didn't know where, but I needed to run away from it, from him. I continued south, running through trees now as I left the perimeter of the city and headed into south Seattle. I ran past the airport and continued further south than last time, running until I reached Federal Way, stopping again near the Sound at Point Defiance. I was panting; I hadn't ever run like this without shifting, but I couldn't shift. My damn wolf would take me back north and Lyle was north. He would take me back to him. I collapsed in exhaustion on the beach and panted wildly.

*Why would he confront me and why, dear nature? Why did he have to wear my sweatshirt again?* Our scents commingled tortured me and made me squirm with arousal. I already knew he picked up on the lie as soon as I'd said it, he was not the type to let it go. I was so glad when Phisher had agreed with me that it would be fun to do a race across the lake instead of going as a group. I knew it would upset him, but he would push me. I was having a hard time lying to him. I could smell the sadness. It made me sad too, but it was for his own good. I couldn't tell him the truth. I am bound to my pack and to the Union to never tell a human what we are. I'd had to leave again, walking with the other guys, and not being with Lyle hurt. I had to lie to them to get away. I shouldn't worry so much about them, but they'd believed my lie so easily — much easier than Lyle would have been able to. I'd shifted and gone to check on him. We raced across the lake and watched from the bushes as Lyle talked about me with his friends. He was still sad. My wolf kept thinking, *no, no sad Lyle. Lyle be happy, be happy.* He wanted to go to Lyle and rub against him, but I had to force the shift back to keep my giant wolf from galloping up alongside the three humans like it was no big deal.

*Lyle would know it's us,* he'd thought happily as I'd shifted back into human form. *No, he would not,* I thought back. *He would be terrified of you, of us, and he would run.* We'd both felt sad at that thought. It was only when the human parts of ourselves were at odds with our wolves that this flow of communication occurred. I was so out of connection with myself that the two sides of me argued over him. I'd run back to camp to put my clothes back on before going to my family's home like I'd said I was going to do. Maybe that's why my lie was so believable this time, I'd thought as I laid down on the lawn in front of our house. No one was home like I'd been told, and I'd felt a few moments of peace. I'd drifted off to sleep, not meaning to and by the time I woke up, I could smell they were back at camp cooking dinner. I'd run back to him. He was so happy to see me; I was so happy to see him, he still had my sweatshirt on, I really liked that. We ate and joked and were happy again. I was sad when he went to bed early, but I knew I had frustrated him. I understood. I was sure I didn't wake him that night as I snuck out of my tent; I'd checked before I left. He was asleep. He didn't have some kind of super hearing; he was just a human; he was perfectly normal. *He is perfect.* I'd gone further away that night than the night before shifting again and running out toward the ocean. I was on my way back when I heard my name, softly, and it surprised us. My wolf was so excited because he knew well before I did that it was him calling for us and he ran toward him. I'd tried to stop and force the shift, but he wouldn't let me. He lept toward Lyle in excitement, wanting so badly to finally meet him that we hit him and knocked him over. I panicked and tried to force us away and he bit, trying to hold on to him. He didn't want to let Lyle go once he finally had him near. I gained control and ran away mid-shift. I felt Lyle's blood in my mouth and loved it; I had wanted to bite him from the moment I'd met him. Bite him and claim him as mine. It was wrong, though. He didn't know what it would mean, that my wolf wanted him, to claim him, to mark him. It was not to kill and, as a wolf, it never could kill, but Lyle was human. One mistake could have cost him his life. I'd run into the lake and washed off his blood in the water. I heard him cry out. I panicked. He needed me. I ran fast; throwing my pants on as quickly as I could and, by the time I got to him, he was bleeding so much and wincing in pain at the wound in his side. I knew instantly I had broken his ribs and that the bite was too deep. I kept him close. I did everything right; I did everything he needed. Why did he keep apologizing to me? I was a monster; he didn't know that, but I was. I'd hurt him and I couldn't stand myself.

I leapt up and started running away again. My thoughts like lava in my brain. I couldn't stop replaying them over and over in my head. I ran hard and fast, going further and further south into the night. I made it to Tacoma before finally stopping again. I felt like my lungs might explode from how hard I was pushing the human half of myself. It would be nothing for the wolf, but it burned. I deserved it, though.

I thought of Lyle in the hospital. I was terrified that he would find out that it was me, that I was the monster who'd done this to him. I wanted to hold him and keep him safe, but I was also the one who'd hurt him. The nurse tried to keep me from him, but I wouldn't allow anyone to separate us. I kept his heart rate down. I was worried he might be in shock. I needed to be sure. They asked him to get into a gown and I finally felt like I should leave, but I didn't know. I needed to know he would be fine. He asked me to turn away again. He was nervous, I could smell it, he was shy and was scared for me to see him nude. It wasn't a big deal for wolves, but it was for him. He tried to take his shirt off and I heard him cry a sharp pain at the motion. My insides twitched and hurt with pains of sympathy everywhere he'd been injured. I wanted to take the pain away from him so badly, it should be me who was broken. I was the one who had done something wrong. He needed my help. I gently lifted his shirt and saw the bruising and deformed ribs against his side as he took a sharp breath in. I nearly tore his collar in half, trying to get it to stretch wide enough to pull over his head without resistance. He looked up at me afterward and smiled. *Why would he do that? Why would he smile at me?* I saw him shirtless for the first time and he was so badly bruised that the rainbow of red and deep purple wrapped around from his back all the way across his torso. I tried to gently cover up what I'd done with the gown, disgusted with myself, as I carefully secured the gown behind his neck. I let him know before taking off his pants and his breath staggered. I gently grabbed his waistband and pulled them down, being careful not to hurt him , but he.... he felt aroused. I could smell the pheromones coming off of him in waves as he tried desperately to hide it. I continued to take off his pants carefully and got him back into bed. He was blushing when I covered him with the blanket and I gave no hint that I knew the secret he was so desperately trying to hide. I sat quietly. I knew then for sure, this had to stop. I had to leave him alone. He was too fragile, he had no place being around a monster like me, a monster who couldn't control himself. As soon as the doctor said he was fine and that he wouldn't die from his injuries, I felt a wave of relief. The nurse came in quickly saying that our friends had arrived, which meant he would not be here in the hospital alone anymore. I had to rip myself away from him as quickly as possible or I would never leave his side again. I couldn't even look at him and I felt the pain it caused him as soon as I left, but I had to leave. He would never know, but I had to run.

I stood again and ran. I kept running as far as I could. I ran past Olympia and kept going. My lungs burned and my legs ached as I pushed them further. I collapsed in the woods near the Oregon border and the earth, lights, and sound went out as I fell to the ground.

# Chapter Thirteen

It had been four weeks. Four damn weeks and I still hadn't heard a single word from him. I knew he was at least alive and that his phone was working because he still texted and worked out with Phisher. Phisher told me Chess had said nothing about it and wouldn't talk about me with him at all.

*What could I have done to cause this?* I wondered and cried quietly inside. There was more happening that I didn't understand and more unexplainable things had continued to happen ever since that night. My hair started turning a darker red amidst all the blonde. I ended up telling Jesse and Hunter that I'd dyed it because I wanted a change, but I had no clue why it was happening. My body hair was growing in thicker than it ever had before, it was to the point where I was trimming my facial hair every morning before going to school. I even started smelling everything around me, the good and the bad. This was unfortunate because, being in the city, there were so many unpleasant smells.

I had gone into the student health center where they confirmed my rib had healed. They also confirmed that the bite was healing properly even though it had only been 3 weeks. They explained that there was a possibility they had misdiagnosed the severity of the bite at the rural hospital I was taken to initially due to a lack of the more sophisticated medical technology available to the university's medical school. I asked them if I had rabies and if I should get a shot. They performed a rabies test, taking samples of my skin and saliva, but they gave me the shot anyway saying that it was best if there was a high probability of exposure. It was explained that I was likely suffering from Post-Traumatic Stress Disorder and I was likely experiencing heightened senses as a result of my body trying to be more aware of my surroundings. I bought into it at first, but, what I was experiencing seemed a bit extreme, I wondered if it was something else.

Even my body started changing, gradually at first and then more quickly. I had never been a super muscular guy. I'd had well-defined arms before, a decent chest maybe, but always a soft squishy core with very subtle love handles. I went from what Hunter described as an 'otter' in the gay community to something else. My arms were larger, my shoulders were broader, my chest gained a lot of definition that it'd never had before, and I knew things were getting weird when my squishy center started turning hard with the definition of a four pack emerging where there had never been one before. When my friends started taking notice, I said I was working out at night but I really was just sitting alone in the quad at night trying to sort through what was going on with me.

I was still angry at Chess for disappearing. I felt like if I could talk to him about all of this, I wouldn't have to hide it from everyone. I started to feel crazy and, if only to make matters worse, I started hearing things. Small mutterings at first, but then sounds that I would have never heard before. It was like eavesdropping yards away or clearly overhearing Kay and Andy from across the apartment. Things that there was no way I could be hearing. I was nervous and I wondered if I was going to start shooting spider webs out of my wrist or something worse. I felt alone in all of it, who wants to share that they think they are going crazy, and I was dying inside for someone to talk to. I wanted to talk to my friends. I didn't though. I was terrified they would think I was just gone and wouldn't want to be my friends anymore. I was thankful we were only one week from winter break and I couldn't be happier to have time to take my mind off school. I'd brought all my grades up to 'A's. I was even doing well in biology with the help of Jaime. She didn't explain things like Chess had, but it had all started making a lot more sense.

On my way to biology, I met up with Jacob for coffee. We weren't together, nor were we dating, but he made me feel less alone, I think. I became more invested in listening to his stories and problems because it took me away from my own. I felt guilty, like I was using him slightly, and I think he knew that because after hanging out with him a few more times I told him that I didn't have romantic feelings for him. I could tell it made him sad, but still he enjoyed being friends and having me around. So maybe the usury was mutual. We walked into class and sat in the same spots we had sat in since after the attack. We were casually engaging in some small talk before the lecture started when...

"Good afternoon class, I'm Mr. Beck, and I will be covering your class today. Dr. Derby is out sick," Chess said, walking in from the professor's office and introducing himself to the class. I felt sick to my stomach and a feeling of rage kept popping up in my chest. A compounding mass of emotions took over when he and I made eye contact from afar. He began to speak and address the rest of the class as I shot daggers with my eyes through his forehead. My gums started to itch and the hair that had grown thicker on my arms raised. I gripped the little note desk attached to the chair, and as I squeezed, it broke, crumpling in my hands. The entire class turned and I could see Chess' eyes widen as I decimated the little desk with almost no effort. I grabbed my things and left, knowing I had just caused a scene. I had busted through the science hall doors with such frustration, rage, and sadness that I had thought I might have broken them too. I started taking off at what I thought was a slow pace when in reality, I was running way too fast and people were looking at me. I stopped, reaching for my phone, and called Jesse;

"..... Hello?"

"Jesse?"

"Yeah, what's up, Lyle?"

"Are you free? I need to talk to somebody."

"Yeah, I can be free. What is going on?"

"I don't know. I just saw Chess and everything just happened so fast, I just need somebody right now."

"Okay, yup. I'm on my way now. Where do you want me to meet you? I am walking out now."

"Uh. I don't know," I choked up a little. "How about the cafe?"

"Perfect, I will be there in fifteen minutes. We will figure it out. Are you safe?"

"Yeah, I'm good. I'm just frazzled."

"Okay, good. I'm coming. I'll see you in a few."

"Thank you, Jesse."

We disconnected the phone, and I started walking toward the cafe. I had taken two steps before I felt that familiar feeling rising across the back of my neck.

"Lyle!" Chess yelled from behind me. I turned toward him, tears still clinging to my cheek, and frustration boiled to the surface again.

"Leave me alone, Chess," I turned and kept walking.

"Wait, Lyle. What is going on with you? What was that back there?" He grabbed my shoulder to stop me and I turned.

"No. You do not get to disappear while I go through all this shit and then decide to reappear weeks later to ask what's going on. You would already know if you wouldn't have left," I said, spitting the words out at him and feeling my chest growl. My gums itched again and I felt my arms get heavy.

"Woah, Lyle. Calm down. It's okay," he started.

"DO NOT TELL ME TO CALM DOWN. IT SURE AS HELL IS NOT OKAY." I yelled at him and felt all the repressed rage channel and escape in my voice. My gums stopped itching and my arms felt fine.

"You left Chess. You left me in a hospital. You don't care. People don't do that to people they care about. You fucking left me and I needed you. I know we weren't anything and I know you didn't owe me anything, but I needed you and you left. You didn't even just leave, you fucking disappeared," I said, pacing. I could feel him examining me, seeing the changes that have happened since he'd last seen me. I felt his eyes grow wide again and burn into the side of my face.

"Lyle, I know. I'm sorry, but I'm here now. I'm here. I won't."

"Damn right you won't! You don't get to decide when you are going to be here or not be here. I'm fine now and I'm leaving," I started wiping the tears off my face, as a small crowd stopped to watch the scene. "I don't need you now, I'm fine. No broken ribs, no bite. I'm all fine again. I don't need you anymore," I yelled as Chess raised his arms up at me as I paced back and forth.

"Lyle, I know. I'm a monster and I'm so sorry, but please let's just talk. Let's just go somewhere so we can talk, please." He looked sincere, and I definitely agreed that he was a monster.

"I don't want to go anywhere with you. You hurt me, Chess, and I never want to feel that way again." I had stopped pacing and, as I did, Jesse came running up from behind me, hearing the shouting.

"What's going on?" she asked, running up concerned.

"Nothing," I said, staring at Chess.

"Jesse, Lyle and I need to talk. I didn't know..." Chess said, trying to convince her to let me go with him.

"He does not NEED to go anywhere with you. You unbelievable asshole," she shouted back as she looked at me before looking back at him. "You broke him and you are not going to just waltz back in and ruin his life again. I thought I knew you Chess, I thought you were a good guy, but you're a prick." She grabbed my hand, standing in front of me. She raised her finger to his face. "If you ever try to screw with him again Chess, I will find you and I will hurt you," she turned and pulled my hand as I followed, "come on Lyle."

I had never seen this side of Jesse before. She'd scared me a bit with the ferocity with which she would defend someone she loved. As we walked away, I could feel Chess's sadness, confusion, and desperation calling out to me and it hurt. I did my best to ignore it as I followed her to the cafe where she ordered herself an Americano and me an iced white chocolate mocha.

We sat at our table and I finally told her the truth about everything. She sat patiently and listened closely as I spoke, giving no judgment to my explanation of the insane things that had been going on with me since that night. I finished telling her everything and we sat still for a while. We sipped our coffee and I waited while she processed the information.

"Well," she said, "it's about time. I was waiting for you to tell me the truth for weeks now and apparently that was it. Not what I expected it to be, but I can tell that it's the truth." I looked at her. "Gym at night? Hair dye? We were all taking bets that you were on steroids or something." I looked at her, dazed and a little incredulous.

"Well, I wish it was steroids, Jesse. At least then I would have an idea of why everything is happening. What do you think it is?" I looked at her, desperate for some kind of answer.

"I think you already have one, Lyle. I think you have PTSD like the doctor said. Trauma can cause a lot of weird things to happen and it's different for everyone. Albeit I've never heard of it causing changes in hair color or explaining changes in physique, but the mind is a powerful thing and, in theory, I imagine it could make those things happen." She didn't sound super convinced at her explanation either, but maybe she was right. "Look, we won't figure it out all at once, but we will work on figuring it out together, yeah?" She said, looking at me, and I nodded. As we continued to drink our coffees, I felt myself relax.

"One thing is for sure." She started.

"What's that?"

"You are better off without him," she said. Her words hurt, but I nodded in agreement nonetheless. Deep down though, I'd begged for him for so long. I'd pleaded with the universe that he would talk to me and acknowledge me again and he finally had. However, the frustration I felt made it difficult to see past it. If Jesse hadn't shown up, and if he'd kept pushing, I would have gone with him. As we left, I felt my core call out to him, and I felt him call out to me. Another unexplainable phenomenon, but it was there.

* * *

Jesse didn't leave my side after we left the coffee shop and headed toward my apartment. She had Reese come over to my place so that we could all hang out together. She called Hunter and Phisher to come over, but I overheard Hunter tell Jesse that Chess was at their place talking to Phisher about what had happened. She said little, but she told him she understood and that they would catch up later. Andy and Kay came home before long. They were inseparable at this point. I was envious of that. Jesse had Reese stop and buy copious amounts of chocolate and candy. He rented several horror movies and Andy ordered a pizza. Jesse said there was one surefire way to mend a broken heart and that was through sugar, carbs, and slasher movies. I laughed. We blew up the air mattress again for extra seating and I couldn't help but feel all the love surrounding me as they were there for me in one of the darkest times I'd felt in my life. We stayed up late, before all passing out around the tv.

The next morning, after everyone left, I resolved to still go to my morning class. It was the only one on Friday and it wasn't difficult to go for just an hour. That and it felt like a little normality would help take my mind off things. As I walked through campus, I kept feeling the hairs on my neck rise and fall while I sauntered across campus. I knew he was somewhere nearby, watching me. He was worried about something, I could tell, but I wasn't ready to talk to him and kept walking like I didn't know he was there. I made it to class and felt satisfied that he hadn't followed me inside, that he stayed in the quad. I tried to push out everything from my mind in order to just focus on the class, Focusing on the lecture felt impossible given how horribly everything had gone yesterday. I decided about 30 minutes into class that I would talk to Chess afterward so that he would stop following me everywhere I went. I got the sense that he wouldn't stop until we did at this point. I wished he'd had that same perseverance before he ran off and left me in a hospital bed alone. I tried to rationalize that we weren't even together and that I shouldn't be that upset with him because he didn't owe me anything.

As class came to an end, I gathered my things and gave myself a quick pep talk in the hall before going outside again. I couldn't see him, but I knew he was nearby. I walked toward the library, stopping at the bench where he'd found me in the rain. It was cold out, but I didn't feel the cold the same anymore. I was always warm. I took a seat on the bench and sat my bag down beside me.

"I know you're there, Chess. Come out. I won't yell at you again," I said feeling him approaching and then seeing him walking up the walkway from the library. He eyed me and sat down next to me. He tried to take my hand, but I pulled it away.

"Lyle, I am so sorry. I can explain everything... I... I don't know where to start."

"You do not need to explain anything. I understand what you chose and I accept that. Now you need to accept the choice you made too," I said, sounding so pious that it hurt me, too.

"You don't mean that," he started, "Lyle, I can tell you know how I feel and I know you feel it too. I can tell you what's wrong with you if you give me the chance."

"There's nothing wrong with me, Chess. I am fine. I have PTSD and I am responding to trauma."

"You're right... I'm sorry... there isn't anything wrong with you... but Lyle, come on. I know you don't believe that's the truth." He tried to grab my hand again. I stood up.

"I think this was a mistake. I don't want you to touch me. I am trying to show you I'm fine so that you'll just go away and, as you can see, I'm fine. I'm a little damaged now and I know it's hard to take, but I'm fine." I said, trying to convince us both.

"Lyle. I need you to hear me when I tell you this, but you are not fine. I should have never..." he stopped. I could tell that it hurt him too somehow, but that didn't matter.

"Chess. I just can't do this with you. I am trying to process everything and, to be honest, you're making it harder for me." I leaned down to grab my bag and he grabbed my hand.

"Lyle, you can't process this on your own. Please come with me. Let's go back to my place and we can talk. Please." I felt him rub his thumb across my knuckles and it felt so good to feel him again, but I couldn't trust him. I pulled my hand away after just a second more.

"I need to go home." I started walking away from him and he tried to follow. "Chess, I'm serious. It's time to let me go. I need to let go of you and you are the one making it hard for me to do that. Just stop." He stopped again. I felt crazy saying those words because, at the same time, part of me didn't want that, but I needed to. I walked away and felt the pull back to him for a long time, but he didn't follow. I went home, climbed into my bed, and tried to forget.

# Chapter Fourteen

I t wasn't possible; it couldn't be possible, but it's happening. Lyle is in transition. I bit him and he was transitioning into a wolf — this wasn't how it was supposed to work. I know that once it was possible, all wolves know that, but we haven't been able to turn a wolf using a bite in centuries. Our records didn't even agree when the last bitten wolf was turned, but it was happening here right in front of my eyes.

I panicked. It wasn't possible; it had to be something else, but I could smell it on him now. It was faint, but it was there. He doesn't know. He clearly hadn't completed his transition yet.

*Is there a way to stop it?* I wondered. *How can I help him? He needs to know now. I need to tell him the truth about everything, but how? He won't let me near him long enough. He won't talk to me; he doesn't trust me and for good reason.* My chest ached. I should've stayed longer, I should have checked-in, I would have seen this sooner, caught it sooner. *I'm in over my head,* I thought as I started walking home. It was time to call my family. This was too big. I needed their help. I would have to explain myself. I was going to have severe consequences, but it was too much. He's a baby wolf and soon he's going to transition. I pulled out my phone and for a second I didn't know who to call, but I pulled up a phone number and dialed.

"Hello, Aunt Jenn? I need your help." She could hear the urgency in my voice and told me she was on her way to the loft.

As it turned out, she wasn't far away. She was just south, doing some scouting in the woods of Mt. Rainer for a winter herb and was going to meet my mother for dinner in Olympia. I had gotten home and sat tensely as I waited for her to arrive. I heard the call for the elevator and held my breath as it ascended again. I could smell my aunt's scent as the lift pulled to a stop and I could sense her worry as she lifted the gate and walked toward the door. I stood and walked over to let her in, she smiled at me as she walked into the loft. She didn't look worried or angry, yet, but I could sense that it wouldn't be far behind after I told her.

"Chess, it's okay, relax. I could smell the anxiety from the lobby," she said, winking at me and smiling as she took a seat on the sofa.

"I'm sorry Jenn, but it's not okay. I really screwed up this time. I can't fix this," I said closing the door and walking over to sit next to her. She grabbed my hand and pushed her other hand through my hair.

"It's okay, honey. We'll fix it together then." She looked a little worried. "Just start from the beginning."

"Well, there's this boy...." I continued to tell her everything about Lyle. Everything I knew, everything I felt, everything I tried to do to stay away from him, and how I'd failed. I told her how we went camping, how I bit him, how I left, and how he was transitioning. She stayed silent and listened carefully to everything I had to say. She stood from the sofa and paced. She ran her hand through her hair and sighed.

"Chess. I thought maybe someone just saw you shift or something like that, but this is bigger than you or I. I love you, honey, I really do." She moved back to kneel before me, took my hands in hers and looked me directly in my eyes. "Are you absolutely certain he's in transition?" She asked me.

"Yes, Jenn. I can smell the wolf in him," I said, looking away from her eyes, feeling so disappointed and ashamed of myself. She pulled me into a hug.

"We need to call the pack. We need to call your father," she said as I nodded and a tear swelled in my eye at the fear I felt knowing what this meant. "Have you told this boy? What does he know?"

"I tried to talk to him, but I hurt him so badly. He doesn't trust me anymore. I can't say I blame him." I responded and put my head into my hands. "Are you going to tell him about my feelings for him?" I asked.

"No, not yet. Though there will be holes in this, your father is a smart man, it won't be long before he puts the pieces together. Especially after he talks to him," she sighed. "I'm glad you called me Chess and I'm sorry that this happened, but the only way out now is through and, unfortunately for this boy, he has no choice in the matter. He may not forgive you for that, if he loves you too he will in time. I'm going to call now." She stood and walked over to the window, looking out over the city. She pulled out her phone and called my father. "Noah," she said, "it's time to call the family home. We have a situation."

Things moved rather quickly after that. I left with Jenn and we headed home. My father would have called my mother, who would have gone to get my siblings. The drive was long and quiet. My aunt continued to comfort me along the route home. The dread I felt inside grew as we hit the ferry, docked on the other side, and with every mile marker that moved us closer to our pack's territory. I had never wanted to be so far away from home in my life. We pulled into the driveway. My father was already waiting on the porch with my mother standing behind him. It looked like they hadn't brought everyone yet like I had assumed they would, but it wouldn't be long until they all knew. My aunt pushed her hand through my hair one last time and asked, "are you ready?" I nodded even though I wasn't. We opened the car doors and I immediately felt the stare of the alpha land on me as I shut the door behind me and drifted toward the house.

Aunt Jenn walked ahead of me and spoke first. "Noah, it's going to be important for you to keep yourself in check for what we are about to tell you. There is nothing you can say or do that Chess isn't already killing himself over and I am still your older sister, alpha or not, and I will not hesitate to hurt you if you get mean." His eyes flashed at her, but he nodded. My mother looked worried and put her hand on my father's shoulder.

"Let's go inside," my father said sternly as he turned and everyone followed him into the house. I trailed behind last as I followed them into the dining room and we all sat down around the table. We all sat quietly as I tried to build up the nerve to tell my parents the truth.

After a minute or two, Jenn offered to tell them, but I shook my head. "No, Jenn, I need to tell them." My parents both looked worried and my father grabbed my hand in an unusual gesture of comfort saying, "It's okay son, we are your family and your pack. There's nothing you are going to tell us that is going to change that."

I started just as I had with Aunt Jenn, leaving nothing out. My mother and father kept their composure, as they always did, and during my pauses they would ask questions.

"What's the boy's name?" My mother asked.

"Lyle."

"How did you two meet?" My father asked.

"The professor I assist assigned him to me for tutoring."

"And you have feelings for Lyle?" My mother asked. I nodded.

"When did they start?" My father.

"The moment I met him."

They continued to listen as I built to the night I bit him, including how it happened, how I'd cared for him, and how I'd left as soon as I knew he was okay. How I ran until I collapsed trying to escape what I'd done. How I tried to cut him from my life, tried to avoid hurting him anymore than I already had. How I saw him in class and what he did. How I went to confront him and could smell the wolf pacing within him. How I would have never left him alone if I had any thought that this was a possibility.

My father leaned forward in his hands, troubled with the truth, and trying to process everything I had confessed. "Chess, it's not possible for humans to transition from a bite. It's just not possible."

My aunt reached out and grabbed my father's shoulder. "Noah. It's true. This boy is transitioning and, from the sound of it, he doesn't have long before he'll make his first shift." My father looked at her, a look of fear and disbelief in his eyes. My mother looked around the room and then her eyes settled on me.

"Have you told him yet?" My mother asked me quietly.

"No," I hesitated, "I tried, but he won't listen to me. I broke his heart."

Everyone sat quietly at the table for a while, taking in the situation's severity.

"Do we..," I started trailing off as everyone looked at me, "need to call the Union?" I asked quietly.

"Absolutely not," my father stated firmly.

"Chess, I don't know who this young man is to you, but we can't be certain that his body will survive the transition at this point. We don't know what will happen. There is no record that exists. All we have are myths and legends. This could kill him." My heart broke and inside, my wolf cried with horror. I hadn't even thought of that as a possibility. I tried to hold my composure, but my wolf was frantic at the thought of Lyle dying.

"Noah," my mother started, "Lyle needs to be brought here. He needs to be told and, if he survives the transition....," she paused. "How long are we going to hide an unregistered wolf from the Union?"

He grabbed her hand. "One thing at a time, love."

He turned to look at me, "Chess, I love you and it is very important that you know that. I do not have words for the amount of danger this situation has put us all in, but if the boy survives, there will be a lot of questions. It is your responsibility to tell this boy what is going on and to bring him back here. There, unfortunately, is no other option at this point. I won't add kidnapping to the list of atrocities that are going to be inflicted on this poor boy. So, you need to bring him back here of his own will. He will stay here with us for the winter break. We will meet him and prepare him for what is about to happen." I shuddered at the thought and felt completely drained, but I nodded.

"What's going to happen?" I asked, waiting to hear if there would be some sort of punishment from my alpha.

He put his hand on my shoulder. "Son, there is no greater punishment I can inflict on you than what you have inflicted upon yourself. You may have just ended this boy's life and we can only hope to save it now so that his death does not fall on you. We will deal with the rest later."

"Go back to the city and bring him back here as soon as possible."

"Em," my father looked over to my mother, "bring the kids home early. We all need to be here now."

My mother looked at me again, gave a soft smile, and then left the room. My aunt followed her. My father and I sat in the dining room quietly for a while.

"Chess," my father said and I turned to look at him, "if I am right, he is going to need you to survive this transition. He won't make it without you. I don't know everything that's broken. I don't need to know right now, but do everything you can to fix it. His life is going to depend on you. I know you are not ready for that type of responsibility, but I hope you will find it within you to do this." His words hit hard, but I knew there wasn't anything in the world I wouldn't do to save him.

*Whatever it takes*, I thought.

# Chapter Fifteen

The rest of the day was a blur after I left Chess standing in the quad. I went home and considered everything that Chess had said. I wanted so badly for him to talk more, but I think Jesse had been right in that I needed to stay away from him. We planned to go out on Saturday to a bar on Capitol Hill. While Hunter hadn't been there, he and Jesse continued to text about making plans for us to hang out. I normally wouldn't have agreed to a night of drinking, but I thought maybe it couldn't hurt with the end of the break coming and me having passed all of my classes. At least I felt good about school.

Saturday morning had come and gone and I was partially looking forward to going out, but, just like every other day over the past four weeks, my heart hung heavy and I wondered if I would ever feel the joy I had felt when I first arrived in the city. I went to the mirror in my room and splashed my face with water - I was almost unrecogniz-able from the person that had stepped out of the Uber back in the fall. My hair had continued to change color from blonde to auburn as did the rest of the newly found body hair. My face looked the same, but my body had continued to change. I grew bulkier and had more defined muscles showing than I thought was humanly possible. PTSD was definitely not what was going on with me, but I didn't have a rational answer for the changes either. It was all out of my control at this point anyway. I checked my phone and saw a message from Jesse.

JESSE

Will be there to pick you up in about an hour! See you soon.

I decided it would be nice to dress up and look halfway decent for the night out. I went to my closet and pulled out a couple of shirts that I thought might look nice. I tried on three and nearly everything was too small, fitting my torso like a glove. I squeezed into a black v-neck that I thought highlighted my new physique decently enough. One that also didn't rise above my navel when I lifted my arms. I picked out a pair of jeans and the only jacket that I had that still fit. I returned to the mirror and splashed some water on my face and thought about shaving, but I felt like the reddish shadow across my face highlighted my jawline and that served me better than going without at this point in the day. I grabbed some pomade and rubbed it into my hair, styling it into a slight curve to the right with some mess to it. I decided against cologne because at this point the smell of it was so strong it hurt my nose. I gave myself one last look in the mirror and probably, for the first time in my life, felt like I was pretty attractive. It was all for naught though. There was no one else's approval I wanted than his and he would never see me like this. I checked my phone, another message from Jesse.

JESSE

We are on our way! Are you ready?

I didn't think it had been an hour already, but looking at the time, it had. My senses were all over the place. I sent back a quick message.

**The Last Red Wolf**

LYLE



I left my room and said a quick hello to Andy and Kay. I really liked Kay. He was down to earth and he loved Andy's quirky humor. They were cute together, though I could tell Andy tried to keep things low-key when I was in the room. Trying not to hurt my feelings. I told him the other day he didn't have to do that and he had acted like he didn't know what I was talking about. I rolled my eyes and laughed. He was a great roommate and an even better friend. I said goodbye and wished them both a good night before leaving to head downstairs.

By the time I had gotten to the front doors, Jesse and Reese had parked out front. I climbed into the back seat and greeted them both.

"Where are Phisher and Hunter?" I asked, buckling my seat belt.

"They are going to meet us there. They're finishing their fancy dinner date," Reese said, pulling out into the street.

Jesse nudged him a bit, trying to keep him from talking about dates. I had told them all I was fine and not to worry about all that, but a few of them still didn't believe me apparently. Jesse was singing karaoke in the car on the way to the bar and I was enjoying having the music loud enough that I didn't have to hear my own thoughts. I got into the rhythm of it and danced awkwardly in the back seat.

We had to park a way off from the bars, but we were still at a better walking distance now than we had been at the apartment. We started walking toward the first bar and Jesse complimented me on how nice I looked. Reese made a comment that I was going to 'get some' tonight, at which Jesse nudged him with her elbow again as we walked past the bouncer. There was a very nice low-key vibe inside the bar and it had several fireplaces, couches, and plenty of tables to sit at. Jesse ordered her and me a rum and coke, while Reese ordered a beer. We took a seat near one fireplace and started joking and having fun. We had moved through three drinks before Phisher and Hunter joined us, they both had clearly had a few drinks at dinner as well. Hunter greeted everyone with a smooch and then laid out across Jesse's and my lap.

"You two look hot," he said, taking his finger and booping me on the nose.

"Thanks," I chuckled a little awkwardly. I took the final swig of my drink and choked it down.

*This isn't very good,* I thought to myself, but said nothing to Jesse about it.

"What are you two drinking?" Hunter asked as he made a quick assessment of my glass.

"Jesse, no. You are not having him drink rum and coke, are you? That is disgusting. Here sweetie, come with me," he said, jumping off our laps and pulling me by the hand back to the bar. I admittedly felt a little tipsy at that point and should have probably slowed down. Hunter ordered me a vodka sprite with lemon and lime and told me I would really like it. The drink came, I took a sip, and it was great. I couldn't really taste any alcohol in it and it tasted like a normal sprite. I took another big sip.

"This is great." I told him as he took me by the hand and dragged me back to the couch. I sat back down in the spot I had been occupying before and listened in on Phisher and Reese talking about sports... again. I didn't ever really mind sports, but I also wasn't super invested in them like they were. I continued to sip my drink and enjoyed being out with my friends. We stayed at the bar for about another twenty minutes before Hunter and Jesse wanted to go dancing. I finished my drink and we walked toward the next bar. At this point I was feeling a bit more than tipsy and thought to myself that I needed to take a breather at the next bar before having another round. We walked up to a small line and waited patiently to go inside. I could feel the bass of the music playing through the cement walls of the building and was a little nervous about going in. I followed my friends and we went inside. We all went to the bar first and ordered a drink. I tried to order water, but Hunter ordered me another vodka sprite instead. I smiled at him and took the drink.

"Did you come out to party or to play sober sister?" Hunter yelled out jokingly over the music.

"I don't know," I hollered back. He smiled and swayed to the music. I followed the four of them through a back room into a long hallway with some stairs that took us to another bar, just below the one we had entered. There were fake vines from floor to ceiling that lined the walls and it had another counter to order drinks from in this room along with playing the same loud music. We found a small table where everyone set their drinks and the four of them made their way to the dance floor. They pushed for me to join them, but I was feeling a little lightheaded and the music hurt my head.

"Lyle?" a voice from behind me yelled my name out over the music. I turned around and saw Jacob standing there, smiling.

"Oh, hi Jacob," I tried saying back. He smiled at me.

"What are you doing here?" He asked me, excited that he was running into me.

"I am... uh, out with friends." I pointed toward everyone on the dance floor and he turned and looked.

"That's fun. Me too!" He said, pointing over at the table with two other guys sitting at it. I waved over at them and they waved back at me, smiling.

"What are you drinking?" He asked me as the song changed to something equally loud.

"Uhhh... Hunter got it for me. It's...uhhh. Vodka Sprite." I said back.

"Do you want another one?" He asked me.

"Sure." I said, shrugging my shoulders. He took me by the hand and I followed him up to the bar. He ordered me another one and got himself one of whatever he was drinking too. It sounded complicated. He passed me my fresh drink as I finished the other. He tried talking to me more, but I couldn't hear him over the music being so loud, I nodded and pretended I did anyway.

"Do you want to dance?" he asked me again.

"I don't know how," I told him.

"That's okay. I'll show you." He said taking me by the hand and pulling me out onto the dance floor. My friends watched as I started looking as intoxicated as I felt. Jacob put his hands on my shoulders and began helping me sway back and forth. He bucked his hips into mine for a moment before turning around and pushing his back into me. I felt confused and things went a little blurry. He turned back around and I felt his hands reach up around my neck and then felt his lips on mine. I couldn't see any of it happen, but I felt it. He was kissing me. I backed away from it and he pushed his lips on mine harder. I started coming back in my head just before I felt Jacob being shoved away and a hand spun me so fast it made the world spin. I heard shouting and made out a face from the spinning. "Chess?" I said before feeling the earth beneath my feet disappear and the rest going black.

I started coming back. In and out at first. I felt motion. It hurt my head. I opened my eyes and felt like I was seeing blurred images from being in the backseat of a car. Someone was driving. I could see the blur of an arm and a hand holding a steering wheel. The images faded again. Smell, I could smell something. What was that? It smelled like spruce, fresh rainfall, and.... Chess? It fell away again.

In what I assumed was several hours later I woke up. It was bright outside. I was laying down in the backseat of a car. I sat up and looked around. I was in the back of Chess's Jeep. He was not in the car. I looked out the windows and all I could see was white every-where. Some green poked out from underneath the heavy snowfall that clung to the trees all around me. I opened the car door and climbed out into the snowy tundra that surrounded the Jeep. I looked around. There were clear skies, but where was I? I turned around and, in the distance, I could see Chess sitting on a fallen tree stump staring out into the woods. I could feel the movement in my chest again, though it was wobbly. It pushed me toward him cautiously; I wanted to be near him, but I also wanted to run away. I wanted to scream at him and I wanted him to hold me.

"Ouch," I said, crying out a little as I grabbed my head with one hand. Thinking hurt, feeling hurt, moving hurt, but I continued to walk forward through the snow toward him. I made my way to him and, as I walked around the stump, I could tell he had been crying. His peculiar and beautiful eyes looked up at me, full of regret and worry. I decided then I would not yell at him. I sighed quietly and sat down next to him. He grabbed my hand. I let him. He rubbed his thumb over my knuckles like he had that day in the quad and it felt nice. I didn't pull my hand away from him. We sat silently for several minutes, just staring into the distance.

"Where are we?" I asked him, breaking the silence, and looking at him through squinted eyes.

"Mt. Rainier," he said flatly.

"Why are we on Mt. Rainier?"

"I need to talk to you, Ly.... Lyle, I need to tell you the truth." He was struggling to get words out. He gripped my hand a little tighter.

"How are you feeling?" He asked me.

"My head hurts, but other than that, I think I'll live." I tried to joke, but he was not laughing.

"Why would you do that?" He asked. I could hear the frustration in his voice.

"Do what?" I asked him, confused.

"Drink all that poison, and.... and... kiss that human?" The last word came out in disgust and I could feel the hair on his hands rise with anger.

"What are you talking about?" I asked him, a little frustrated.

"That guy... I pushed him off you. I should not have done that, but I... I shoved him." He said staggering backward.

"What guy?" I asked. "What... Ohhhh." Images and flashes suddenly returning to me, "Jacob? I ran into Jacob.... and.... and... he kissed me?" I remembered it now. It made my stomach turn sour. "Oh... Oh God." I leaned over the edge of the log before hurling a bunch of bile and sour from my stomach into the snow. Chess moved to rub my back as it came out.

"I see," he said, as I finished spitting the awful taste out of my mouth, "you didn't kiss him."

"No, I would never kiss Jacob. He is just... He's been a... distraction," I said.

"A distraction?" Chess asked me, confused.

"Yes, when I'm around him, he talks so much that he makes me forget," I started, stopping myself after realizing what I was saying.

"Forget what?" He kept his hand on my back and rubbed in small circles.

I turned to look him in his eyes, "you.... Everything that has been happening to me. My hair, my body, feelings that come suddenly, senses, and just other things that I should not be able to do or that I don't understand. He talks so much that it all goes away and I needed that, but," I sighed and looked away from him and felt guilty, "but I never meant for him to fall for me or think there was anything more than friendship between us. I thought I was clear," I sighed, not clear enough.

"It's not your fault," he said, pulling my face back up. "He would never have been able to stop feeling what he feels for you. Especially now." He continued to look into my eyes and dropped his hand to mine, taking it back in his. "Lyle, these changes. They are not your fault and they're not from trauma. You experienced trauma, but that isn't what is changing you. This is happening because of me, because of what I did." I sat, listening. He was being honest for the first time. There was no hesitation in his voice about what he was telling me now. "Lyle, I'm... I'm a werewolf and the bite you got when we were camping wasn't from a mountain lion, it was.... from me," he paused, taking in a sharp breath, "and now.... that bite is turning you into one too." As soon as he finished, he broke the connection between our gazes and hung his head low. I felt a tear drop fall and hit the top of my hand.

The words echoed in my head. *Werewolf. Bite. Him. Me?* I heard him and I believed he was telling me the truth, but werewolves? "Werewolves... werewolves don't exist Chess. What are you talking about?" I started eyeing him strangely before Chess lifted his hand from mine and, as he did, hair grew out of his skin as if on demand. His fingers cracked and moved as his fingernails grew out, turned black, and curled into claws. I stared dazed at seeing his hand twist and morph into something it was not before and then, just as suddenly, morph back again into a normal hand. He returned his hand to mine and gripped it tight. He spoke cautiously, probably thinking that I would pull away from him in horror now that I knew, but he was hurting and the only sense I had in my chest was to comfort him.

"Stop," he whispered.

"Stop what?" I asked him.

"Stop rationalizing it and making it okay. Yell at me, scream, cry, hit me, run, do something, but do not make it okay," he said looking up at me.

"I..," I didn't know what to think, it overwhelmed me and consumed me with the knowledge of what he was, what he was saying he did, and with the realizations falling into place that made sense, but could not possibly be reality. "So this is why my hair is changing, why I can hear, smell, see, and sense things I shouldn't be able to, why my body changed and healed like it was never broken before?" I asked him. He nodded.

"It should never have happened, Lyle. I should not have allowed myself to get close to you like I did. I shouldn't have bitten you. I should not have left you. We can't make wolves from bites. It shouldn't have been possible, but it is happening. It is happening to you and while I can't take it away from you or change it now, I'm so sorry." He cried, "I've cursed you and I could have prevented it if I had only been a little stronger." It pained me to see him like this, I don't know how or when, but I somehow had already accepted it. It didn't feel like a choice and, as the dots aligned and the connections fit together, I felt whole, and I felt like me. I wasn't angry at him. I didn't feel cursed or anything of the sort.

I pulled him into my arms and stroked his hair. Scents of him rose in waves and it brought me even more peace. "Chess. It's okay. I'm fine."

"But you're not fine Lyle. This... This could kill you. We don't know if a human can even survive the transition. There isn't anyone alive that knows or that can remember when a wolf was ever turned." He said, looking at me trying to gauge my honesty.

*Killed*, I hear him say it, *this could kill me?* I felt movement in my chest again and a warmth near my heart that had never been there before. It felt like it was responding, rising up to meet my thoughts that I would be fine. I don't know how I knew, but I knew. "You said we?" I asked him. "Who are we?"

"My family, my pack. They want to meet you and we want to help you," he said. "My Dad, he... he's our alpha. He can help you, we can, we can help you survive it."

"Chess, I'm not going to die," I told him. I didn't know how I knew that, but I just felt it.

"You don't know that. There is so much you don't know, but I... I can be here now and I promise to never disappear again. I will show you what you need to know," he said, sounding so earnest and hopeful.

I felt hesitant. My head rushed with all the information again, werewolf, bite, him, me, death, family, pack. The information hit my head hard again and it hurt. I believed him, but it was a lot. I think he felt it, the enormity of the pain that I felt. He winced as if some kind of physical force had struck him. "I know," he cried. "I know it hurts. I hurt you. I know I hurt you, and I'm sorry, but Lyle, I need you to trust me again. I won't betray that trust - I know you can feel that."

My head swam with uncertainty, but it was automatic. I didn't even have to think about it. "I trust you," I said. He smiled at me. "I just think maybe I need some time to process all of this before anything else."

"Lyle, there isn't time. There's no way of knowing when the full transition will happen, but we know it's soon. We need to leave for my family's home and prepare — today," he said, sounding worried.

*There isn't time. The transition will happen soon. More information to process.* As he said the words, I knew he was right. I could feel it now. I didn't know what it was before, but I knew. The changes were near complete. I could feel that, which must also mean that would be when it would happen. "Okay," I said, "I'll go with you." I was so confused at my answer and, at the same time, I wasn't. My head questioned everything, but my instinct spoke for me knowing it was the right thing to do. Chess smiled and it was the brightest smile I think I had ever seen cross his face. I was glad that I'd made him happy, but inside I had so many questions and a fear of uncertainty for what would happen next that I couldn't even put into words. Chess rose from the log and pulled me up to standing. I was still shorter than him, but now we were both as bulky as one another. He hugged me for the first time and I laid my head against his chest, which felt like the first time even though I had done the same when he'd carried me out of the woods, but, somehow, this time it was different.

"We have one other problem," he said as he held me close.

I pulled away and looked back into his eyes. "And what's that?" I asked.

"Jesse may very well kill me the next time she sees me," he said looking scared and for the first time in weeks I laughed, I laughed hard.

Time was of the essence now. We were driving off the mountain, headed back to my apartment to get some things for me to take to Chess' family's place. Chess told me a little more about his family, now that I knew the truth. His dad, Noah, was the Alpha of their pack, Pack Beck. His mom, Emily, was the Beta and she was more likely to be reserved. His aunt, Jenn, was his dad's older sister and she was the one he'd called first when he found out about me. His sister and brother, Valorie and George, were both younger and about to finish high school. His cousin Rupert was Jenn's son and the same age as the twins. He held back on telling me everything and I could sense that, but he gave me enough to know who I was going to meet and what I might expect without overwhelming me with the details. It was nearing mid-afternoon when we arrived at my apartment. Chess shared that he could smell Jesse, Reese, Hunter, Andy, and someone else in my apartment and that they smelled anxious. I looked for my phone, which I found under the seat in the back, and it was dead.

"You can smell all that?" I asked him as we left the car.

"Yeah. You will be able to as well at some point. Your senses must not be finished transitioning." He half smiled at me. I could sense my transition worried him a lot. He was trying to remain confident, but I knew that he was not.

I buzzed us into the building and we headed up to the elevator. Chess stayed behind me a little, preparing to use me as a wolfie shield should Jesse decide to launch herself at him again like she had last night apparently.

"Scaredy wolf," I teased as I tried to make a clever joke and smiled at him. He didn't look amused but I got a kick out of it.

I opened the door and, as expected, saw all their eyes fall on me and then shift to Chess.

"Where the hell have you been?" Jesse asked, clearly a little more than irritated.

"Uh, Chess took me back to his place until I regained consciousness this morning. We.... uh. had a lot to talk about," I said.

"And what was all of this conversation concerning?," she started, "clearly it was enough to clear the air it appears."

"Yeah, it was... illuminating to say the least and I understand now why everything happened the way it did," I said.

"And why was that?" She asked, staring Chess down, looking for an answer.

"I... uh... needed to come out to my family first?... and... I... needed to take some time with that," Chess said. He was trying to spin a lie with a truth and it seemed to be working.

"See Jesse! I told you that Chess was just trying to figure things out. I knew he couldn't just leave Lyle like that without a reason," Hunter said, smiling.

"Is that the truth, Lyle?" She said, looking at me. She was a freaking human lie detector. That girl could sniff out a lie in any situation. I knew I had to do my best with Jesse in her personal detective mode and I used the technique Chess had just employed.

"Yeah, it's the truth. We came back so I could get some things. He told his parents and then told them about me. They want to meet me, they invited me to spend winter break with them. I know it seems kind of sudden, but," I looked back at Chess, smiled, turned back to Jesse, "I trust him."

They all stared at each other, except for Jesse. She continued to look at me and stare. I felt her looking for any tell that I may be lying to her, but, after what seemed like forever, I could feel her relax a little and then, satisfied with the response I had given her, she said, "fine." Then she walked up toward Chess and put a finger to his chest saying, "I do not know how many chances Lyle will give you, but I only give one. Screw this up again and I will hurt you." He smiled at her and nodded, understanding the sincerity in her warning.

The mood in the room shifted and everyone looked relieved to see that I was still alive. Glad that they didn't have to worry anymore. Hunter followed Chess and I into my bedroom and said that he thought it was so romantic that I was going home to meet his family. He said he would want all the details when we came back. Chess played along and, even though I was going home to meet his parents, I knew it was not because we were in love or boyfriends, or even dating, but that he wanted me to survive my transition, and believed being with his family was the only way that was going to happen. I had my reservations for sure, but I knew for some strange reason that I wouldn't die. I had questions of my own and I didn't know if Chess was going to be the one to answer them for me, but I was excited at the prospect of getting some clarity on my current situation. I packed my bags and bid my friends farewell for the holidays. Chess carried my bag down on the elevator and to the car. We climbed in the car and buckled in.

As Chess started the car, he grabbed my hand and I looked over at him.

"Are you ready?" he asked softly.

I knew there was no turning back, there was no stopping this from happening, no mystical, magical cure to lycanthropy, but at this moment, I felt okay.

I knew everything was going to change, but I knew that Chess would be by my side. I looked over and stared back into his eyes and said, "Yeah, let's go."

# Chapter Sixteen

The drive back toward the coast was much different this time around. I was different. I felt alive inside for maybe the first time in my entire life. Chess continued to look at me in a way he never had before. I think it was because he could finally be honest with someone outside of his pack. The way he'd talked about them this time differed from the last time he'd told me about them. It was very clear they were closer than I would consider a normal family. Chess said it's because they're a pack, but I didn't even know what having a genuine family felt like for comparison's sake so the concept of something deeper than that was hard for me to fully grasp.

After boarding the ferry, we went back up to the observation deck. Only this time, there was no argument that needed mending; it was just us. My senses were alive. I could smell the salt in the sea and the woods nearby on the shore. I could hear the waves clapping against the hull of the ferry in a rhythm I hadn't heard before. I could see along the coastline to where the waves smacked against the shore and then raked the sand back into the ocean. Chess held me like he had before, but it wasn't because I was cold. I hadn't felt cold for a while now. He held me because he wanted to and I wanted him to as well. It was a perfect moment, one of the few I'd created as an adult. I couldn't recall feeling any perfect moments as a child or a teen. I had existed in a world that only tolerated me. Here, now, and from the moment I had landed in Seattle, I felt like I had finally started living.

Chess was happy, too. I could feel it somehow. I could sense him more now than I ever could have before. I could always sense his presence before, but I felt like his emotions were readily available to me now as well. I could sense his feelings and not just his physical presence. It was complicated though,  his emotions came to me as like a small stream of consciousness that I had to focus on in order to truly feel. I could even sense his fear, the internal anxiety he kept buried deep down inside himself. I knew part of this was his concern for me, my safety, and my life, but there was more. I wanted to feel it more, I could tell that there was more, but my ability to delve into his feelings stopped there. He kept this part of himself tucked away from any ability I had to access it.

"Stop it," Chess said, whispering in my ear patiently. He wasn't mad, but it surprised me.

"Stop what?"

"I can feel you doing that," he said. It took me back a little, not understanding.

"Doing what?"

"Searching my feelings. I can sense yours too, but you are digging too deep." He said it so matter-of-factly, that it was so obvious that I should have known he would know. I turned around and looked at him.

"What? You can feel it?" I was genuinely curious.

"It's a wolf thing" he said, grinning so that all of his teeth showed. "Listen and feel."

I stood quietly while he closed his eyes. I felt nothing at first, but then certain thoughts and feelings which were tucked away slowly emerged on their own. I recalled the first time I met Jesse and her friends, how nervous I was, and excited I had been that they had wanted me to join them.

"They are really great people," he said, smiling at me. I could feel only slightly that it was him pushing them to the surface, that he was feeling the emotions I was feeling.

"Is that a thing for all wolves?" I asked nervously, to see if his family could invade my emotions and thoughts.

"No," he said, "it is something only mates can do, but I could do it to you even when we first met and you were human. I think you could kind of do it too now that I think about it all, but it is odd that you and I can do that because we are not mates." He said it so plainly. It hurt my feelings a little.

"No, not like that. Mating is something different entirely for wolves. I will explain it to you more later, but don't let it hurt you. We are about to dock. Let's head back to the car." He said, keeping my hand in his and we headed back toward the car.

I kept feeling like as soon as I found out one thing about wolves, there were three more things I didn't know. I was relieved to know that his family couldn't feel my feelings or pick away at my memories. I was a little nervous that Chess could do it so easily. "So, you have access to everything I'm feeling and all of my memories?" I asked as we climbed into the car.

"No, I don't. I can sense your emotions easier than you can mine, but pulling up a memory is a lot more difficult. Even then, I can't see it the way you do. It's the feelings related to it you can sense." He explained.

"Huh." I said, settling back into the seat, mulling it all over. It was so crazy, but cool at the same time. "Is it because you bit me?" I asked.

"I don't think so. Like I said, it was there before all of this." He smiled again. I think maybe he was getting a kick out of answering all my questions. I tried bringing up mates again, but he refused to talk about it. "You won't understand until after the transition." He continued to tell me, but every time he thought of the transition, his anxiety would spike.

After leaving the ferry terminal we took the same route that we had traveled for the camping trip, passing the turnoff we had used when we had gone camping. There was snow on the ground and some snow that clung to the evergreens like on Mt. Rainer, but less so here. I got nervous the further we drove, feeling our impending arrival growing closer.

*What if they didn't like me, so many other families hadn't liked me and had sent me away? What if they do it too?* I thought to myself as I started fidgeting with my hands. I'd never worried about not being liked before because I had never felt there would have been an actual sense of loss, a family could just pass me along, but what if Chess' family rejected me and then he did? I didn't want to think about that. I could feel somehow that we were getting close to our destination.

"Hush." Chess finally said, grabbing my hand instinctively.

"Okay, that might get annoying." I said, even though I felt a sense of relief with his hand on mine. He grinned childishly, as if to say, 'get used to it.'

"We're here." He announced as he slowed the car and turned into a tree-lined driveway. He pulled up around the trees which opened to a beautifully renovated farmhouse with lots of windows, a wrap-around porch, and a matching detached garage. The exterior was all white, just like the surrounding snow, with black accents outlining the windows, porch, and trim. It was massive, just like the property behind it, which had a large old barn which had been re-done to match the house.

"Pretty," I said as he pulled up to the garage and put the car in park. I looked out the window and could see people gathering on the front porch. They all looked so stunning, each of them stood out distinctly from one another, but they looked like they belonged together at the same time. They were all dressed in what I assumed would be their casual wear, but were clean and stylish. They looked like they belonged on the cover of a fashion magazine or something. I was supposed to get out of the car, but I hesitated. Chess instinctively did what he always did and walked around the car opening my door.

"Breathe," he whispered, "you're safe here." He reached out his hand and I took it. He helped me out of the car and I looked down at my clothes suddenly feeling so underdressed and out of place amongst all of them. Chess wasn't dressed as nicely, but his looks fit in with his family's all the same. He grabbed our bags from the car as I reached for mine. He didn't want to give it to me at first, but I insisted so that I could use it to cover my outfit slightly even though my backpack was just as ragged looking. I fidgeted a little before Chess gave me his hand again, pulling me along the pathway that led to the porch. We approached as I hid my core from view with my bag and stayed slightly behind Chess. We stopped at the bottom step and I struggled to look up at all of them. I could feel their eyes on me, assessing me, and I felt like if Chess let go of my hand I might start shaking.

"Lyle, this is my family," Chess said and I finally looked up. They all were smiling politely and some waved. "Family this is Lyle." I pulled a smile across my face, but I had never been more nervous to meet people in my entire life.

I made out Noah right away. He was tall and broad; he had the same eyes as Chess, which I found to be interesting. He radiated an energy that I could feel pulse into me. It was not a terrible energy, but it made me nervous. He was very handsome and I could tell that Chess and he shared similar features beyond just their eyes.

The woman to his left spoke first, "Hi Lyle, it is very nice to meet you. We're all so glad you agreed to come home with Chess for the break. Would you like to come inside?" Her voice sounded so warm and smooth as she spoke, it was very comforting and welcoming. I nodded as Chess squeezed my hand slightly and smiled at me. They all turned and everyone walked inside. Chess moved up the stairs, pulling me along behind him. We moved into what I assumed must be the formal living room. The woman who had invited me in, I assumed this was Chess' mom Emily, ushered the three younger kids upstairs which left Chess, me, Noah, another woman who must have been Jenn, and Emily. Chess grabbed the bag that I had been clinging to for additional comfort and gave it a tug. At first, I didn't let go, but he gave my hand another squeeze and I relinquished it. He set it next to the door and we walked into the living room. I noticed that as we walked past Noah, Chess instinctively twitched his head to the side.

*That was weird,* I thought privately. Chess had me sit next to him on a two-person sofa, as his parents and aunt did the same on two other sofas that made a small 'U' around an expensive looking coffee table. I looked around slightly and noticed how nice everything was. It was very well decorated, very high end. It put Chess's loft to shame.

"Chess?," the woman spoke again, "maybe more direct introductions might be helpful for Lyle?" She said, smiling at me.

"Of course," Chess started, "Lyle this is my father Noah," got that one correct, "my mother Emily," correct again, "and my aunt Jenn." I did well.

"It's very nice to meet you," Emily spoke. She was beautiful; she had a perfect complexion, long blonde wavy hair that she had styled to frame her face, her eyes were a dark green, and she looked like she could have come directly out of an old Hollywood movie. Her voice sounded like honey and was so smooth.

I finally spoke, "I...it's nice to meet you too." My voice cracked slightly, like it had in the lab when I first met Chess.

His aunt finally spoke, "we know you must be terrified and nervous, but we want to assure you that you are safe here and that you are most welcome to be here." Her voice was very pleasing as well. Not as smooth as Emily's, but also very comforting. She was equally beautiful. She had a lot of features in her cheeks and eyes that were similar to Chess' and his dad's. She was older, with dark brown hair that had a slight tinge of gray mixed throughout. She had two brown eyes, this differed from her brother and Chess, and slight crow's feet that showed at the corners of her eyes. She radiated energy that was serene and calming.

"Th... Thank you." I said and smiled at her. She smiled back and looked over at her brother.

I turned to look at him too, even seated he was quite tall and intimidating. I was not scared of him, but I was worried about what he thought of me. What had he thought of me grabbing his son's hand so tightly, maybe he felt I was a problem to be dealt with. We made eye contact and I immediately shot my eyes down, nervous to see his expression. As soon as I did that, he leaned over and grabbed my knee softly.

"Hey," he started, "you don't have to be scared here. I'm sure you must already be terrified, but you have nothing to fear from us." I had thought he would have spoken as sternly as he looked, but he didn't. He was comforting as well and his voice matched up with him, it was very fatherly and easy. I looked back up and made eye contact with him again, this time not looking away. "See, not so scary." He said, finally smiling at me. "Welcome to our home," he said. "We will need to chat later, just you and I, but until then let's get you settled, shall we?" He stood and everyone else followed. Looking around, I stood seconds later than everyone else.

I followed them up the winding staircase and down the hall. Chess had grabbed our bags so quickly I didn't even notice he had them in his hand. His father went past a door before Chess spoke up, "I thought Lyle might stay with me, at least for tonight, until he's comfortable." I had felt an emotion off him that read hopeful. I thought about it briefly before hiding a slight blush that may have turned my cheeks red if I hadn't stopped it. I had only slept next to him once before on his couch by accident and hadn't even thought about the possibility of sleeping next to him in bed.

"No," his father said sternly, but still kindly, "Lyle is going to have his own room here. Your mother has decorated it nicely for him. He will be alright." Chess did not like that and could feel a small growl even while I was standing at his side. It made me tense up a little and he responded with a small squeeze of my hand and we both relaxed. We passed two more doors before Noah opened the third. We all walked into the room and it was just as beautiful as the rest of the house. Three walls were white and one was a deep navy blue. There was an antique queen size bed with brass finishings pushed up against the navy blue wall. There were two wire end tables with a light brown leather top, a lamp on each side. Above the bed hung a golden mount of a deer head that gave a modern feel to the space. There was a dresser with a large mirror above it that stood next to the door to the small bathroom, decorated to match the bedroom. On the right side of the bed was a small basket full of blankets next to a small chair. Both items sat under a giant window that looked out at the barn behind the house where you could see a line of snow touching the evergreens. It was by far one of the nicest spaces I had ever been in. Their entire house was. I had never thought that in my lifetime I would I ever get to sleep in a place as nice as this.

"Do you like it?" Emily asked softly.

"I... I don't think I have ever been to a more beautiful place than your house or this room," I said honestly.

"I'm so glad," she said smiling. "If you want to change anything, let me know. I have no problem taking you shopping and letting you pick out your own things if you would like. I also purchased you a few outfits, however I am afraid they may be a little small. I hadn't expected you to be as broad shouldered as you are, but that's easily fixed. The sweaters I bought should fit fine, though."

"Oh, uh... you didn't have to do that. I couldn't even think of changing anything." I mumbled.

"Well, what does your room look like at home?" she asked. I fidgeted a little, not really knowing how to respond, and I could feel their eyes on me.

"I don't really know, I guess," I described my room in my apartment a bit and claimed it as my childhood home, but I could feel Chess grow suspicious. "This is far nicer than any room I could have probably dreamed of, though. Thank you." I started saying similar things I would say to my foster parents when I would move into their homes. They would show me where I would sleep and ask similar questions. I was thankful she accepted that answer.

"Let's let Lyle get settled in. It has been a big day for him," Noah shared, "Chess, let's have a word while Lyle is getting settled."

I looked over at Chess. He gave my hand one more squeeze and let go. "I'll come back in a bit, okay?" he said.

"Okay." I said and with that they all left the room. As each of them walked out they would lightly touch one another with a hand on the arm or the shoulder or, as Emily did with Chess, put their hand through the other's hair. I thought it odd, but would try and remember to talk to Chess about it later. They left, including Chess, who closed  the door behind himself. I walked up to the bed and touched the navy comforter. It was so soft. I sat down and looked around the room feeling like an alien and utterly out of place in it. I had never had nice things like this and had never even had thought to want them, but, as I sat there, it felt warm and comfortable. I grabbed my backpack and started unpacking the clothes I had brought. When I opened drawers, they were filled with new clothes that were very stylish and far nicer than anything I'd brought with me. I discovered a new pack of socks and a pack of boxers that hadn't been opened in another drawer. It reminded me of many of the foster homes I'd cycled through where they would often have extra packs of clothes in the closet for kids who came with nothing or very close to nothing. I combined some shirts in one drawer with some sweaters in another to make space for what I had brought. I didn't even want to think of ruining one of the nice outfits Emily had bought for me, just in case they wanted them back at some point. I grabbed the few bathroom essentials I had brought, heading into the bathroom to put them away and I found the same. A new toothbrush, new deodorant, razors, hair products of all varieties, and the shower fully stocked with shampoo, conditioner, and body wash. I set my few things inside an empty drawer and walked back into the bedroom. I pulled out my phone to check the time and to see if I had any messages. It was 4:00 PM and I had one message from Jesse.

JESSE

I am glad things worked out for you two,
but if you need me, Reese and I will be
there as fast as we can to pick you up. Let
me know when you get there.

I felt comforted, knowing that I could have an escape plan if I needed to. I sent her a small text back, but discovered that it took a while to send as I had poor cell service.

LYLE

Thank you. Me too. We made it. They are all
very nice. I will keep that in mind.

I sat back down on the bed and stared in the mirror. I was glad my face wasn't changing. My hair seemed to have lightened up some, but was still significantly red over it's original blonde. I hoped that this whole thing wouldn't change who I was. After I had finished my transition, I wanted it to still be me inside. Chess had said it wouldn't be much longer before the transition had completed and that, when it was through, I would shift for the first time. I wondered when it would happen, today, tomorrow, in a week. I had jokingly said to Chess on the drive that it would probably happen under the light of the full moon, to which he assured me that the full moon did nothing more for wolves than providing a brilliant light to go on a night run. I thought it would be funny though if that was how it would happen. That would be next Thursday. I had looked it up, trying to be funny. It made us both laugh.

Laying back on the bed I heard a quiet knock on the door and sat up. "You can come in," I said, hoping it would be Chess, but it wasn't. Instead, it was Chess's sister.

"Hi," she said politely as she walked into the room, "I'm Valorie. Chess's sister. Can I come in?"

"Yeah," I said back politely. She looked a lot like her mom, an old-time beauty with blonde hair. She walked into the room quietly and sat in the chair under the window. I moved over to the other side of the bed to face her.

"How are you?" she asked

"I'm okay," I told her, "Maybe a little nervous."

She smiled at me, "your name is Lyle, right?"

"Yeah, that's me." I smiled back.

"This must all be so crazy for you," she said. "I have a lot of human friends and this would totally melt their brains."

"It has been a lot to take in for sure, but I think I'm doing okay."

"Are you scared?" she asked me.

"A little."

"I'm scared too."

"Why are you scared?" I asked.

"I don't think my brother would be the same if you," she paused, "you know."

"Oh.." I said, "I wouldn't be scared of that if I were you. I am not scared of that. In fact, I have a pretty good feeling everything is going to be just fine."

"Then what are you scared of?" she asked me.

"Silly things." I told her. "Things I shouldn't fear."

"Like what?" she asked again.

"Hmmm," I thought for a second, there were lots of things I was afraid of with Chess, their family, and my friends, but I would never tell her that, "does it hurt?"

"That's what you're afraid of?" she snickered.

"Well, I don't know. I've never done it before." I joked back.

"I don't think it does, but I really don't know how it will be for you. I hope it doesn't," she said nicely.

"Me too."

We talked a little more about school, how she wanted to go to college to be an artist. She asked if I would look at some of her paintings sometime in the next few weeks and I told her I would. She asked if I liked her brother and I told her I did. She told me she didn't think he liked anyone other than himself, but it was clear that she loved him and looked up to him. She told me I smelled funny, and I asked her how, but she couldn't give me an answer. She said it was weird, but that everyone could smell it and that it was different. Not bad, just different. We had talked for about thirty minutes before there was another knock at the door. This time it was Chess. He walked in surprised to see Valorie sitting in the chair and us talking.

"What are you doing in here?" he asked her.

"Getting to know your friend." She said, "He seems like a good guy. Too bad he met you." She smiled. I winked at her and she stood to leave. She bumped into Chess on her way out in a similar way the rest of them did as they had left earlier.

Chess shut the door behind her and came to sit on the bed. "How are you doing?" he asked.

"I'm doing alright."

"Did she bother you?"

"No, not at all. She was great company." I smiled.

"I'll pretend I didn't just hear you say that." He laughed. I laughed a little too. I went quiet for a moment and he moved closer.

"What's wrong?" He asked.

"Nothing is wrong. It's just all this is just..." I started.

"It's just what?" he encouraged me.

"Familiar. Overwhelming I guess."

"Being in a house full of werewolves is familiar?" he joked.

"No, just the bedroom, the clothes, the things. It just reminds me of growing up. I'm being silly. I'm fine, honestly." I smiled at him and gripped his hand. "What did your dad want?" I asked him.

"Nothing important. Just to remind me of certain expectations."

"Expectations? Like what?" I encouraged him to share.

"It's not important. Are you ready to eat?" he asked.

"Eat?"

"Yeah, dinner is almost ready,"

"Oh, well, yeah.... sure." I smiled.

I followed him into the hallway, feeling nervous about being in a room with everyone again. He didn't take my hand this time, but I followed close behind him, matching his pace. We descended the stairs and went into the dining room. I was thankful that there were two seats left next to each other. I went to take the corner seat before Chess tapped me and had me sit between that seat and his sister.

"Dad sits at the head and I have to sit to his right." He whispered in my ear, but I was certain by this point that, in a room full of wolves, they all could hear a small whisper. I sat in the seat I had been instructed to sit in. Emily was seated to the left of where Noah would sit, someone that I assumed to be George sat next to her, and then the youngest looking one, Rupert, sat next to him. Opposite of Noah's seat was where Jenn sat, to her left sat Valorie, and then me. By Chess's hint, I imagined there was some sort of order to why everyone sat where they did, but I couldn't decipher what it was, beyond the placements of Chess and Emily. Their seats made sense being the eldest son and wife.

The table was spread with an assortment of food that almost looked too beautiful to be eaten, like a picture in a catalog. There were several options for meat, a roast chicken, what I assumed was beef brisket, and some sliced ham. There were rolls, mashed potatoes, steamed carrots, broccoli, and green beans. Someone displayed and plated all the food like we were in a 5-star restaurant. Everyone waited patiently for Noah to join us before plating their food. As we waited, Emily and Jenn introduced me to George and Rupert. George seemed nervous and, wanting to make a good impression, as soon as the introduction was made he shoved his hand across the table to shake mine, knocking over an empty glass and shifting the table in the process. He turned red and Emily reminded him of using proper etiquette. I was nervous when she said that and I realized that I didn't know what proper etiquette was. George settled for a small wave and told me he was happy to meet me. Rupert sat quietly, saying hi and smiling. He seemed much more reserved than the others, but was still nice. Valorie surprised me when she rubbed her hand through my hair, she smiled and told me she loved the color.

"Thank you," I told her. "I had to get used to it kind of quickly. It has just changed to this in the last few weeks." I said chuckling a little, but the rest of them did not.

"You mean your hair color wasn't naturally this way?" Emily asked.

"No," I said, a little confused. "It was one of the first changes I noticed before everything else. It finally settled after about two weeks into what it is now." I explained.

"Interesting." Jenn said, "I wouldn't have thought that a transition would do that, but I imagine you're about the biggest expert in the room on what is and isn't normal for a human in transition." She smiled at me. I wished I knew what was normal and what was not, I reflected. I was clearly one of a kind, so all bets were off on what else may happen in the next few days or weeks leading to my shift.

"What's interesting?" Noah asked, as he entered the room. He touched the tops of Valorie, my, and Chess's heads softly, scratching our heads. When he did, Valorie and Chess tilted their heads ever so slightly like Chess had done when we first arrived. I was not used to all these brief notes of affection and as they had slowly approached me over the course of the day nudging me, touching my arm, or running their hands through my hair I had been startled, but I didn't want to say anything either.

"Lyle was just saying one of the first things that happened in his transition was that the pigment in his hair changed to what it is now." Emily shared as Noah kissed her cheek softly. As he did, she did the head thing, too.

"Oh, that is interesting," he said looking over at me as he took his seat, "what was it before?" He asked.

"I guess like a dull blonde color," I said. "I've heard the term dish-water blonde once."

"Well, this color looks more natural on you, definitely more so than blonde would have." Valorie said, touching the back of it again.

Noah's food was plated and the rest of them had begun as well. Chess made me a plate rather quickly. I eyed him quizzically, think-ing, *why did he do that?*

He responded, "Don't look at me like that. You hardly ever eat. You're a wolf now. You need to eat as much as your body is going to burn. You don't want to look like a mangy wolf." He smiled and his siblings chuckled. I took the plate and waited for everyone else to have their food. They turned to look at Noah again and, as he took the first bite, everyone else started eating.

"So, Lyle," Emily started talking, "have you given any thought to how we might approach talking to your parents? I know we have a lot more to worry about, but do they know where you are right now?" She said looking at me, worried slightly. I figured it was a normal question to ask and, if I'd had parents, I could only imagine how much more difficult this all could have been. Especially with most of them fearing I would die during my first shift.

"Oh... I... uh. I don't have any parents," I said, "so I guess there's no need to worry about what to tell anyone." I shrugged my shoulders, very matter of fact over it, but it clearly raised an alarm for her. Chess looked at me and grabbed my knee to comfort me, but I was honestly fine. Silence fell over the room. I'd clearly struck a cord that they didn't expect to hear.

"I... I'm so sorry," Emily started, "I hope you will forgive me."

"Nothing to forgive," I said. "I never knew them."

"Well, is there anyone we should try to reach out to?" Noah asked. "A guardian or anyone?"

"No," I said, "maybe my friends?" I looked over to Chess, shrugging my shoulders a bit. "They already know I'm here though." The room sat quietly for a minute and I felt a little awkward again. Chess shifted the conversation away from me for a bit, but I knew there were a lot of questions they wanted to ask me, and I had a few that I would like to have answered as well.

As we finished our first meal together I felt that, overall, it had gone well. I felt slightly more comfortable than when I had first arrived. Emily continued to watch me throughout dinner. Her eyes with a sad expression in them and I could tell my not having parents or a family had broken her heart.

I really liked Chess's siblings. George was hilarious and very mischievous. He told us about school and how he was really trying not to get kicked out this time. I wondered how many times he had been kicked out. He seemed a lot less mature than his twin sister, still a little rebellious, and with a lot of extra energy to burn. I helped Emily clear the table, and started doing some dishes before she looked at me funny.

"What are you doing?" she asked, amused.

"Helping clean up?"

"That is so kind of you, but honestly sweetie, you don't need to do that. That is George's and Rupert's chore." She responded.

"I really don't mind though." I spoke. George ran up from behind me and rubbed his hand through the back of my hair quickly.

"It's cool, bro. We got it!" he said, jumping in and starting to wash. I backed away in agreement, and Emily walked up to me and laid the small mess he had turned my hair into back down flat.

"Why do you all do that?" I finally asked.

"Do what?" she asked, looking slightly confused.

"Everyone kind of just nudges and slightly touches one another. I haven't ever really seen anyone do that before. Is it a wolf thing?" I asked her politely.

"Well, beyond being a gesture of welcoming and love, I suppose yes, it would be a wolf thing. We scent mark each other through touch. It makes everyone feel safe, marking you as safe, and making you feel safe with us." She rested her hand on my shoulder. "It's marking you as one of us." She smiled at me.

*Scent marking*, I thought to myself. I started recalling all the subtle times Chess had done that to me and realized he had been marking me with his scent since the first day we met.

"Do you have questions?" She asked me.

"Not at the moment, I don't think." I shared back honestly.

"Well, if you do, please don't be scared to ask. There are a lot of things that are going to be new to you, and we are here to help." She gave my shoulder another squeeze before pulling me into a hug. It surprised me a bit, but she hugged me tightly. I had differentiated some scents walking in, but hadn't attributed them to any of the surrounding people. However, now, with her hugging me, I could smell honey, lavender, and a breeze. It immediately comforted me and I wrapped my arms back around her.

Chess walked in, "glad to see you're feeling more comfortable." He said, smiling, as he leaned against the doorway to the kitchen. I turned and gave him a smile. "Dad would like to talk to you if that's okay," he said to Emily.

"Sure," Emily said, giving my shoulder another squeeze, and I followed Chess out of the kitchen. We walked through the dining room into the living room where I had officially met Chess' family earlier in the day. Noah was seated immersed in something on his phone. Chess and I sat on the sofa facing him.

"You can go Chess," Noah said, finishing up whatever he had been looking at, "Lyle and I will be fine." Chess looked at me for a second, as if to confirm my agreement with Noah's assertion, before standing and walking out of the room.

"Lyle," Noah said as I turned to look at him, "I just wanted to start off by telling you that we are truly happy that you are here, but..." he trailed off for a moment, and leaned forward slightly, "I also want to apologize to you for what has happened. This was not your choice and I cannot put into words a way that would  express how sorry we all are that we are having you here under these circumstances." He sounded slightly worried, but only for a split second and then his sense of worry passed. He quickly shifted back to a state of being very composed.

"I... I'm not mad or upset," I muttered. "Chess told me I should be and maybe your family feels that way as well, but I'm not."

"I'm glad to hear that," he said, smiling. "There will be a lot of time for us to get to know each other more over the next few weeks, but it's important to me and important to all of us that you know how glad we are that you are here."

"Thank you," I said, "and I do feel that." He stood at that point and walked over to my side,  running his fingers through my hair like the rest of the family had done.

"Well, if you're ready then Chess has been chomping at the bit to take you for a run ever since you arrived."

"A run?" I asked.

"Well, as I understand it, you have yet to see a proper shift and seeing as you have transitioned as far as you have, you should have no problem keeping up with him shifted or not." He smiled and said, "head on outside, Chess will show you the way."

I stood and headed out the front door. Upon opening the door and walking out onto the porch I was met with a shock.  "HOLY, gahhh...." I said, as I flushed bright red, my eyes immediately landing on Chess standing in the front yard, completely naked. I gazed at him head to toe before covering my eyes and turning away. "I'm sorry..." I said.

Chess laughed, "for what?" He sounded amused. "Come on pup, if you are going to be a wolf, there is going to be a lot of nudity in your future. No time to get embarrassed now."

I turned back toward him, feeling totally embarrassed at how casual he was being about it. I had only ever seen him shirtless and despite knowing that I wanted to see him naked, many many times, I hadn't expected it to be like this. He could see how red my face was and his only response was to do a little dance out in the yard, completing a hip roll and gyrating to accentuate the full nudity of his body. *This really gives a new meaning to disco stick,* I thought to myself as he kept going with his dance party of one, my blush gradually incorporating a smirk. *Why couldn't I look away? Why did he have to take everything and make it so much...well, more?*

"Will you stop that?!?" I said as he continued to chuckle at how funny he thought he was, "Oh and don't call me that!"

"Don't call you what? A pup? Well, technically, that is what you are, maybe you would prefer I call you baby wolf?" He mused, a slight upturn at the corner of his lip highlighting his brattiness in regard to the power dynamic that now existed between us. I felt it again, the stirring in my chest and I let out a small growl instinctually for the first time surprising myself.

"Oh, is that so pup?" he said in response, smiling. "Take off your clothes."

"Absolutely not!" I stammered and felt my face flush.

"You can't go running through the woods like that," he said, smiling.

"Like what?"

"Like a human. You are a wolf now, pup, time to start acting like it." He quickly shortened the distance between us and was suddenly standing on the porch in front of me. He grabbed the bottom of my shirt and played with it a little. He sucked his bottom lip in between his teeth, "So, pup, how 'bout it , you ready to be a wolf?" The words poured out of his mouth so smooth and thick I realized that if my face hadn't already been as red as a tomato it would have been now and I was glad that Chess wouldn't get the satisfaction of seeing me blush even further, letting him in on the knowledge that his actions were affecting me.

I hesitated for a second and then let him lift my shirt up and off. He lingered as the shirt was pulled up over my head, arms in the air, shirt over my face, and I felt him take the measure of my changed body. Taking in the changes that had occurred with it during my transition and appreciating how it had shifted and defined itself to take shape around  the newly formed muscles that I hadn't even known existed. "Very nice," he said and I could hear an approving warmth in his voice.

"Shut up," I said, giving him a small nudge.

"Ouch, pup I am your elder," he said as he winked and laughed, "you're quite a bit stronger now too, you know."

"Don't call me that," I repeated, feeling my lips betray me as they twitched at the corners revealing a small smile.

"Oh I see how this is going to be," he said, "take your shoes and socks off." I hesitated. "Take your shoes and socks off," he repeated,

"It's not cold for you anymore. You'll be fine." I reached down and pulled off both shoes and socks, leaving them on the porch.

Chess sauntered back toward me, leaving little space between the two of us. His breath landed on my face warm and heavy. He grinned  as I looked deep into his mismatched irises and smelled a subtle hint of mint on his breath. He stood there for what felt like an eternity, barely leaving a gap between our bodies, I flushed slightly at the awkwardness. He was so close to me that my body couldn't help but respond and just as I felt myself stir he grabbed the waistline of my pants, moving to unfasten the button on my jeans.

"No, Chess! That's enough for now." I said firmly as a low growl grew from my chest again. He pulled both of his hands up into the air, raising them childishly as if he had been caught touching something he shouldn't and slowly backed away from me.

"Fine. Fine," he said, smiling, "You forget though."

"Forget what?" I asked him.

"I've already seen it once." He smiled, a snicker in his eyes, and my face grew bright red. I went to say something in rebuttal before I could he leapt off the porch and, right before my eyes, I saw him shift in mid air. His body went flying up and, as it did, he quickly changed from the man I knew into a wolf, hitting the ground gracefully with his front paws and proceeding to prance around the yard in what could only be an imitation of his dance from earlier, but now in wolf form I stared at the wolf in front of me and couldn't help still feeling a little flustered by his last comment.

"You know shifting isn't getting you off the hook for that comment," I said. The gray and white wolf danced around on the ground before me, clearly still humored by what he had just done. It was funny to me though, even as a wolf, he still looked like Chess. The same blue and green eyes still stared back at me. He was big and bulky like Chess. His markings were striking just as Chess' looks had been. In particular, I found there was a small spot just below his neck with a solid white diamond that drew my eyes. *That might be my favorite part*, I thought, taking a few steps down from the porch, hesitating for a moment before stepping barefoot into the snow. I felt my foot slide into the soft powder. Just like Chess had said, it wasn't cold. I continued walking out into the yard toward Chess and the snow continued to feel like powder beneath my feet. Chess ran up to my side and rubbed his head into my right thigh, circling back and doing the same to my left. I reached down and scratched him on the head, giving him a good scratch behind the ear. He chuffed and danced around, obviously he liked that. He gave a small woof as if to ask me if I was ready. I nodded and we started running. He ran slowly at first to make sure I was keeping up, we ran through the trees, jumping over fallen logs and running through jagged terrain. Chess started running slightly faster and I matched his pace. He glanced over his haunches at me as I caught up, returning to his side and he ran faster. I pushed harder. In wolf form he had the clear advantage, but I wanted to give him a run for his money. I dug my feet into the earth and sprang forward harder and harder with each thrust until I was back up beside him and we were neck and neck. He glanced at me again, I could tell he was running at full speed. Trees zoomed by in blurs, I didn't know how fast we were going and I didn't really care. I'd never felt so free in my life. I continued to follow his lead as we exited the tree line and ran out onto a sandy beach in the clouded dark of night. Chess stopped at the edge of the water and I watched as the wolf at the shoreline grew back into the man I knew. I couldn't help but stare at his butt while he shifted and stood at the edge of the ocean. He stood there for a moment and as the moon broke through a cloud it shone down on him illuminating his backside in a silver glow.

"What are you staring at, Lyle?!" he asked as a large, toothy grin stretched across his face.

"Uh... Nothing," I said, as my face flushed once again. He started walking toward the sea and took a dive into the water.

He breached the surface, pulling in a breath of air, "This is why you should have let me take your pants off, so you could swim with me, but seeing as how you are so terribly shy I guess you will just have to watch from shore." He teased, splashing in an attempt to engage me.

I looked around, reassuring myself that no one else was around. *You can do this; you can do this.* I hummed to myself softly in an effort to psych myself up before I unfastened my pants, slipped out of them, and walked toward the shore. Chess watched quietly the entire time, I could feel his emotions churning even from the shore. I felt oddly powerful at that moment. I walked into the water and dove in, just as Chess had. I swam out to meet him and we both treaded water silently.

After a few silent moments passed, I broke the stillness. "Is that what you wanted?" I asked, breathing a little heavily. He nodded.

"Lyle?" he asked quietly.

"Yeah?" I replied.

"I hope you know, that I uh...," he paused, I felt my pulse race as I waited, "I uh... totally schooled you back there on that run."

I felt a little disappointed, hoping for something deeper, but splashed him in the face and he was hit with a mouth full of water that he was not expecting. I swam back to the shore, walking out of the water a bit before turning and sitting in the sand.

*This is crazy,* I thought to myself, being on a beach in winter. We should be freezing, but here we are swimming in water that must be near arctic temperatures, sitting on cold sand not phased in the slightest. Chess swam out of the water, walking up the beach and eyeing me carefully before sitting down next to me.

"What's on your mind?" he asked.

"Can't you already tell?" I mused jokingly.

"No, actually," he replied.

"It's just all of this. It just seems so unreal. It's a fantasy and yet I can't think of a time in my life where I felt more myself."

"It definitely looks good on you," he said, falling quiet for a moment.

"You know, I am glad you bit me. I know you regret it, but I don't." I looked over at him as he watched me carefully, "You can feel that, can't you?"

"I can," he sighed, "but your life would have been normal if it weren't for me. I... I'm glad it happened too, though. I'm glad you're here now... with me."

"Chess, I didn't have a life before you. Sure, I had just started making friends, but before that, all those years, I just existed. You can sense that too, right?"

"Kind of. It's not exact, but I can feel it," he said, smiling at me.

"Chess?" I asked.

"Yeah?" He said, looking over at me, I continued to keep my eye on the moon reflecting on the water.

"Do you still like me? Like, the same as you did before." I said, regretting asking the question the moment it came out.

"Of course I do," he started, "but it's complicated...."

"What's complicated about it?"

"It comes back to mates and what it means for a wolf to be mated. I can touch you, hold you, cuddle you, even kiss you, but we can't ever be more than that. That's what mates are." He said, sounding sad.

"Why? What does mating have to do with us not being able to be together?" I asked.

"Lyle," he said, it was clear he didn't want to talk about it yet and I was pushing, "wolves only mate once and, when it's done, it can't be undone. It is a union of souls. It's like marriage between humans, but it is far deeper than that. The two souls combine into one." I sat quietly, absorbing the information.

We sat and stared into the night for a while again before I asked, "and you don't want that with me?"

"Lyle.." A long pause passed before he finally continued, "nothing would make me happier than that possibility, but it's not that easy. I.... I'm to be the next alpha of my family's pack. It's not just because I'm the eldest son, it's more than that. In our pack, the next wolf born with heterochromia is destined to be the next alpha." He explained. The alpha part made sense to me. It was why he and his dad had the same eyes, it was the alpha trait. What I didn't understand was how that had anything to do with mating.

"I don't understand. So, because you are the next alpha, we can't ever be together?" I asked.

"Wolves don't get to choose their own mate. We are matched with potential mates from other packs and we must choose a female wolf to be mated with, it happens that way so that we don't become extinct." He tried to explain it the best he could, but I could also feel he didn't like the answer either, based on his tone. "There is only one way to make sure our species survives, and wolves, until you, can only be born, not bitten. Two male wolves cannot produce a child. I said before that I don't believe in gay or straight when you asked me and that's because for wolves it matters very little, but we don't have the luxury of a choice in the end."

"That sounds awful Chess. How can you not have the choice?" I tried to wrap my brain around the idea of not being able to choose who you wanted to be with. *How could we never be allowed to be any more than we were right now?* I became anxious and felt overexposed realizing that I was sitting here naked next to a man who was saying that we could never be together.

"Hey, Lyle, it's okay. It'll be okay," he said, moving swiftly behind me and wrapping his arms around my shoulders. He pulled me in close. "You're not wrong. It's not right. I have feelings for you. We have a connection. Your feelings are not wrong. I understand and I don't like it either." He said laying his head on my shoulder. I didn't know how he always knew what to say and I didn't know how it was all going to be okay, but I knew I believed him.

"It's getting late. We should head back" he said, running his fingers through my hair. I nodded. We stood again, I walked over to grab my pants.

"Lyle, at some point, you are going to have to get used to me and everyone else seeing you nude. It's part of being a wolf. You can't shift with your clothes on," he said matter-of-factly.

"Well, I can't shift today, so until that happens I'll wear my pants." He laughed as I slid back into my pants. "Are you going to shift for the run back?"

"No, I figured we'd run together like this until you're able to shift," he said. I felt the heat run to my face again and we began the run back.

We made it to the house in little time at all with Chess knowing I could keep pace. We walked up to the porch, I looked for the rest of my clothes, but they had been moved.

"Mom, probably put them in your room," Chess said, as he saw me looking for them. We walked inside, everyone had already gone to bed. We walked upstairs and Chess followed me to my room.

"Well, I guess I'll see you in the morning." I said quietly so we wouldn't wake anyone up. He looked at me, confused, and he sat on the edge of the bed.

"I thought I might stay here with you," he said, making himself slightly more comfortable.

"Oh, no you are not. Go!" I told him, laughing and smiling.

"Are you sure?" He said, laying himself out on my bed.

"Yes... Can you go put some shorts on or something?" He started making silly faces at me and I rolled my eyes.

"I'll put some on if you say I can stay," he said, wagging his eyebrows at me.

"No, not tonight. Your parents made it clear they wanted us in separate bedrooms." Chess stood up and walked over to me.

"Okay, but if you change your mind. My room is just two doors down... I'll leave the door unlocked in case you have a bad dream." I rolled my eyes and he raked his fingers through my hair again. I finally reached up and did the same for the first time. He blinked at me slightly before smiling. He wished me a good night and went to his room. I was exhausted and I laid down on the bed, it wasn't long before I fell asleep.

* * *

Suddenly I was jarred awake, I had been sweating and felt it, once again, seeping into my sheets. It felt like this was becoming more frequent. I came to slowly, realizing that Noah had been saying my name and was shaking my shoulders gently. Chess was seated on the other side of me with Emily and Jenn at the end of the bed watching. I could see concern on their faces, but didn't understand why.

"What's going on?" I asked.

"Are you okay?" Noah asked me with both hands still gripping my shoulders.

"Yeah, I'm fine. What's going on?" I asked again.

"You were screaming like you were in pain. You kept screaming, 'save him, please save him'." Chess said.

"I was?" I asked.

"Yes," Noah said, "do you remember anything that happened?"

"No... I don't." I spoke.

"Let's go downstairs. I'll make some tea," Jenn said.

"Are you sure you're, okay?" Noah asked me again.

"I think so. I feel fine."  He helped me out of bed and we walked to the kitchen. Jenn pulled out some herbs from a cupboard and Emily put some water on the stove to warm. They asked me to try and remember anything about my dream, but it was all a blank. I could tell from their expressions that it made them even more nervous with the upcoming shift, but I could feel at my core a feeling that I would be fine. We each drank a small glass of tea that Jenn said would calm the nerves before going back up to bed. Everyone made sure I got back to my room and asked again if everything was alright. I insisted I was fine and everyone left. I pulled off the sheets that were still wet with sweat and climbed back into bed. Just as I turned out the lights, Chess quietly opened my door and was walking back in.

"What are you doing?" I asked him.

"You think I'm going to let you sleep alone after something like that?" He said.

"Chess, I don't know if that's a good idea." He sat down on the edge of the bed.

"I'm scared Lyle," he looked out the window into the night, "I'm scared that I'm going to lose you."

I sat back up and put my hand on his shoulder, "you're not going to lose me, I'm not going anywhere. I'm going to be fine."

He reached his hand up and grabbed mine as it rested on his shoulder. "If I shift, will you let me stay with you?" he asked. I thought for a second about it and I would have been lying to myself if I'd said I didn't want him to stay with me, but I was already in so deep with my feelings for him and, hearing him tell me we would never be together, I wanted to safeguard some parts of myself in the hope of protecting me from a potential future without him again. He turned to look me in the face, still gripping my hand softly and gave it a gentle squeeze.

"Yes," I finally told him. He stood and pulled the shorts he had been wearing down to his ankles before shifting back into his wolf. He jumped up on the bed, sat toward the bottom, and looked at me. He whimpered slightly and I reached over and scratched him behind the ear. He panted and closed his eyes at the touch. After receiving what he must have felt were enough ear scratches, he got up, sauntering into a small circle just before curling into a ball at the foot of the bed, laying his head on top of my shin. I laid back down, feeling more relaxed than before, and we both fell asleep.

Over the next few days I spent a lot of time with Chess, but also spent time with the rest of the family. Noah took Chess and I on walks throughout the property and talked about what it meant to be an alpha, what it meant to be a man, and shared a lot of his ideals including asking us about our own. At first, I thought it was a little weird, but then I grew to really enjoy talking with him and began eagerly anticipating our conversations. I enjoyed hearing his personal philosophies and him taking the time to hear my own, each of us growing by expanding our minds to learn new possibilities that we hadn't considered before. Noah told me that living means always learning and that just when you think you are on the cusp of knowing what it all means, you find that you weren't even remotely close. He was wise, I grew to respect him. Chess told me it was just because he was the alpha and that wolves always respect their alpha, but I disagreed. It was something more than that, he had unique perspectives and knew a lot, but he was never arrogant. He felt like the world's best teacher and I thought Chess and his siblings were so lucky to have him as their dad.

Emily appeared to take a shine to me the very first night in their home. I became her chef's assistant and she always wanted to know where I was and how I was feeling. She didn't hover, but she showed time and time again that she cared about everything and anything that I was feeling. She must have answered thousands of questions by now, but took the time to answer them all as thoroughly as she could. Some questions she would defer to Noah, but she was truly remarkable. She had taught me how to cook and so much more. She had said it was a near full-time job feeding a pack of wolves and she was happy that I enjoyed helping and keeping her company with our conversations.

I found out that the house had a cellar and that everything that was stored in it had been grown, picked, canned, and preserved by her with the help of her family. She thought it was very important that we live green and healthy, but she also never turned down a good iced caramel macchiato from her favorite coffee shop. She said it was a balance. She was wise like Noah, but their wisdom lay in different realms. She loved gardening, taking care of the planet in her way, and caring for her family. She was truly one of the most impressive people I had ever met. I told her that, in some ways, she reminded me of my best friend Jesse and she had asked a lot about her. I also told her about Reese, Hunter, Phisher, Andy, and recently Kay. She said that she was honored to be compared to someone like Jesse and insisted that she get to meet her and the rest of my friends someday. I didn't know why I felt so giddy about that, but no one had ever asked me questions about the people I cared about before or took the time to hear what I liked about them. She had asked me a couple days after arriving if the clothes she had gotten fit and I'd told her I was scared to wear them because I didn't want to ruin them. She looked at me, a bit saddened by that, before taking me upstairs and grabbing a shirt from the top of the pile on the dresser. She raised her hand and shifted so that her claws were out and she ripped the shirt in half. She grabbed another and handed it to me, smiling before saying it was my turn. I laughed, because she was so insistent that I couldn't ruin a single thing in the world, especially something that was just clothes. I ripped the shirt slightly and she clapped and cheered in response. She told me that the only thing she was worried about me ruining was myself, but that they were there to make sure that didn't happen. After that she took me shopping and Chess asked to come. She told him no, that he would just have to suffer for a few hours without me because she and I were spending time together. I shrugged at him and he smiled.

I overheard Jenn and Chess talking one morning, I probably shouldn't have been listening, as she told Chess that she thought I was hot and a total catch. I had heard him agree and they both laughed. I was nervous at first at the thought of spending time with her because she was one of Chess's best friends. Even in his most scared and panicked moments after he had learned the truth about what was happening to me, he hadn't called his mom or dad. He'd called her. To me, that showed how close their bond was, and it made me feel like it was important that she liked me. I was quiet around her at first, but quickly warmed up. It was easy to feel at ease around her. She was a free spirit and loved to have fun. She came out to help Valorie, George, Rupert, and me when we were trying to build a snow wolf and, just as we finished, she started a snowball fight. She showed me the Materia Medica that she used to aid in formulating homeopathic cures for various concerns or ailments that might occur. The book was very old, having been passed down through the family, each wolf that had come into its possession adding their own notes through the years. She let me help harvest, store, and  categorize her herbs, adding them to her apothecary in the barn. She told me that wolves rarely get sick, but that they occasionally needed help with accelerated healing or antidotes in the event that they accidentally ingested wolfsbane, which was poisonous, including how to reverse its effects if it was accidentally eaten. She had recipes for emotional ailments and healing the soul. Her favorites to make either smelled or tasted good. She told me more about mates and what happens when two wolves become one. I appreciated that information because I hadn't felt comfortable broaching that subject with Chess's parents and he still tried to keep parts of it a secret. She told me how mating is supposed to happen and how, despite our best plans, destiny would always have her own plans in the mix regardless of how much the Union tried to regulate it. She let me feel hopeful that it was possible for Chess and I to be together someday. She never said so directly, only hinting at it. She and the others continued to shy away from talking about the Union. All I learned was that they were officially called the Union of the Wolves and I was instructed to understand the gist of its purpose, but the way they skirted around discussing it made me think it was a much bigger part of being a wolf than they were ready to share.

Intermittently, I spent time with Valorie, George, and Rupert. I really enjoyed getting to know all three of them, but found that Rupert was the odd man out in the family. Valorie and George explained to me what had happened with Rupert's dad and how Rupert had blamed  Noah for his death. Even though they said it had happened a long time ago, Rupert hadn't seemed to move past the death of his father. Rupert seemed nice enough and he came around occasionally, Valorie and George, however, appeared to be fascinated by me and tried to join in on everything Chess and I did. Chess would often tell them no and I tried to make it up to them when we would come back from our time together. Valorie showed me her paintings and I found them to be fantastic. She painted the unique landscapes she saw when running as a wolf, places that normal humans would really struggle to get to, but that she had no problem with reaching. She also had drawings she had done about shifting that beautifully captured the different aspects of how the body morphed and changed into the wolf. She started painting a portrait of me, which sat on the easel in her painting studio. She was more kindly in her depiction of me than I would have been of myself, but strangely only half of my face was complete. I asked her why she had left the piece undone and she told me that the other half would be my wolf likeness  and she smiled at my compliments of amazement in regard to her design.

George was into sports and had wanted to be a professional athlete when he was younger. Unfortunately, he'd had to back out of sports because of the unfair advantage he had over the human boys on the teams. His passion hadn't waned in the slightest though and he had switched gears, deciding that he wanted to go into Sports Medicine. While he couldn't play due to a risk of exposing himself and the family through his obvious talent, which had caused questions amongst coaches and other players, he could help others play, and, if he got a spot as one of his favorite team's doctors, it would be almost as good as being on the field and he felt that it was the fairest tradeoff with him being unable to take part in the actual sport.

Rupert didn't tell me much about himself. He said he would probably just find a job with the Union at some point, but, like everyone else, didn't tell me anything further about them. He kept to himself. I thought Chess was one of the luckiest people in the world to have a family as great as they all were.

Chess and I ran almost every night. Sometimes his family would join us. They all found my anxiety about nudity quite funny and, just as Chess had expressed, they asserted that at some point it would pass and encouraged me not to think of nudity by the terms of humanity. They tried to remind me that all animals in nature, with the exception of humans, are nude and they reassured me that once my transition was complete I would shift and everything I was wearing would shred anyway. I listened to them, but I kept my pants on all the same for the time being. Chess continued to shift and sleep at the foot of my bed every night since I had arrived. Some nights I would have the nightmare and some nights I would not. I wished I could remember what it was about after waking, but every time I woke up the slate was wiped clean. It had been five days since I'd first arrived, I had been so nervous and scared of everything and everyone, but, in such a short amount of time, I felt connected to all of them and they made me feel like I was one of them too. Tonight was the full moon and the family was planning to go for a run since the sky would be clear and the forest would be full of light. Chess and I spent the day with his dad  discussing some of the unique abilities I may or may not possess after the shift.

In all packs, wolves had the abilities to control their shifts. They had heightened senses, speed, strength, and an increased ability to heal, but all packs also possessed a unique skill that was specific to them. For the Becks it was superior sight, they could see much farther than others of their kind, their alphas also had a specialized ability to anticipate movements and could see where others would move based on their trajectory and muscle movements. Upon hearing this, it became clear that Chess had tracked the movement of my fall, catching me just before I would have hit the floor of the lab when I passed out during our first meeting. Some packs had a superior sense of smell and could see the scent trail of others. Some could move much faster than other wolves and some had enhanced hearing. It seemed like each pack had it's own superior sense with their alpha's displaying their packs trait to an extent that took the trait even further. Noah and Chess led me to assume that with the speed I could move without even shifting that I would probably be even faster as a wolf. Chess had seen the abilities in each blood line through his lab work at the university. He'd mapped out the bloodlines of the packs that existed within the world at present and had also been secretly studying the genetic history of wolves for some time. I found everything they came to tell me incredibly interesting, but when I tried to ask about other packs both of them danced around the subject which was increasingly frustrating. Returning home that afternoon, it was time for me to help Emily with dinner. We again cooked a wide array of proteins and sides before sitting down with the pack and enjoying the meal together. Afterward, we each did our own thing until it was time to run. We gathered out on the lawn and everyone shifted. I removed my shirt and shoes and we started for the woods. I stayed near Chess when we ran with the family and sometimes he and I would veer off and go to the beach for a swim. Tonight was no different. Chess slowed and bumped me as we ran playfully and I chased him in return. I'd found over time that it was no problem for me to catch him, but I also was not convinced that he didn't slow down ever so slightly as I approached so that I could reach him. We came to the edge of the water where each time I would inevitably agree to strip and join Chess in the water. We had such a good time swimming and splashing each other in the water but as we walked out of the water I could tell something was off.

"Chess?" I said before a burning sensation cracked in my chest and I collapsed at the edge of the sand. My eyes burned and I could feel cracks in my chest. I screamed out as I felt a giant crack in my ribs. I could sense Chess running back to my side.

"Lyle, what's wrong?" He said frantically before another bone in my waist snapped and I fell to my side.

"I...I think it's happening," I said through gritted teeth. Chess watched through horrified eyes as the bones in my body kept snapping and breaking. I cried out into the night as the bones inside my body cracked and twisted.

"Lyle... Lyle, it will be okay. Just hold on." He sounded so panicked. He grabbed my arm just before it snapped and he pulled my head into his lap. I coughed and as I did, blood spurted into my mouth. I could feel the heat and the thick sludge that tasted like iron as it filled my mouth. "Oh God," Chess said, whimpering slightly as he watched blood beginning to seep out of my ears and I continued to cough up blood a little bit at a time. Chess had shouted out for his family, for any form of help as I lay there in agony. My bones seemed to have stopped breaking and I could feel waves hit my feet as some of the pain subsided. I still tasted the blood in my mouth and my gums itched terribly. The burning in my chest remained, an odd presence that I continued to feel, one that felt like something was scratching and tearing at my insides. I winced as it tried to get out. I opened my eyes, looking up at Chess and  I could see him screaming and looking toward the edge of the trees, but I couldn't hear him anymore. The sound had faded away. The waves continued to splash against my feet, but slowly I felt their sensation fade away into nothing as well. I looked up toward the sky and saw the stars and the moon. They looked so beautiful.

"Ch... Ch. Chess?" I said as the sensations started fading into some sort of nothingness. Chess looked back down at me and shifted my head a little on his leg. I felt some of the blood that had pooled drain out of my ear.

"Lyle... What can I do? What do you need?" And I realized he'd started crying. It took a lot of effort but I pushed life into my limb and was able to move the broken pieces up to take Chess's hand.

"Lll... Look Chess. The moon. It's full." I said, smiling at him as I felt a final tear hit my cheek. He grabbed the side of my face with his other hand and I saw his mouth say something, but I couldn't hear it. I wished I could feel his hands on me. The warmth might feel nice. I could feel my breathing slow as the sensation in my chest continued to rip and scratch and tear even as I felt my lungs fill with blood.

*You lied to me. I am dying,* I thought to myself, feeling upset at the untruth I had been told by the center of my being which was now destroying me from the inside. I looked up at Chess again and the light of the world started dimming at the corners of my eyes, growing darker and darker as it worked its way toward the center. I wanted to say something to Chess, but couldn't get it out. *I love you,* ran through my mind as I took in the last image of him and the darkness sealed him from my sight.

# Chapter Seventeen

*Am I dead?* I thought to myself. I lay still and numb in the darkness of my mind. My body long shut off.

*No.* Something in the darkness answered back, another thought from a separate consciousness entering my mind.

*Then what is happening?* I thought.

No response. I waited.

No response. Nothing.

*The cage is breaking,* it said.

A small light started glowing in the distance and I tried to focus in on it. I felt myself moving toward it. I tried to look around, to see my hands, my feet, but could only see the light. Moving closer, the light grew bigger and, as it did, faces emerged as if I were looking through a window in the darkness. I moved closer and as the faces became more clear; I realized that I recognized these people. I didn't know how, but I did. I moved closer to see more and, as I did, I fell through the window.

Recognizing that I was still in my consciousness, I tried to look around, but my head wasn't moving. I was sitting on a stool in a small wooden room. It was dark outside, but the light of the full moon poured in through the window. Small candles were lit and I was holding the hand of a beautiful woman with soft features, blonde hair, and green eyes. She was lying on a bed and I looked down to see another woman who was older seated at the end of the bed. The woman laying down had her legs up, a blanket covered them. I could see their mouths moving and hear slight murmurs as they spoke. I could see now that the woman was in labor and was just about to give birth. I watched her face as she screamed and pushed one last time before the older woman pulled the child from her and lifted it into the air. My ears took in the sound as the child began to scream and cry.

"It's a boy!" the older woman said as she quickly snipped the cord and passed him up to the woman.

"He's beautiful." She said as she looked at him. "John," she said, looking over at me, "John, we have a son." I looked over at the baby boy that lay in her arms. He had subtle red hair and blinked at me with blue eyes.

"We have a son." I felt myself speaking, but the words were not mine. I felt tears of joy run down my face as I reached out and touched the small child in front of me. As I did, I realized this was not me. The woman who had delivered the baby reached out to me and grabbed my shoulder.

"Congratulations, my son." She said as she pulled me into a hug. I embraced her as my own mother and turned back toward the child, my son. We all sat staring at him.

"Rebecca," I said, speaking to my mate who was holding our child, "thank you for giving us a son. You have blessed our pack with the future Alpha of our people." She smiled back at me.

She handed my son to me and I stood with him. I walked over to a small wooden bucket that sat on a stool and washed him. I stared into the water and saw myself, but it was not me. I looked much older, my hair was longer and shaggier. I had a small red beard that hugged my face. My eyes were still blue, but in the reflection flecks of green glowed back at me.

We could be twins. I thought to myself as I continued to watch as this John washed his son. I finished washing him and returned him to my mate, who then fed him.

"He's beautiful." My mother said, sitting next to Rebecca, the baby's little hands wrapped around her pinky.

"Thank you, Sarah," Rebecca said to her. We all sat in the room watching him as he cooed and nursed.

"What should we name him?" Rebecca asked.

I pondered for a moment as she shared a few names I turned down. I finally thought of a name, and said, "Lyle. His name will be Lyle."

"Lyle," she said, "That's perfect."

We continued to sit in bliss as we watched baby Lyle nurse in peace. Suddenly, a man burst into the small wooden room. I stood quickly and walked over to him.

"John," the man said, "we have been betrayed. The men they have come." He was panicking.

"We need to go." I said, "Quick, gather the others and run for the woods. We will lose them there." The man nodded and ran off. I listened carefully for a moment and heard a gunshot off in the distance. I returned to my mate's side.

"Rebecca, we must go now. It's not safe," I said. She nodded and pulled Lyle from her breast and wrapped him in a blanket. "Mother," I said, turning, "we must go."

"You go, run. You won't both be able to shift with the baby, you must both go. I will hold them back as long as I can." She said just before shifting into an enormous wolf with mostly gray hair and red that ran along her back. She burst through a window and took off toward the sound of the gunshots. Rebecca was standing slightly now and reached her hand out to me. I grabbed it and we left the cabin. Others ran past, shifted, and headed off toward the fight while others still ran into the woods. The man who'd told me the news had returned.

"Brother," he said, as he ran toward us, "Most of our people have run, but others insisted upon running to the front to give you time. You three must survive."

I grabbed his arm. "You must come with us, Victor," I said, pleading with him.

"No, I'm going to fight," he said, turning to look at Rebecca, "my queen" he said, bowing and tilting his head to show his neck.

She nodded at him, "Thank you Victor."

"Go now, all of you, quickly. You must survive, the pup you hold is our future," he yelled back before shifting into a reddish wolf with black and white markings running full-speed toward the gun shots. I turned back and could see an eerie red-orange glow from the forest as the humans set fire to the trees. Rebecca and I started rushing toward the woods. As we reached the border, we heard another patrol of men entering our home from the river. They were too close and we hurried. Rebecca held Lyle tightly to her chest as we ran through the trees. I looked over at her and yelled for her to run as I heard shots ring from behind us. We ran as fast as we could. I turned toward Rebecca again just as a shot hit her. She rolled, tumbling toward the earth. I ran and knelt at her side. She coughed and blood spewed from her mouth.

"Take him." She cried. "Take him." A mother's desperate plea for the life of her child.

I took Lyle from her as she cried, insisting we leave her. She howled at the moon above. "Go!" she yelled. She shifted and ran toward the men. She leapt at one and ripped out his throat before taking another shot to the side. I ran again as I felt my soul, my love, my mate take her last breath and our connection severed. A part of me died alongside her, but her dying wish propelled me onward, taking me away from the agony of my grief. Her wish spurred me on and urged me to continue my mission to save the child that she had paid for with her life. I held Lyle tight to my chest as I ran, my only thought was to keep him safe. He must survive, he must. I took a shot to the side and fell. Looking at my rib, I saw blood pooling in my shirt. I stood again and ran.

As John ran, I watched. He moved quickly as he changed directions and ran somewhere off into the distance. The light moved farther away as I slipped back into the darkness.

*Broken*, the thought came to me again. *It is broken. Open your eyes, open them.*

My eyes shot open and I felt my lungs fill with air. My bones shifted and moved, refastening themselves as I felt the rage that built in my chest burn move to all the corners of my body. I looked up to see Chess being held by his mother and father, all three turning to look at me in shock as I tilted my head back and howled to the moon. I looked down, seeing paws where my hands would be. I turned to look back and saw a tail, my tail.

*I survived.* I felt the thought stream to the others.

*We survived.* The thought flowed back to me. I stood and as I did; the others looked at me, expressionless. I walked toward Chess slowly and laid down, placing my head on his lap.

"L... Lyle?" He said, blinking his eyes slowly in disbelief. I let out a small gruff in agreement that it was me. As soon as I did, he leapt onto me and wrapped his arms around my neck, burying his face in my chest. I hugged my head back into his body and he held me, crying.

"You died, Lyle," he cried out, "you died."

I felt my body shudder slightly and the wolf dissipated as I shifted back into human and wrapped my arms around him. "I know, I'm sorry," I told him. "I came back, though. I'm here now," I said, feeling Noah and Emily put their hands on my shoulder and I looked up to both of them. They, too, had been crying.

"We need to go now." Noah said, looking around carefully, "Lyle, don't shift."

# Chapter Eighteen

We returned to the farmhouse. I hadn't shifted, as Noah had said. I'd tried to put my pants back on, but I found that post shift I was much larger than I had been before. My legs, torso, and arms were bulkier, and my clothes didn't fit. I found it odd, but being nude didn't bother me like it had before and I folded my clothes and held them under my arm as we walked back. At the house, we all went to our rooms and dressed again. I quickly found, however, as with my pants, none of my clothes fit me now. I slipped into a pair of loose shorts and found that Chess's purple hoodie, the one he had given me as a human and that I previously drowned in, was one of the few things left that would fit me. Even though now it was a much tighter fit. Chess burst into my room, barely able to contain himself. He was dressed and was obviously still working through the trauma of my near death. He gripped me tightly. We were much closer in height now and I no longer had to look up to look in his eyes. He looked deeply into my eyes.

"Lyle, your eyes changed," he said.

"What do you mean?" I asked.

"Well, they're still blue, but there are specks of green in them now," he replied.

I walked to the mirror and looked closely at my reflection. Chess was right. They had changed. When I investigated my reflection again, I saw a lot more of John in myself than before. We were the same size now, but my hair was still short and shaggy and I didn't have a beard, so long as you didn't count the red stubble that had run along my jaw. Now, though, we had the same eyes. I stared at myself longer, trying to assess if anything had changed within me. I searched for my feelings, my beliefs, my friends, my Chess, and myself. I was still me. I breathed a sigh of relief. The man in the mirror looked back at me approvingly. I was me now. This was me.

I turned back to Chess, "You're right. They have changed, but Chess, even though my outside has changed some, I am still me in here. This has been me all along, I think."

He looked at me and grabbed my hand. "You're right. This is who I saw whenever I looked at you and I am so glad that you're here." He quickly and sweetly flashed his face forward and gave me a small kiss on the mouth. It was tight-lipped and it was only for a moment, but he did it. I felt my face burn hot and felt the moment my face turned red with blush. It was only a fraction of a second, but I didn't care. I thought it was perfect.

"My dad wants to speak with us," He said, breaking the intimacy of the moment. "Are you sure you're, okay?" He eyed me carefully.

"Yeah, I'm fine." I smiled at him, "let's go."

I followed him into the hall as we walked down, past the stairs, and toward two giant wooden doors. I knew this was Noah's office, but I hadn't ever gone inside it until now. Chess pushed the doors open and we walked inside. Noah, Jenn, and Emily were all standing around the fireplace. There was something clearly on their mind, I could feel that they were worried.

"Ah, boys come in," Noah said, as we walked through the door. "Have a seat."

We pulled up chairs around the fireplace and I waited to hear what was on their mind.

"Lyle, we can't be certain if it's a random coincidence of being bitten or more, but we need to know, when you shifted, what happened? We need you to tell us everything you can." Noah sounded mostly himself, but there was also a sound of concern in his voice.

I wanted to tell them everything, but the feeling in the center of my chest, fully awakened now, was hesitant. I responded by taking a deep breath, which seemed to put him at ease, and I told them starting with my bones and body breaking as the shift began, telling them how everything had faded out, and then about the dream. I told them about John, Rebecca, Sarah, Victor, and Lyle. About the fire and the humans with guns, how Sarah and Victor ran off as wolves to go stall the humans, and died in the fight so that Rebecca, John, and Lyle could escape. How more humans had used the river to surround the three and had chased them into the woods. How Rebecca had been shot and fell. How she'd begged me to run with Lyle as she shifted and killed two humans before being killed herself. How I ran with Lyle until they shot me, but then I got up and kept running to save him, and then how I had watched as John and Lyle ran into the woods. Then I told them about the other consciousness within me and how he told me that a cage had broken, that it was time for me to open my eyes, and that when I had, I felt the shift.

Noah stood and walked to the fireplace, leaning against it heavily. "What's wrong?" I asked, "is there something wrong?"

Noah began muttering to himself, "it's not possible. It's just not possible."

Emily leaned in. "Lyle, when you shifted your coat, it was red. Your fur was red, like the color of your hair."

"What does that have to do with anything?" I asked. I looked over at Chess and he looked at me as if a lightbulb had suddenly gone off in his head, as if he had now connected the dots for himself. I looked at him searching for answers, "What? What is going on?"

"Sweetie," Emily took my hand, "there are no red wolves left. They all died a long, long time ago. The pack of the red wolves, well…" she trailed off.

"Well, what?" I asked her.

Jenn finally leaned in and put her hand on Emily's shoulder. "Lyle, supposedly they were all murdered. No one knows what happened or how it happened. Most of our knowledge of wolves and our kind wasn't compiled until little over a century ago and they were supposed to have existed in the 1600s. But, there was no real proof they had ever really existed to begin with only children's stories about the king and queen and their fur of red. All we have are myths and legends of them, their pack, their abilities, and the collective suspicion that they were the first."

"The first what?" I asked.

"The first wolves," Chess said.

"It's not possible." Noah said again. "It must just be a coincidence. You are a human bitten and turned. It must be a mutation that caused it." He went on, "Chess, you have done extensive studies on wolves, genealogy, and our chromosomes, correct?"

"Yes." He said.

"Have you finished cataloging and creating a profile from all the packs in the Union?" He asked.

"Yes, I have, but what has that got to do with all of this?" Chess asked.

"We need to run a profile to see what happened with Lyle. Why was he able to be turned, compare his genes with the rest and see what you find?" Noah turned to me. "Lyle, what do you know about your birth parents?"

"Uhhh. Not much," I said. I thought longer and shared what I knew or what I'd heard without ever knowing if there was any truth to it, "They said my father died of an overdose before my mother knew she was pregnant and that after she gave birth to me, she took her own life." I said this kind of matter-of-factly. It never really bothered me before, thinking about it or saying it, but this time I felt a moment of sadness pulse through me. "I... I don't even have a picture of them." I said, feeling my loss for what felt like the first time.

"It's going to be important that we know who they were, their families, and where they came from," Noah paused, "Lyle, I know I'm asking a lot of you, but are you willing to request those records and look into your family's history? We need to know more information to be sure."

"What if it is true?" Chess asked.

"We will cross that bridge when we can be certain, but Lyle, can you walk down this path? You are my son now. I won't put this on you if you don't think you can handle it, but we really need to know the truth." Noah said, gazing at me searching my face for an answer.

My heart swelled at hearing him call me his son and nearly brought me to tears - I belonged to their family, their pack. I knew what he was asking and it frightened me a bit to dig into my family's past to try and uncover more. Even if he hadn't asked, I needed to know who those people were in my dream, if they were real, if I was related to them, and why the baby's name and my name were the same. "Yes," I said, "I will."

"We need to be cautious," Jenn said. "The Union can't know anything about Lyle or this."

"Agreed," Noah responded. "Lyle, the fact that you were turned from a bite puts us all at risk on its own, but if you are in fact a true red wolf..." he trailed off. "It would change everything."

Chess grabbed my hand and rubbed his thumb across my knuckles, like he did when he knew I was stressed or upset. It brought me so much comfort. I looked over at him and nodded. The tension never left the air and now that one worry had been solved, ten more had emerged. They continued to ask more questions about my dream and when they seemed satisfied, plans were made and agreed upon for all of us to follow before finally calling it a night. As I headed toward my room, Chess trailed behind me and followed me inside.

I sat on the bed and a wave of exhaustion hit me. Physically I felt perfect, healthy, and not an ounce of pain anywhere from the shift.

Mentally, however, I was drained. I looked down at the mattress. Since the shift, the bed seemed much smaller than it had the night before. Chess sat down next to me and it was clear that it wouldn't accommodate both of us. I looked over at Chess and said, "I don't think we will both fit on here anymore." Disappointment hanging in my tone.

"My bed is bigger." He replied with a hint of a smile curling at the edge of his mouth. Through his smile though I could see that my shift had taken an even greater toll on him. His eyes were still red from the tears he'd shed as I'd laid there lifeless in the sand. It had traumatized him and even though I felt like maybe I should stay in my room I knew that wasn't an option for him. I nodded and stood to follow him.

I had been in his room before, but I was nervous as I walked down the hall and went inside. He sat on the edge of his bed and he was right it definitely was bigger. It smelled like him, his scent emanated from every corner of the room. It hit me in waves and his scent filled my nose and I reveled in it. Now, as a wolf, it smelled even better, more complex, and it was the combination of all my favorite smells in the world. He patted the other side of the bed where he wanted me to sit and I followed his gesture. I took off the purple sweatshirt, pulled up the comforter, sat down, and swung my legs underneath the covers. Chess stood and I thought he was going to shift after taking off his clothes, but he grabbed the other corner of the comforter and pulled it down to climb in bed.

"What are you doing?" I asked him.

"Getting into bed?" He said, looking confused.

"You... You're not going to shift?" I asked.

"Lyle, I thought you died earlier tonight," he stopped, the memory still haunting his mind, "I don't want to sleep near you as a wolf. I want to lie next to you as a man. Can that be okay, please?" He stared at my face, trying to read my expression. I'd slept in the same bed with him every night since arriving here, but I had been sleeping next to the wolf, not the man and, even though

I'd wanted to, I still felt a slight blush and a twinge of nervousness at the idea.

"O...okay," I said, "that's fine." He smiled at me and climbed into the bed. I rolled to face him and I felt my cheeks flush. He did the same and we looked at each other.

"Is this okay?" He asked.

"Yeah, it's nice," he said, smiling. He reached his hand up and ran his fingers through my hair and it felt amazing. I finally understood how the scent marking worked because I could smell my scent float into the air as he wiggled his fingers through my hair. He liked it too.

"You smell really good," he said as he continued to play with my hair.

"So do you," I whispered. I closed my eyes as he continued to rub my hair. I felt sleep coming as a heaviness hit my eyelids. I opened them slightly to look at him.

"Lyle?"

"Yeah?"

"Can I hold you?" Chess said and I nodded without hesitation as he moved closer to me and wrapped me in an embrace. I snuggled my head into his arm and shoulder. Waves of scent fell off him, commingling with mine. It was the most relaxed and sedated I had ever felt.

"I think I'm going to fall asleep now," I whispered.

"That's okay," he whispered back and I slowly faded into sleep.

I awoke the next morning just before Chess. I was facing the wall and Chess was holding me in a tight grasp. I felt his arms around me, one under my head and the other draped over my side, across my chest. It felt nice. His feet were tangled with mine and his legs matched the curve of mine. I shifted slightly and I felt something hard against my rear. My body grew slightly rigid as I knew exactly what it was and Chess stirred.

"Good morning." He whispered as he rubbed his nose into the back of my head.

"Good morning," I said, "Chess?" I asked.

"Yeah?" he replied.

"Is that your.... um, You know... at my back?" I asked, a little dry in the mouth.

"Oh... um... yeah it is," he said pushing forward a little and I jumped out of bed.

"Chess!" I said a little too loudly.

"What?" He laughed, a little amused.

"Why did you do that?"

"Because I was happy to see you." He smiled. "Looks like you are too." He said as his eyes trailed down from mine. I looked down and realized what he had been referencing. I flushed and covered myself. "Look, it isn't a big deal. Just come back to bed." He moved his hands in a waving motion, calling me back to bed. I settled slightly and climbed back into bed.

"You said we can't do things like that." I mentioned to him as he put his arms back around me.

"I know, but it doesn't mean I don't want to." He replied. He made it so difficult for me sometimes. Hearing that he wanted it too made my heart soar and that electric feeling hummed back alive in my belly after I'd forced it away when he'd told me we couldn't ever be more. "Let's not talk about it right now," he said. "it's gone now anyway. No need to worry about it."

I was worried about it though, often. We walked such a knife's edge with everything we did and, as I'd laid there dying last night, I'd tried to tell him the words I wanted to say so badly, but couldn't. I was slightly relieved now that I wasn't able to say it and saddened me at the same time. I didn't know if my shifting had changed things, those moments I'd hung in the balance of life and death, or now that I may even be the last red wolf. Would any of that change things for us? Would he be able to look at me like he did before last night, before he held me broken and bleeding? I wondered, but I assumed by his response that it hadn't and maybe he was just trying harder in order to make up for what happened.

I'd tried to accept it before, but it felt harder to accept now. Maybe if he knew, if I'd said it, he would say it back. Should I say it now? I reflected as we laid there, tangled in each other's arms, but I didn't. It wasn't much longer before we heard his sister knock on the door, letting us know it was time to get up. We looked into each other's eyes for a moment more and moved out of bed to get ready for the day.

The rest of winter break sped by and as it came to and end Chess and I began to get things prepared for our return to the world outside of our pack's home. After being at the farmhouse for three weeks, being accepted by the pack, and finishing my transition, I had easily felt like I had become one of them. Noah helped me request the sealed records of my foster history and the records pertaining to my birth parents. After arriving back at the university, Chess and I would also begin looking at my chromosomes and genetic make-up to see if anything could be found about my background through a scientific route. Noah got us each a burner phone that we could use to contact him with any news pertaining to our research or to inform him of receiving any records about my parentage. He asked that we give him updates as we uncovered information and said that he would do his best to cover our tracks with the Union, especially as they grew more impatient in regard to Chess choosing a mate. Our research was a top priority and while uncovering my past would not be easy we at least had a start. We rehearsed what we would tell my friends so that we didn't raise suspicions. I didn't like that I had to keep lying to them, but we were already treading in dangerous water and we couldn't risk putting them in harm's way.

Over the last days of the break, I learned more about the Union and why they were so dangerous. They were made up of representatives from all the packs left in the world. There were 12 packs in total. The most notable, besides the Becks, were the Lumi, the Coinin, the Adalwuf, the Volkov, and the Dubois. Not that the other packs weren't as important, but those five were the largest and by far the most dangerous to the Becks. They had made a large part of the Union's rules, alongside the Becks, and were less than forgiving when other packs had broken Union rules. Often finding the smallest infractions as an excuse to steal territory from the offending pack along with forcing their alphas into a position of submission. They were a threat and, I was told, that was all I needed to know for the time being. Chess and I continued our dance of awkward moments of connection while I learned more about being a wolf. We continued to sleep together every night, but neither of us gave any indication of pushing for more. I learned that the feeling in the center of my chest and the subconscious thoughts that were pushed forward from time to time came from my wolf. We were the same, but the wolf was an extension of myself and would have feelings and desires that were not governed by our frontal cortex, an area where our human consciousness maintained control. The wolf would make what it wanted known and our human consciousness had to govern whether they received their wants and desires. For me and my wolf, that desire was Chess. I tried using our connection to get a sense of Chess' feelings, his wants and needs, but I found the connection harder to read now that my wolf often would spoke up and interrupted my focus. A few times, Chess felt my attempts and flirtatiously denied me the information I searched for. He knew I kept digging for something, but admitted he didn't know for what and that, if I wanted to know something, all I had to do was ask.

*Oh yeah, ask him if he loves me too. That's a great idea*, I thought sarcastically, but never said what it was I was truly looking for.

We had one final run together before going back to the university in the morning. It was the first time we had gone back to the beach since my shift. Once we reached the edge of the water, Chess stopped.

"Is everything okay?" I asked.

"Yeah, I think so."

"You think so?"

"Yeah," he turned and smiled, "this just used to be my favorite place to run to growing up and I always loved swimming here in the water at night, but now I don't know if it's the same."

"Is it because of me?"

"I want to say no, but I lost you here and while the blood has washed away it's still all I can think about," he paused, "It's also the place where you came back though, so I don't know," he said, shrugging.

"I'm sorry," I said. "I didn't mean to scare you like that. I didn't know that would happen, but I kept my promise that I would survive."

He smiled at me. "That you did."

"I also have a new favorite place," he said.

"Where is that?" I asked.

"Everywhere you and I are together," he said.

"Chess," I sighed and paused.

"What?" He asked

"I need you to stop saying things like that to me."

"What? Why?"

"It's starting to hurt me."

"What is?"

"Hearing you tell me all the things I want you to say and knowing that nothing more can ever happen. It hurts me, Chess."

"Oh," he breathed. I waited. I'd hoped he would say something more, that he would tell me what I wanted to hear, but nothing came. He kicked his feet in the water and sand sadly. I walked up to him and gave him a hug. He hugged me back tightly and we said nothing. We shifted and our wolves played together like normal. Noah really didn't want me shifting, but had agreed it would be okay as long as we stayed well within our pack's territory. He didn't want to risk anyone potentially seeing my red coat. Chess and I continued to play as we ran back home, but inside my heart was hurting for more. That night Chess stayed, shifted as we went to bed, slept on my leg like he had the first night and I felt like I had my answer. We woke up the next morning, said goodbye to everyone and headed back to school.

# Chapter Nineteen

A fter being back at school for a few weeks we settled back into our routines. Our reunion with our friends had gone great, though the same questions I had been wondering myself since the night of my shift were also on all their minds. *Were Chess and I together or were we not?* We hadn't slept together since that last night in his bed and it was tearing a hole in me.

I hadn't known what to expect from him when we had returned to campus. *Would I move in with him? Would we still stay the night with each other?* I knew that by the time we'd left the pack that I could hardly sleep without him and the purple sweatshirt had started to lose his scent. It was still there slightly and I had worn it less and less to preserve what little scent it had left.

Jesse asked for the run down of the break shortly after our return and I told her most of the details, with the exception of the fact that I was now a werewolf, oh and that he was too, and that we also couldn't be together because when werewolves mate it's for life and that he had to mate with a woman so that he could have pups and carry on his whole werewolf legacy... but I really wanted to, I would have loved to tell her all of it. If I could have told her, it might have made more sense to her as to why Chess and I were having such a 'road-block' as she put it in our relationship. She pushed me to just tell him how I felt, telling me it would jumpstart things, but she didn't know the whole story. I shrugged and pushed it off. Knowing her and, even worse, knowing Hunter, it was not something that would be let go of so easily.

I received some of the files that Noah had helped me request about my time in foster care from the Department of Child Services and most of the information was completely useless. The documents had the names of all the families I'd lived with for short periods of time and a birth certificate, but it was incomplete. It said the same thing that the copy I had said, J. Larson for Father and A. Larson for Mother. I reached out to the hospital I had been born at in the hope that I might find more information, but the hospital said they only kept birth records until they were sent over to the state and that this had happened shortly after my birth. I reached out to Carol Nettles, the woman who'd told me about my parents' unfortunate end, but my attempts at contacting her were left unreturned. I knew that there would be something that would break eventually and give us a better lead, but I couldn't think of where to go next in hopes of finding out more.

Chess had taken several blood samples from me when we'd gotten back to campus and had started building my genetic profile. I thought it was going to go much quicker, but he said he was still working on it. He was spending more and more time in the lab, but thankfully hadn't completely disappeared. We were texting regularly, but I longed for the time we'd spent together over the break to come back again. My wolf was relentless inside of me, constantly pushing me to run with Chess again like we had every night at the farmhouse. It was like having a toddler constantly pushing for something and then having to tell them 'no' over and over again. Chess had tried to hang out with our friends and I much more frequently, even though they would tease us for not figuring things out, and I think their relentless chiding made the situation even harder for him.

I was lying in bed thinking through everything and trying to figure out how I could change the way things were between Chess and I. The wolf inside me would not stop being chatty and really thought we just needed to tell him again how we felt and that it would fix everything. While I had immediately felt myself after the shift, the constant intrusion of thoughts I was trying to avoid being thrown back into my mind constantly by my wolf was annoying. I growled and nearly shredded a pillow with my frustration before my phone went off.

CHESS

I got the results finished. Can you come to the Lab?

The electricity zoomed in my stomach at seeing his name and I sighed, trying to force the excitement away. My wolf danced at the opportunity to see him too, but I knew I would end up leaving alone, again. I pulled up the message and replied.

LYLE

Sure thing. I'llll head that way now.

I pressed send and jumped out of bed to leave. In the living room, Andy and Kay were playing a video game.

"Hey, you heading out?" Andy asked as I shut the door to my room.

"Yeah, I'm going to meet up with Chess for a bit. I'll be back in a couple of hours."

"You can always bring him back here. We could all watch a movie together," Kay suggested kindly.

"Yeah, that might be nice. I will see what he has going on afterwards." I replied hopeful, even though I knew I wouldn't be bringing Chess back with me.

They waved a small goodbye and I left our building, heading toward the science hall. It was 5:30 PM, so the Lab would be almost empty and the traffic on campus had pretty much cleared out. I enjoyed taking advantage of the new speed I had gained, and, while I never ran due to the possibility of being seen, I moved much faster than I usually would have. I slowed slightly when I could sense somebody in the distance who might be close enough to watch me. I made it to the hall in exceptional time and was heading up to the lab by 5:40. As I walked into Chess' lab, I enjoyed his scent as it filled my nostrils and put me at ease. He had been here for a while now. I could smell that he had been working hard. He'd positioned himself standing at the giant monitor that hung in the center of the room. I watched as he pulled up a bunch of graphs on one side that were smaller, and then one big one pulled up next to them.

"Hey," I said casually as I walked into the lab.

"Hi," he replied, "I'm glad you were free." He flashed that full toothy grin at me again and the electricity hummed back alive. My wolf jumped inside of me. I thought back to him to cool it and he growled.

"Yeah, me too," I started, "so what's up? What is all of this?" I asked, gesturing toward the circular graphs on the monitor.

"Uh... Yeah," he said, moving and positioning me so that I was standing front and center for his presentation, "so I ran your samples multiple times, trying to figure it all out, and every time they come back, the same."

"Okay?"

"This one, right here," he pointed to the big graph, "this is you. All these little markers outside around the edges are your genetic profile."

"Okay," I said again, "is that normal?"

"It is. These first markers are all the ones that show your human side. These three additional markers show the wolf genes that everyone who is a werewolf has."

"Okay, then," I said, looking at the graph closely. "What are these?" I asked, gesturing outwards toward a group of markers that he hadn't provided any explanation for.

"That's where I got really confused, it's what drove me to run them multiple times." He pulled up some other of the small graphs next to mine. "These are the genetic samples from every pack that exists today. This one is our family's pack." He said overlaying the sample of his genetics on mine, only one of the other markers was covered.

"Okay, what does that mean?" I asked him cluelessly.

"That is our genetic marker for our heightened vision trait. You have it too." He said, smiling at me. "This one is the Lumi Pack, speed." He moved the profile over mine, another marker was accounted for as it overlaid mine. "The Coinin, scent. The Adalwuf, sound. The Volkovs, touch. The Dubois, taste. And here are the rest." He pressed a button and the genetic profiles of all other packs overlaid mine and filled in most of the remaining profile. "Lyle," he paused, reaching over to grab my hand, "you have them all."

I looked at the screen in disbelief. "How.... How is that possible?" I asked him.

"I don't know, but I know you possess every marker for every special ability we know of and then some. This is more evidence to support that you more than likely descended from one of the first of our kind, a pack that has been lost for ages, and yet, somehow, here you are." He smiled and laughed slightly in disbelief and amazement.

The electricity inside me zoomed around with the way he looked at me and I quickly looked back at the screen. "What do these four markers here mean?" I pointed to the remaining markers on the graph that remained uncovered.

"I have no idea," Chess shared, "could be anything. We don't quite know what you are and aren't able to do if you're one of the first."

He pulled the graph out to the full screen and I looked at all the markers that had indicated the different blood lines that made up mine. I felt satisfied somehow that this was just more evidence that I, in fact, belonged to those beautiful and amazing wolves from my dream. John, Rebecca, Sarah, Victor, and Lyle. I wanted to know more about them, to find out what happened that night after John continued to run into the woods. I stared at the screen longer wondering and processing the gravity of this reality.

*Could I really be their descendent? Could I really be the last of them? The last red wolf.* I thought to myself.

"Lyle?" Chess spoke, breaking my concentration on my thoughts.

"Yeah?" I asked, continuing to look at the screen. A moment of silence passed and I turned to look at him. He was staring down at the ground and fidgeting.

*What is he doing?* I thought to myself. *He never fidgets.* "What's wrong?" I said, concerned.

"Uhh. nothing. Nothing is wrong." He said pausing again while I waited for him to speak, "I...," he cleared his throat, "I've been thinking a lot, and uhhh... I.... really don't know what all of this means yet, but I.. ummm. I know I've made things confusing for you and I think that is partly because I was confused and I'm... umm ...not confused anymore and so I," he said, pausing again.

*What is he talking about?* I thought to myself. I continued to wait for him to find the words he wanted to say.

"I know what I said about the expectations on me and, I know it won't be easy and we might end up getting into a lot of trouble, but would you maybe, I don't know, I guess what I'm trying to ask you is.. uhhh," he paused yet again, "will you go on a date with me?"

"What?!?" I asked, a little stunned. *Did I hear him right? He's asking me on a date?* I was a little taken aback. *Please let this be real, please don't take it back.* I thought.

"I said, will you go on a date with me?" My heart raced and I could feel my wolf hopping and dancing around inside of me.

"You want to go on a date with me?"

"Yes," he said, smiling and staring at me slightly more confidently now. It was so bizarre to see him feeling uncertain of himself, anxious and fidgeting uncomfortably. It was usually me who was left unsure about where I stood with him.

"Why? What's changed?" *Just say yes, you idiot,* I thought to myself as I asked him.

"You... Me... Us.... All of it." He paused thinking of what he wanted to say next, "Lyle my entire life I knew what the expectations were for me and my entire life I've fought them and hoped that something would come along and change things for me. Just when I'd finally started accepting the inevitable future that had been laid out for me, you happened. It scared me at first and I hesitated, but I shouldn't have. You are what I'd always hoped for and I'm sorry for not embracing that sooner."

I was a little speechless. His words were perfectly chosen and, at this moment, I was elated. I said, "Yes."

He smiled wider than I knew he could. I could feel a rush between us and in this moment things that I had been trying so hard not to feel for him suddenly came to me and I finally knew that he wanted me as badly as I wanted him. I could feel our wolves reach out to one another as we stood there smiling.

"So, tomorrow night?" he asked.

"Tomorrow it is." I said, sounding so cheesy but there was no helping it, I was sure I looked just as cheesy as I sounded with a permanent grin running across my face from ear to ear. I could sense his wolf was dancing as wildly as mine and I was so elated in my feelings that I nearly forgot about all the things we had just uncovered and so I asked, turning back to the reason for our meeting, "What are we going to do about all of this though?"

"Oh... yeah... right," he said, switching his focus back to the results, "I will call my dad and let him know what we've found. Have you made any headway with finding out your parent's names?"

"No," I said, "I reached out to the foster mom who told me what had happened, but she hasn't called me back."

"Hmm," he said, "well maybe we'll make a house visit then," he said, grinning at me. I could sense his determination to find out more and I couldn't help but feel it too. The genetics were just part of the puzzle and now we needed to know more.

"Maybe we should," I admitted, "but for now, let's just get through this weekend." I said smiling and he nodded.

"Agreed," he said. "Can I walk you home?"

"Sure," I told him. He quickly shut off his lab equipment, grabbed his bag, and we left the science hall. We talked all the way back to my place about classes, our friends, and where we might go on our date. He admitted he'd never gone on one before and I suddenly wished that I'd waited for us to be each other's first date. Chess ended up deciding that he knew where we were going to go and that it was a secret. I would just have to wait and see. As we reached my apartment, I asked him if he wanted to come up and hang out for a while. He politely declined, saying he had a lot to do between now and tomorrow to get ready for our date. He hugged me and held onto me longer than a typical hug should last before heading off into the night. I immediately went upstairs and pulled out my phone to text Jesse and Hunter. I told them both that Chess had asked me out on a date for tomorrow night and they both were as excited as I was that this was finally happening.

The next day, I spent a lot of time getting ready. Jesse and I went shopping early in the morning so that I could get a new outfit to wear. It turned out to be a bit of a struggle to find clothes that would fit me. Jesse had noticed some of the larger changes that occurred over winter break and I'd had to cover by telling her how amazing their home gym had been and how Chess has a really rigid workout routine that he'd insisted I try. It was a little hard for her to buy into, given that she was very good at sorting out the truth in nearly every situation, but she didn't seem to give any indication of not believing me. Sometimes, I found maybe it didn't really matter to her overall, as long as we were happy. I really wanted to tell her everything about Chess and the rest of the pack. She was my first real best friend. Someday. When it's safe, I thought to myself as I pushed the truth to the back of my mind. We settled on a decent pair of dark wash blue jeans, a white v-neck, and a striped blue button up. I looked in the mirror of the dressing room and felt uniquely satisfied with how I appeared in front of myself. Jesse said that the color of the shirt really complimented my new hair color and made my eyes stand out. I flushed at the compliment, but I had to agree with her. This was going to be the perfect date. I just knew it.

I looked at the clock and 5:30 came faster than I could have anticipated, Chess knocked at the door, he was right on time. I'd texted him all day trying to find out what all we were going to do for our date and he'd continued to insist that it would be a surprise. It made the anticipation of it even sweeter. He knocked on the door and when I opened it; he was standing there, holding a small bouquet of red roses, and he was dressed to kill. He had put on a nice pair of black jeans, a brown leather jacket that he wore over a white button up, and he even had a small black tie that hung down against his chest. I smiled while staring at him because he had also gone and gotten a high fade undercut with a bit off the top, and had styled his hair with some product that pushed it over to the left. He'd trimmed his facial hair back and he looked so handsome.

"Hi," I said to him as I held the door open for him to come in.

He smiled back at me in return. "Hey. I... uh. Got these for you," he said as he handed me the roses wrapped in floral paper.

"Thank you," I told him. I had never received flowers from anyone before and suddenly every romantic movie where the guy gives the girl flowers made total sense. It ignited deep sparks within me as I took them from him and I felt like my skin must have been glowing with how special it made me feel. "You didn't have to bring flowers, you know. I was already happy just to go out with you, but I am glad you did," I said, pulling them up to my face and taking a small whiff. The smell of them was so much more complex than flowers had ever smelt before and they were amazing.

"I know," he said, "but this is special, and I wanted to make sure that you knew exactly how special you are to me." He looked down at the ground, made eye contact with me, smiled, looked away, and then looked back at me again, subtly biting his lip. He was flirting and it was working. I moved into the kitchen and pulled out a large glass cup, filled it with water, and set the roses in it. It was no vase, but it would work for now. "Are you ready to go?" He asked.

"Yeah, I am," I told him, turning around, and walking out of the kitchen.

"Great!" He replied as he held the door open for me to walk out. As I walked by, he put his hand against the small of my back and followed me into the hallway. I locked the door behind us and we headed for the lobby. Out front, the Jeep was parked against the curb and, as we approached it, he opened the door for me, like he always had.

"Thank you." I said to him as I climbed inside. He scampered around the car and into the driver's seat. "So, can you tell me where we are going now?" I asked him.

"Nope. Just sit tight. We will be there soon." He put the car in drive and pulled off into the street. We had been driving for a while before I quickly found out that he was taking us back to his loft, and it made me curious what all he had planned.

"What are we doing here?" I asked him.

"You'll see." He said, parking the car near the entrance. He rounded the car and opened my door for me again, taking my hand before heading inside. We followed the same route down the hallway and up the freight elevator to the top floor. I started walking toward his door before he took my hand again and instructed me to follow him. I followed him as we walked down another small hallway and around the corner toward a door. He opened it and we started ascending the stairs toward the roof. "Close your eyes." He instructed me as we reached the top and started opening the door. I walked out onto the roof with my hands over my eyes, and I heard a loud clunk as Chess pulled something. He walked up to my side and put his arm around my waist. "You can open them now."

I dropped my hands from my eyes and opened them. I'd never been to the rooftop of his apartment dont before, but it was lit up with strung Edison lights that glowed a soft orange in the darkness. They illuminated a small table set for two, several dozen roses in white and red that were positioned scattered around the rooftop. "Did you do all this?" I asked him incredulously, staring at how beautiful everything was.

"Yeah," he said optimistically, "do you like it?"

"Do I like it?" I asked in disbelief, "Chess, this is amazing. I couldn't have pictured you doing anything even close to this." I turned to look at him and took his hand. "Thank you." I whispered as water collected in the corners of my eyes.

"Well, don't thank me yet," he said, walking toward the table, "you haven't tried my cooking." I walked with him as he pulled out my chair and I sat down. He walked over to a hot bag where our food was being kept warm. He pulled out a giant box revealing pizza from the pizzeria where I'd gone with my friends and had a surprise encounter with Chess after our awkward first meeting. I started laughing uncontrollably when I saw it. It was perfect. "What are you laughing at?" he said, chuckling, pulling out a couple of slices of pepperoni pizza and setting them on my plate. He served up two more for himself and returned the box to the bag.

"Nothing, I just wasn't expecting something as high class as this for dinner." I said sarcastically.

"Woah, hey, you know me - I'm all class." He said jokingly, taking a bite of pizza. We continued to eat, talk, and laugh about everything. Chess pulled out two more slices for each of us and we continued to enjoy each other's company and conversation. Afterward, Chess stood up from the table and pulled a tiny remote out of his pocket, pushing a button. When he did, music started playing, and he reached out his hand for mine.

"Oh no," I said, "Chess, I can't dance." He looked at me and smiled.

"I know," he said. "Remember, I walked in on you attempting to dance several weeks ago?" I flushed at the thought of it, but he walked up closer and grabbed my hand. "However, this isn't that kind of dancing." He pulled me up and put his hand on my waist and held my hand in the other. I blushed and smiled, rolling my eyes at him before putting my hand on his shoulder. He started swaying us back and forth slowly as we moved in rhythm with the slow instrumental music that played from a small speaker he'd no doubt set up as he'd planned for this exact moment.

"Chess?" I said, looking into his eyes as I followed his lead around the gravel roof top.

"Yeah?" He asked, I paused. I thought maybe this was the perfect moment to tell him the last thoughts I had that night on the beach before everything went black, but I hesitated.

"This is by far the cheesiest and absolute best first date I think that anyone could have ever given me," I leaned in and rested my head on his shoulder, he ran his fingers through my hair, "thank you." We continued to sway in motion and I let myself move into him closely, keeping my head on his shoulder.

"Well then, are you ready for part two?" He asked.

"Part two?" I lifted my head, looking at him surprised.

"Well, we are wolves, Lyle," he smiled at me mischievously, "what kind of first date would it be if we didn't go for a run together next?" He said grinning.

"I guess an incomplete one." I said, returning his grin and following his lead by walking down from the rooftop back toward his car.

We drove several miles until we hit the woods past Issaquah. We disrobed in the car, taking our time helping each other remove our outfits and placing them to the side. The moon was out, lighting up the forest all the way to the mountains. We shifted and started running through the trees, dancing and jumping around each other as we did. We ran deep into the mountainside and stopped once we'd reached the top. We sat next to each other and I rubbed into his side as we looked out over the lights of the city. Chess was the first to shift out of wolf and he stood next to me for a moment, scratching me behind the ears. I shifted shortly after and took his hand.

"Chess... I.. There's something I've been wanting to tell y..." I started before being cut off by him.

"You talk too much." He said quickly before taking me by the waist and pulling me into a deep kiss. He had kissed me only once before, slightly, and quick, but that was different. This was our first proper kiss. He pushed his lips into mine and he didn't pull away immediately like he had then. I kissed him back. I didn't know how to kiss, but I wrapped my hands around him slightly and pushed my lips back into his. The curves of them fit perfectly together and I could feel the stubble on his chin rubbing against mine. He surprised me slightly when I felt him push his tongue against my teeth, I opened my mouth slightly as he did. I fell into it, the passion I felt pouring out between us, and I never wanted it to end. I followed his lead and moved my hands against his body, touching his chest and sliding my hands down around his torso and across his stomach. I felt a growl grow in his chest as I did. He did the same and I moved my hands down even lower and touched him for the first time. He pulled away then quickly, "Sorry," he said as he did, "I'm sorry, we can't yet." His breath was heavy and so was mine. I felt a twinge of sadness at the loss of his mouth on mine, but he was right. It was too fast.

"I'm sorry too," I panted, "I... I got carried away." I side-smiled at him and he returned it.

"You have nothing to be sorry for." He said walking back closer and he kissed me again, but it was much briefer and not as heavy as the first time. I couldn't have imagined this date going any more perfectly than this. I could feel that he felt the same and he smacked my behind slightly for poking around for his feelings again.

"You do that a lot, you know." He said, with a small devilish look in his eye. "If you want to know what I'm feeling Lyle, all you have to do is ask me."

"Okay," I said, "are you happy?"

"Yes Lyle, I am very, very happy." He said putting his arms around me again and we stood at the top of the mountain watching as the night set and the sun peeked over the horizon before we shifted and returned to the city.

# Chapter Twenty

Two more weeks had gone by with no word in regard to the information we were looking for about my parents. We were moving into March and we kept running into the same red tape that we had been all along. We'd met with Noah in Chess' lab less than a week ago and, with the new information regarding my genetics, he had been equally as perplexed as he was before. I know he'd done his best to hide it, but the results troubled him more than they made him feel relieved. I'd thought my being a descendant of the first wolves was a good thing, but I could see that it brought further fear and worry for him. I confided in Chess and he did his best to reassure my concerns. He told me it would never matter to his dad whether I was a descendant. I was part of their pack; I was family and that he would always be there for me just like he was for Chess. That brought me some comfort. Noah had decided that he would make some calls to see if he could find out more than we could, but the burner phones stayed silent.

Chess and I decided that it would be for the best to keep our relationship hidden from the pack for now. There was so much stress on them to hide me from the Union and keep them from pushing Chess to choose a mate. All our moves for information had to be quiet. Everyone had their roles to play and we were doing ours.

I spent most of my nights in the loft with Chess and we had gone on several other dates. Soon, after our third date, he announced to all our friends that I was his boyfriend and our relationship continued to flourish. We had grown closer than we even thought possible and, as we did, our wolf bond grew stronger. I could show him some memories of what I had seen when I died that night on the beach. He hated thinking about that night, but he saw John and Rebecca and it brought me a lot of joy to share that with him. He shared some of his childhood memories with me and I finally found out what the deal with the head twitching thing was for them all. Chess had explained that it is a sign of respect and acknowledgement toward the alpha. It had nothing to do with a head nod, but was exposing the neck, a show of vulnerability and fealty that displayed their respect. There were a lot of things about being a wolf that I had yet to learn, but I was doing my best to find out what I could.

Chess and I were on the sofa in the loft watching a movie. I had my head on his thigh and he was running his hands through my hair. "Lyle?" he said.

"Hmm?" I responded.

"I think it's time we visit this Carol Nettles in person," he paused, "we've tried calling multiple times and she hasn't returned any of them."

I heard what he was saying and I knew he was right, but I had been avoiding the topic for fear of actually going. This woman hadn't wanted me to stay with her as a kid and now, as an adult, she wouldn't even take my phone call. It seemed clear to me that she wanted nothing to do with me, so going to her house seemed like a terrible idea. "I don't know Chess," I said rolling onto my back and looking up at him, "it's pretty clear she doesn't want to talk to me. Maybe we should keep looking at other avenues. Noah said that he was going to cut through some red tape to find out more. Maybe we should wait and see what he comes up with." I could sense that wasn't the answer Chess was hoping for.

He took a deep sigh and said, "Lyle, it has been months since we returned from winter break. All we have done so far is find out that you have every werewolf ability, but we are making zero headway on finding out who your parents were. Don't you still want to know?"

He ran his hands through my hair. "Of course I do. I guess I'm just scared. She sent me back to be moved to another house when I was little and now she doesn't want to talk. It just feels like if we show up on her doorstep, she's going to slam the door in our face."

"We don't know that, Lyle. There could be a ton of reasons she hasn't called back, but time isn't on our side to continue waiting. It's important that we know about your parents before the Union finds out about you."

I understood and agreed. "You're right..... We can go this week-end." I said, rolling back to face the TV and we continued to watch the movie.

The week zoomed by and well before I was anywhere near ready we were already in the car, heading toward Spokane and Carol Nettles. I'd told Jesse and Hunter about the trip and what we were going to do. They thought it was great that I had taken an interest in finding out more about my parents and Hunter had offered to assist us in the search once we found out their names. His passion for digging into the past might be useful once we had more information to go off of. We passed through Ellensburg and were deep into the barren fields of sagebrush and dirt that made up most of Eastern Washington. I had grown up on this side of the state and returning now showed me how much I hadn't missed it. Chess thought it had its own type of beauty, he thought all nature was beautiful. He was right to a certain degree, but the boy I was here had hardly any relation to the man I had become. This side of the state didn't want me, I'd never felt a chip on my shoulder about any of it until now, but I'd been alone nearly every day of my life growing up in this area and thinking about how much of an outcast it had made me and how lonely I'd felt hurt me. This was especially poignant in contrast to my life in Seattle, because now that I knew what it was to have people, loved ones, family, friends, and a pack it made me sad for the boy that never got to know those things and should have.

I tried to keep my feelings hidden from Chess throughout the drive. I didn't want him to feel sad for me or angry about everything that had happened. He knew I'd moved frequently, but I'd never told him how frequent it was or how many families hadn't wanted me. Jesse knew and her knowing was hard enough. I didn't want my friends, my new family, to feel sorry for me. To know how unwanted I was by so many, it made me feel vulnerable, as if they would see that something was wrong with me and no longer want me too.

As we pulled closer into the edge of Spokane, we followed the GPS as it guided us back to the place I'd once called home albeit for a very short time. When we arrived, I had to admit that I didn't recognize it. There was nothing familiar about the junk piled in the yard, winding its way onto the front porch. The paint on the sides of the house peeled slightly and several broken boards on the porch made us watch our step as we walked toward the door. Chess knocked on the door and we waited quietly for a few moments before a woman in leggings and an old dirty tank top answered the door.

"Whatcha want?" she asked, irritated.

"Hi, we are looking for Carol Nettles," Chess said. "Does she still live here?"

"Uh huh," the woman spoke, "whatcha want with my mama for?"

"She used to be my foster mom," I said. "She'd known more information about who my actual parents were than the state did. Do you think it would be okay if we spoke to her for a couple of minutes?" I asked her nicely.

"Don't know how much use she'll be to ya; she's gone senile," she said, looking at both of us, "but yeah, you can talk to her." She opened the door wider and walked down the hall as we followed her inside. The house's interior was in the same disheveled condition as it was outside. The walls were dirty, the rare areas where the carpet hadn't been worn through were covered in stains, and floor boards were broken and missing as we walked down the hallway. The smell of cigarettes and cat pee clung to every surface of the house, it was difficult to take. The ceilings and their corners had all yellowed, no doubt for the same reasons as the pungent smells. "MA!" the woman yelled as we walked down the hallway and followed her into the kitchen.

"WHAT?!" an older woman sitting at a small kitchen table yelled back at her as she held a cigarette in one hand, a book in the other.

"This man said you used to be his foster mom," and the older woman turned to look at us, squinting as the younger one asked, "that true?"

She held the cigarette to her lips and pulled a deep drag that caused the end of the ash to burn bright as it followed the direction of the smoke. "Well, I'll be goddamned," she said. "Lyle is that chu?" she asked, exhaling the smoke from her lungs.

"You remember me?" I asked.

"Course I do," she said. "You look different now, but I'd remember that mug of yours anywhere." She smiled and, as she did, I saw that the teeth that she had remaining were all stained deep yellow. I wished I could say that I remembered her as well, but there was very little about this woman that I could recall. She motioned for us to come in and have a seat. We approached the tiny table and sat with her as she flicked the ash into a tray and took another drag. I looked at her closely, trying to recall her. Her's was one of the first homes I could remember being in. Her hair was thinning and gray. She had it pulled back into a ponytail. She was much larger in the middle, thinner in her face and legs, and if she had stood, she might have resembled an egg. I looked at her face and finally saw that she bore a bit of a resemblance to the woman I had pulled into my mind. Time and smoking had taken its toll on her, but around the eyes she looked like the Carol I'd known. "What can I do for you?" She asked, while breathing out another enormous cloud of smoke.

"I was wondering if you could tell us anything you remember about my parents. We have been trying to find their names and it doesn't look like anything about them was documented in my records." I looked at her as I spoke and she smiled a little.

"Yeah, I knew your folks," she said, "Ashley and Jeremy Larson." She took another drag. "I was friends with your mom when they moved here."

"I... I didn't know that." I said, surprised.

"Yup. I told her when she found out she was pregnant with cha that I'd take care of cha if anything ever happen to her and it did." She took another long drag of her cigarette. "Had cha too until them bastards found ya and hauled you off into the system." She finished smoking her cigarette and lit another one. "I woulda tried to get ya back, but found out I's pregnant with this lousy bitch."

Her daughter interrupted her, "eh fuck you. You miserable cow."

Carol started laughing, "Well anyway I couldn't do both of cha so I let them take ya."

"So, you knew my mom and dad well, then?" I asked her.

"Well, I probably wouldn't say well." She took a drag. "Your pa was a real son of a bitch. Mean as a snake. Can't say I wasn't glad when I heard he died." She started coughing as she blew out another breath of smoke. "Your mom, though. Probably one of the nicest gals that I had ever met. Real pretty too. Lot like you. Red hair, blue eyes, pleasant face. I had told her she was too good for that bastard of a husband and then he wouldn't let her come round here no more. I was sad when that place called and told me she had died. She put me down as her next of kin. Bit of a surprise to be honest, but figuring out what she did, and what I had told her when she found out she's pregnant with cha, well, I guess she'd felt you had a place to go. Was a waste, I thought to myself when I heard, but then they'd told me you's was born and I came and got ya. Had yas up till near 6 years old before that damn school called me in for saying I neglected ya. After that though, there was nothing I coulda done to keep ya. You wasn't mine." She took a long pause and smoked the rest of her cigarette. "Wish you was though. You were smart, funny, kind, and a damn good-looking kid. You were all hers through and through, no doubt about it."

Chess finally spoke up, "What place called to say she had died?"

"The state hospital out toward Medical Lake. She checked herself in there shortly after shit for brains died. Said she had to get clean for ya. Said she felt you was gonna be important." She lit up another and continued to smoke. "Other than that, I didn't know much about em I'm 'fraid. Might check with the hospital though."

I sat and absorbed all the information she just shared. "Thank you," I said to her, standing to leave. "I really appreciate your time."

"No problem, sugar," she waddled her way up out of the chair, "y'all don't have to rush off either now."

I had started walking and Chess spoke up, "I'm sorry, but we unfortunately have to get going."

"Well okay now, y'all don't be 'fraid come back and pay me a visit again. I would love to know how ya got along." I heard her say as I reached the front porch and walked back into the fresh air. I was having such a strong emotion stirring in my chest, I had to leave.

*I looked like her*, I thought to myself as I opened the door to the Jeep and climbed inside. As soon as I closed the door, I felt tears hit my lap. I hadn't even realized I'd started crying until that moment. I'd never cared to know these things. It'd never piqued my interest or caused me any distress before this moment, but I looked like her. She knew them. Chess climbed into the driver's seat and sped off as Carol's daughter walked out onto the front porch to see what was going on. I never even knew that her name was Ashley or that she had red hair or blue eyes like me, that she was kind and pretty.

*How could I have never cared?* I asked myself, as I could feel Chess poking around in my feelings. He almost never did that and I looked over at him with tears in my eyes.

"You never had to know. You just survived. You were alone and you did what you needed to do to get through it. You feel safe now and that's the only reason you are even able to allow yourself to feel these things " He said, responding to my inner thoughts. My inner wolf howled in my chest, responding to the news as well. We both missed a person we had never even met, had never even thought to miss until this moment.

"I want to know her." I said, as Chess pulled back onto the interstate.

"I know," he replied. "Where do you think I'm headed?" He pulled out his phone and in the GPS he already had directions routing us toward the hospital Carol had told us about. He reached over and ran his fingers through my hair. "We will figure this out."

The hospital was not far from Spokane and, when we pulled up, we could see that it had been there a while. The brick building was imposing and the sign out front said Eastern State Hospital. I hadn't put the two together when Carol had called the hospital by the city it was located in instead of it's actual name. Growing up in the foster system it wasn't uncommon to hear stories from other kids or to over-hear discussions between foster parents about which of the kids' parents were incarcerated and whether they were in jail or in prison, but it was always in hushed tones and partially hidden conversations that you would hear about someone's parents who were at "Eastern State", more commonly known and referred to by the other foster kids as 'the mental hospital'.

We walked up toward the imposing brick facade that looked more like a prison than a hospital, we climbed the front stairs and went inside, heading up toward a desk behind a glass window for help. I didn't really know what I was supposed to say or ask when we got there, but here we were. A young woman was seated at a computer. She looked up from the computer screen and said, "Hi, how can I help you?"

"I'm looking for some information on my mom. She was a patient here about 21 years ago?" I said.

"Okay, I will just need to take a peek at your ID. What was her name?" she asked.

"Ashley Larson, I'm her son Lyle Larson." I told her as she started typing the name on the computer.

"Now that's a name I haven't heard in a long, long time," said a woman from the back office walking out toward the window. She was older, hair pulled back tight into a bun, and there was less of a hustle to her step, clearly having worked here for a long time. "Kenya, sweetie, I'll help them."

She walked around the desk to our side of the counter. "I wondered if I might ever get to see you again someday." She said as she walked up to me. She reached out and took my hand and grabbed it.

"I'm sorry," I said, "do I know you?" I asked her as she looked up at me with tears in her eyes.

"No," she said, "but I was here the night you were born. I'm Rosie." She motioned for us to follow her. I looked back at Chess and he shooed me with his hands in an effort to get me to follow her. We walked back down the hall and followed her into a small office with multiple chairs. She sat down and we followed suit. "So, what would you like to know?" She asked me when we were all seated.

"I guess as much as you do?" I told her matter-of-factly. "Today was the first day I ever knew her first name." I told her honestly.

"Oh, that hurts my heart to hear that." She said, pausing a moment.

"Well, there is barely a day that goes by that I don't think about Miss Ashley. She came to us and checked herself in. She said that she was pregnant, that she had to get clean, and that she was ill. I didn't meet her then, but she was checked-in and given a room. I came on as her nurse a few days later. She was going through withdrawal and I asked her if she had anyone she wanted me to call for support, she said she didn't have anyone. She just said she had to get through it for you and that it didn't matter what happened to her. I stayed with her after that and saw her through the next couple of weeks while the drugs passed out of her system. After that she seemed like a whole new person, so kind and sweet. I'd like to think that even though I was her nurse that I was her friend too. Even on days when I wasn't on her rotation, I would come by after my shift to check on her. We would sit and talk for hours about the other nurses and the patients around the floor. She shied away from sharing too much about herself while she was here, but one thing I knew for sure is that she loved you."

*She loved me?* I thought to myself. I paid close attention to every word she had to share even as inside I was breaking.

"She would often spend time in the sunroom and would just sing to you and rub her belly in the rocker. I'd hoped that by the time you were born, she would find the strength she was looking for to carry on, but she hadn't. She never really let it show, but there was a deep well of sadness she carried with her everywhere she went around the hospital. You could always feel it from her, but with the way she would talk to you and about you, I'd hoped she would turn it around. She wanted so badly for you to come out healthy and, when you finally did, the sadness disappeared for a while. We continued to do everything we could to help her, but she would say that half of her was missing and that part of her would never be okay again. She never said what it was, just that half of her was gone. We kept everything potentially harmful away to prevent her from being lost to us, but, after you were born, she spent two days with you and then she passed. We never could find out what caused her death officially, but it was like she'd lost the will to live and once she'd made sure you survived and that you were healthy, she was gone."

I sat quietly. I couldn't find thoughts or feelings at first and then, like a wave, they hit all at once. I held it together on the outside, but inside I was falling apart. She'd loved me and she'd wanted me, but it was not enough to keep her here. I wasn't enough to help her find the will to live. I felt small tears edge up on the corners of my eyes, but kept them from falling. "Thank you." I told her, "There was so much I never knew, so thank you for telling me that." I rose to leave and Chess stood too, taking my hand.

"Well, don't you want her things?" Rosie asked as we prepared to leave.

"What things?" Chess asked.

"Well, I assumed you were here to claim her possessions, but when you got here, I knew we had to speak," she said as she stood and walked up to me, holding her hand against my cheek, "I can only imagine how difficult this all is, but, if you would like her things, you can follow me." I nodded and we followed her further down the hallway, into a stairwell and down to the basement. We walked into a storage room filled with shelves that held boxes with patient names written on them. She asked us to pause at a table while she went to the back corner of the room and came back with a white box labeled 'A. Larson'. "There isn't much, but there are a few things that I think you may want to keep."

She opened the lid and slid the box over to us. Inside there was a small journal she had written in, a few drawings she had done while being at the hospital, a hairbrush, and at the bottom was a picture of her. I had never seen a picture of her before and I picked it up and held it closer so that the light could shine on it. It was a picture of her in a green dress, leaning up against the brick outside of the hospital. You could see she was pregnant with the baby bump she was holding, and she had turned and smiled at the camera. "Is this her?" I asked, knowing full well it was.

"Yes," Rosie said, "I took this photo of her and had it developed. I hoped if she could see how happy she was that maybe it would help her somehow." The world fell away for a moment, this was the first and only picture in the world of her and I. She was as beautiful as both Carol and Rosie had said she was, with curly red hair that hung down over her shoulders and deep blue eyes, like mine, that you could see even in this photo at a distance. She had a pretty smile and looked short in the photo. A tear finally escaped and fell off my face and hit the photo. Chess put his hand on my back and looked at the photo too.

"She's beautiful." He commented. I nodded.

Rosie rounded the table and threw her arms around me. "I'm so sorry, sweetie, but just remember, she loved you with everything she had left to give." She pulled away.

"Thank you." I told her. Chess picked up the box, and we headed upstairs. "Is she buried nearby?" I asked as we reached the top of the stairs.

"Yes, she is," Rosie said. "If you would like, I can give you the address of the cemetery and how to find her when you get there. I take fresh flowers once a month."

"Thank you." I told her as I nodded. We headed back toward the nurses' station and Rosie wrote the instructions on how to get there. She gave me another hug and wrote her phone number if I ever wanted to call her and talk to her. I thought that was nice. She truly loved my mother as a friend and was just as crushed by her passing as anyone else in her life would have been if she had been close to anyone. She would have probably been someone I would have called auntie, a sort of chosen family member, if my mother hadn't passed and their friendship resumed, I thought briefly. What a different life I could have had if she'd lived.

We reached the car and Chess put the box of her things into the back of the Jeep. Before opening the door for me like he enjoyed doing, he scooped me into a giant hug and held me close to his chest. I gripped him tightly, knowing he was searching my feelings again. "If things hadn't gone the way they did, Chess, I may have never met you, and my life would have been incomplete. I have a newfound love for her, but please don't think I regret how my life turned out because I have you and our friends and our pack." I said, speaking into his chest and then, finally, I felt him stop searching.

He pulled back slightly and kissed me. "Do you want to go see her?" he asked before letting me go.

"I would like to, I think, yeah." He pulled open the door and I climbed inside. As he walked around to get in, I reached back and pulled out the picture, the drawings, and her journal. Chess drove toward the cemetery and I continued to look at her photo. She was entrancing to look at. I couldn't believe I had never had the curiosity to search for her sooner. I flipped past the photo and looked at her drawings. I found it so strange that she drew wolves of all things while being at the hospital, they were so beautifully drawn.

*She was talented,* I thought to myself, looking at them.

As we pulled into the cemetery, I put the photo and drawings back in the box and pulled open the journal. "Oh, my God!" I said, reading the first couple of pages.

Chess slammed on the brakes suddenly and we jerked forward in our seats, "What? What's wrong?" He asked, looking around.

"This," I said, holding the journal, "it's about me." Chess drove again as I flipped through the pages. She had taken notes when she found out she was pregnant with me, when she could finally see the baby bump, the first kicks, and her heartburn. She wrote about Jeremy, my father, and how much she missed him and how his death had hurt her. She wrote about her dreams she'd had for them and ones she'd had for me. At the very back, her last entry was addressed to me directly.

"We're here." Chess said as he put the car in park. I stuck my finger in the journal at the last entry and held it. We left the car and began walking toward the grave site that Rosie had given us directions to. It took a bit to find her, but when we did, I fell to my knees.

*Ashley Larson, Beloved Friend and Mother*

It appeared that Rosie had paid for a nice headstone and epitaph to be written for her. Next to her grave, Chess pointed out my father. He had nothing but his name written on a stone on the ground. I didn't hate him or even dislike him, but I couldn't help feeling that maybe he wasn't the greatest man, but my mother had clearly loved him with everything she had so that was enough. "Hi dad." I said as I knelt in the grass. I turned back to my mom's grave and said, "Hi, mom."

Chess leaned down behind me and wrapped his arms around me. "What's that you're holding marked?" He asked.

"It's an entry she wrote for me to read." I told him.

"Do you want me to wait in the car?" He asked.

"No," I said, "will you read it with me?" I asked him and he nodded, keeping his arms around me. I opened the journal back to the page I had marked and read it out loud.

*My Dearest Lyle,*

*I cannot begin to tell you how sorry I am for not being able to find the will to go on. I can't help but believe that you will be better off without your father and me. I hope that I am right in that belief. We have not lived the best life for ourselves and we certainly did not know how we could have done it better for you. Maybe that makes us terrible people, but it never, for one second, makes us love you any less. You were the greatest thing we ever could have possibly achieved and, even after your father passed, I knew I had to do everything I could to make sure you would be here. Over the past three months, I have dreamed more than I ever have in my entire life. My favorite dream has been about a woman with blonde hair. She and her husband had a son and they named him Lyle. I took it as a sign that it needed to be your name too and, now that you are here and I'm holding you, I know it was the right thing to do. I dreamt of that same couple night after night and, as crazy as it sounds, they turned into wolves and ran through the woods. I know that's impossible, but watching them in my dreams made me feel free and wonder what that might be like. I know you may never read this, and that's okay if you don't, but if by some small chance you do, I hope you get to feel that type of freedom in this world. This world has been a less than kind place to me, but I hope it is kinder to you. The only thing I want you to know is that we loved you with everything we had and that, if there is a heaven and we get to go there, we will always be watching over you. I must go now. You are getting a little hungry. Be good my love.*

*Love,*

*Your Mom, Ashley*

# Chapter Twenty-One

Chess and I had returned home to Seattle two weeks ago. We enlisted the help of Hunter and Phisher in trying to find out as much information about my parents as possible. We had updated Noah on their names and he was doing as much as he could to find out more about them. In the meantime, Chess and I were studying for finals and preparing to go back home for Spring Break. We had only grown closer and closer as the weeks ran by. He had asked me to stop sleeping at my place and I'd nearly completely moved into the loft with him. I'd asked him if we were officially living together yet and he said no, but that he didn't like nights where I wasn't there with him anymore. I thought it was cute. We continued to go on runs in the mountains where we had shared our first kiss and continued to kiss each other regularly. I still hadn't told him about the night I'd shifted, but I really wanted to. I just needed to find the right time.

We were on our way to meet Hunter and Phisher at the library on campus to see if they'd found out anything new about my parents when Jesse and Reese ran up behind us.

"Hey lovebirds!" Reese shouted as Jesse leapt and grabbed my shoulders. We knew they had been coming a ways off, but I was getting good at acting surprised.

"Hey y'all," I said, turning around and getting a big hug from Jesse.

"Where are you two going?" She asked.

"We're on our way to meet Hunter and Phisher," Chess said.

"Oh sweet, have they found out anything more about your mom and dad?" Jesse asked, looking at me. I hadn't told Chess that everyone knew about our new research project, but he played like he knew.

"That's actually what we are going to find out right now," Chess replied, looking over at me and smiling.

"Awesome! Can we join you?" she asked, looking over at Chess.

"Of course you can! We were just thinking of texting you to come too," he said with a hint of sarcasm. She did an exaggerated laugh at his comment and then grabbed Reese's hand.

"What are you two up to?" I asked them as we continued to walk toward the library.

"Scheming," Jesse responded. Chess gave me a side eye and a bit of a smile.

"Scheming?" I asked her, "for what?"

"For a triple movie date, silly," she said. "I've only been planning it with your boyfriend for a week now." Chess's small smile turned into a full grin.

"Oh, really?" I said, a little surprised.

"Yeah, I can't believe you didn't notice," she said.

"And just when were you going to tell me you were planning dates with my best friend now?" I asked Chess.

"I believe we just did," he said as he gave Jesse a high-five and they both laughed.

"Ok well, I definitely don't know if I like this," I said, turning around and pointing my finger back and forth between the two of them.

"I'm not sure you have much of a choice. Right Chess?" Jesse said, as she turned to look at him.

"Nope, not a ton," he said. I started laughing and rolled my eyes.

"You two are just too much," I said, as we continued to walk into the library. Phisher and Hunter were downstairs, sitting at a table toward the back of the library. They both had their computers open and were still searching for information when we arrived.

"Hey guys," I said as we all walked up to the table.

"Hey queens," Hunter replied as we pulled up chairs around the table.

"Anything yet?" I asked, sitting between Hunter and Chess.

"Actually, yeah," Phisher started as we all turned to look at him, "a couple of things." They stared up at each other and we waited for them to share. They continued to pause.

I looked back and forth between the two of them. "Well, what did you find out?" I asked eagerly.

"Well, your dad has a bit of a sordid history. No living relatives, several arrest records for possession and intent to distribute, traumatic childhood, dropped out of school to name a few," Phisher shared. The information didn't surprise me too much. From what I had learned from Carol and my mom's journal, it fit the image I had drafted in my head about him. "Also, when your parents got married, he took your mom's last name over his. His actual last name is Landon. We can't be sure why they chose that, but Larson is your mom's maiden name."

"What about my mom?" I asked.

Hunter chimed in, "Your mom is different. She has no arrest records or any negative records of any kind. She graduated from her high school in Massachusetts with honors and had been accepted into Salem State University. It looks like she met your father sometime between the two because she never went to the University." That frustrated me a bit. She had been having a good life before meeting him. Maybe if she never met him, she would still be alive, but then neither would I. "Also, it might be interesting to note that your mom was adopted at birth."

"She what?" I asked them.

"Her birth records show different parents. Her adoption records show they adopted her the day after she was born," Hunter added.

"So then, I could have family that's still alive?" I asked them, feeling slightly hopeful that there may be someone that could help fill in some of the missing pieces.

"No, I'm afraid not," Phisher said. "We looked into that too, but her biological parents' death records are from a week after she was born. They both died in a 'suspicious' car accident from the police report, but both deaths were ruled to be caused by the accident. It was filed as a hit and run. Her adoptive parents died a little less than a year ago. We couldn't find any other records about relatives in either her biological or adopted families." I was stunned.

*How could it be possible that they all were dead?* I looked around the table while everyone tried to assess how the news made me feel, and to make sure I was okay. In truth, I was not. I was furious that they were all dead, and that it really made me the last one alive in my family line.

"What was her birth name?" Chess asked.

"Oh, hold on one-second, I have it here," Hunter said sifting through a manilla folder that sat next to him, "Conri. Her birth name was Ashley Conri." I felt a shift in Chess's mood and I looked over at him. His affect looked the same and he showed no hint of the change, but I could sense it.

*What would her birth name have to do with anything?* I wondered to myself.

"There's more," Hunter said. "They own a house in Salem and they left the deed to their daughter and, with her gone, the house would go to Lyle." I remained silent and tried to sift out what Chess was thinking, but couldn't.

"Lyle, are you okay?" Jesse asked, finally breaking the small silence.

"Yeah," I lied, "I'm good. I'm not totally surprised. I mean, if I had any living relatives, I would have assumed the system would have found them and placed me with them instead of foster homes, right?" I had gotten better at masking some of the true feelings I had about things. "It was worth looking into though I think because at least now I know, right? Besides, if things hadn't happened the way they did, I may have never met any of you, and that would be more heart-breaking to think about than people I never knew."

I felt the mood lighten a little and Reese finally intervened, "well, I think that's enough of that then, right? Should we head to the movie theater?" He asked. Everyone agreed and stood as Phisher and Hunter put their things away. I grabbed Chess's hand and gave it a squeeze. He smiled at me and nodded. I knew there was more that needed to be discussed later, but it couldn't be shared with our friends. I wanted to know now rather than wait until we were alone again and it made me wish we could have included our friends into it so that they knew the truth. I knew it wouldn't matter to them, and that they wouldn't say anything, but I also made a promise to Noah and Chess that I wouldn't.

The movie date went well. We all really enjoyed the movie and I really loved watching Chess become better friends with everyone. Before all of this, he had been a lot more reserved with people and had mostly kept to himself. I was feeling eager to get back to the loft so that Chess could finally tell me what it was he had been holding in. I tried to text him and ask what was up, his only response was to talk about it later. I loved that about him, but it also drove me crazy. We had taken Phisher and Hunter home afterwards, and when we were finally in the car alone, I asked him.

"So, what's up?" I started, "clearly something they said struck a chord somehow. What was it?"

"You can't just relax for fifteen minutes until we get home, can you?" He teased and I crossed my arms. "Fine," he said, "the last name 'Conri' I have seen it noted somewhere before when I was an intern with the Union. I don't remember what it means though, we will need to call dad."

"Well, let's call him then," I said.

"Lyle, relax," he reached over and grabbed my hand, "we will call him when we get home. I know you are excited, but you have got to calm down a little."

"How can I calm down?" I asked. "It has been weeks since we've gotten anywhere and now we finally have something that could link back to the wolves. It's huge."

"I agree," he said, "all the more reason we aren't in a car driving when we call." I agreed, but the drive back to the loft felt like it took hours instead of minutes. When we arrived, a car was parked out front. "I may have already texted him," Chess admitted, parking behind Noah's vehicle. We went upstairs and sure enough, Noah and Jenn were both there waiting for us to get there.

"There you two are. We have been waiting for a while now," Noah said as Chess slid the door behind us shut.

"Sorry we were at a prior commitment that we couldn't get out of," Chess explained as we walked toward and sat down on the sofa.

"What did you two find out?" Jenn asked.

"Well, our friends have been doing some digging to help me find if I have any family left alive, and it turns out that my mother was adopted a few days after being born, and her biological parents died in a car accident a little less than a week later," I told them, "But Chess said that there's a connection between their last name and the Union."

"What's the name?" Noah asked.

"Conri," Chess said, "the last name is Conri." Both Jenn's and Noah's expressions changed and the feeling in the room grew tense.

"What, what does it mean?" I asked.

"Lyle," Noah said, "Conri is a term used by the Union when referring to the highest position in our order. It's a very old name and we believe it to be the name of the first pack."

"It means King Wolf." Jenn added.

"A member of the Dubois Pack was sentenced to death many years ago over killing a human family with the last name and saying they were descendants of the first wolves. We all thought it was nonsense, of course, and he endured the ultimate penalty for taking human life." Noah shared.

"The Dubois pack are the worst of us," Jenn added, "they are sneaky, bloodthirsty, and power-hungry beasts. Their alpha Gerard is the worst among them."

"So, you're saying that there's definitely a possibility that the mad wolf could have been, right?" Chess asked.

"I think there's a very good chance of that, but it makes little sense." Noah paused. "Werewolves don't just stop being werewolves. There is no way a descendant could have survived and just couldn't have been a wolf."

"Unless," Chess said, looking at me.

"Unless, what?" Noah asked.

"Lyle, you told me in your vision that night you saw John continue to run with their son into the woods." Chess started.

"I did."

"What if, and I'm just saying what if, he got their son out to someone who could have suppressed it," he paused, and the tension in the room intensified, "what if he went to a witch?"

"There's no way," Noah said immediately. "a wolf would never turn to a witch for help. They are serpents, tricksters, and their magic only helps themselves. Even if a wolf had, they would have never agreed to help a wolf."

"I know, I'm just saying what if he did?" Chess repeated.

"Even then, there's not a witch alive today that would possess enough power to do that to a wolf." Jenn said.

"That we know of," Chess continued, "their records and histories far extend our own and didn't we fasten ourselves in the same fashion as they had to collect our own history?"

"We did." Noah agreed.

"Then it would be possible." Chess said. "What better way to protect his bloodline than to suppress it under everyone's noses than to make him human?"

"We'd need proof." Noah added, and a long silence took hold over everyone. I sat and remained in disbelief.

"There's a house," I shared, breaking the silence.

"What?" Noah asked.

"My mother's parents, they left their house and property to her, but I guess it's mine now," I said.

"What does that have to do with anything?" Chess added.

"I would like to go there. Maybe there is something there. Maybe they knew something," I said.

"Lyle," Chess said, "that's not possible."

"Why not?" I asked.

"The house is in the center of Dubois territory. We would never be able to get there undetected by their pack, and if we tried, we'd be breaking the law." Chess said.

"The laws have already been broken." Noah added. "Lyle is right. The two of you need to go to Salem and go to this house. I will make the arrangements to ensure the lawyers in possession of the deed know to meet you to claim it."

"Dad, how are we going to get in undetected?" Chess asked.

"Keep a low profile and mask your scents as much as you can. It will be difficult, but it can be done. No one knows about Lyle yet and that is an advantage. If anyone asks, Lyle is a client we are assisting with claiming his family home and, if you keep your scents covered, they won't know he's a wolf," Noah said.

"Noah, this is extremely dangerous," Jenn added. "If the Union or the Dubois suspect anything, we could all be in danger. That is even if the Dubois let them live if they are discovered."

"Oh, they'll let him live." Noah added. "Gerard wants Chess to mate with one of his daughters. He would not risk losing the potential match by killing him off."

"So, Salem, then?" Chess asked.

Noah responded, "Yes, boys. Salem."

# Chapter Twenty-Two

We landed in Salem on a Monday morning only a few days after our meeting with Noah and Jenn. Noah had arranged for us to meet with the estate lawyer mid-morning the next day. As we took a taxi from the airport to our hotel, I noticed that the beauty and history of this place was breath-taking. Spring had just begun and the trees were bright and green, so different from back home in Seattle. We arrived at a small hotel that looked like it had seen better days. Chess told me that our accommodations would be less than humble to help prevent discovery while we were here. Our directions were to get in, look around for anything that might aid in finding out the truth of my parentage, and then get out. We spent the first night ordering pizza and watching some basic cable TV in the hotel room. Chess had booked the room for two beds instead of just one, just in case we attracted unwanted visitors, but we had no intention of ever getting into the other bed. The next morning, we woke up and ordered another taxi to take us to our meeting with the estate lawyer at the house. Before leaving, we nearly drowned ourselves in enough cologne to make us sick in an effort to mask our scent, but this also had the unwanted effect of making our taxi driver less than enthusiastic about having us in his vehicle. After an awkwardly quiet drive, we finally pulled up to the house and stepped out of the taxi onto the pavement.

"It's beautiful," I said, staring up at the old colonial style home. The house's facade was red brick with white trim accenting the front door and windows. Some of the paint had peeled and the yard looked like it had needed some tending, but overall, the magnificent giant of a home stood tall and proud. The black iron gate hadn't yet been unlocked, so we stood impatiently on the sidewalk gazing through the gate toward the house that I hoped held the keys to my past and waited for the lawyer to arrive.

"It really is something," Chess said, agreeing with me.

"I never expected the estate to look like this or had any thought that they came from the type of money that could afford a place like this," I said. "Why would they have given my mother up for adoption?" I asked quietly.

"They must have suspected something bad was going to happen," he responded. "It's unlikely that the Dubois would just kill them without first stalking and trying to find out more information about them," he added and I realized he was right, they had probably done it in an attempt to safeguard her.

"You're probably right," I said, continuing to look at the house in awe. We waited for a few minutes longer when a small black Prius pulled up to the curb and a short older man emerged with a briefcase from the driver's side of the car.

"Mr. Conri and Mr. Beck, I presume?" He asked, approaching us. He wore a dark gray suit and had thin metal framed glasses, which he adjusted before offering his hand to shake ours.

"Yes, I'm Mr. Beck and this is our client, Mr. Conri," Chess pushed his hand forward and into the man's and shook it firmly.

"Ah, yes, of course," the man said, "I'm Mr. Farley."

I followed suit, albeit with a less firm shake, and said, "Nice to meet you, Mr. Farley."

"Well, seems like we should get to it," he said as he opened his briefcase and pulled out a set of keys. He slipped the smallest key in the lock chained to the front gate and had some trouble getting it to turn and set the locking mechanism free. After a few jangles and a swift shake the lock popped, he pulled it through the now loosened chain, opened the gate, and walked inside, gesturing for us to follow. As we walked he began to tell us about the home, the first part of the house had been built in the early 1800s. He said that it had been expanded to become the house we saw in front of us closer to the end of the same century. The house in its current state had eight bedrooms, four bathrooms, a conservatory off the kitchen, and many other unique features that were uncommon for the time the home was built.

We walked up to the front door and Mr. Farley handed me the set of keys. "Might as well let you open this beauty seeing as she is yours," he said and waved toward the imposing double door entrance of the home. I looked down at the keys in my hand.

*Mine?!?* I thought. I'd never thought about having a family home, let alone owning it and it all felt incredibly surreal. I pulled aside the key that Mr. Farley indicated would fit into the brass deadbolt and slid it into the keyhole. Turning it to the side I could feel the mechanism release, it's tooling fitting into the notches in the key like fingers in a glove. The deadbolt clicked back into place, unlocking what could be the only door standing between me and my past, I reached down and  touched the knob. Suddenly, I felt a strange peace as a small chill kissed my cheek. I looked over to Chess who appeared to feel nothing, standing unperturbed and waiting to head inside. I rubbed at the spot on my cheek where the cool sensation had occurred and walked into the house with Chess and Mr. Farley following behind.

It was nothing like I had ever seen before. Walking into the open foyer of the home's entryway I could see that there were dark wooden floors spanning the entirety of the lower level. The dark wood was accented by ivory-colored walls, which were themselves framed out in ornate molding. They had neatly covered all the original furnishings with white sheets in every room. It was apparent that no one had been in the home for some time as a small layer of dust could be seen covering the floors and surrounding surfaces.

"If you two would follow me into the kitchen, I have a few forms for Mr. Conri to sign and then the house is all yours," Mr. Farley said.

"Certainly," Chess replied, gesturing for me to follow him with one hand. We walked into a room to the left and then followed a corridor past several closed doors, ending our journey in the kitchen. The kitchen was, unsurprisingly, equally as stunning as the entryway with exposed brick walls and black iron fixtures. Someone must have updated it before my mother's family's deaths and it was easily seen that no expense was spared.

Mr. Farley rested his briefcase on the counter and withdrew several documents. He reorganized and ordered them and then pulled out a pen which he handed to me. He had me initial and sign several places on each page with Chess carefully examining each page to ensure everything was being handled correctly. Mr. Farley took the pages and placed them back into his briefcase withdrawing two envelopes which he then passed to me.

"What are these?" I asked him, taking the envelopes.

"The first is the deed to the house and the final balance of all the late Conri's estates that have been accumulating interest over the last few years. I already provided details to Mr. Beck's office on how to transfer future funds into a bank account under your name. The other accounts have been liquidated," Mr. Farley explained.

"Thank you, Mr. Farley," Chess said, as he closed his briefcase.

"Well, gentlemen, if there isn't anything else, I will be on my way," Mr. Farley said.

Chess thanked him and walked him back to the front door. I stayed in the kitchen and opened both envelopes. The first, like he'd said, held the original deed to the house and surrounding property. I opened the second envelope and pulled out a cashier's check for five hundred million dollars. I'd nearly fainted before Chess must have sensed it, returning to me just in time to steady my descent to the floor. I looked over at him and realized that he didn't seem nearly as surprised as I was.

"Did you know about all of this?" I asked him.

"Yes," he explained, "when Dad reached out, we found out that it wasn't just the house and that there was so much more to the Conri family than this building alone. I thought it would be a pleasant surprise for you."

"Wha...," I started, staring blankly at him, the check, and the house, "How is all this possible?"

"Lyle, your family owns most of the land that this town is built on. The town pays the Conri estate for being built on their land," Chess explained.

"How is that even possible?" I asked in disbelief. He shrugged his shoulders and sat down on a stool nearby. It took a moment for all of it to settle in before I was able to return to the task at hand.

"Where should we begin?" I asked, after having had a few minutes to clear my head. Chess suggested we start upstairs. We found most of the bedrooms had been cleaned out with the exception of the furnishings that sat covered in white sheets mimicking the scene from the rooms we had seen downstairs. The dressers had all been emptied and the end tables were the same. Returning to the first floor we found an office space, but every drawer had been emptied as well. We continued walking through the empty hallways, rooms, and furniture hoping to stumble on something to no success. When we'd finally finished searching the larger portions of the house we descended the staircase into the cellar below the kitchen. We walked down the small wooden staircase into the darkness, as our bodies dipped below the plane of the first level of the home we realized that the stairs opened into a vast space that was lined with wooden shelves that were empty except for strings of cobwebs and thick layers of dust. The walls of the cellar were lined with brick and the room was dimly lit. We walked along one side of the cellar against the brick walls and I felt the wisp of coolness touch my cheek again. It was much cooler than before and it startled me slightly.

"What's wrong?" Chess asked, turning around.

"Nothing," I said, "just a cool rush on the side of my face. It happened when we were at the front door and it just began again down here," I explained to him.

"That's not nothing," he said before I felt a small growl expand in his chest.

"What is it then?" I asked him.

"It's witchcraft," he growled again. "There must be a spell here that only you can sense. Try to feel where it is the coolest and touch it," he said cautiously.

I followed along the wall, trying to feel for the temperature change again. As I neared the back of the cellar, I felt a rush of a cool blow against my hand into my face again. I reached out toward the wall and my hand pushed through.

"It's an illusion spell," Chess said, walking up and touching the brick where my hand had passed through, "and a strong one too. It looks like only members of your family can cross it."

I pulled my hand back through and looked at him. "What do you think is behind it?" I asked.

"I don't know, but it looks like only you can find out," he said, shrugging his shoulders.

I put my hand back up to the brick and it passed through again with ease. "I'll be right back," I said, looking at him anxiously. He nodded and I took a step through the wall. As I did, the breeze that had kissed my cheek, passed through my entire body, and I found myself in a smaller room on the other side of the brick wall. I turned around and could see Chess standing on the other side of the brick. It was clear he couldn't see me, but the dim lights of the cellar helped to illuminate the tiny room I had stepped into. It didn't look like anybody had been in this room for a much longer period of time than only the limited time since my grandparents had died. It was dark and the remnants of a candle and some old matches were sitting on a table. The furniture was all made of wood, it was much older than anything we had seen upstairs. There was a desk with a large leather book on top and to the right there was another small wooden door. I leafed through the book carefully, finding a catalog of names with birthdates, death dates, and locations written next to the names across the page. All the last names read as Conri. As I scanned the names, I was surprised by how many of them had died young. The last entry was dated in 1810, Sebastian Conri, Born January 9, 1810. There was no death date listed. *This must have been when the family stopped tracking,* I thought quietly.

I closed the book and opened the small door which I found led to another room with old papers and diagrams hanging all over the walls. There were drawings of human and wolf anatomy, notes, and papers that were written in a language I couldn't understand. On another table, a smaller leather notebook sat next to what appeared to be the remnants of a quill and a small glass jar that had once held ink. I opened the notebook and on the first page it read, "This journal is the property of Lyle Conri". I couldn't believe it. I turned to the next page and there was the first entry, it had been dated for June 1693. I was shocked.

*Could this really be him? The baby that was born in my dreams? This was his journal?* My thoughts raced as I flipped through the pages. In most of his notes, he wrote about searching for a way to break a curse and how he had been unsuccessful in his quest. He wrote about building the house on the site where his family had been massacred and reclaiming the land that had been stolen from them. Reading through the journal I realized that his earlier entries were much more coherent and, the further through the journal I went and the more time that had passed, his writing and thoughts appeared much more scrambled and unclear. I looked through the images on the walls and my eyes watered as I realized he'd been looking for a way to become a wolf again and that he had failed. He'd spent his life trying to regain a connection that had been severed and taken from him. It had driven him crazy, his never ending pursuit of his lost wolf and the need to break the curse that had taken it from him. Scanning the room with what little light I had, I found a small portrait that hung on the wall. The painting showed a family of three. I assumed it must have been Lyle and his family. He had a wife and a son, but never talked about them in his journal. It looked like his  mission had been to regain the connection to his wolf and it made me sad for him. Sad for all of my ancestors that had lived their lives not knowing who they really were and potentially not even knowing that a part of them was missing. I wept quietly thinking of their pain.

"Lyle?" Chess called out in a hard whisper. I wiped my eyes and put the book back down on the table.

"Lyle?!" He said again with much more urgency. I left the room and looked through the doorway as he knelt with his back against the wall and looked toward the ceiling. He was growling slowly, and the hair on the back of his neck raised. I blew out the candle and walked back through the doorway.

"What's wrong?" I whispered.

"We have company." He hushed back and, as he did, I heard a footstep land on the floor above us. I could smell them from here. They were wolves and there were several of them.

We listened carefully and, somehow, I could make out five figures standing in the kitchen overhead. I could see an outline of their scent trailing off them through the floorboards. Chess looked over at me, "What is it?" he whispered.

"There are five of them. I can see them through the floor" I whispered back. He nodded his head.

"You can come up now," a voice called from the kitchen, "no one here is going to hurt you."

Chess growled again. "Stay behind me," he instructed firmly as we made our way down the cellar wall and back toward the stairs. As we walked up the stairs and entered the kitchen five wolves were standing exactly as I'd seen them.

"I have to say," said a man washing his hands in the sink, "it was quite rude of you and your father to not let us know you were coming. We would have been more than happy to accommodate you and your guest for your time in Salem." His words came out smooth and raspy. He was young, probably around the same age as Chess, with thick black hair and dark eyes to match. He was smaller than Chess and I, skinnier too. I looked at his hands as he washed them in the sink and watched as the red blood fell from his hands into the drain. He looked up and smiled at me with a wink. His features were very sharp and narrow.

"What do you want, Lucas?" Chess asked, sounding furious.

"I don't want anything from you Chess," he shook off his hands into the sink and turned toward us, "my father on the other hand would love for you to join us for a meal this evening." He said, smiling menacingly.

"Fine, but I would like to take my client back to our hotel first," Chess said.

"Chess, Chess, Chess," Lucas stated and waved his finger, "you should know better than to think that we wouldn't find out about your little wolf pal here." He looked directly at me and said, "you really should have done without so much cologne to save us all the burnt nostrils, your scent is far more pungent than anything you could ever try to cover it up with." He chuckled to himself and looked back at Chess, "You'll come with us now or we could make you. Kind of a 'choose your own adventure' I guess." He snickered and I felt a growl instinctively grow in my chest. As the growl became audible I was surprised to see the other wolves behind Lucas react with a hint of hesitation.

"My, my you are a ferocious little thing aren't you," Lucas replied dubiously.

"Lyle, that's enough," Chess instructed. I tried to back down, but the wolf inside me stayed on high alert. I felt my eyes itch and, as they did, I could see the other wolf's arteries pulse and their veins glow, starting from their hearts and moving throughout their bodies' forming a network. As their arteries pulsed rhythmically they glowed bright and I knew some sense inside me was providing me with markers, showing me where I could tear into them and rip them out of this life in seconds if I'd wanted to. Chess must have sensed me tensing and he grabbed my hand. I looked down to see that I had instinctively started to shift and that my claws had grown outward from my fingers into sharp points as a preparation to strike.

"My, what big eyes you have," Lucas said, laughing like a hyena and finding himself very funny. Chess looked back at me and in the reflection of his eyes I could see that mine had shifted, the flecks of green glowing and expanding into the blue. In Chess' eyes they glowed, reflecting back at me.

"Relax," Chess whispered. Lucas clapped his hand loudly as I closed my eyes and felt the green retreat into the small flecks it had been before.

"What a marvel your little pet wolf is Chess. Tell me, where did you find him?" Lucas asked.

"Let's just go," Chess stated, angered.

"Fine. Fine. Keep your secret for now. It will all come to the light soon enough," Lucas said as he danced past the others and down the hallway toward the front door. Chess followed and I stayed close behind him. The four other wolves stayed close behind me, ready for us to run or to try and attack. We walked out the front door and the scent of blood filled the air. I followed the scent trail in my mind to Mr. Farley's car, still parked out front. In the back of the trunk, I could see a dead body stored and the blood continuing to pool around him as I visualized the figure through the metal. We continued walking toward the car and Chess pieced together what I just had and stared at the trunk. "Ah, yes. Well, I am afraid dear Mr. Farley remains as useless as ever." Lucas shared carelessly, "Ignoring our attempts to buy this dump over the years and then he didn't even have the courtesy of telling us once the owner had been found. What a waste." Lucas smiled again before opening the rear door of Mr. Farley's car and instructing me to climb in. Chess nodded and I climbed into the back. Before Chess could climb in, Lucas took the empty seat next to me, "Oh dear, I guess there is no more room in this car Chess. You will have to take the other car." He shut the door and two of the other wolves climbed into the front seats. I watched closely as Chess walked to the car Lucas and his cronies had brought. Chess climbed into the back with one wolf and another took the driver's seat.

"So, little wolf," Lucas said, putting his arm over my shoulder, "where have the Becks been hiding a handsome little devil like yourself all this time?"

I growled instinctively and he removed his arm. *Good, glad to know he is not a complete idiot,* I thought to myself. He had minimal tells, but he had a healthy sensibility for doing what was needed to stay alive. "I haven't been hiding." I said, both angered and annoyed at their imposition on our time and their disrespect for the Beck's pack.

"Oh, but you have Lyle. You have been hiding for a very, very long time," he said, laughing again. Lucas continued to talk, asking questions about me, my life, and about Chess and the Becks. I ignored him and stared out the window. I could sense Chess, if I focused, but the cackling of the hyena next to me made it difficult. Chess was scared and angry, but he was holding it together. I tried to push back to him that I was fine, but I was unsure if he would be able to feel it. Lucas put his hand on my thigh as he said something else I intended to tune out and, as he did, I felt my eyes glow and I turned my face toward him, growling harder than I ever had. His pulse quickened, his arteries glowing brighter with the adrenaline my reaction had triggered in his system.

"Apologies, little wolf," he said. "It's not every day that you get to sit next to a prince, though, is it?" He smiled his disgustingly smug grin at me again and I wanted to vomit. He continued drolling on about how amazed I was going to be at their chateau and how I was a guest of honor to them. He assured me that I would be treated much better than I had been in the company of the Becks and, as he continued, we pulled into a private driveway in an area that I realized was far outside the city limits. The driveway wound up a hill toward what could only be called a mansion that was too grandiose for its own good. A large fountain made of black-and-white marble that matched the marble columns that lined the front of the chateau stood at the center of the circular driveway. The cars parked in front of the marble steps at the entrance of the home and, standing at the top of the stairs were an older man, a woman, and two girls similar in age to Lucas.

Lucas opened the door and climbed out first. He reached out his hand for mine and I climbed out of the car, rejecting his assistance. One of the wolves that drove Chess opened the back door of their car and Chess climbed out of the back seat. I instinctively moved to stand next to him before Lucas put his hand on my chest, stopping me from doing so. The older wolf descended the stairs toward us, smiling. He had sharp features that were similar to Lucas' and it seemed grossly clear that this was the great Gerard I had heard so much about from the Becks. He didn't look like much, but from what Noah and Chess had explained, he was one of the most dangerous wolves in the Union.

"Aw, Chess, Lyle, thank you so much for joining us. I am so glad to have heard about your arrival in Salem," he said smiling at me. He turned to Chess before letting his smile diminish. "Of course, I would rather have known you were coming so that proper arrangements could have been made, but, all the same you are here now, which is what matters most, I suppose. Come now, let's head inside."

I followed Chess's lead and walked toward the front door, following Gerard. "May I have the honor of introducing my wife, Dahlia?" Gerard said as the woman curtsied politely. She may as well have been growling and lashing out for our throats. She was by far the scariest looking wolf present. She was equally as pretty as she was terrifying and had long black hair that laid straight against the edges of her face.

"Please, meet my two daughters, Angelica and Angelene. Both took after their mother with their looks and equally upsetting demeanors. And, of course, you both have already met my son, Lucas," said Gerard as Lucas continued to follow behind me at a distance that was too close for comfort. I could feel Lucas' eyes on me and I shifted uncomfortably at the attention.

"Welcome to our home." Dahlia said.

I imagined that if thorns on a rose could speak they would have sounded very similar. It was exquisite, but also had a dangerous ferocity to it. My eyes hadn't stopped glowing and I could still subtly see every heartbeat and vein of everyone present.

We walked into the foyer and I was able to take in more of the grotesquely expansive and gaudily decorated palace they called home. As we paused in the foyer for a moment, Gerard approached me and spoke, "my dear boy, it's one thing to be entering into the home of another wolf reeking of that awful manmade stench, but it is just vulgar of you to be tracing our arteries every second like you are. You are a welcome guest here and I would very much appreciate it if you would stop shining your eyes at my family." I took a step back with surprise that he knew exactly what I was doing and also that he knew what I could do. Chess looked at me surprised as well, maybe not knowing the skill I had found, but also with the knowledge that Gerard knew.

"Being a guest would imply that we would be free to leave if we chose and I feel that Chess and I are not free to do so," I said in reply, dimming the shine in my eyes as he'd requested.

He smiled at me, "I suppose you are correct, but it would be quite rude of you both to leave before having dinner and before we have the opportunity to get to know one another. It is not every day an extinct bloodline re-emerges and I would think that you may want to get to know every pack your great family created, not just the Becks. After all, your ancestors choose each of our packs at one point or another for a reason."

I wasn't sure how he knew as much as he did, but it put me on edge to think of all the knowledge he possessed that others didn't know. "Very well," I said graciously, "thank you for having us in your home."

"Now, that's much better," Gerard said, grinning ear to ear. "I have a request, if you both wouldn't mind," he started, "please go upstairs and wash that awful smell off you. We will have fresh clothes provided for you both to change into for dinner."

Chess continued to keep quiet. "Very well," I stated, "may I then request that my friend and I be allowed to use the same chambers, I would very much like a word with him in private since we have not been afforded that opportunity since meeting your son. Since we are guests, I would not think that would be too much to ask."

"Indeed, granted." Gerard stated, nodding at my request.

"But fath...." Lucas spoke up to protest, but with a wave of his hand, the rest of the wolves backed off.

"My daughters will show you both to your room. May their behavior be far more hospitable than my sons," Gerard said, motioning the girls forward. "We will send a human for you when dinner is ready."

We followed the girls up the stairs and down another corridor. They were both very cordial and polite as they led us through the hallways of their massive home.

"We apologize for the gruffness of our brother," Angelica said as we walked further along.

"He's well," Angelene started, "malleable... soft." The two of them laughed a little as they teased their brother at his own expense.

"We all are, in fact, quite glad to finally meet you both," they shared. "Father has been working quite hard on arranging our meetings, Chess," Angelica shared

"Well, yes, it is true. However, he has been far more excited with the knowledge of you, Conri boy, over Chess I mean," Angelene shared.

"Why is that?" I asked before Chess grabbed at my wrist and encouraged me to not take part in the conversation.

"Well, it's one thing to be mated to the next alpha of the Beck pack," Angelene started. "It's another to be mated to the next king of our kind" Angelica finished and they both stopped, looking me up and down uncomfortably.

"Here is your room, boys," Angelene said, pushing open a door and gesturing for us to walk inside. There was a king size bed with two suits laid out over the comforter. *Was there no room in this house that was not just as gaudy as the rest of it?* I wondered silently as I looked around the room that was decorated in a sort of classless opulence, just as the rest of the house had been. "A human will be along shortly to escort you back to dinner," Angelene said, closing the door slowly behind us. I turned around and could sense waves coming off the door and a scent that burned, so I backed further away from it.

"It's wolfsbane." Chess admitted as I backed into him.

I turned around and looked at him, "what the hell Chess, you didn't say anything."

"They had no interest in talking to me," he admitted. "you're the prize they want to please this evening. I am surprised they let us come up here together."

"I'm no one's prize," I scoffed. "We need to find a way out of here." I stated.

"Oh, they'll let us go when they're ready," Chess said blatantly. "If they knew who you are and wanted you dead, they would have killed us at your family's home, but it appears they have other hopes for you."

"Yeah and I can guess what that is too, gross," I said. He was acting defeated and his demeanor was upsetting. "Chess, what's wrong?"

"It may be better for you to hear him out rather than to fight it. If they want to instate you as the king of our kind, that would be better than them wanting you dead," he said.

"What the hell are you talking about?" I asked him, a little pissed off. "I don't want to be the king of anything. I just want to be with you." I grabbed him by the shoulders. "We need to find a way out of this and we need to get back to Seattle. Do you understand me? There is no way I am going to end up stuck here in this scary hell den of wolves. Get your game face on and play the damn game alpha boy.

I need you." He looked frazzled a bit, but he started to snap out of it. He wrapped his arms around me tightly and pulled me into him.

"You're right. I'm sorry," he said with his face pushed into my shoulder.

He pulled away and I grabbed his face. "Good. Now let's rinse off and change into these ugly suits before they come back." Chess nodded and we headed for the bathroom to wash up.

Just as we'd finished putting on the suit jackets, we heard a small knock on the door. "Come in," Chess said.

A skinny man entered the room, looking scared and hesitant. "You can come in," I said. "It's okay." He stood dressed in a butler's uniform and asked us to follow him to dinner. I didn't understand how the Dubois could have a human working for them, he seemed scared out of his wits, and if it was illegal for us to disclose what we were to humans, it seemed out of place. I felt bad for the man. He had clearly been abused judging by his demeanor and I felt an urge to protect him somehow. I knew, however, that there was very little I could do to help him given our current situation. We followed him down into the foyer before he stopped outside a set of large double doors. The doors cracked open and another human, who stood inside the room, asked our names. We gave them to him and he opened the door for us to enter. As we did, he announced our arrival to a packed dining hall which was much more than I had been expecting. The room was filled with wolves and due to the similarity in their features I figured that they all must be the extended family of the Dubois pack. Gerard came forward and wrapped his arms around each of us, providing us with a small polite embrace. It appeared he envisioned himself as a royal of sorts amongst the wolves and was fully committed to playing the role. He paraded us around the large dining table, introducing us to his siblings, uncles, and cousins. He took particular attention in mentioning who and what I was - making it known to all that I was the last red wolf. As he introduced me to everyone in attendance along with the title he had bestowed upon me, some reacted with eyes wide open in surprise, quickly exchanging glances and murmurs at the table with their neighbors, others still seemed to  doubt his claim as he continued his introductions, making me publicly known to everyone in attendance. I politely whispered to him I would prefer to remain discreet, but he took no notice and continued on in the fashion of his own choosing. After Gerard was satisfied with his theatrics, he announced to the human waitstaff stationed around the room that dinner would now begin. Gerard escorted us to the head of the table and gestured for us to sit in the two seats next to him on the right, a position I had learned from the Becks was significant. I expected Dahlia to sit to his left, as Emily would have with Noah. The seat, however, remained empty with Dahlia sitting with one empty chair between her and her husband. I thought that was odd and I looked at Chess as the rest of the pack took their seats around the table.

As I stared into Chess's eyes, a scent filled my nose, and it was like nothing I had ever experienced. It smelled like spice and electricity. It was pleasant to me, but I could tell from everyone else's disgusted reactions that this was not the common experience and the other wolves appeared to actually be repulsed by the odor,  Itching their noses and acting as if the scent burned them. Everyone turned toward the double doors and the human attendant opened them, announcing the presence of a newcomer.

"Announcing Mistress Willow Foster." He opened the doors and,  as he did, a woman with flowing, dark brown hair entered the room. She was the most beautiful woman I had ever seen. Her fair skin and delicate features far outshined any other woman in the room. Her skin seemed to shimmer with light that sparkled from within. Her large, doe-like eyes were a hazel green and her cheek had a natural blush. She looked otherworldly to me, the smell of spice and electricity hummed inside of me. Her eyes locked with mine and she watched me carefully as she descended into the room. I leaned into Chess, "Why is she glowing like that?" I whispered.

"She's not glowing, Lyle, she's just a witch," he whispered back unimpressed. Her eyes never left me as she floated around the table, past a bunch of wolves who were clearly disturbed by her presence. Unflustered, she made her way to the chair to the left of Gerard and he stood to embrace her.

"Willow, thank you so much for agreeing to attend," he said to her, her eyes still fixated on mine.

"Of course, my dear Gerard. How could I refuse when you promised such exciting house guests?" As she spoke her voice rang out through the air. The wolves around the table appeared as if the sound hurt their ears, like a dog whistle being blown too loud, but her voice sounded light and airy to me — like a breeze blowing in the forest. I didn't wince as she spoke, as the rest of them did, and at my stillness her expression changed, her gaze growing curious as she looked at me with intrigue. "Is this him?" she asked, gesturing toward me.

"Yes," Gerard turned toward me and gestured for me to stand. "Willow, may I introduce Lyle Conri?"

I bowed slightly, regarding her. I didn't understand why all the other wolves winced away from her. She was ethereal and bright. I felt no fear in her presence and found her to be  calming. "Lyle?" she raised her brow slightly before nodding at me.

"Gerard," she laughed, "are you sure this is a true Conri and not some great pretender?"

"I assure you, mistress, he truly is a Conri. I am not sure how it happened, but it's him," he said musing excitedly as he pulled out the chair for her to sit.

"Well, well," she said, "I'm sure we will all have many questions for him then won't we." She smiled, finally breaking her eye contact with me, and turned to look at Gerard, "but that's for another time. I am absolutely famished, Gerard. Will dinner be served soon?" She asked.

Gerard waved his arm and as he did humans emerged from another door bringing in silver covered plates like we were at some medieval dinner party. As they set the plates in front of us, I heard a humming inside my head and I pushed back against it. The silver covers were lifted and steam rose from the food inside. Large T-Bone steaks had been freshly prepared for all in attendance. The humming continued and through the steam of the plates I could see that Willow was staring at me with a sense of urgency.

*Lyle? Lyle? Can you hear me?* It was her. She was speaking to me inside of my head.

*Yes,* I thought back.

*Good, listen to me. You and your friend are in great danger. If you want to save his life, you are going to have to do everything I say and you are going to have to trust me. Can you do that?*

*Who are you?* I thought back to her.

*Someone who places the value of your life above all else, but I can also clearly see the bonds strung between the two of you. So, if you value his life, please trust me.* Her voice rang clear as day in my head now.

*What do I need to do?* I thought back to her.

*Agree with everything Gerard says, he will ask you to stay here for the night. Agree. He won't let you two return to the same room this evening. Agree. Once this ordeal of a dinner is over, I will come for both of you. Be ready.*

*Okay. I will. Are you speaking to Chess too, does he know?* I thought to her, taking a bite of my meal and smiling at Gerard as we continued to speak privately.

*He won't let me in, he doesn't trust me. They will hurt him, but if you agree with Gerard and go along with what he says, they won't kill him.* My throat went dry at the thought of Chess being hurt, and my wolf grew restless in my chest. *Calm down, wolf, or you will give us away!* She smiled and politely engaged in small talk with Dahlia as the dinner went on. *Send him a message through your bond. He won't hear you like this, but he will sense it. Do it now. Gerard is about to start.*

I pushed with all of my might out to Chess to tell him to trust me and to trust Willow. I pleaded with him to not fight and to just follow my lead. I pushed out through the bonds I could feel between us and begged for him to hear me. He moved slightly and his knee rubbed mine. Relief washed over me just as Gerard stood to speak.

"I would like to make a toast," Gerard said as he raised his glass, "for too long we have been without our King. Tonight, our Prince returns to us after being taken away for too long. He will join our house and become the next alpha of our pack." The other wolves cheered, "he will choose one of our daughters as his mate," he said, gesturing toward Angelica and Angelene. The wolves cheered louder than before. "With his help we will take our rightful place above the humans, announce ourselves to the world, and will usher in the next generation of red wolves. A generation which will descend from the Dubois pack line" The other wolves became rowdy, clanking glasses, banging at the table, howling, and cheering at his announcement.

Gerard turned to me. "Lyle, please stand." I looked over at Willow and back at Chess in panic. I rose as he had asked. The rest of the wolves grew silent, a pit began to grow in my stomach.

"Will you take your rightful place within our pack, call yourself my son, and take one of my daughters as your mate?" He asked as I looked around, panicked. I had hoped this was not what Willow had asked me to agree to.

*Did she know he was planning this?* I began to search the room as the rest of the wolves waited eagerly for me to respond. I looked at Chess, who was just as frazzled as I was, and the fear in his eyes grew as I sensed that this was the moment he believed he might lose me. I knew Willow had told me to agree, but looking into Chess's eyes, I knew I couldn't. The next words I spoke would matter the most to Chess and to me and, in the end, there was no other choice.

"I..." I looked around the room again, Willow's face pleading to agree, Chess waiting to have his heart broken, and I murmured, "I can't." The words just fell out and I could see Chess' eyes flow with tears of relief.

"What do you mean you can't?" Gerard said, slamming his palms on the table, his eyes wide and his face clearly angered.

"I have been claimed as a son to another pack and I accepted. If I am to be a wolf of my word, I cannot break that bond even in place of another offer such as your own." I tried to steady the waters before this situation turned into a storm.

"Who do you think I am?" Gerard said, "I don't give a damn what you've promised another pack. I will have you in this pack and I don't care how long it takes for you to decide to do it." The wolves flew into a furry, some started shifting before snarling and biting toward us. I jumped back from the table and Chess followed. I was ready for an attack and my eyes grew brightly awaiting whomever made the mistake to move too close. Every living thing in the room turned into nothing more than a buzzing hum of veins and heart beats as I focused in on those who threatened Chess and myself. My teeth grew longer and I felt my fangs emerge as, simultaneously, claws grew from my fingertips. Just before I launched into an attack, a bright light from across the room flashed and I felt myself fall to the ground, everything fading to black.

# Chapter Twenty-Three

I woke up what felt like moments later and found myself tied to a bed. I looked around the room and found that I was back where Chess and I had gotten ready for dinner. My head was pounding and my skin was burned. I pulled against one of my restraints as Gerard walked into the room.

"Oh, you're awake," he said, walking up next to the bed, "Lyle, Lyle, Lyle, I had hoped we could be more civilized about all of this." He sauntered closer. "I will see my pack rise to the position it rightfully deserves. My ancestors and I have followed your family line for centuries, waiting for a wolf to re-emerge, but, for whatever reason, your line was all human. We did everything we could to keep your family our little secret, and, until I became alpha, we kept them under surveillance but stayed out of their affairs." He leaned in close to my face hovering over me and he rubbed his hands against my chest. It burned. I looked down toward his hand and realized I was shirtless. He took a deep breath taking in my scent, shuddering as he did. "I knew your family needed interactions with wolves to remind you of what you were. So, when I approached your grandparents about arranging my marriage to their daughter, they panicked. What

I didn't know was that after I left, they rushed to get the baby as far away from me as possible. When I was finally able to track her down, I sent one of my cousins to retrieve her and to kill her husband, but the idiot botched the job and he told me, before his untimely death, that he'd ended up killing them both," he winced at the thought of losing my mother, "I truly believed that both of them had died in that car accident." His eyes started pooling with tears at the corners. "But, low and behold, the imbecile was wrong and now, blessing of all blessings, here you are — delivered to me courtesy of the generosity and kindness of the Becks. All of their willingness to help you figure out your own story has led you here ... to me ... my pack and I were able to find you easily right where you belonged, in the Conri family home. I will have to send the Becks a gift basket as a thank you. Do they prefer fruit and nuts or just candy?" He said, smirking as I pulled at the restraints in an attempt to break free and kill him, I had never felt the amount of rage that was currently pulsing inside of me all aimed at my desire to see this man, who I didn't really even know but that had taken so much from me, dead.

"Oh don't bother with that, we have you injected with so much wolfsbane that it should've killed you by now. Given what you are, I knew you'd survive it. I would never doubt you, my dear boy. You truly are one of a kind, you are far more than I'd ever hoped you would be." he took my face in his hands and kissed me deeply. My eyes grew wide and my brain smacked of confusion, as he continued his attack on my consciousness. I snapped back into my mind and the only thing I could think of was to bite him. I grabbed his bottom lip with my teeth and felt my fangs emerge as I sliced through the flesh of his lower lip with little resistance. He pulled away, slapping me across the face, "you see, even now you don't disappoint me," he smiled a bloody red grin, "you are a fighter, you are everything I'd ever heard you would be, and with your bloodline incorporated into ours we will become the next ruling pack by both strength and lineage. You just wait and see." He pulled my face to his again and bit my lip hard, drawing blood that filled my mouth and his. I threw my head forward and back as fast as I could to throw his face away from mine. He pulled back smiling.

"You're crazy," I yelled. "What the hell makes you think I will ever be a part of your pack?" As I spoke the mixture of our blood spat out of my mouth.

He wiped the blood off his face and placed his hand on my thigh. "My dear boy, I don't need you to be a part of my pack. Now that I know you're a wolf, all I need are a few of your pups to raise as my own, you are just my link to the bloodline." He rose from the bed and headed toward the door. "And, there is more than one way to get pups out of you," he said, laughing. He hollered as he reached the door and a human opened it. Before leaving he turned around and said, "plus, I sure as hell don't need some half-assed Beck wolf for my daughters now that we have you." He chuckled and I heard him continue to laugh to himself, as the door closed and he walked down the hall.

Rage coursed inside me like nothing I had never felt before. I had seen evil in the world, but nothing like this. Had he just threatened me, I wouldn't have been nearly as mad as I was now that he had threatened Chess. He threatened the love of my life, my everything, the person I died and came back for, my mate. I didn't care that we hadn't mated yet. He was mine and I was his, I felt it in the intertwining of our souls and the knowledge that if anything happened to Chess a part of me would be irreparably broken. My blood boiled, burning through the wolfsbane they had injected into me. I felt my strength return. My eyes burned and glowed as I pulled on the restraints feeling stronger as the muscle fibers tensed, recruiting more strength as my body awakened. I snarled and snapped in the air like a caged beast until I felt the restraints break and my hands were free. I heard a struggle behind the door and I hopped out of the bed, ready to attack, as Willow burst into the room, her hands glowing with white flame as she walked through the door.

"Good, you're awake," she said walking up and touching my

shoulder, "we need to move. We may be stronger than them, but we are not strong enough for them all."

"You lied to me," I breathed heavily, staring at her, enraged.

"I did no such thing. This would have gone so much easier if you just had the sensibility to just agree and lie to that bastard's face." She said, appearing equally upset as to how things had gone. "We can discuss the intricacies of what you should do when you say you are going to trust someone later, but right now we need to go. If you want to save Chess, we need to move now." She gave me a shove, pushing me toward the door.

Leaving the room she began to run and I followed her. I was surprised with her speed, seeing as she was a witch and not a wolf, and we kept pace as we moved through the house. She led me through back stairways and corridors that led out to the rear of the chateau. I smelled Chess instantly as the back door swung open. He was hurt. I scoured the grounds frantically, the terrain moving and my brain processing with a speed I had never thought possible as I traced the scent toward a small wooden shed. I moved past Willow, running at full speed. On approach, I could smell the five wolves who had met us at the Conri home, including Lucas. I felt rage course through me again as my nostrils filled with their scent. My muscles coiled and my bones snapped. I thought I was shifting into my wolf, but in my rage the shift had changed. I fell to the ground for a few moments as I felt my chest expand and my jaw protrude from my face into a snout. My gums itched as my teeth grew sharp and elongated. As I stood, I realized I was more beast than wolf as the rage continued to tear its way through me. I stood on my hind paws, much taller than my wolf would normally have been, and, as I rose to stand, I heard Chess cry out as they continued to assault him. I tore into the ground with all the strength I had, leaving prints in the ground where I started my run from a stand still, and I was at the shed in a matter of seconds. I smashed through the side of the shack and stared in horror at the reddened hues on the ground and at Chess lying in a pool of blood on the floor, scratch marks cutting deep into his flesh. A growl that had been growing deep and harsh inside of me snuck out as Chess looked up at me and smiled. The other wolves, having recovered from the shock of something smashing through the side of the building, turned to look at me and screamed in horror. I stepped forward as Lucas kicked Chess one last time in the head knocking him unconscious. I howled in a fit of fury before I grabbed him by his neck. The other wolves howled and shifted as they tried to run around me to escape. I nearly felt the life of that sick bastard slip away in my hand before one of the smaller wolves leapt on me in a fitful bout of courage, making the poor choice of biting my arm. I threw Lucas across the room like a rag doll. I grabbed the wolf and shoved his head against the wall, pushing my forearm deep into his mouth. The muscle in my forearm expanded as he tried to open and release the bite. I pushed harder and growled. I felt my face elongate further into the beast and my fangs grew sharper as I heard the wolf's skull crack from the pressure. I turned faster than the other wolves ran and slashed through the remaining three before returning to Chess. He continued to lay unconscious, and, as I went to move toward him, my rage was quelled with fear and grief. The beast fell away as I knelt beside him. He was breathing through ragged and gurgled breaths with blood in his lungs. I looked over and saw Lucas was lying broken on the other side of the shed, but that he continued to breathe. I stood again, my rage turning in my chest, and I started toward him to finish the job, but, as I did, Willow caught up to me.

"Lyle, there's no time." She screamed jumping over the rubble and corpses of the wolves. "Grab Chess, we have to go!" I snapped back to my grief in response to his name. I turned back to him and ignored the desire to shred through the weak wolf that I could still hear, struggling to breathe as Chess was.

I leaned down and carefully lifted my love's broken body from the ground, cradling him against my chest. *I'll carry you now*, I thought, trying to push the feeling into him, not knowing if he could feel anything beyond the pain. I turned and followed Willow out of the shed, running carefully so as not to hurt Chess any further. He opened his eyes slowly and looked up at me before closing them again. I had never imagined I would ever see him like this. He was so much stronger than me, bigger than me, and smarter than me. It burned in my heart how much pain he had endured because of me. At this moment, I finally understood why he left me like he did so many months ago. I would do anything to spare him the pain he was feeling now, including walking away if I had known things would ever come to this. Willow stopped, she waved her arms through the air and told me to go.

"Where? Where is safe?" I asked her.

"Your motel, it's spelled, they won't find you there. And, if I can focus, they won't be able to find your scents either. Now go. I will find you soon." She was fierce and I could sense now that she would do anything for me. I didn't know who she was to me, but I trusted her completely.

I ran as fast as my feet could carry me through the streets of Salem in the darkness of the night. The sky was black and the chill in the air nipped into my flesh as I moved quickly back to the motel room, back to the place we had arrived just over twenty-four hours ago. Chess had slowly regained some semblance of consciousness as I approached the door to our room. I opened it and laid him down on the bed, continuing on toward the bathroom. I filled the ice bucket with warm water and grabbed a washcloth as I made my way back to Chess' side. I cleaned his wounds and as I washed the blood away I could see that he wasn't healing. He blinked at me slowly and struggled to breathe. I tried to ask him what to do, but he couldn't speak. I pleaded with him to heal and to breathe, but he continued to lie there, blinking at me while making weak gurgling breaths. Panic began to set in as the door opened, Willow burst into the room and hurried to the side of the bed. I watched her as she scanned over Chess, assessing his wounds.

"He's not healing," I cried, "Wha.... What....? Is there anything you can do?" I asked her, speaking raggedly as I choked through my tears.

"No, but you can," she said.

"What do you mean? You can't do anything? You're a witch. What can I do that you can't do?" I asked.

"Look Lyle, I wish there was more time for us to talk and for you to learn, but I only bend nature. I maintain the balance, but you," she paused, "you are nature and there are potentially limitless possibilities for what you can do. Focus on him. The wolfsbane is preventing him from healing. Take it from him." I blinked at her, trying to assess what she was saying, but my mind couldn't break away from Chess and how she needed to do something to fix him.

I glared at her and protested as she forcefully grabbed my hand and put it on one of his bleeding wounds. "Take it from him."

"How?" I asked her, feeling his blood flow beneath my hand, a warm steady current coming from the wound.

"You know how, trust yourself. Focus!" She yelled at me.

I closed my eyes and focused on the wolfsbane, trying to take it out of him. I focused as hard as I could, but nothing was happening, his ragged breaths were breaking my heart. "It's not working!" I screamed at her.

"You're focusing on the wrong thing. Take his pain away." She encouraged me.

I panicked. *What could I do?* I continued to look at him, blinking at me, struggling to breathe. I didn't know what else to do. I moved, pulling my hands up to his face, "Chess, I need you to listen to me. That night I turned, when I died in your arms. The last thing I tried to tell you was that I loved you," I started to cry, "do you hear me, I love you, I need you, and I have to save you." I pulled his face to mine and kissed him, crushing my mouth into his fierce and hard. I felt it then, deep into the depths of my being, a small burning that I'd never felt before. I pulled away and put my hands on his wounds, "I can do this," I whispered to myself and focused on pushing the heat from my core up through my arms and into his body. Chess howled out in pain as I held my hands over the deep crevices that scarred his torso. I could sense the wolfsbane within him and imagined it burning as I pushed the heat into him. Several seconds passed as Chess continued to scream, but I couldn't stop, I pushed harder and as I did his breathing steadied and the large gashes underneath my hands began to close.

Willow rose and left the room. I didn't know where she went and, at this moment, I didn't care. I knew I would see her again. As the wounds beneath my hands closed, I pulled away and watched as Chess fell back into unconsciousness. I laid there next to him for a while and listened to his breathing, steady and regular. *I did it*, I thought to myself. I leaned over and kissed his forehead lightly before standing and walking toward the bathroom. As I walked into the small space, I turned on the water and splashed a little on my face. I looked into the mirror and sighed deeply, it was a breath full of relief and I finally felt safe for the first moment in I didn't know how many hours. I stared into the mirror and looked at myself. I was covered in blood. I could hardly recognize the person looking back at me. I was still me, but I was so much more than just me. I looked into the mirror and saw a man staring back at me.

Thoughts rushed through my mind, as I replayed the trauma that had just occurred. The assault on Chess and on me. My stomach wretched when I recalled the deaths of the four wolves. It wretched again at the thought that I had actually killed someone. I didn't know if I would ever be able to process that. I reached up toward my head, continuing to scrub at the blood that had begun crusting along my hairline. I bowed down slightly trying to duck my head under the sink faucet, all the while trying to shove the intrusive thoughts about the events of the day into the back of my mind. I reached back behind me into the shower and turned on the water. Pulling the curtain to the side, I stepped in. Climbing inside the water singed my skin and I watched as blood ran off my body and down the drain. I scrubbed and scrubbed until the water coming off of me ran clear and then I let my head rest on the shower wall under the hot water, allowing myself to feel the water running through my hair, a part of me secretly hoping that it would also wash away the thoughts that kept creeping into my mind. I was so lost in everything that time seemed to slip away. I didn't know how much time had passed, but as I was drowning in the sensations I didn't hear Chess wake or climb into the shower behind me. He reached out and grabbed my shoulder, startling me. I stood upright and turned toward him. He put his hand behind my head before I could speak and pulled me in to kiss him. It was as deep and as passionate as our first kiss on that cliff's edge. As he pressed against me, I could smell the blood washing off his body, trailing down toward the drain as the water splashed between us, I motioned to pull back. Chess didn't stop and he only pulled me in and kissed me harder. He pushed his tongue into my mouth and I opened it to him. I wanted to be with him more now than ever and as the thought drifted across my mind, I felt him slide his hand down and touch me for the first time. I pulled away at the touch of his hand, knowing what it meant.

"What are you doing?" I asked him.

"I'm taking you as mine," he said, pushing his mouth back onto mine and I let him, against all hesitation, I fell deep into his kiss.

*I have always been yours*, I thought to myself, and now he was finally ready to claim me.

My emotions churned within me questioning whether I should trust what was going on, all the while my wolf yearned for him pushing me toward the ritual to cement our bond. I am not sure how, but I found the will within me and pulled away. "Chess, is this because I told you that I loved you and because I saved your life or is this because you are truly ready?" I was both terrified and ecstatic to hear his answer, but with all the trauma and emotions that had surrounded us this felt like way too big a decision for him, for me, for us, and I felt the need to make sure he wasn't making a hasty decision that he wouldn't be able to take back based on the emotion of the moment. I waited as seconds ran by like hours.

He stood before me and I stared into his peculiar eyes, the look that he returned scared me and excited me all at the same time. He panted heavily and stood confidently. He took my face in his hands and his eyes bore into mine, "Lyle," he breathed heavily, "I've been hiding something from you." He pulled me into him slightly , kissing me lightly and grinned, "That night on the beach, as you lay in my arms and breathed what I thought was your last breath - I told you I loved you." He kissed me swiftly and his stubble grazed against mine as he spoke. "I loved you then, I've loved you since, and I love you now. I have always been yours." He said, chuckling, "It wasn't even fair how fast you knocked me off my feet, but from the moment I met you, I was yours and I knew that I would never be whole without you." My heart danced and my wolf leapt within me to hear him speak the words I had longed to hear him say. Joy tore through me harder than any emotion had ever experienced before.

"You don't even realize how special you are," he began, reaching his hands around my waist and gliding them up my back, "You'll change everything and I want nothing more than to be at your side when you do, as your mate." He pulled me back into him and held his hand firmly against my lower back to ensure I wouldn't back away again. I could feel him against me and the heat that burned between us was hotter than the water's continuous stream down my back. He slid his hands down my back, grazed them over my butt and grabbed me firmly from the back of my thighs, hoisting me into the air. As he did, I wrapped my legs around him. He carried me from the shower back to the bed and I felt my wolf leap out to his. I felt love as they danced around with one another just as our human bodies were. Chess lowered me down onto the mattress and I continued to hold my legs around him. I felt him move against me and he looked into my eyes for approval. I leaned up into his ear and whispered, "I've always been yours." His eyes flashed a little at my proclamation and his wolf stirred to the surface in acknowledgement. My eyes flashed back in a similar fashion. Chess moved swiftly then and, in less than a moment, we had become one. It was only then that I knew what this meant to him and what it meant to me. Part of my soul intertwined with his and part of his intertwined with mine. Our wolves continued to dance and play together in a field between us as we moved against each other in complete ecstasy. I'd never thought a moment would mean this much or would be as defining as the moment I was experiencing right now. I felt his breath quicken and his speed hasten. I knew the moment was coming where the ritual would be complete and we would belong to each other forever. I cried out his name and pulled his face into mine, kissing him wildly as I felt him come to a halt and we both hit an intense wave of ecstasy that exploded as we fell back into reality and I knew then that his soul and mine had forever become a part of one another. His chest moved up and down wildly as he remained over the top of me. I kissed his forehead gently before he rolled over onto his side and I pushed my head into his chest. He held me close and whispered, "I love you."

We lay there quietly for what felt like a blissful eternity. I had never felt so much love from or for another person in my entire life. To have a person truly be mine after being alone for so long. We shifted slightly and watched as the sun rose in the sky between the creases in the curtains that hung over the window.

"Oh crap, I forgot something." Chess cried out in urgency. He fumbled off the bed and reached into his bag for something. He pulled out something I couldn't see and crawled back into bed.

"What is it?" I asked him, laughing slightly at his dorkiness.

"I... Um.... I was waiting for a perfect time, but there wasn't a more perfect time than our moment, and that came and went, but Lyle?" He asked me, fumbling over some of his words.

"Yeah?" I asked him.

"Will you marry me?" He pulled out from behind his back a beautiful single gold band and presented it to me.

I laughed instantly. "Chess, werewolves don't believe in marriage? Why are you asking me to marry you?"

"Because you do." He paused, moving in closer. "You grew up in the human world with thoughts of marriage and finding true love. I grew up in the wolf world of assigned mating. I want our union to not only be representative of me and the way I was raised, but to also honor you and your upbringing," I smiled back at him and laughed slightly, "so Lyle Conri Larson, I'll ask you one more time. Will you marry me?" His grin was so cheesy and he was so in earnest holding the little gold band up as he slipped it onto my ring finger.

"I thought I already did, but a thousand times over, yes. Yes Chess, I will marry you." He pulled me back into another deep kiss before I felt his mood lighten.

"I have one more question." He managed to say between kisses.

"What's that?"

"Can we do it again?"

# Chapter Twenty-Four

Chess and I woke up late in the afternoon. I laid in bed and stared at the ceiling; my head rested against Chess's side. The small bonds that had been tied between Chess and I were now cemented, stronger than I ever knew they could be. I could feel all of his feelings and, if I pushed, I could call up memories with ease and access things about him I'd never thought possible. I knew that meant he could do the same to me and that thought frightened me. I didn't have any secrets from him, but I worried he might tap into the deep sea of loneliness and longing I'd felt for most of my life before him, before our pack, and before our friends. Those feelings had long since dissipated thanks to the people I now had in my life, but being here in Salem, finding out everything about my family and my legacy had brought me into a new sense of sadness and loss that I didn't know existed until now. My heart bled for them all, my ancestors, my family, my pack. Somewhere along the way jealousy, secrets, and betrayal had taken hold in the hearts of those to whom my ancestors had turned toward for help, those that they had trusted. My soul ached for the Conri pack and all of my ancestors who had been denied the right to their full and complete selves for centuries. They had spent that time looking for a missing piece of themselves, but never understanding what had been taken. All of this pain had been at the hands of  wolves who had sworn to protect them and their desire to want what someone else had.

Chess stirred, sensing my feelings, and moved to comfort me. He pulled me in close and kissed the top of my head. "What are you thinking about?" He asked quietly.

"Nothing," I said, "nothing important."

"If it's nothing important, then why are you so sad?" He asked.

I groaned slightly in the humor that he was also using this new found connection between us and found it frivolous to hide it from him. "I can't help but think about my family and how everything that happened to them was so horrible. I can't even think about how my life would have turned out if it hadn't been for you." I admitted.

"Well, thankfully, you won't ever have to." He said, pulling me in tighter and squeezing me with reassurance. A knock came at the door and we both jumped with alarm.

"It's just me," Willow said, standing behind the door, "if you two are quite done canoodling, I'd very much like to come inside now." She opened the door and walked into the small room. "Right then. I think it is time we talked." She closed the door behind her and shot light from her hand at the door handle. She'd carried a small bag with her this time and set it down on the dresser across from the bed before taking a seat in the chair next to it.

Chess swung his legs over the side of the bed and went to grab a pair of shorts. "Just who do you think you are, witch?" He retorted as he bent down, putting one leg through his shorts.

"I believe what you meant to say was thank you." She replied as Chess finished pulling up his shorts.

"Thank you," I said to her, reaching for my own shorts at the edge of the bed.

She bowed her head slightly. "I'm sure you probably have over a thousand questions," she said, speaking directly toward me. "And perhaps I can answer some of them by explaining our family's history."

I nodded toward her. "As you both heard last night, I am Willow Foster. You already know that I am a witch and that I am obviously quite powerful." She narrowed her eyes slightly at Chess. "I have been posing as a witch consult to the Dubois, hoping to someday find you before that evil bastard did," she looked over at me, "you have proven to be quite difficult to find Lyle, even through magic."

"That doesn't tell us who you are to us," Chess retorted.

She narrowed her eyes toward Chess again, "I am getting to that," she said glaring and Chess growled.

"Enough," I said, "Chess, just let her speak, please." He sat back down on the edge of the bed with me and listened.

"Thank you," she cleared her throat, "as I was saying, I am the last Foster witch alive today. Our families extend back to the night that John Conri brought your namesake to my great ancestors' hut for aid. My family is the reason that yours survived, but at a significant cost. I am not sure how it happened, but my family, like all witches, lost most of its magic that night. My family has continued to protect yours through the centuries and we have searched for a way to undo the spell that rendered your family human ever since your namesake was old enough to defend himself and his family. He thought that, by having a family, his child would not be born with the same affliction, but that child's wolf was also absent. We have continued to search for a way to restore your family to the throne of your people, but as the centuries passed, we began to lose hope. Then one night several months ago, the coven's and my magic returned out of nowhere, and I knew that somewhere in the world you had turned. I have been looking for you ever since."

"Why?" I asked her, "Why did restoring my family matter so much to you? From what I know about witches, and I know very little, our kind hate each other."

"When I arrived last night and all the other wolves hissed and groaned at my scent and the sound of my voice, did you?" She asked.

"No."

"Chess," she looked over to him, "now that you are mated to Lyle, does the sound of my voice or my scent repulse you?"

He looked surprised when she asked and then thinking said, "No. You don't"

"I told you last night that you are nature's son. You and your family were created by nature herself,  as servants to nature's will, we are bound to you and your family. The magic that was performed that night was an assault on nature and her family. As such she rejected witches for a time and many of us were slaughtered in the years that followed. This included the witch that cast the spell to make your ancestor human, Ann Foster. Wolves, even the turned packs that exist today, reject us because of whatever my ancestor did to protect yours on that night. Even though it was another pack that betrayed your family, taking away your birthright was a greater assault on your kind than the slaughter of your entire royal family. Through the reclamations of Lyle's wolf, however, we are no longer rejected and the balance has started to be restored."

"This is heavy." Chess stated, taking in all the information.

"Agreed," I shared, "so then, do you know what actually happened that night with John and Ann?"

"I don't," she said and I sighed.

"Willow, the night I turned I had a dream that I was John. I watched as the forest burned and my family was killed. I re-emerged from that dream fully transitioned into my wolf moments after Rebecca was killed and John was shot. I watched as John continued to run, injured, into the forest and then it faded away. I need to know what happened next. Can you help me figure that out?" I asked her.

She looked shocked. "You saw it all happen?" I nodded. "Then the memories must remain with your wolf. He must have been there that night then. That shouldn't be possible, but then again, nothing is impossible when it comes to your family." She stood from the chair and began pacing. "I think I can help you, but it will be dangerous. We will have to return to your family's home for it to work."

"I don't think we should." Chess protested. "Lyle, we need to leave Salem and get back to our territory. The Union prevents me from attacking another wolf in their territory."

"This isn't their territory, Chess," Willow explained, "it's the Conri's territory. They are the imposters laying claim to a land that isn't theirs and after what they did to you last night I would hope that wouldn't stop you."

"I don't want to cause a war between anybody," I said, looking at Chess and stroking his cheek, "but I need to know what happened. Please help me." He paused for a moment and I could sense conflict within him, but he nodded in agreement all the same.

"Very well," Willow summarized. "I have masked your scents and covered our trail for the time being. They will expect that we will return to your home and we will need to expect the worst when we arrive."

"We need to avoid killing any more wolves," Chess stated.

"Agreed," I said, "Incapacitate, not kill." He nodded in agreement.

"Once we find out what you need to know, Lyle, we will have to leave quickly. Salem won't be safe for any of us after this," Willow explained.

"Will you come with us?" I asked her. "I am in your debt for your help in saving Chess's life and our pack will help protect you"

"I will have some much needed work to do after this night, but yes eventually I will come back to you." She exclaimed and I nodded in acceptance.

We planned how we would make our move back to my family's home. Chess and Willow continued their bickering as disagreements occurred and I played the mediator. While nature and I forgave the witches, I could see that it would take time for the rift between the wolves and the witches to narrow again. As we waited, Chess received a call from his father and briefly updated him on the situation, leaving out a few key details regarding Willow that we undoubtedly would have to address upon our return home. Noah would take care of the travel arrangements. He was angered at our insistence to return to my family home one last time. He didn't command us to return, however, reluctantly allowing us the time we needed to complete our last task. Worry crept into my mind at the thought of what lay ahead at the house and, as it did, Chess reached over and grabbed my hand in silent acknowledgement as he and his father finished their phone call. I sat quietly at the edge of the bed, looking down at the gold band on my finger. I felt love inside me and the part of Chess's soul that had merged with mine hugged my heart warmly, but the anxiety continued to worsen. Chess set the phone down on the bed and turned to me.

"Don't." He said calmly.

"Don't what?" I asked him stupidly.

He grabbed my chin and turned my face to his, his thumb rubbing against stubble on my jaw, "Don't doubt what we've done or ever worry that it was a mistake, we are one now and nothing will ever change that." He paused. "Not even my father."

I hesitated to say anything because I had a great deal of love, admiration, and respect for his family, especially his father whom I had accepted as my alpha. I knew this would hurt the pack and hurt his father who, above all else, wanted to protect us. I found relief in Chess's words and shoved the fear aside as I accepted his gestures of reassurance. I smiled back at him, "I don't think we made a mistake and I am as much yours now as I ever have been."

"Good," he replied with a breath of relief. Choosing to become mates could never be undone, but knowing that choice would hurt others weighed on me.

Willow returned to the motel room after having made several calls outside. "Are you ready?" she asked, holding the door open.

"We are." I replied as I stood up from the bed with Chess at my side. We gathered our belongings and set out quietly into the night. Willow fastened two bracelets made of twine to our wrists.

"These will help cover your scents, but they won't last forever. We need to be quick. The other witches in the city will help us, but they aren't as strong as they will become. If the Dubois show up in force, we will still be no match for them. Lyle, I will send you back into the memory, but it will be up to you to be quick. Find what you need and then we must leave," she said, clearly anxious.

"I will," I assured her.

"Let's go," Chess exclaimed. We moved into the night swiftly, cautiously moving toward my family's home. We passed two other witches along our path through the city. They were out walking the city streets, allowing their scent to seep into the night to aid us in our mission. We approached my family home and, as we did, we were surprised to smell only two other wolves in the house. I followed Chess quietly as we climbed the fence and made our approach to enter the house. We crept in quietly through the back and the wolves inside immediately went on the attack. Having been expecting us, they shifted quickly and tore at us with all they could. We quickly subdued them. Willow pulled out a needle from her bag and stabbed them with it.

"Wolfsbane," she proclaimed as we looked at her, "I assure you it won't kill them, but it will keep them from waking for a while. Come, we need to hurry."

We rushed back down to the cellar. Willow pulled out several other items from her bag and drew symbols onto the floor. "Okay Lyle, you lay down here and Chess you here."

"Why do I need to lie there?" He asked her, confused. I looked at her with a look of confusion as well.

"This spell won't just work on Lyle, it will affect you too, now that you've mated. All of Lyle will need to go back and now part of him lives within you, so you have to go as well." We followed her direction and laid on the floor. "It will be dangerous for Chess to be there with you Lyle, you must hold on to him so his soul doesn't become lost." She began chanting and the symbols began to glow around us, she turned once more and asked, "are you sure you want to do this?"

"We've come too far to turn back now," I looked at Chess and he nodded, "We're ready." Chess proclaimed.

Willow nodded and continued speaking in a language I had never heard before and the symbols began to glow brighter. I grabbed Chess's hand and squeezed it tightly and I felt him say it would be alright. As the last symbol grew brighter, the world below us seemed to fade away and we fell into darkness. Chess's hand was still in mine and we looked at each other. We stood and looked around in the darkness seeing nothing.

*Where are we?* Chess thought quietly.

*I'm not sure,* I responded.

We began walking forward into the darkness. As we walked, nothing but darkness appeared to stretch forever around us and we couldn't see each other as we moved. I could only feel his hand and thoughts.

*What are we supposed to do now?* He thought to me.

*I'm not sure, I think last time the wolf took me the rest of the way.* I thought back to him as we continued to walk.

*Try thinking about that night again, try calling up the memory,* he thought back to me. I did as he suggested and the darkness faded slightly as we continued to walk forward. I could see now that we were walking into the small cabin where my vision had begun, only this time I was still myself and Chess was here with me. Rebecca was in labor and John was at her bedside as she birthed my ancestor into the world. We continued to walk through the memory side by side with John and Rebecca as the tragedy of that night unfolded in front of me again. I began to cry and Chess pulled me in closer. We reached the point where Rebecca gave Lyle to John and shifted to protect them both, giving her life. I wept next to John as he fell to his knees at the loss of his mate and Chess cried too.

*It's too much, I thought to him. I can't do this again.*

Chess moved beside me and wrapped his arm around my waist. *You're not alone this time. I'm here. We can do this together.* As John moved to his feet and continued we followed him, back to where I re-awoke as a wolf and the darkness returned.

*What's happening*, Chess thought to me.

*This is where my memory ends*, I thought back to him, beginning to panic.

*We need your wolf*, Chess pushed his thought to mine and I knew he was right. I reached internally and tried to push a shift, but couldn't. I looked over to Chess as the memory continued to fade. We continued to look at each other when a red wolf emerged walking toward us from the darkness. Just behind him, a darker wolf jotted along with one green eye and one blue.

*Could it be?* I thought as the wolves approached and sat next to our sides. The red one chuffed in agreement that it was. I looked over to Chess in amazement and he looked just as bewildered as I was as we had come face to face with our inner selves. I knelt down to look my wolf in the eye and Chess followed me. His wolf rubbed up against the side of him as we did.

*I need to see the rest. Please show us what happened.* I thought to him. He resisted slightly before pulling his head back into a silent howl into the darkness. Chess's wolf followed mine and the darkness that prevented us from moving forward fell away, we returned to the memory standing in the woods just as before. I acknowledged the pain that flowed from my wolves' eyes and followed him forward, into the woods, chasing after John. We followed John through the woods as he continued to be pursued. He made his way into a clearing, having thrown off the humans, who continued to search for him nearby. Toward the edge of the clearing, John knelt, pounding on the door of a hut in the middle of the woods, with little Lyle crying out into the night. A small woman opened the door and pulled them inside with haste. We followed them inside and observed.

"Ann, I need you to strip Lyle of his wolf. I'm dying and this is the only way we can protect him." John pleaded with Ann.

"John, I can't," she resisted. "It would go against the laws of nature to strip your son of this. It goes against everything we believe in and is against the balance. You know I cannot do this."

"There is no other choice," John cried out in pain as blood pooled at his feet. "The Conri will die here tonight if we do nothing. The others will find him and kill him if we do nothing." Ann was quiet.

John fell to the ground no longer able to keep his stance, "Ann, there isn't much time. I'm dying and I need to lure them away. Please, Ann, save my son." John pleaded and coughed, blood spattering the corners of his mouth and teeth.

"Okay John, you're right. I will do it." Ann sighed in defeat. "You need to know though, John, he and his descendants will never be whole. They will always search for belonging and will never find it for as long as they are disconnected from this side of themselves. They will live a half-life. They may suffer from madness and ailments unknown, but they will be alive. Is this the life you want for your son and your descendants?"

"Yes, Ann, please. Save him." John pleaded again.

"Okay." Ann sighed. She took Lyle from John and laid him on a table. She unwrapped the tiny swaddle that was wrapped tightly around him. She began chanting in the same language we heard Willow speak to send us here. As she did, tears of blood emerged and she appeared to be in pain as she spoke.

She held her hands over Lyle and continued to chant. We watched in horror as the veins in her hands grew black, trembling as she spoke. Blood trickled from her ears and the blood from her eyes continued to fall in drops on the table around Lyle, but she didn't stop chanting.

Her knees buckled and she fell onto the table before Lyle, but did not stop. The pain appeared unbearable but her chanting continued. The wind outside the hut grew wild and the surrounding trees shook the hut violently. Ann fought her way back to her feet and appeared to be pleading with another in the same language as she continued to deal with great pain.

She put her hand on Lyle, now completely black, it appeared

dead. Blood flowed from the beds of her fingernails as she continued to chant. She appeared to grab a glowing substance from Lyle and pulled it up and away from him. Before her, an astral wolf cub dangled from her hand as she held it from the back of its neck. Strands connecting the cub to Lyle still clung between them as it fought against her to return to Lyle.

Ann's face began to sink and wither as she continued to chant and in her other hand a white flame encompassed her entire arm. She continued to chant and weep, staring into something we could not see. Her hair turned white from the roots as she did. She pulled her arm back and in one fell swoop, the flames cut the strands that connected the astral cub to Lyle. The wolf at my side let out a sorrowful yelp and clung to my side as he did. As soon as the strands were cut, the astral cub faded from view, and Ann collapsed to the floor. She turned her head toward John, who sat quietly in the corner.

"It's done," her appearance aged and the blood still wet on her cheeks, "he will be safe here, but you have to go now."

John stood and said one last goodbye to Lyle with tears in his eyes, "goodbye my son." John turned and left the hut, leaping into the air and shifting one last time into his wolf as he tore toward the forest.

My wolf pushed on my leg and encouraged us to follow John. I pulled on Chess's hand, he was continuing to look at baby Lyle, tears pouring out of his eyes at what he just witnessed. He pulled away with me and we followed our wolves out of the hut and after John into the night. We caught up with John as he bore into the last human, tearing his throat from his neck. He had several more bullet wounds, all with dark red blood flowing out, making his red fur appear black and tacky in the moonlight. We watched quietly as John laid down amongst the carnage.

He shifted back to the human just before three wolves walked out of the forest. John laid naked and exposed to them. We went to move closer, but Chess's wolf attempted to hold Chess back. Chess continued forward with me anyway, and his wolf followed with his tail between his legs. My wolf attended his side, urging him forward. As we approached, we could see the lead wolf that walked up to John. Its coat was dark and in the moonlight Chess and I could clearly make out one green eye and one blue. Chess's thoughts flooded into mine. *It can't be true. No, no, this isn't happening.* As he did, the wolves shifted in front of us and the Beck ancestor knelt down at John's side.

"Traitor," John spit blood at him in anger with the last bit of energy that he had.

"Come now John," he said, "that's no way to speak to your new alpha." He let out a chuckle and, laughing with the others, said, "Now tell us, John, where's that pup of yours? Stash him nearby, did you?" The other wolves spread out and searched for a scent trail.

"He's dead," John cried. "They killed him."

"What?" The Beck wolf grew angry. "John, how could you let them get to him?" He paced angrily, "No, no, no. It wasn't supposed to happen like this."

"Beck, you said there was no way the humans would have killed the infant." Another wolf growled.

"It wasn't part of the plan." He growled back.

John laughed slightly. "Was that your plan, Beck? Steal my son for yourself?"

The Beck wolf grew even angrier. "Beck, you know what this means?" The other wolf proclaimed, panicked, "we'll all die out. Without Conri, we can't make more wolves."

"I know that, you idiot," he growled again. "Where is he, John?" he grabbed John by the shoulders and hauled him up. "Where is he?" The wolf sounded crazed. As he continued to yell and shake John violently, we watched as the light fell from John's eyes and the last of the original Conri alphas died.

# Chapter Twenty-Five

We were on the plane flying back to Seattle. Chess and I still hadn't talked about what we saw and the discovery of who had betrayed my ancestral pack. Upon the death of John, both Chess and I awoke in the basement of my family's home. Willow looked drained from the amount of magic it had taken her to send us into the memory. We had been surprised at the knowledge that no other wolves had come for us. The two we had dealt with on our entry to the home were still out cold as we snuck back out of the house and into the night. We made our way through the streets of Salem to an old storefront where Chess and his father had arranged a driver to meet us. I begged Willow to join us on the return to Seattle, but she was insistent that she had to return to the greater coven and attend to business. She assured me we would reunite soon, but she had to attend to the things that had been set in motion. I trusted her and so did Chess, mostly. The cognitive dissonance within me churned as we sat next to each other on the flight home. I wanted to use our newfound connection to peek inside of him and find out how he was feeling, but in light of the delicate nature of what we had witnessed I did not. I hadn't even figured out how I felt knowing that the ancestral alpha of the Beck's had been the wolf to betray my family with a plan not all too different from the one Gerard had about using me to legitimize his supreme rule over the wolves by infusing my bloodline into his pack. It was all just too much.

I sighed. As I did, Chess turned his head in my direction and flashed me a half-smile. It still dazzled me and yet I knew he was feeling the weight of the knowledge of the past just as I was. He reached over and grabbed my hand before turning away and looking out the window. I looked down at my hand, at the little gold band hugging my finger like it had always belonged there. This should have been the happiest time of our lives, I thought to myself as the gold caught the light overhead. I felt content, though. I had longed with every fiber of my being to be with Chess and now we would be together forever. I could feel his soul settling against my heart and I felt peaceful. *That would always be there,* I thought to myself, and it brought me comfort. There was never a doubt for Chess either. He had gone out and bought this ring before we'd mated. He had already decided that we would be together forever, even before we knew who I was. I grew warm inside at the thought.

He sighed this time. I turned and looked over at him. He was facing forward now and I stared at the side of his face and took all of his features in. I didn't know how it was possible for someone like him to be mine. He flashed a look in my direction again and caught me staring.

"What is it?" he whispered quietly while the other passengers slept around us.

"Nothing." I responded. He gave my hand a small squeeze and smirked at me. I hated when he did that. It was the most adorable look he had in his repertoire and I felt like he only used it on select occasions knowing it would make me sweat.

"Come on now, it's not nothing." He responded.

"Well... it's just that..." I paused, hesitating to bring it up.

"Just what?" He looked concerned.

"Well... I mean... Should we talk about it?" I whispered back at him.

"We can if you want to." He whispered back to me. Of course, I wanted to, but I didn't know what to say. *Oh hey, so what do you think about your great great whoever killing my great great whoever?*, I thought to myself. *How was this supposed to make me feel and did it change the way he felt about me?*

"I do," I responded, louder than I'd meant to. A few people shifted in their seats around us and I blushed.

He smiled at me, "Okay, what about it would you like to talk about?" he said quieter than he had before. I grew annoyed, I didn't want to be the one to bring it up and yet here he was, being perfect, and willing to talk about anything I wanted and yet wouldn't take the ownership to discuss the one thing that I knew we had both been replaying in our heads since we witnessed it.

"You're insufferable."

He chuckled a bit. "Oh yeah? How so?"

"You know what I want to talk about," I rebutted.

"Well, I have an idea, but I am not a mind reader, Lyle. If you want to discuss it, address it."

"What are you talking about? Of course, you are a mind reader." I spoke softer when mentioning the mind reader. "You're telling me you don't know?"

"Well, if I read your mind for everything, there'd be no need for us to talk and I'm quite fond of hearing your voice." He smiled, thinking he was being smooth. I lowered my brow at him in annoyance, but felt relieved that he still liked my voice.

"I want to talk about what happened to John." His smile softened and his face returned to his more serious self.

"I do too." I sighed with relief to hear him say that. "What, in particular, would you like to discuss?"

"Well... I guess.... Does it change things for you?" I asked and stared down at my feet, preparing to hear the worst and hoping for the best.

"Change things?" I turned to look at him as his face twisted into a look of confusion.

"About me... you and me.... us?" I asked, continuing to eye the floor of the plane. A silent pause went by and I feared the worst before Chess's hand took me from under my chin and turned me into a deep kiss. His stubble tickled as he pushed his lips hard into mine and all the tension in my body melted into the floor. A small intentional cough from the man in the seat across the aisle from us pulled us apart. Chess let a small growl escape from his chest toward the man, who then turned away rapidly. He gave me one more soft kiss. "Nothing would change how I feel about you, Lyle. You are mine now and always."

I flushed hearing him say that, "Does it change things for you?" he whispered. I was not quite prepared for him to ask me that, "Of course not!" I exclaimed, "But don't you think that it is going to complicate things further? We are already returning, mated, and engaged.  Now, we have the news that your family killed my family. I mean, what are we going to do? Hide it all forever?" My mouth vomited all the things I had been thinking and Chess just sat there and listened to all my concerns, staying cool and calm before responding.

"We will talk about it when we get home." He exhaled. "Try to get some rest. We will land in another hour or two." I went to push him more, but we had awoken another passenger from our conversation in the seat behind us and I resisted. He turned back to face forward and I did the same. I leaned my head back against the headrest but found no relaxation there. I continued to resist the temptation to listen in through our bond, but knew, sitting next to him, he also wasn't finding any rest on this crowded plane.

The rest of the time passed by slowly, but eventually the plane landed and we made our way through the passages of the airport to Chess's Jeep parked in the garage. Stepping out of the automated doors and back into the cool wet breeze of the Pacific Northwest had a calming effect on us both. It was raining heavily and as it hit our skin on the way to the garage; I knew we were both glad to be back in one piece. We remained silent as we made our way back up through the downtown exits of Seattle and  toward Chess's loft. We arrived as the sun rose slowly above clouds that continued to pour down rain and the black skies started to turn gray. I went to open the door to the Jeep when Chess suddenly spoke. "Wait!"

I pulled my hand back from the door handle and turned quickly toward him. "What?" I asked him, startled. With a huge grin pulled back from ear to ear, he responded, "let me get that for you." I rolled my eyes as he jumped out the driver's side and ran around to my door rather quickly. He opened my door and extended his hand out to mine. "you're a little ridiculous sometimes," I proclaimed as I took his hand and stepped out of the Jeep.

"Oh, you ain't seen nothing yet." He growled deliciously before sweeping me off the ground faster than I had ever been.

"Chess!" I screamed. "What are you doing?" and I laughed a little.

"Well, I'm carrying you into our home, dear." He stated proudly, walking toward the door to the loft. "Isn't this a human custom when two people get married that the man carries his mate into their home?"

In between laughing and bouncing up and down as he walked, I said, "Yes, but.... we aren't married yet."

That didn't stop him and he carried me with remarkable ease through the hallway and into the lift that would take us up to the loft. I was surprised at how easy it was for him even though I was much larger than the last time, but he maneuvered around the building with ease, keeping me in his arms the entire time. I  thought for sure he was going to struggle with unlocking the giant sliding door with how he was carrying me, but he merely flipped me over his shoulder, dug out his keys, and opened the door.

"Welcome home," he said as he walked through the door and gave me a swat on the behind. *Home*, I thought to myself, realizing that this beautiful loft was my home now, too. I could hardly believe it as I took it in, and became a little overwhelmed with the truth of it.

"Wait," I said to Chess, "please put me down." He lifted me off his shoulder and helped me to the couch.

"What... What is it?" Chess said, confused.

"Home," I said, "this is my home now too?" I felt like I was acknowledging a truth, but it came out sounding like a question.

Chess knelt on the ground in front of me and took my hands. "Of course, it is. We are mated now and everything I once had is now yours too." He smiled at me and brought one of his giant hands to my face.

I continued to sit, looking around the room at everything, feeling the warmth of Chess' hands against my cheeks and took a long deep look into his eyes. I was not naïve and I knew the gravity of what being mated had meant when it happened, but being back and being 'home' now made it more real somehow. I didn't know how to explain it in the moment, but I continued to feel the swell of happiness within me sitting with the man I loved in front of me and scared shit-less all in the same moment. "Chess," I said, "I've never had anything in my life as nice as any of this and I'd never let myself want anything like this, in fact one of the very few things I've ever wanted in this world is you, and I guess I just hadn't thought about anything beyond just being with you until now, and this....," I paused, "this is my home now too."

He smiled before jokingly stating, "Well, I guess if you really wanted, we could move into your apartment with Andy." I laughed somewhat before taking his hand that had moved from my cheek to my shoulder and kissed it lightly once.... then twice... then a third time on the finger that would also need a ring of its own in time before I looked back up at him. His peculiar eyes held my gaze and the look in them turned from humor toward love and then more carnal as they flashed at me in the same way they did that night in the hotel room. His musk filled my nostrils, and I unwaveringly fell into its heavy scent. It was at that same moment that Chess smelled my scent as well, "Damn, you smell so good," he said before smashing his lips against mine and pushing me back into the sofa.

He climbed on top of me and continued to assault my mouth with his own. I pushed my hands up his waist and under his shirt where I could feel the fuzzy warmth of the hair that clung to his abs and I felt his muscles twitch underneath my touch. He stopped and leaned back to pull his shirt off and over his head much faster than I had ever seen. He put his hands against my chest and ripped open my flannel with such force that the buttons scattered across the floor in every direction. He put his mouth back on mine and felt his hands cover every inch of my torso and lower abdomen. I put my hands on his waist and made a quick movement that ended with him laying on his back against the couch while I hovered over him. He panted for a moment and paused, looking at me, intimidated. "What's wrong?" I asked him.

He moved his hands up toward my belt, undoing it swiftly and unfastening the top of my jeans. "Does it hurt?" he asked cautiously. I understood fully what he was asking at that moment and chuckled lightly. "Don't laugh at me," he said, partially amused and irritated in the same breath.

"Only a little." I replied, amused, and put my mouth back on his. I reached down and pulled the small bow at his waistband free to loosen the sweatpants that hung around his hips perfectly and helped him push them down. He kicked them free and I commented, "No underwear?" before putting my mouth on his neck and grazing my teeth against his skin. He moaned slightly and I felt his pulse beat into my mouth. My gums itched a little and my fangs sharpened against his skin slightly. He felt the pricks of them push against his skin and he moaned louder, exposing his neck further to provide access. I continued to kiss his neck and bit him softly. As I did, he pushed my pants down lower and freed me from their constriction. Musk filled the room as we both ground into each other, our lust enveloping us. He wrapped his legs around my waist and gave me a nod, urging me to proceed. I made a swift motion and as I did, he gritted his teeth together. I could see that his fangs had sharpened slightly as well. We moved as perfectly and rhythmically as the first few times before, only now I was taking him. It wasn't long before we found ecstasy again and I collapsed on top of his chest.

I rolled to my side to face him and we laid there together, staring into each other, for what felt like moments, but time seemed to move differently when we laid together like this. His peculiar eyes creased in the corners as a grin stretched out across his face. I smiled back at him. "What is it?" I asked.

"Nothing. I was just thinking about how much I love you." I felt my face flush and felt so safe and warm.

"I love you too," I whispered back softly.

After a few moments more, we finally moved to go clean up and adjourned upstairs to climb into the giant king sized bed at the top of the loft. Laying in his... *our* bed I found myself looking out over the railing at the city skyline and sinking into the cool comforting sheets left me with a feeling of pure contentment. I leaned my head against his chest and listened to his heartbeat as the rain pattered against the surrounding windows.

"That wasn't quite what I expected." Chess finally said, breaking the silence.

"What wasn't?" I was amused.

"I didn't think I was going to like it and, in fact, I wasn't sure how you liked it at all, but I get it now." I could feel the smile stretch across his face while I continued to lay my head on his chest. "I don't know that I'd want to do that every time, but I think I'm going to like it." I laughed.

"So you're?.... Oh what did Hunter call it?... A vers queen?" I was amused. I turned to look back up at his face and we both started laughing.

"What does that even mean?" He asked, still laughing.

"I think it means you like it both ways, but honestly, I just heard Hunter say it once." We settled back in and looked out at the gray horizon and overcast morning before my thoughts shifted away from us and our newfound happiness to the stress and anxiety of what's yet to come. I didn't want to think about it, but it eventually creeped its way back into my mind.

"Chess?" I whispered, trying to assess if he was still awake.

"Mhmm?" He responded softly, though evidently tired.

"What happens next?" I asked nervously.

Chess reached his arm around my back and pulled me in closer to him. "I don't know, but whatever it is, we will face it together."

I sighed, content with that comforting thought and let myself fall back into Chess, losing myself in his embrace before finally drifting off to sleep.

# Chapter Twenty-Six

We stole two more days from the world upon our return from Salem and used them to hide out and just to be together, away from everyone. We ordered delivery, watched trashy horror movies, and lost ourselves in each other's presence. However, pressure from Noah, Jesse, and Phisher continued to attack our perfect oasis until we couldn't ignore the world any longer. We convinced Noah that we needed time to settle things in the city before returning home to the pack, but we had reached the point where there was no choice other than to head back to the Beck family home.

I was so nervous as we drove the route that had, by now, become all too familiar, but tried to play it cool. We chatted slightly more casually about the weather, how pretty the Sound looked as we crossed the ferry, and even sang a little with the radio. It felt like a near perfect afternoon despite the uncertainty we were driving toward. As we left the ferry terminal in Kingston, my nerves got the better of me.

"Chess?" I asked quietly.

He reached over and turned down the radio slightly. "Yeah?" he asked.

"What do you think is going to happen when we show up?" I asked, "Should I take my ring off and leave it in the car or what are we going to do?"

He sighed softly. "You can if you want to, but honestly, it won't make any difference."

"What do you mean?" I asked.

"They'll know as soon as we pull into the driveway that we've mated," he responded, sounding super casual.

"What do you mean they'll know?" I asked sheepishly.

"They'll smell it on us," He replied.

"They'll smell it on us!" I was appalled by his statement. "What will they smell?"

"They will smell us, our scents. They are different now that they've mixed." He continued to sound casual. I stupidly sniffed myself to see if I smelt differently, but couldn't tell any difference.

"I don't smell different,"

"Well, of course you don't, but once wolves' mate, it happens. It is how other wolves know when another wolf is claimed. You can smell it." I was stunned. There was still so much I needed to learn about myself now.

"How is it I still don't know all of this?"

"Well, there is a bit of a learning curve, I suppose," he replied. "I guess it just never occurred to me to tell you until it came up, but now that it has." He shrugged his shoulders slightly. On the outside and in his voice, he sounded calm and collected, but I knew we were both worried about the reactions we were about to receive.

"Are you worried?"

"Yes." He replied. "But no matter what happens, I know that I'll still have you and, despite their response, that won't change." He flashed me a toothy grin, and I settled into the seat, slightly comforted by his words.

"Have you given any thought to our wedding?" he asked me.

"What?" I looked over at him as his eyes looked at me with that curious boy look he does and couldn't help but smile. "No," I laughed, "When in the last few days would I have had time to think about our wedding?" I asked.

"Hmm," he responded jokingly, "I have."

"Oh, really?" I said back to him.

"Yeah." He replied confidently.

"Well, what have you thought about?" I was interested.

"Nothing much, just something small," he responded.

"Something small?" I reiterated.

"Yeah, something hopefully out here on the peninsula. Our family and friends. Then one epic race between you and me through the woods." He smiled.

"A race?" I repeated back to him, amused.

"Yeah, it has been too long since we've just gotten to run and play, babe. Aren't you dying inside to get back out into the forest?" He was earnest and excited about the need to go run through the woods and, to be honest, so was I, but I got hung up on the first ever 'babe' to come out of his mouth.

"Babe?" I asked him back.

He laughed, "Yeah, babe."

"Born a werewolf and there's still no better term for a mate except babe?" I laughed.

"Yeah, I'm still working on it." He admitted, running his hand through his hair. I reached over and grabbed his hand and gave it a small kiss.

Another hour had gone by and we reached the northern end of Lake Crescent and began driving further south toward the house. The entire family had been home for a few days because we could smell them as we drove up into the driveway. My stomach sat uneasily and the hair on the back of my neck stood on end as we pulled up to the garage and Chess put the Jeep in park. I had refused to look out my window but felt the eyes of Noah, Emily, and Jenn as we sat there. Chess put his hand on my knee. "You ready?"

he asked reassuringly and I nodded. He pulled open his door and I waited momentarily to open mine until he was rounding the back end of the car so that he would be the first to see his family's faces. I turned to step out onto the concrete driveway and heard nothing. Chess waited for me to step up next to him, and we started toward the porch together. I still hadn't looked, but could feel mixed feelings as we approached. I stopped toe to toe with Chess as we reached the bottom of the porch and held my breath as Chess said, "Dad."

I looked up then and held my head high as I made eye contact with them. Noah stood in an alpha stance, clearly upset, but not angry. Emily's face only showed concern, and Jenn's face shared a firm look of approval.

"Inside. Now." Noah's voice sounded harsh and short. We responded in line with his directions and walked up the stairs to head into the house. Chess opened the door and the rest of us followed behind him. I followed Chess's lead of holding his head up high and showing that we had done nothing wrong. We walked into the sitting room where I had initially met them all those months ago and I sat next to Chess on the sofa. Jenn took a seat in the chair next to the fireplace and we all sat in silence, waiting for someone to break. I looked over at Chess, who was staring directly into his father's eyes as the two of them continued to stare each other down for some sort of dominance over the other. Several more moments passed and the air felt heavy and thick. I looked over at Jenn, who gave a passive shrug, and then at Emily as she smiled at me softly.

Then Chess broke the stalemate. "Did you know?" he asked, gruff and hard.

His father continued to bear down on Chess with eyes glowing slightly. "Know what?" He asked.

"That this was some wild goose chase and you'd known all along that Lyle was, in fact, Conri?" The tone hadn't changed. Noah's disposition wavered slightly. And if you hadn't been watching, you would have never seen it.

"Of course not," Noah replied. "I would have never put either of you in danger like that, but let's not get away from the problem here."

"And what problem would that be?" Chess cut Noah off and a growl stirred in his chest. The hairs on the back of his neck rose, and his canines showed.

"You went off to Salem to mate with another man and bring shame onto your pack despite me specifically telling you it would not be tolerated?" Noah growled and I felt myself grow angry at the display of aggression toward Chess.

"That is not what happened and you know it. You knew I loved him since the moment I brought him here. You felt the bond between us from the moment he turned. This was meant to happen. Lyle and I are mated and there's nothing you can do to undo that." Chess shouted back at Noah and then the two of them both were up on their feet, snarling at each other.

I tried my best to stay out of it, but my wolf started tearing out from inside and I jumped to my feet, too. I started growing in size like I had that night in the shed, before Chess turned quickly and stood between me and Noah.

"Woah Lyle. Calm down, it's okay." Chess proclaimed as the shift on my face began. I reined it back in and felt myself calm down, feeling terrible for losing it so suddenly. As I sat back down, Chess turned back to Noah.

He stared back at Noah, repeating his initial question, "Did you know?" Noah sat back down on the sofa and gestured for Chess to do the same. Chess followed his suggestion and settled down into the seat next to me.

"Can you elaborate on what you think I might know?" Noah asked with a cooler head. Chess continued to burn hot next to me, trying to contain this rage inside so I spoke instead.

"That it was your family who betrayed my family." I stated quietly.

Noah turned and looked at me. He was clearly upset that I was now Chess's mate, but for the moment he looked at me like he had before when I was one of his pack, his son, and he looked sad.

He took a deep sigh and his eyes moved toward the floor. "I did." Chess growled aggressively toward Noah and Emily spoke. "Noah!" Her voice filled with overwhelming disapproval and disbelief. We all sat silently for a while as we digested the truth and settled into an uncomfortable silence.

"Why didn't you say anything?" Chess finally asked.

"This was a secret passed down from Alpha to Alpha in our pack. It is our deepest shame and you would have found out eventually, when I passed the pack on to you." Noah admitted.

Jenn sat in shock just as Emily did, but remained silent.

Noah turned his attention back to me, "Lyle, I never intended for you to find out this way and I am truly sorry for the atrocity that was caused by my family and how it affected your pack and, eventually, you. We can never make it right, but none of this changes the fact that you and Chess cannot be together."

"You don't get to have a say in that." Jenn said, finally speaking up. "These two are bound by both natural bond and mating and, despite everything, they have found their way to each other. Are you truly too blind to see it or do you just choose not to, Noah? They are true mates. I have felt it since the two of them found each other and now that what's done is done and their bond is even stronger."

"This isn't a decision for you to make, Jenn. This is dangerous. It won't be long before Gerard takes the knowledge he's learned to the Union and they will demand for us to bring him forth. What will we do then? Go to war with the Union? Our numbers are growing smaller and smaller. We don't have the wolf power to keep any of us safe from them, especially Lyle. He's the last Conri. Some packs will want him dead, others will want him for their own, and Chess, being mated to him, puts us in the crossfire alongside him."

"Well, if that's where it puts me, then so be it!" Chess spoke back up, "Lyle is mine and I will die to keep him safe!"

The arguments continued to go round and round, about what we had done, what my lineage meant, and that the only thing any of this meant was danger. Danger not only for myself, but for these people I said I loved. I leaned back into the couch as images of Chess lying broken in the shack flooded my mind again.

*How could I be so selfish?* I thought to myself. Destiny, war, death. Everything kept coming back to the impending doom my existence created and how all of it could have been avoided if only Chess and I had stayed apart. My heart sank lower into my chest as words continued to fly around the room like bullets amongst the family.

Round and round they went arguing as to what was to be done with me and the problems my existence would cause. As they did, the arguments began to sound more and more like the conversations I'd heard amongst the multiple foster families that had no longer wanted me. The only difference now was Chess. He was actively fighting, fighting for me and telling his family that he would gladly lay down his life to protect my own. I watched as the first person to love me as his own, to claim me as his husband, started to break apart his own family to be with me.

*I never wanted that,* I thought. I never wanted any of this to happen to the people I loved. All I'd wanted was to find my place in the world, to change my life, and to create a family who would want me for me. I thought I had found that here with the Becks and certainly knew I'd found it with Chess, but now knowing who I was and watching my family break apart over the decision of whether or not to put their lives in danger just so that I could have what I wanted?

*No,* I thought to myself. I couldn't put this weight on them and I certainly won't sit by idly, watching them fall for me as Chess did in Salem. I felt the part of Chess within me grip my heart tightly in disagreement with the thoughts that were rushing through my head as they all continued to fire bullets about war, fighting, and death amongst each other, and how anything to do with me would certainly lead to one if not all three of those things. I immediately hated and resented everything I was for allowing this to happen. Somehow, inside of me, I believed this was the right outcome.

*How could I have ever truly believed that my life would amount to anything more than the reject I had always been?* I hated everything about who I had become, for who I was, and I hated being the last red wolf.

"No." I finally said quietly, the words burning my throat as the wolf inside me pulled back. I looked around the room as bullets continued to zoom through the air between the pack members. My eyes connected with Emily as her eyes glistened.

"No." I said it again, slightly louder, fighting against the beast inside me. I winced at the turmoil it was causing me before opening my eyes to see Chess looking at me, canines sharpened and ready to continue arguing. The room fell quiet and everyone waited for my response. I flushed under the pressure, as all the eyes in the room turned in my direction. I looked away momentarily to see Chess's siblings listening from the stairwell, clearly stirred with emotion as well. I couldn't let these people...... This family..... My family die because of me or because of the love I had for their son, their brother, and their future alpha. In my pursuit of and feelings for Chess I had never really considered the cost and I couldn't bear the pain our love was bringing to our family. I knew it was going to cause problems, but images of Chess's body continued to flood my brain. My stomach grew into knots as I began to envision all the Becks laying similarly to how I had found him and I couldn't bear it. Their lives could be ruined and it's all my fault.

"No one is going to die because of me." I made a blanket statement and another long pause settled into the room. "I...I never meant for any of this." I stared into Noah's eyes and tears filled the corners of mine. "I.. I only ever wanted to be a part of your family and only ever loved your son, but the cost is too hig.."

"Shut your mouth," Chess yelled, flashing his eyes at me. I could feel him poking around in my head, discovering what I was about to say. I could feel his stare tear through me like the words that had been flying around the room. I continued to stare at Noah and tried to ignore Chess' protests.

"The cost is too high," I continued, "this was the first place that ever felt like home to me and I won't..."

"Stop it." Chess shouted aggressively as I tried to push through his continued assault in my mind. My wolf growled in protest as I fought through and Chess's wolf wrapped itself so tight around my heart it made it hard to breathe.

I stood from my seat and looked at Noah again, "I'm sorry." I turned and headed toward the front door. Chess was hot on my heels, telling me to sit back down and to stop. I glanced at Chess' brother and sister on the stairs, clearly upset over the confrontation and continued to keep walking. I opened the door and stepped out onto the porch before Chess tackled me to the ground. He pinned me to the porch and his eyes flashed as he resisted transitioning out of rage and the desperation to stop my leaving, it came off of him in waves.

"What are you doing?" he shouted, I looked into his eyes and could see the pain I was causing him.

"Leaving." I said coldly.

"No, you're not." He growled at my throat. "You are mine and I am yours," his anger subsided slightly, "forever." His voice sounded wounded now. I was hurting too, but the images of all them laying pooled on the floor continued to swirl in my mind, I had to leave. It was the only way to prevent what would come now that more people knew the truth of who I am - what I am. I was naïve to think that I would ever get what I wanted from this life and that I could just be with the person I loved and live happily ever after. Time and time again, this world always showed me I could never have the things I wanted. Only now it meant costing people their lives to pursue the life I wanted.

"I have to." I whimpered, sounding defeated. I turned my head away from him and laid it against the wood porch. It took all the will I had inside of me to command myself to hold my composure despite his pleas. To remain cold. To save him from the curse I barred.

"No," he said again, this time letting go of one of my wrists and twisting my face back to his and pushing his lips into mine. "You can't go," he whispered through my lips and into my mouth. "I'll never let you...." He stopped before going limp and collapsed on top of me. I looked past him to see Noah standing above us, having injected something into Chess to make him pass out.

He hauled Chess's body off of me and allowed me to stand to my feet. I could hear Jenn in the background, raging and shifting inside the house. The sounds of fabric tearing and glass breaking all while Emily stood at the door watching behind tear soaked eyes. I lowered my head. *This is all my fault*, I thought.

"It's time for you to go," Noah stated as he positioned Chess's arm around his neck and stabilized his body to carry him inside. Hearing the words come out of his mouth echoed through my mind and, while I'd heard it so many times before ,the sting of it shattered a part of me I had kept armored throughout my childhood to protect against this pain, a part of my heart where I had only recently learned to drop my guard.

"Don't let anything bad happen to him." I said back through gritted teeth, continuing to stare at the ground.

"He'll be fine. Just make sure you stay on the move. They'll be coming for you." I looked up at him, Noah's demeanor wavering slightly, as if he wasn't sure what we were doing was the right thing, but he didn't budge. His lips held tight in a line stretched across his stern face. I turned and walked off the front porch, running toward the tree line. Each step felt heavier and heavier as I moved away from him. I pushed down all my instincts, against the beast tearing at my back urging me to turn around and let him save me, but it was too late. I crossed through the trees and vanished out of sight.

# Chapter Twenty-Seven

I awoke in bed, head spinning and heart aching. My stomach churned and I rolled over the edge of the bed to spew vomit onto the floor. I cracked my eyes and looked out through the haze, I was in my room. I moved to sit up in bed and failed miserably as I fell back down onto the mattress. I looked to my left and saw that the other side of the bed was empty.

*Where is he?* I thought to myself, *Where is Lyle?*

My heart was wretched in my chest and the part of Lyle that had lived happily in my chest was waning. I could still feel him there, but the warm sensation that normally accompanied him was cold and hollow. My stomach bellowed again and another wave of nausea came rushing out. I had just enough time to turn again and add it to the growing pile on the floor next to me. I looked out the window after to see that the moon was shining in on me, the day had passed by. Anger bellowed in my core and I pushed myself to sit again, to get up, to go after him, but failed again and again. My wolf and I pulled into ourselves and felt the waves of sorrow move through my human body. Everything ached within me as I continued to fight against whatever it was that  prevented me from going. I fell to the floor, trying to reach for the door. My vision wavered and the room began to spin before my wolf and I sang out our turmoil into the hollowness that bore through us. I tried to shift and, as I pushed outwards and forced some of the bones to shatter and change, I was consumed with waves of nausea and vertigo. I pushed harder, but failed as the cracking of bones only worsened the ongoing state I found myself in. Letting out another howl into the night, I heard my door open. I turned and through my blurred gaze, made out my father standing in the doorway.

"Where is he?" My voice said, groggy and slurred as I continued to fight.

"Gone," I tried to focus my vision on his face as the word hit my ears, he sounded remorseful. For the first time in my life, my father sounded unsure of himself, the shroud of unyielding confidence I'd known my whole life absent in one spoken word.

"How could you let him leave?!" I slurred out the words in anger as my head continued to spin not knowing if the words were even discernible from the mumbling.

"If he would have stayed....." He trailed of, "I.. I can't lose you. You're my son. They'll kill him and you." Defeat and grief hung on every word.

"Then I'll die fighting! Lyle is mine....." The slurs sounded even less discernible than before, "my mate, my alpha" My stomach wretched and I clung to it as the pains continued, "I would die for him a million times over." I growled.

"He is not your alpha. I am still your alpha until you take over that role in this pack." He growled.

"Lyle is the alpha." I spit out between gritted teeth, "he is the last. I have to protect him." I howled again as I continued to fight against the spinning and the pain to push myself up from the floor trying to stand and face him before collapsing again.

He remained silent. "What did you do to me?"

"I.... I saved you from yourself." He whispered, still sounding unsure.

"Save me?" I scoffed, "From the moment he stumbled into my life, he has been the one." I fought through the slurs. "Everything in my life made sense the moment we mated and I will be damned if I let anyone keep us apart. I will leave this pack and make my own with him as my alpha, if that's what it takes. I may be a Beck and your son, but despite - and possibly in spite of those things - I alone will make the choices that are best for me. Lye is the choice that is best for me." I forced myself to sit upright before falling back, hitting the edge of the bed. I sat up breathing heavily, holding my ground, and waiting for a response, but got nothing. A moment or two passed as we faced off with one another in the doorway of my bedroom before I lost the fight and I felt everything going limp, my body moving back toward the floor. My dad swooped in and grabbed me just before my head hit the ground, lifting me back up with ease.

"I know, son," he said as he laid me back down in bed. My vision flurried again and made the lights flicker in and out. "Rest now, we will figure it out when you wake." I looked up at his face and saw my father cry. I went to say something again, but the drugs took me before the thought could escape my mouth.

"He's right, you know," Jenn spoke from the doorway, peering into Chess's room. "There's nothing that can be done except to embrace what destiny or maybe karma has brought back to our doorstep."

Noah stood and shook the uncertainty and tears from his eyes before turning to his sister. "You're right," he said, "I should have never let him leave....I failed them both."

"No," she said, her face full of concern as she moved forward and placed her hand on his shoulder, "you haven't failed them yet. There's still time to fix it."

"He's so angry with me, Jenn. How can I fix it?" He replied with defeat hanging on every word.

"We let him go," said Emily, walking in the room toward Noah.

"He needs to find Lyle and while he's searching, we will prepare for whatever comes next."

"What?" Noah asked, sounding displaced, as she planted a kiss on his cheek.

She repeated herself, "we let him go find Lyle and bring him back by whatever means necessary. Then we make sure that boy knows he is as much our son as the rest of our pack. We will defend him like we would our own." Jenn nodded in agreement and she waited with Emily for Noah to respond.

"You're right," he said, hanging his head low. "I should have never let him leave."

Emily reached out and put her hand to his face. "That's not important now. The only thing we can control is what we do next." Noah nodded in agreement, looking back at Chess passed out on the bed, "I just hope he will forgive me."

I woke up to the warmth of the sun shining through the windows. My head still spun, but I was finally able to focus my eyes toward the wall. The control over my motor functions seemed to be restored and I sat up even though my head ached and pounded in my skull. It was nothing compared to the hole I felt in my heart and the pain I was enduring by not having Lyle near me. My heart felt as cold and hollow as it had the last time I'd awoken. My soul had shattered and, for reasons I didn't understand, I flung my hand to my chest and felt my lungs start to move sporadically.

*Where is he?* I panicked, and turned inward, searching for the part of Lyle that was within me. My chest felt tight and water began falling from my eyes as I grabbed my chest harder and began gasping for air. Jenn rushed into the room and sat down beside me, placing her hand on my back.

"It's okay Chess," she said, "calm down, it's okay. You're having a panic attack." She continued to rub my back and kept talking to me,

"Breathe with me Chess, slow it down." She started taking deep, slow breaths and encouraged me to copy. I couldn't stop. *Where is he?* My mind flooding, my heart empty, and my wolf feeling utterly helpless as he too began searching.

"Chess!" She yelled at me, continuing to mimic the breaths. "I... I... I can't... I can't feel him." I felt myself choking on air as I tried to speak. Jenn pulled my hands down and put her hands on my chest. "Chess here. He's right here." She looked into my eyes, "focus and breathe." I started following her lead.

"That's it, keep breathing." I watched her and felt the warmth of her hand push against my chest hard.

"It's okay, Chess. It's all going to be okay." She said, trying to reassure me.

As my breath continued to slow I finally managed a response, "no... no, it's not... Lyle's gone. I can still feel him, but he's not there like before." I looked around the room, for anything of his. Starting to feel panic creep back in. "I have to find him." I said stood up suddenly and felt my knees shake as I moved toward the bedroom door.

Jenn grabbed my arm and pulled me back. "And you will find him, but you won't be able to if you don't calm down and rest."

I sat back at the edge of the bed and continued to breathe as the drugs continued to wear off. "I can't rest, Jenn. I have to find him. Something is wrong. What if the Dubois took him? He can't survive on his own; a wolf needs his pack. I need to get to him."

"And he will have the pack." Noah stated as he turned the corner and walked into the room.

"He will?"

"He will." Jenn agreed approvingly.

"Chess, I was wrong to have behaved as I did. You are both my son, and I am so sorry that in that moment I failed you." My father knelt down next to Jenn and looked me in the eyes. "It's a father's and an alpha's duty to protect his pack from any threat and what I thought was best for our pack was wrong. I should have never betrayed the two of you that way and I'm sorry." He bowed his head to me, signaling respect and submission. "We need to find Lyle and do everything we can to bring him back home. We have a lot to prepare for and, you're right, he is not safe."

I nodded in agreement but couldn't find the words to acknowledge all that my father had just said. As I stood, my dad rose from the ground and said, "I love you, son."

"I love you too."

I headed toward my closet, grabbing a backpack from inside, and started shoving clothes into it from my dresser drawers. I quickly removed my vomit stained shirt and swapped it for something clean as my mom walked in.

"Where would Lyle have gone?"

"I'm fairly certain he would have gone to see his best friend Jesse before doing anything. I'm going to start with her and go on from there." I said, leaving my room and walking down the hall.

"Dad, do you still have access to Lyle's account?" I asked as I continued to move forward.

"I do," he responded.

"Will you please watch to see if he uses it and keep me updated about where purchases are made?" I asked him. He nodded in agreement as they followed me.

"You and Lyle are really mated?" George asked as I rounded the corner headed toward the stairs. Valorie was with him and I paused slightly as it hadn't occurred to me that no one had probably spoken to either of them about everything. I could tell they had a lot of questions to ask me. If time weren't so important at this moment, I would have given them the time that both of them deserved.

"Yes, we are." I said plainly as I kept moving past them toward the stairs.

"So you're gay?" Valorie asked, slightly confused.

"I don't know what I am Valorie..." I shook my head in frustration trying to leave, "all I know is that for me it's Lyle and that's all I know."

"Well, I think it's... uhh... you know.... cool," George said, trying to sound supportive following me.

I stopped and turned to them both. "Cool, is it?" I asked him back.

"Yeah... I mean. I think it's great that you found someone who... well... you know, is yours?" His response came out more of a question, but it made me smile.

"Well, you've never acted gay?" Valorie shared, still confused.

"Does it matter to you if I'm gay or not?" I asked her back.

"No." She said, "I just know a lot of gay people and never thought you were."

"You know that it's not the same for wolves. It was just him. That was it. If that means I'm gay, then sure, that's what it means. All I know right now is I have to find him and fix this or I won't ever have a mate at all."

"Right. Well, cool." She said pausing again, processing everything before adding, "he's way too good for you, ya know." She replied sarcastically.

"On that, we can totally agree." I said, reaching for the door and opening it just before she flung her arms around my neck and gave me a wildly unexpected hug.

"Be safe and bring both my brothers home. Okay?" She said as she pulled away and I nodded at her.

I walked out onto the porch and my family followed me outside as I headed toward my car. "Bring home our boy," Mom called out one last time as I reached the driver's side door.

"I will. You can count on it." I replied as I hopped into the car and pulled out of the driveway. As I drove out onto the highway, I reached for my cell and called him. I knew it would be a long shot that he'd even answer, but I had to start somewhere. The dial tone rang once before a recorded message informed me that the number was no longer in service. That's bullshit, I thought to myself, knowing Lyle had blocked my number.

There was only one thing left to do, I thought to myself and I turned inwards, pulling on what connection to Lyle I still had. At first, the only emotions I felt were despair, loneliness, and emptiness, but I couldn't stop. I continued reaching out for him, trying to feel him, to sense where he might be. I was driving way too fast, but I had to. He had so much lead time to run that I knew I would have to do everything in my power to catch up to him. Trees zoomed by the windows in the car and minutes already felt like hours.

*Come on, Lyle*, I thought to myself, continuing to feel for him, for anything that could tell me where he was or how he was feeling, and for the next hour, nothing.

"Got you!" I said to myself as an image of Lyle finally flashed as I saw him sitting on a ferry boat. He looked so sad and it broke my heart more to see him look that way. I wanted to be there to grab him and hold him close to make his pain go away. I tried to push out to him and to tell him I was coming for him, but he didn't get it. I could feel that he didn't. All that mattered now was for me to get to him. I knew it wouldn't be easy. He wasn't going to make it easy. He was equally brave and stubborn and if he thought his leaving was going to save everyone, he wouldn't change his mind unless I was right there in front of him. I hated him for that, but all that mattered now was getting to him.

# Chapter Twenty-Eight

I sat alone on a bench in the upper canopy of the ferry on the long ride back to Seattle. I had already called Jesse as I caught a bus that brought me back to Port Townsend, but she hadn't answered. I sent her a text briefly as I sat down on the bus before she called me in a furry. I managed to once again talk her through some of the information without revealing too much, but I knew she knew more of what was going on than just what I had been telling her.

She would be waiting for me as soon as I walked off the ferry and would drive me back to my apartment in the city. I would have very little time to explain things, how do you explain to someone that they are incredibly dear to you but that you could never talk to them again? It wouldn't be safe for any of them to be my friend. I had to be quick, I knew I wouldn't be able to stay much longer before someone came looking for me. I also knew it would most likely be Chess. There was no way a sedative was going to keep him from coming for me and no amount of sway or power that Noah had that would keep him at heel.

*I wish this had never happened;* I thought to myself, staring out at the horizon as the sun rose. I wanted so much more in life and look at what happened.

*Be careful what you wish for*, crossed my mind, and I could feel my wolf rustle slightly inside. I took it back. I'd felt more myself in the last several months than I had in my entire life, but I had never known what the cost of this life would be. Still, I wouldn't take back knowing Chess even though the thought of him felt like a long sharp piece of ice sinking deeper and deeper into my heart. The physical pain I had created, knowing that I was leaving him, was insurmountable to any other pain I had ever experienced, and yet I had to leave. It was the only way to keep him and the others safe. My existence is a danger to those I love and the only way to keep them safe is to keep my pursuers moving toward me and away from them. A tear fell from my eye and landed on the gold band wrapped around my finger. I looked down at it again and I contemplated taking it off, for the third time since running into the woods, but I couldn't do it. Nothing meant more to me in the world than knowing that someone like Chess could love someone like me. Truly love me for me, even though I could no longer be with him at least I could keep this to remind me of why I had to stay away from the ones I loved.

I tried to think of what I was going to say to Jesse, attempting to rehearse some kind of story to tell her, even though I knew I wouldn't be able to just disappear without telling her the truth. I also knew that it would be hard for her to understand and I worried about the problems it may cause for Chess and his family later, but I knew I had to do what I had to do. The ferry pulled into the harbor and docked just as the daylight grew brighter, stretching its light through the spaces between the city's buildings. I gathered myself and headed down to the lower deck.

I walked off the ferry and onto the boardwalk toward where Jesse said she would meet me. As I approached, I could see her waiting. She had leaned up against her car, waiting patiently and alone. She waved at me as she saw me walking toward her.

"Hey," I said as I got closer.

"Hey," she said, smiling back at me sweetly, as she gestured for me to get in the car. I looped around and hopped in the passenger seat. She followed suit, moving to the driver's side just before I finished getting buckled in. She put the car in drive and we ascended the city streets heading toward north Seattle. We sat quietly for most of the drive as I continued to look out the window and then back down at the ring on my finger.

"You hungry?" She asked, breaking the silence as she took the exit off the highway heading toward the apartments.

"I am."

"Good." She smiled over at me and headed down the road toward what I know thought of as "our pizza place."

She pulled up to the first place we had eaten together and I smiled. "Pizza? For breakfast?" I asked her quizzically.

"Is there even a better alternative?" she said sarcastically. We both laughed and walked into the parlor and grabbing our normal table in the back. We gave our order to our waiter and settled into the chairs. As we did I prepared myself for a good old-fashioned interrogation.

"So what happened?" Jesse finally asked. "Before you two left to go back to his parents, we couldn't pry either of you out of his place. How can you go from that to being over in a matter of hours?"

"It's so much more complicated than all of that Jess." I sighed, "I don't even know where to begin other than that I have been keeping a lot from you, and I know I shouldn't have, but once you know you can't ever not know and it may not be safe for you to know."

"Safe for me to know?" She chuckled, "What is Chess, some sort of super spy or something?" She said as she continued to laugh.

"No. It's nothing like that." I paused and hesitated for a longer moment, reconsidering everything I was about to say.

"It's just that I'm...... Chess and I, we are uhhh......" I struggled to find the words to say. *How do you even tell someone this?* I thought to myself.

"Oh, come on now, out with it." She said, growing slightly impatiently.

"We are.... Uhhh...," I paused again, looking around the empty parlor before mouthing werewolves with no auditory output of any kind.

"I'm sorry... What?"

I sighed... gathered up the courage again and whispered, "We are werewolves." Barely an octave above mouthing the words. She looked at me for a second, confused, and then laughed.

"This isn't funny." I looked at her dead serious and she paused.

"Lyle, I'm sorry, but I really can't take this seriously. Werewolves don't exis...." I stretched my hand across the table and covered her mouth. "Shhhhhh, not so loud!" I whispered.

She nodded in acknowledgement and I pulled my hand away. I tried to think of how to make her believe me and my only thought was to show her. I looked around the parlor again before laying my hand out on the table in front of me, behind the salt, pepper, and cheese sitting in the middle of the table. I shifted it slightly, showing the claws grow out of my hands and the hair thicken into a coat of red fur on top of my hand and down my arm before letting it vanish. She stared fiercely at my hand. I couldn't tell if she was scared and about to run or what she was going to do, but she just kept staring at me.

"Lyle.... I... uhh... I don't know what to say." She said, looking speechless.

"Don't say anything." I proclaimed quietly, "like I said, it's not safe for you to know any of this, but you being you."

"Why are you telling me this now, then?" She asked.

"Because I have to leave and get far away from here and from all of you. I know there's no other way for you to let me go than to tell you the truth." I breathed.

"So you're telling me.... my best friend.... is a" she stopped and mouthed werewolf before continuing "and that now you are leaving?" She sounded irritated.

"Correct." I sighed.

"Uhhh. Absolutely not. You're not going to drop such an awesome bomb like this and then vanish. Whatever it is, we can figure this out." She said, being completely herself.

"No, Jesse.... This isn't all of it. I have to leave. It's not safe for me to be around anyone. It could get everyone killed." I explained.

"You're going to have to explain it to me, then. All of it. There's no scenario in which you leaving will fix anything, but please try and explain. Start from the beginning." She leaned in just as our pizza was dropped off at the table. She thanked our waiter nicely and then waved him to go away. "Begin," she said impatiently.

I sighed deeply and started from the moment I met him, how he terrified me and excited me all in the same stroke. Then how we kept being pulled together like we were and what happened on the camping trip and how, unknowingly, it had caused an ancient curse to be broken. The curse that had really started all of this. I saw the sparkle in her eyes as she started connecting the dots along the time-line of our friendship. I explained my first transition, my family bloodline, what mating means to wolves, about the union, and the Dubois. I left no detail unexplained or elaborated upon. I told her about witches and that I'd killed other wolves, about Chess and I and his family, and how I am the last red wolf and what that means.

We sat there as I explained everything in excruciating detail. Spilling my guts about the trials of the past several months as she listened intently and purposefully. Pausing and asking questions for clarification only, trying not to interrupt or go off on a side conversation that could take much longer than the time we had left together to explain. I reached the end point, where I had  decided I had to leave and to  run in order to keep everyone safe and that it was my conclusion that it was the only way to keep everyone alive.

She reached over after I finally finished and grabbed my hand, "Lyle, I am so sorry that all of this happened to you and I can't imagine what weight you are currently feeling, but in all honesty, and I say this out of love and as your best friend," she paused, "you are an idiot."

I stared at her, hardly blinking as she summed up my entire experience into that. "How am I an idiot?" I asked her plainly.

"Well, frankly, you all are." She took a sip of her drink and leaned back in her chair. "You don't run from the people you love in these situations. You hold them close and fight for what you have. Haven't you ever read one of those epic novels or seen any movies?" She took another sip. "The only way to get through this is together, not alone."

"This isn't some story, Jesse. This is real life and life has taught me things aren't like they are in books or in movies. It's a cluster fuck of a million different things and it all points to me leaving and going into hiding." I tried to explain again.

"With all due respect, love, you're wrong and by running, you are a coward." She paused, "However, this is your journey, not mine, you have to do what you feel is right. I want you to stay and we, your friends, will help you figure this out if you want us to. I will keep your secret if you ask me too, but I want you to know you have choices other than the one you are currently choosing for yourself." She grabbed my hand again. "You will always be my best friend, no matter what you choose to do that won't change. But this isn't the new frontier or the middle ages or whatever it was when your ancestors were murdered, we have law and order now, and if you can't find resolution in the wolfie world, then find it in the human world is what I say."

"That's oversimplifying it a bit." I tried to protest.

"Maybe it is, but you don't have to leave the man you love or the friends you love to keep us safe. Let us keep each other safe." She let go.

A long pause grew between us and silence set in as I contemplated everything she was telling me. *Could she be right?* I thought to myself and thought over my plan again. As I began thinking about the merits she proposed, I felt him.

"I have to go," I announced suddenly.

"Why? What's wrong?" Jesse asked me.

"It's him, it's Chess... He's here." She looked around the restaurant.

"No, he isn't?" she said, puzzled.

"No, he's.... he's in Seattle. I can feel him looking for me." I stood. "If I don't go now, I never will. I'm sorry Jesse, this is just how it has to be." She sighed and stood.

"If you're going to leave, I expect a call at least once a month to know you're safe. You don't have to tell me where you are, but at least do me that favor." I nodded quietly and heavily contemplated everything she said. It was everything I wanted to hear and feel. Even so, it wasn't enough. I didn't want to leave, but the only problem I could see in all of their lives was me. If they had never met me, they wouldn't be in danger like this. My mind was made up and I believed that what I was doing was the right thing for everyone. I'd never had people in my life that loved me as much as I loved them and I would do anything to keep them safe. I felt my entire body shake and quiver. I could feel him searching for me, from the moment his feet touched the Seattle pavement, I knew Chess was coming. I tried to push back the urge to run to him and tried to fight his efforts to find me.

She hugged me. "I hope one day you'll realize you're wrong and come back to us. I love you." She reached into her purse and gave me the key to her car and what money she had in her purse. "Be safe." I nodded in acknowledgement and headed for the door. I resisted the urge to look back once I reached the door and pushed my way through. Every instinct in my body was fighting me to stay. My wolf was pushing back against me as he howled out for Chess, but I kept moving. I got in the car, put it in drive, and drove. I didn't know where I was going, but wherever it was, I went.

# Chapter Twenty-Nine

Three weeks had passed since I pulled out onto the street and drove away from the life I loved. No matter what I did or where I went, I could always feel Chess close behind me. I was parked somewhere along the highway, somewhere just outside of Texas. It wasn't until I stopped in Nevada that I realized Chess was probably watching my account and seeing where I was spending money to stay hot on my trail. I made one last large withdrawal in Vegas before fleeing the state. I sat in my car and counted all I had left. I was amazed at how fast almost two thousand dollars had been spent.

Who knew being on the run was going to be so expensive? I had about 800 dollars left and didn't know how much more I was going to need to keep running. I leaned my head into the steering wheel and felt an overwhelming rush of grief and frustration. I started slapping my hands on the dashboard and screamed out loud until my hand went down and straight through the dashboard.

"Shit." I said to myself, pulling my hand out of the dashboard. I opened the door and stepped out onto the highway. Not a car for miles and endless dirt as far as the eye could see. I walked around to the other side, leaned up against the trunk, and looked out towards the horizon. *How did I think this was going to go? I couldn't go into hiding when the love of my life was just as relentless at finding me as I was about running from him to keep him safe.* I closed my eyes and quietly thought to myself, *just let me go.* A tear ran down my cheek and I reached up to wipe it away. As I did, another consciousness entered my mind and echoed — *never.* The thought brought a sense of relief to my mind and a hug wrapped around my heart.

*Damn it Chess,* I thought to myself quickly. He was close again, just close enough to hear faint thoughts from one another. I pulled myself together and returned to the driver's seat, taking off again.

Time continued to blur as another week passed, I found a decent stop in New Orleans. I took refuge in an abandoned home at the edge of town where windows were broken and the walls had deteriorated. I sat on the floor with my back leaned up against the wall and was eating the last good meal I was going to be able to afford. This would never end. This cat-and-mouse game where Chess and I pitted our wills against one another. I chuckled at the irony of it. In all the time I'd recently had alone to think I would relive the memories of all the months where I was truly happy for the first time in my life. It was all I had left to hold on to and by thinking of happy times, I couldn't help but think about how sad an existence I was going to live. I thought of my mom a lot and wondered if her turmoil in the end was like my own now.

I wish I could have known her; I wish it wasn't just me left. I wondered how much longer I could go on like this. I'd reached the bottom of the barrel and no longer could afford anything except the gas to keep moving. The thought came to me to give up. To let Chess come and save me from this mess I'd created and to go back to everything and everyone like it never happened. There was nothing more I wanted than that. My life had become physical agony day in and day out, constantly feeling the tearing sensation in my heart as I'd run just far enough away from him so that I could no longer feel him. Each time it happened, it would get harder and harder, with my resolve for our game of chase growing weaker. I felt sorry for myself and resented who I was and what I represented as the last red wolf. I could no longer feel my wolf inside of me, as if he resented me as much as I resented myself. All this time had passed in between the massacre and the mess of a life all the members of my family had lived through each lifetime since and how all of it inexplicably fell onto my shoulders.

*What did that even mean? What the hell I was supposed to do as the last red wolf, the last Conri?* I scoffed at the thought.

If only my family could see me now and the low level we had fallen to. *John should have just let it all end that night,* I thought, although I immediately took it back. He had done everything, both of them, to keep their son safe and to see our lineage survive, but at what cost? I pushed my head back against the peeled wallpaper and let myself drift off into a restless sleep.

The next morning, I took a walk through the French Quarter and enjoyed myself for a moment, listening to the hustle and bustle of the crowds. The jazz music seemed to infect everyone that it touched and even I found some of my spirits lifted. I enjoyed looking at the street art for sale and watched as a man painted his next masterpiece in front of the world. I stalled for a bit to watch him use all his reds, browns, and blacks as he poured his heart into the piece. It made me think about how cold my heart had become and how that place within me that was once full and warm was now empty. A tear pooled in my eye as an older woman passed by. I don't know what prompted her to approach me, but she was walking right toward me with intent in her eyes.

"What troubles you sha?" She walked right up to me and put her hand on my shoulder. Her accent was thick with a cajun dialect, she was dressed in what looked like an older dark red gown with gold rings hanging on the side of her hip, dark green sleeves, and golden embroidery laced throughout. She had grays flowing through her thick and wild black hair. Her dark complexion and crows feet that hugged her eyes made her seem caring and wise, but a no nonsense look all the same. She reminded me of what I would consider a mother to the world.

"Oh... uhh... nothing..." I started, "I.. I'm fine." I rubbed my eye slightly and pushed back my feelings back below the surface.

"You don't be a fooling me you, I know what I see in front of me. You looks lost to me sha, needin' some help you do." She smiled. "Come with me, you, Mama Lootie, will help you." She gripped my hands in hers and rubbed the top slightly. Her touch was comforting and very soothing, her very presence made my troubles lessen to a simmer. I thought about taking her up on her offer, but also felt that it was getting close for me to be moving along soon. Staying in one place too long puts me at risk of losing my lead from Chess.

"Oh... Well... Actually, I was just about to be on my way." I told her politely.

"No, yous aren't a leaving until Mama Lootie sees you fed. You come with Mama now." She pulled on my hand, which showed some incredible strength on her part. I did as she beckoned and followed her. She led me through some of the back way streets to a small apartment tucked in an alley back out of view. Part of me thought maybe I should be afraid of being pulled so far off the open path, but nothing she did or said felt anything but welcoming and hospitable. Walking into her apartment revealed further revelations that this was no ordinary elderly woman. Her house was filled with herbs drying on the walls, rows upon rows of old spice jars, and many signs of occult type decor throughout. She had a pot of food cooking on the stove and it smelt superb. She waved her hand in the air and wind chimes moved outside the window.

"The sound will soothe the soul, don't ya think?" she asked, enjoying the way the metal bars clanked and sang.

"You're a witch?" I asked her plainly.

"No, no witch, but Mama knows a lone wolf when Mama sees one." She turned and smiled, "Sit, sit. You have nothing to fear from Mama."

"How did you...." I started, "if you're not a witch."

"Spirits be a talkin' in my ear from time to time, young wolf. Mama may be no witch, but spirits tell Mama what she needs to know." She picked up two bowls off the shelf and ladled some contents from the pot into them. "MMMMMmmm, don't tha smell right?" She asked, taking a whiff of her cooking.

"It smells great." I agreed. She handed me a bowl and sat down opposite of me. I watched as she immediately started eating and I took a bite as well. It was... spicy, but very delicious and warmed me all the way through.

"Nothing like some soup in your bowl to fill the soul."

"So you said spirits told you I'm a wolf?" I asked her after a few moments.

"Huh?" she turned her head away and off to the side as if she was listening to someone else talking.

"Spirits have a lot to say about you young wolf," she smiled and took another bite, "why you runnin young wolf?" she asked.

"It's complicated." I shrugged, continuing to eat.

"All life is complicated, but that's not why you run." She waved her hand, and the chimes rang again.

"I... I'm a danger to others." I said.

"No," she turned and looked at me curiously, eyeballing me up and down, "you no danger to others."

"I mean, I put others in danger by being near them." I said. She turned her head again to listen to something I couldn't hear. I tried listening harder and more intently, but nothing.

"Ohhh," she said finally, "you a rare one says them, but that does not make you a danger. That make you special." She smiled again. "You are loved, young wolf. Your Ma loved you very much, ya know."

"My ma?" I blinked. "You mean my mom is talking to you right now?"

"No," she looked off again, listening, "He not tell me who he is, but he loves you too." Her eyes closed in a peaceful acknowledgement. "Mama is at peace."

"He.... Who is he?"

"Looks like you he does," she nodded. "Yes."

"You're not making any sense." I became frustrated. Who was telling her all these things, and who did I look like?

"Mama does not need to make sense to tell you that you are doing things wrong, young one."

Suddenly it occurred to me, "John. Is John the one you are speaking to?"

She sighed. "Why you not be with ones who love you, if you love them?" She asked. Ignoring my question.

"Because of the danger." I repeated. "But is John the spirit who is speaking to you?"

"No, no danger. Only fear you have." She insisted. She turned again and listened before the chimes rang again. "John, he is, and he says you only run out of fear. Red wolves do not run from fear."

I growled, "what do you mean red wolves don't run from fear? We have all been running since he spellbound us. Who the hell is he to tell me what I am doing?"

"This is not something Mama can say, but young wolf, it's time to go home."

I was angry. *How could John be telling her to tell me to stop running when that's exactly what he did?* I wished I could talk to him directly, to yell at him for not being more cautious, to not expect the betrayal. I put all the blame on him for not being a better alpha.

"You fear danger and unknown when you not know what tomorrow brings. Today is all that's given, and tomorrow brings new things. Tomorrow may bring danger, may bring happiness, but today is what have you." She smiled. "Don't blame John, young wolf." She reached her hand across the table and grabbed mine. "He loves you, and he sorry for what has happened. It's time to go home." She rubbed her dry thumb across the top of my knuckles and I felt comforted slightly, even though deep down I was still angry.

I smiled politely and nodded. She turned off again and listened, "Stubborn wolf spirits say." She laughed, "many lessons left to learn you. Go be with those you love, young wolf, world is no place for a wolf so young to be alone."

I nodded and pretended to agree. Neither John nor she could know all the pieces to the story and there's no way that being with those I love will protect them from anything, I thought to myself quietly.

"Huh?!" Mama said again, turning her head. "Your mate wolf," she said.

My stomach flipped. "What about my mate wolf?"

"He be here sha, in the quarter." She said,

"What how?!" I asked. *He can't be here,* I thought to myself. *I would have felt him.*

"Go to him sha, all will be right." She touched my hand again from across the table.

"I'm sorry, I have to.... I have to go now." I stood quickly to head toward the door. Mama followed.

"Stubborn wolf," she murmured, "all be right with you sha, just listen to your beast, your family, and they will guide you home."

"Thank you... uhhh. Mama for the food and the talk, but I really have to go now." I headed out the door and back into the alley. Mama stood at her door and waved behind me as I took the first turn back toward the main road.

*How could he have gotten so close without me knowing?* I thought to myself as I quickly hustled back into the busy street while panic crept its way into my mind. I made my way back toward the abandoned house, moving through the crowds of people. Somehow, the crowds of people seemed to double, and I felt like everything was closing in. I looked for the best route through the mass, and there he was.

My eyes connected with the striking blue and green irises of his and the masses between us seemed to freeze in time. My heart fell into my stomach as I searched his face for intent, feeling, meaning, for anything. His physical prowess called me in like a magnet. I could see that it had been a while since he'd shaved, the hair that clung to his cheeks was far thicker than I had ever seen him allow it to grow before. He seemed thinner, slightly, and he had a darkness that grew under his eyes, probably from the lack of sleep in pursuit of me. He was still as handsome as ever, even after everything I'd put him through. The moment felt like an eternity as we stared at each other. I reached out to see if I could feel his presence standing this close to me once again, but felt nothing.

*Does he no longer love me?* I thought to myself, I've always been able to feel him. How could it be now that our bond was suddenly gone? I felt a sickness boil in my stomach at the thought that Chess no longer loved me, but why would he still be trying to find me? Maybe it's just out of some obligation he feels toward me or maybe he does still care. My head swam with intrusive thoughts. He suddenly shifted his weight in a motion toward me and I turned to run. I pushed through the crowd voraciously, swimming through people like an Olympic athlete trying to get away. I turned to find that Chess was doing the same. I saw an alley opening ahead and went for it. I dove out of the herd of people and into the space. I ran down the alleyway to find a dead end and froze.

*I cornered myself;* I thought briefly before turning to see Chess standing at the end of the alleyway. Until now, I hadn't utilized any of my other wolf abilities other than my sense to run. I was afraid that if I shifted or used too much that my wolf would take control and take me back to him, thinking only with his Id and not with his ego, he surely would only follow his instincts. The only way out now was to use it. If Chess caught up to me and cut through the distance between us, I would no longer be able to resist. Tears swelled in the corner of my eyes as I looked into his eyes once more. I turned, looking toward the roof tops ahead and turned back toward him.

"Don't do it," Chess yelled, pleading, demanding, and calling out to me. His voice pulled me in, hearing him again after all this time rang in my head like the sound of my favorite melody. I wasn't even sure if I could do it at this moment, if I still wanted to, but Chess surely knew I could.

"I'm sorry," I breathed before turning toward the building. I called on my inner beast to give me the strength I needed to escape and felt a surge of power slide down into my legs as I squatted down and pushed out and away from the earth. The force left out the bottom of my feet as I flung myself high into the air and flew toward the top. I landed awkwardly on the shingles and felt a sense of disbelief that I had actually done it. I looked back once more to see Chess slowly leaping onto balconies below, trying to reach me before I bolted across the roof and disappeared from sight.

I continued to run for several hours, leaving the city limits and into the Louisiana wilds. I stopped at what appeared to be an abandoned shack and collected myself. I fell to the dusty floor and pulled myself into a ball. I let out a scream that turned into the saddest wolf call I had ever heard. I did it again. I ran from him, but this time hurt so much more than before, maybe because I could no longer feel what he felt or from seeing how broken I'd left him because of his pursuit of me.

*You're such an idiot*, I thought to myself, and felt self hatred surge through me. The rest of the day turned into night and rain drops started to clink against the broken roof before small drips fell through small holes and landed on my face. I pulled myself from my fetal position and slid myself into a dry corner where no water appeared to be falling. *What am I going to do now?* I thought to myself as a flash of lightning illuminated the small broken shack through the windows. I sat there considering what options remained and the choices remaining seemed to keep shutting faster and faster.

There was one last option to consider. I'd left everything else I had with me in that dilapidated house and there was no way I could go back and get it. Chess had probably already sniffed it all out by now anyhow. I had no more money, no food, and no means of transportation other than my own two feet. At this moment, I just longed for peace. I longed for everything to be over, and I thought maybe it was the last genuine option I had left to take.

There would be no real danger to anyone then, there would be nothing for Chess to chase and he could move on. Maybe not fully, but at least in part. His aunt, sad as she was, had found happiness. Chess could do the same and then the running would be done. Jesse and the rest already had no clue if I was or not, so their moving on had already begun anyway. I played with the idea in my mind and as my hatred toward myself and my self loathing grew, so did the idea. My mom did it, I can too.

The world had already moved on from our legacy. "Red wolves," I scoffed, and I didn't want it anymore. It wasn't fair to begin with. I shoved the thought away before tears bubbled to the surface and leaned my head back against the cool, damp wall. I didn't know where else to go from here, but if that was the option for me, then I at least wanted to go home to where it all started. Where my life, although dismal, was still mine.

The next several days came and went as I moved out of the swamps and into a small town somewhere in the south. I relied on the knowledge I had gained from my foster siblings and ended up lifting an old car that hadn't looked like it had been moved in decades and liberated a snack machine of some food to satiate the hunger pangs that came on day four. I slowly made my way north back toward Washington and stopped in Colorado when the car ran out of gas. I pulled it into a gas station and parked it. I wrote out an apology note to the car's owners and a please return address so that the car might make its way back. I felt terrible for resorting to something so low and decided that I would go the rest of the way on foot. I tried to have an exchange with my inner wolf, tried to feel what small part of Chess remained as I went, but I felt nothing. Everything had gone numb inside and the only feelings that remained were dark and sad.

I tried shifting finally when I reached the corners where Wyoming and Utah met to find some relief from the running and walking. I howled in pain as my teeth itched and tried to force the shift, breaking some bones, and growing some hair, but was unsuc-cessful in completing it fully. It looked like I was on my own here once again and I bottled that hurt back down with all the rest. I considered finishing the job then, but something continued to push me forward toward home, and I found a second wind to take me there.

It took several more days moving at wolf speed to get back to the Washington border and I stopped to rest one last time before finally making it back to Spokane. I figured now was as good a time as any to use my card one last time. I got myself a small motel room for the night, and a few things from a dollar general. The room left a lot to be desired, but was at least clean enough for guests. I went to the bathroom to take a shower before going to bed. Looking at my reflection in the mirror, I felt the need to shave off the red stubble that enveloped my face and clean up; I realized I had lost more mass and looked much skinnier than I had ever seen myself before. I wished I could do something about that before I went and saw my mom one last time, but I also knew I was going to a grave and it wouldn't really matter that much, anyway. I made quick work of the shave and enjoyed a long, hot shower. As I washed over the layer of grime and musk that had accumulated from this long stretch, I found a lot of relief physically and emotionally. I sat down in the tub and let the warm water wash over me, hoping that it would continue to wash more away than just the dirt and sweat. I reconsidered everything, thinking about my friends, the Becks, and Chess and how much I missed them all. I tried leaving out all the negatives and to think back on all the happy memories and the sense of family I had felt. I relived all the happy memories in my mind as I moved from the tub, to the bed and finally into sleep.

The next day, I rented a car and drove the rest of the way. It wouldn't matter anymore if Chess or whoever saw where I was spending money. I had assured myself that there was plenty of space between Chess and me, that he wouldn't be able to catch up. The drive the rest of the way was nice. I had stopped all the thoughts that continued to run through my head and it felt nice to stop thinking so much. I listened to the radio and let it drown everything out. It didn't feel like it had been long before I pulled up to the edge of the cemetery where my mom was buried. I parked the car along the paved edge, walked out toward her grave, and collapsed to my knees in front of her gravestone.

"Hey mom..." I said, putting one hand on the corner of the gravestone. ".. I, uhh, kinda made a mess of things for myself." A tear shed from my eye and fell onto the ledge of the cold cement slab, darkening the gray slightly.

"I met a guy... and well, he's amazing. I think you really would have liked him, though I kind of messed that up, too. We're werewolves..." I choked off and chuckled to myself a bit like I was saying it for the first time, "kind of funny isn't it? Kind of far out there, but I think you may have known that on some level."

"I found out a lot about us and our family. Turns out we were quite something once upon a time. Though, I'm the last one...." I chuckled again, "kind of sucks to be honest." Tears continued to fall as I started pouring out my story to her.

"I think I understand you more now than the last time we met... Why you did what you did, and I want to let you know I forgive you and that I understand..." I sobbed slightly, "I think that may be the option for me too." I cried a little harder and bent over, grabbing at my stomach and sobbed.

"I don't want to do it though...." I said out loud as I sobbed against her grave. I leaned my head into the cement and poured my feelings out to her. As soon as I'd let it all out, I felt a sense of warmth for the first time in a long time. I sat up and leaned against her grave stone, taking in deep breaths of relief. I felt my beast dancing inside slightly again after feeling him abandon me.

*Not abandoned,* a thought not my own entered my mind. *We are always with you, Lyle.* A voice rang in my head like it was carried on the wind that slowly blew across the graveyard.

*What do you mean?* I thought back to myself.

*All your family lives in you. We are all here and we will always be here for you.* The thought felt like an echo in my mind coming again from nowhere. I closed my eyes and tried to follow it back to the source and all I found was my wolf sitting there happily at the center of me, smiling at me. I felt a nudge in my heart and felt waves wash over me as a new sense took over, all this time I was never alone. Maybe I had been alone in person, but in spirit, my family is in me, loving me, and encouraging me to go on. They had been pushing me all along toward Chess, toward my mate, my family, my pack, and all this time I couldn't see it. I heard him then, louder than before. *John;* I acknowledged. My wolf nodded at me.

*No more running young wolf.* The thought rang in my head. I nodded.

*I'm sorry that all this happened to you, but there is no other wolf in our family I am happier to call our next alpha.* My wolf nudged against me again. *You will have trials ahead of you, but with your family, all of your family with you.* I saw images of Chess, the Becks, Jesse, and my friends flashing across my mind. One by one, being brought up in front of me. *No one will stand in your way.*

I nodded again, finally understanding that I had been wrong like everyone had been telling me. *I had been wrong this entire time;* I reflected to myself.

"Yes…. You have," a gruff voice spoke and the sound rang in my ears.

I flung my eyes open and was startled to see Chess dropping to his knees in front of me. He reached his hand up to my cheek and wiped tears from my face, "but it's not too late to fix it."

His hand moved to the back of my head and I felt him slide his fingers through my hair before pulling me into him. I collapsed into him and he reached out his other hand to hold me. I leaned into his shoulder and began sobbing into his shirt. He held me close. I felt his arms around me again and he held me firmly, ensuring there was no way I could escape his embrace. I felt all my feelings rush back into me. Chess motioned slightly, pulling one arm away from me and yanking a cord free from around his neck and suddenly I could hear Chess in my head again repeating, *you're not alone.* He was back.

*How?* I wondered momentarily, but it didn't matter, I could feel him again. The part of him that existed within me danced with my wolf and I embraced all of him again. I leaned back into his chest for what felt like an eternity, his arms wrapped around me feeling like home.

I continued to sob and cried, "I'm sorry.... I'm sorry..." repeatedly between breaths and he continued to hold me and told me it was okay. When I finally stopped crying, I looked up at Chess and looked into those familiar peculiar eyes, seeing nothing but his love staring back at me. The pit of despair I had been feeling lessened and the bonds that I had tried so hard to cut were just as strong as they had ever been. He looked at me quizzically before I finally said, "I'm sorry," again in a more controlled tone.

"Lyle, you don't have to be sorry for anything," he reached up and ran his hand through my hair, "just please don't leave me again." His hand stopped at the back of my head and he pulled me into a deep kiss. I felt all his grief, his longing, his anger, his passion, his love flow through me in that hard, deep kiss. I inhaled through my nostrils and felt his scent fill my head, and I could only think back: *I love you.*

We pulled apart after a moment of eternity and I looked back at him. "How?" I asked, "how did you find me?"

His lips turned up at the corners, and a grin stretched across his face. "Mama Lootie was quite insistent that I would find you here. Something about a spirit telling her where he'd take you."

I smiled back at him and thanked my wolf inside of me softly as he chuffed back in acknowledgment. All this time, all my family was here with me. I turned back to Chess. "This doesn't fix it all, Chess. Everyone is still in danger because of me." Chess cut me off and pulled me back into his chest.

"Lyle, you were in more danger just moments ago than any of us ever were being together. Besides, you have us, all of us." He turned back toward the road and I looked over his shoulder to see Noah approach from a black SUV parked behind my rental. His head hung low, his approach was soft and hesitant. When he reached us, he knelt down next to Chess and me in the grass.

"Lyle, I..." He started and then trailed off as he hung his head down in the same way all the wolves in our family did to him. Exposing his neck to me in the most vulnerable way, something that an alpha never did. "I never meant to hurt you in the way I did." He took a deep breath, "It's a father's duty, an alpha's duty to protect his sons, his family, and I broke my sacred duty to protect you, and I will spend the rest of my life making up what I have done to you and what my family had done to yours so long ago." He turned his gaze to mine. "This I swear to you."

I felt my wolf inside sit proudly, already knowing that my wolf, my family, had never blamed him or held him responsible for the actions of his ancestor. I reached out to Noah with one hand before feeling him grab me into a full embrace, "I love you, son, and I am so sorry that I ever made you feel anything less."

"I love you too," I breathed, as I felt my wolf in my chest nudge his head against Noah from within me. At that moment, I felt like that ancient betrayal was truly forgiven. Noah let go before Chess and he helped me to my feet. I looked at both of them again and felt all their love being reflected on me. Chess leaned his head into mine. "No matter what happens, Lyle, we are a family, a pack, and we will stick together."

I nodded at him just before he motioned us to move back toward the cars. I walked beside Chess and Noah and as Chess opened the car door and reached out his hand to help me in the car, I looked back at my mom's grave.

*I don't know what happens from here, mom, but please know that for now I'm safe, with my pack.* The wolf inside of me howled again, and I felt a beautiful acknowledgement run through me. I turned back and took Chess's hand. He smiled at me and pulled me in for another kiss. I climbed into the car, knowing that whatever happened next would happen with us together.

# Epilogue

Gerard paced impatiently outside the embassy awaiting the invitation that would allow him to enter. His imbecile of a son sat in a black SUV parked against the sidewalk. He didn't understand what he could possibly have done wrong in his life that caused him to deserve such a failure for a son and command the weak excuses for wolves that made up his pack. How could it have gone so wrong after decades of planning finally came to fruition? The Dubois should be revered as the highest and most prestigious pack that exists amongst all these other wolves, but he was stuck with wolves like his. He mused over the necessary changes. He was the only one that could bring his pack to the ranking it deserved, even if he had to kill his son to make him the wolf he needed to be, he would do it. Gerard hated being in D.C. and hated that he would have to resort to involving the Union in order to get what he wanted. He knew he would have to be manipulative and careful, but until his pack could be addressed he would need assistance.

The doors to the embassy opened and a petite woman in a red business suit with short black hair stood at the top of the steps.

"The Union is ready for you now," she said, addressing Gerard.

Gerard ascended the steps of the large historic building where the Union of Wolves assembled themselves in their eastern location. The building was set to match itself to the others that made up the pathetic excuse for a human government that existed, but even Gerard could see the benefits of hiding in plain sight. He much preferred the more modern, but classy embassy to the west. However, considering its proximity to Beck territory, this would have to do. They crossed the marble lobby and made their way past the wolf secretaries in human form that upheld the appearance that the Union was merely some form of governmental department that existed as a part and parcel of the United States. Gerard admitted that Aiyana Lumi had cleaned up shop as the leader of the Union, even though it really should have been him leading.

He followed the petite woman down the hall to an ornate set of double doors carved to depict a forest scene with wolves running throughout their wooden facade, above the doors were adorned with a wooden wolf's head mount, carved in the same intricate style. It seemed to peer down upon those who entered, as if they didn't already know why they were here. He appreciated the irony and thought to himself that maybe he and Aiyana would have been a better mated pair than that bitch Dahlia who had given him weak cubs and soiled the Dubois legacy. With Aiyana at least then he would have been able to pass down the speed of the Lumi pack to his offspring, rather than bestowing upon them the petite size of the Faolan wolves that his forced mate Dahlia had come from. He had always resented not being mated with a wolf from the top five packs. The woman opened the doors and stopped just inside the large open chamber where the Alphas of the other packs sat in a semicircle with Aiyana at the center.

"Gerard Dubois, Alpha to the Dubois pack and the reining pack of Massachusetts." The woman announced as he took the floor. He walked up toward the podium in the center of the room to address the other Alphas. He looked at the ten Alphas present. Good, he thought to himself as he looked around the room, all the other alphas, except for Noah Beck, had responded to the summons. One over to Aiyana's right sat Jasper Coinin, the pack known for its exceptional sense of scent, and to her right sat Sierra Hemming, big brute of a wolf, herself definitely being one of the largest amongst the other exceptionally big Hemming wolves. Lincoln Adalwuf and Gregor Volkov also sat closer to the center, their abilities with sound and touch were equally desirable. The least useful abilities sat further to the sides. Cobalt Faolan, cousin to his mate and a tiny beast of a man, Clarke Otsoko, a smart wolf, but a major pain in the ass and know it all, Dixon Wulfric, strength, but without the ability to control it all he is good for is smashing rocks to dust, Maia Bleiz, a youthful beauty even in her older age, and Petra Clell, faster regeneration than the rest of us, but still an ability we all share. Beck's seat sat empty to the right hand of Aiyana having been intentionally left out of this summons.

"Alright Dubois, you have the floor. What reason do you have for bringing together this secret summons?" Aiyana stated.

Gerard went to speak, but was cut off by Clarke Otsoko. "Excuse me, Aiyana, but shouldn't we wait for Noah to join us?"

"The Becks won't be joining this summons, Otsoko," Aiyana explained. "Proceed Gerard." She gestured for Gerard to begin.

"My fellow Alphas," Gerard began, "I have summoned you all here today to share the most troubling news I have learned regarding Noah Beck and his son." Gerard moved from the podium and walked the half circle of Alphas, "I recently had the pleasure of hosting our young future Alpha Beck in my home, which came as a bit of shock considering the boy entered my territory absent invitation, and, to my horror fellow alphas, Chess was in the company of a new wolf."

"New wolf?" Maia Bleiz asked.

"Yes, Alpha Bleiz," Gerard responded, "a new wolf. You see, it has come to my attention that Chess Beck bit the boy some time ago, and seems to have created a new line."

"You're way off base here, Gerard. The Becks do not possess the ability to make new wolves," Clarke exclaimed. "No wolf possesses such an ability."

"Thank you, Clarke, for your wonderful insight, as always." Cobalt Faolan said, annoyed.

"How have you come by this information Gerard," Jasper Coinin asked, "up to your old games?" He smirked and leaned back into his chair, amused at the potential embarrassment Gerard was bringing on himself.

"My fellow Alphas," Aiyana growled, "let Gerard speak!" The rest of the alphas settled and resumed listening.

"Thank you, Alpha Lumi." Gerard gave a slight bow to acknowledge her station above the rest. Gerard motioned toward the door where his idiot of a son waltzed into the room with a large stack of portfolios. He hurried around the room, passing out a black leatherbound folder to each Alpha. "If it pleases you, my fellow Alphas, please open the folders you have just been given." The Alphas responded accordingly and opened the leather portfolio that contained several images of Lyle, stolen genetic profiles from the university that Chess Beck had completed himself, as well as a family tree tracing back to a family all the wolves present had made a ruling on before.

"My fellow Alphas, it is my greatest honor to introduce to you Lyle Larson, or should I say Lyle Conri." Gerard shared a grin as the fellow Alphas looked through the portfolios put together on the boy and the information that Gerard and his pack had pieced together through means of thievery, manipulation, and any other means they felt necessary to get what they needed. A weight fell over the room as the other Alphas finished flipping through the information.

"What makes you believe this boy is a Conri wolf?" Sierra Hemming stated, finally joining the conversation.

"Well, my dear lady," Gerard explained, slightly annoyed," this boy possesses all the genetic markers for every unique ability present in this room, and more. If you'll all open the back pocket and take one last look for me, please." The alphas followed and removed a small stack of photos of Lyle in his red wolf form, as well as a snapshot from his own security footage of Lyle as a beast. Small gasps and side conversations emerged as they processed the information amongst themselves.

"There's just no way this boy could be a Conri, Gerard," Gregor professed. "We would have known if a small line of Conri wolves had survived the massacre."

"Aww, you see Alpha Volkov, you are absolutely correct, unless the boy and his family had been spellbound." Gerard added.

"Spellbound?" Clarke inquired, "What witch in their right mind would have spell bound a Conri?"

"What witch indeed," Gerard exclaimed, "we all know that the witches have been less and less of a threat over the years and their powers had waned. I believe this to be due to a witch having done the unthinkable, spellbinding John and Rebecca Conri's last heir." Gerard paused, feeling his plan coming to a sweet, sweet conclusion. He had them all eating out of the palm of his hand. "We'd all assumed that Rebecca died with the pup still in her belly, but my fellow alphas this.... is.... a.... lie. The Conri line, my fellow Alphas, is alive and well, having been awoken by the bite of our dear Chess Beck. Hidden from sight by Noah Beck and the rest of his pack. The red wolf is back."

The remaining Alphas began growling and arguing in an uproar of disbelief and uncertainty. Some proclaimed they should kill the boy, that he should be taken and protected, and others sat silent.

Aiyana let out a large howl, amplified by the acoustics of the room. The other Alphas calmed themselves and sat back into their seats, although the air in the room had changed significantly.

"Gerard," Aiyana started, "you have provided us with a lot of illuminating information this evening. These accusations will, of course, be substantiated and investigated thoroughly. We will dismiss and reconvene in the western chambers, where a summons for the Becks and this boy, Lyle, will be called forth for questioning. Should this boy, in fact, be a Conri, a committee will determine what is to be done." She leaned forward, assessing that some of the other Alphas were not in line with her decision. "Until then, the Becks and the boy are to remain untouched. None of you will alarm the Becks until then." Aiyana was trying to assert law and order to the room, which is the opposite of what Gerard intended. "I was elected as lead alpha for a reason," Aiyana continued. "We may be werewolves, but we are not animals."

"One more thing, my dear Alphas." Gerard started.

"What's that Gerard?" Asked Aiyana.

"The boys. Chess Beck and Lyle Conri." He smiled.

"What about them?" Asked Lincoln.

"They're mated." As the wolves returned to a loud series of fighting and howling, Aiyana, attempting to cool the situation, Gerard turned and headed out toward the exit, smiling contently.

www.ingramcontent.com/pod-product-compliance
Lightning Source LLC
Chambersburg PA
CBHW070610300726
48975CB00006B/1777